E

GARDEN."

Olivia felt as if everything had become perfectly still—the songs of the birds, the rustle of the breeze. Adam took another step and now he was close enough for her to feel his breath against her temple.

She did not move and yet she knew that every fiber of her being was leaning toward him, longing for his touch beyond the whisper of his breath. She closed her eyes and savored his knuckles stroking her cheek and then his finger was under her chin, urging her to look up at him, and, when she did, he whispered her name.

"Olivia." It hung in the air between them like the flutter of a butterfly's wings. Hesitantly she touched his face, and as if that were all the assurance he needed, he swept her into his arms and kissed her with a force that left her senses reeling.

Instinctively she knew that all that was necessary was the slightest resistance—a hand pushing against his chest, a step backward, the merest turn of her face away from his. But she did none of that for she wanted the kiss to go on forever, to continue its magic of transporting her from the humdrum life she had come to accept to the possibility of something far greater, far more thrilling . . .

Dear Readers,

In July of 1999, we launched the Ballad line with four new series, and each month since then we've presented both new and continuing stories set everywhere from medieval England to the American West—the kind of passionate, romantic stories you love best, written by the most gifted authors. At the back of each book, we'll tell you when you can find subsequent books in the series that have captured your heart.

This month, the fabulous Willa Hix returns to historical romance with her new series, *The Golden Door,* which follows the adventures of a pair of half siblings new to America during its lush Gilded Age. In **Cheek to Cheek,** a young woman fleeing an arranged marriage finds herself faced with the possibility of real love—with the man who has hired her as his aging mother's companion. Next up, ever-talented Linda Lea Castle continues the triumphant saga of *The Vaudrys* with **Surrender the Stars,** as King Henry III commands a loyal subject to wed a mysterious woman who may be his doom—or his heart's destiny.

Reader favorite Kathryn Hockett sweeps us back to the turbulent era of *The Vikings* with the **Conqueror,** a warrior sworn to vengeance . . . but tempted by desire. Finally, Cherie Claire concludes the lushly atmospheric story of *The Acadians* with **Delphine,** as fate reunites a dashing smuggler with the girl who once professed to love him—but who has become a woman with wealth, obligations—and desires—of her own. Enjoy!

Kate Duffy
Editorial Director

The Golden Door

CHEEK TO CHEEK

Willa Hix

ZEBRA BOOKS
Kensington Publishing Corp.
http://www.kensingtonbooks.com

ZEBRA BOOKS are published by

Kensington Publishing Corp.
850 Third Avenue
New York, NY 10022

All Kensington titles, imprints, and distributed lines are available at special quantity discounts for bulk purchases for sales promotion, premiums, fund-raising, educational or institutional use.

Special book excerpts or customized printings can also be created to fit specific needs. For details, write or phone the office of the Kensington Special Sales Manager: Kensington Publishing Corp., 850 Third Avenue, New York, NY 10022. Attn. Special Sales Department. Phone: 1-800-221-2647.

First Printing: June 2002
10 9 8 7 6 5 4 3 2 1

Printed in the United States of America

One

London, 1899

If Olivia Marlowe had to endure one more second of listening to her stepfather pontificate about the latest debate in Parliament, she thought she would commit some heinous and totally inappropriate act of violence—possibly against herself. Anything to escape the tedium of another evening in the company of her stepfather, her stepbrother, and her betrothed. On the other hand, the drone of Lord Barrington's voice was assuredly preferable to the snorts and occasional snores emanating from her intended husband, Sir Dudley Cochran.

How was it that men could be rude or boring or crude . . . and occasionally all three at the same time, without the slightest fear of retribution? Women, on the other hand, were expected to be eternally solicitous, entertaining, and proper. When had she begun to notice that inequality? At her mother's knee, no doubt. Perhaps it had been the day when she had overheard the male guests at one of her mother's gatherings discussing the Queen's latest decrees. She recalled being fascinated that a woman—even if she *was* the Queen—could have such power over the thoughts and actions of a group of men.

Even now her stepfather was ranting about the latest

decree from Her Majesty. Here was a man whose sole interest in women lay in what they might do to satisfy his need of the moment, and he was clearly fascinated by the actions of Victoria. Of course, he assumed that powerful men were influencing her decisions. It was obviously impossible to believe the woman might actually have a brain of her own. Olivia had always aspired to model her life on that of Victoria. How had she come to this?

"Olivia, my dear, could I trouble you for another sherry?" her stepfather said, holding out his glass as he returned immediately to the topic at hand.

Olivia set aside her needlework and refilled his glass, making the rounds of the room to refill the glasses of Sir Dudley and her stepbrother as well. Sir Dudley roused himself at her approach and mumbled an appropriate, "Quite right, old boy," in response to Lord Barrington's latest comment. It occurred to her as she restoppered the cut crystal decanter and replaced it on the tray that this was the future . . . her future. Endless evenings like this one. As she passed Sir Dudley on her way back to her chair, she saw that, although he was putting up a bit of a struggle, his eyelids were already drooping and his mouth had gone slack.

Sir Dudley was a member of one of the oldest and most powerful families in London. His family pedigree ran back a dozen generations. He was twice her age and had never married. In his day, he had probably cut quite a striking figure, but too many puddings and years spent in sedentary pleasures had taken their toll. Still, he was undoubtedly her last best hope to marry and provide the heir Sir Dudley now professed to want. At twenty-six, Olivia had long since crossed the invisible boundary that separates eligibility from spinsterhood. She had unfortunately not inherited her late mother's talent for charming the opposite sex. In fact, she had a most distressing habit of speaking her mind—something she was even at this moment trying hard to control.

"Such a stimulating man," her stepbrother, Jeremy, whispered snidely as he crossed the room on his way to refill the very sherry glass that she had just filled for him. He nodded at Sir Dudley and grimaced in disgust before turning to his father. "Father," he shouted to the hard-of-hearing man, "I have an engagement."

He drained his sherry in one long swallow and set the glass on the tray next to Olivia's chair. "I'm sure my charming stepsister will keep you gentlemen amused," he added. "Perhaps you could play something, Olivia dear." He fingered the fringe of the silk paisley shawl draped across the grand piano. "You know how we all enjoy your little concerts."

"Not tonight," Olivia replied tersely.

"Have it your way," he said with a shrug. When he bent to kiss her cheek, Olivia stiffened slightly and was not surprised when he smiled. He tapped her lightly on the nose as he said in a low voice, "I have a plan to escape all of this if you're daring enough to consider it." He glanced over at Sir Dudley who had a bit of drool coursing down his jaw. "On the other hand, he is *extremely* wealthy and you'll certainly want for nothing. You'll probably hang yourself in the attic after a year or so just to break the monotony, but you'll have every comfort."

Before Olivia could respond, he turned back to his father. "I shall be going out, Father," he repeated in a normal voice now that he had his father's full attention.

"You'll be at the office tomorrow," Lord Barrington replied. It was not a question, but a command. Still, Lord Barrington smiled as if he knew how pointless it was to remind his only son of his responsibilities.

"Of course," Jeremy replied with a wave. Satisfied that his father had once again focused his attention on Sir

Dudley, Jeremy lingered. He ran one hand along the back of Olivia's chair. "Marry old Duds or go to New York and be your own woman," he whispered as he passed her.

Olivia rolled her eyes, but Jeremy leaned closer.

"Don't believe me, but I assure you that I not only have a plan—I have the contacts to make it happen. I leave you with but one thought to ponder for the remainder of the evening, my dear Livvy. You don't have to marry ol' Duds." And then he was gone.

Almost from the day Olivia's mother had married Lord Barrington and brought Olivia to live in his home, Jeremy had delighted in taunting her. In those days, Olivia had consoled herself with the idea that she was of age and would certainly be married shortly herself. That had been seven long years ago. Six months after they arrived, her mother had been killed in a foxhunting accident, and Olivia had assumed the role of hostess for the household.

New York indeed, Olivia thought, attacking the lace she was tatting as if it were a noose for Jeremy's neck. It was just like Jeremy to suggest something so completely outside the bounds of reality. He knew of her fascination with novels set in America—the works of Mrs. Edith Wharton, in particular. He was teasing her as usual. She deliberately laid her needlework aside and glanced across the room. "Your grace," she shouted and was gratified to see both her stepfather and her betrothed turn to her with a start. "I'm afraid I am quite exhausted," she said in a softer, more demure voice. "Would you forgive me if I leave the two of you to put right the affairs of Parliament without me?"

Sir Dudley struggled to his feet, his corpulent frame stretching the fabric of his rumpled coat to its limits. "Of course, my treasure," he murmured as he crossed the room and placed a kiss on the fingertips of her extended hand. Olivia straightened her spine to stay the shudder that threatened to rack her from head to toe. He was a good man, a decent man, she reminded herself. *You'll want for nothing, but* . . . she heard Jeremy's voice in her head.

She smiled at both men. "Good evening to you both," she said and pulled the pocket doors closed behind her. She stood for a long moment in the deserted foyer and closed her eyes. *If Jeremy has a plan, the least I can do is humor him and hear him out,* she decided as she climbed the wide curved staircase to her room.

Adam Porterfield was relieved to have completed his business in London and to be going home to New York. It was late March, and he especially enjoyed New York in the spring. From a business standpoint, his visit to London had been a great success—*smashing,* as his new friend and business associate, Jeremy Barrington, might say. The two of them had hit it off from their first meeting at a dinner party at the home of Adam's aunt when he'd come to England several months earlier on another business trip. They had corresponded, and when Jeremy heard that Adam was making a return trip, he had insisted that Adam be his guest at his club and permit him to arrange for entertainment at the opera and theater for the American.

Adam had few illusions about Jeremy, but he liked his new friend's enthusiasm and wit. In a country known for propriety at all costs, Jeremy was a breath of fresh air. The decision to accept the Englishman's proposal to join forces in business as a junior partner in Adam's firm had taken some time. There was no question that Jeremy would bring a rare combination of class and wit to the business. On top of that and most important, the funds he had promised to invest meant that Adam would be able to expand the business at a faster rate than even he had envisioned.

All in all, Adam had accomplished everything he had

come to England to do, except for one thing. He had hoped to find a suitable Englishwoman who might be interested in coming to New York and working as a companion for his mother. It had been nearly two years since his father had died after a sudden illness. His mother had not been the same since. She had sunk into a state of depression that left her irritable and argumentative. Nothing and no one seemed to please her. She tolerated Adam's attempts to get her involved in social and charitable events, but used everything at her disposal to thwart his efforts. Two housekeepers, a chauffeur, and the gardener had left in the past year, saying that she had become too demanding and they could not hope to please her. His mother had dismissed every woman he had interviewed to serve as her companion as too bourgeoise—meaning too American.

Adam had confided his dilemma to Jeremy during one of their late night sessions at a local pub. Ever the person who strove to please, Jeremy had hinted that he might just have the solution. Adam had taken this boast at face value. He suspected that he would be doing that quite a lot in the weeks and months to come as he and Jeremy settled into a business relationship in his investment firm in New York.

"Adam!"

Adam smiled as he watched Jeremy work his way through the crowded pub. He turned and signaled for another ale. "You're late," he said in mock sternness as he led the way to a table away from the noisy group celebrating a cricket win. "I'm two pints ahead already."

"Ah, but should we count the three glasses of port I had with dinner and the double sherry I consumed after dinner, you would be the laggard, my friend," Jeremy said with a laugh. He took a long swallow of the ale and set his glass down. "I believe that I have secured the services of a promising candidate for the position of your mother's companion, if you'll have her," Jeremy announced.

"We sail tomorrow," Adam reminded him. *"Early* tomorrow."

"She'll be ready."

Adam hesitated. As a businessman, he had learned never to make decisions hastily, yet his mother's health was deteriorating almost daily. Since his last visit to London, she had refused to leave the house, claiming that she could not abide the uncouth behavior of common Americans. "My mother has found a certain solace in her English heritage since my father's death," he said, more to himself than to Jeremy. "I had thought that perhaps having someone who shared that heritage that she could talk with might cheer her, but this is rather short notice."

"Those who have lost a dear one are often drawn to those things that have given them comfort in the past," Jeremy said sympathetically. "The woman I have approached with this offer lost her dear mother in a tragic accident just a few years ago."

Adam studied him with interest. "And, this is why she wants to leave England?"

"It is part of her reasoning. Fresh start and all that."

"And she is educated? You know her to be above reproach?"

"Absolutely," Jeremy assured him. "She is a plain-looking and rather staid woman . . . not that she isn't gifted on a number of levels. She's a talented conversationalist, for example, able to converse on any number of topics. Art, music . . ." He ticked the topics off on his fingertips. "Exceptional in the needle arts."

"New York can be seductive. What if she arrives and decides that the city has more to offer than sitting with an old lady day in and out? What of her hopes for marriage and a family?"

"I assure you that she has no such aspirations. She is a spinster and quite content in that role. To be truthful, she does have a bit of a willful streak—nothing that can't be tamed, to be sure, but it has put off more than one potential suitor through the years, and I have no doubt it will be equally unappealing to your American colleagues."

"You seem to know this woman quite well. How is that?"

Jeremy took another swallow of his ale. "She has lived in my father's house for the past six years, managing the household, that sort of thing." He waved a hand as if to dismiss any further details as unimportant. "She's quite capable, I assure you."

Adam smiled. "And were you perhaps one of those who felt the rebuke of her willfulness, Jeremy?"

Jeremy choked on his brew and wiped away the foam with the back of one hand. "Heaven forbid. She is hardly my type, sir."

Adam couldn't help laughing. "Is she that difficult to look at, my friend?"

"She's quite presentable in a very prim sort of way. She's just not to my taste," he added as he smiled seductively at the barmaid and lifted his glass to signal for another ale.

"So, you have made an offer on my behalf?"

Jeremy fingered the rim of his glass. "We've discussed the matter." He glanced away, then back. "Of course, the particulars are left to you . . . salary, responsibilities, that sort of thing."

Adam hid a smile. "I appreciate that. Has this woman no family—no need to put matters in order before she leaves?"

"As I have told you, her mother died a few years ago and her father passed away when she was a mere child . . . an only child."

Adam tapped out an idle rhythm on the table as he worked through the possible pitfalls of the situation. When he had met Jeremy on his last trip to London and Jeremy had begun his campaign to form some sort of partnership, Adam had had his staff make a thorough review of Jeremy's background. In the meantime, Adam had turned his interest to why the man would want to leave a comfortable life and take his chances in America. After meeting Lord Barrington one afternoon at Jeremy's club, Adam believed that he knew exactly what the younger man's motivation might be. His father was a retired military man, quite set in his ways, who obviously doted on his only child as long as Jeremy played according to his father's rules.

The matter of Jeremy and the woman, though, was something else. Still, Jeremy's reaction when Adam had suggested that the Englishman might have an ulterior and purely personal reason for suggesting this particular woman had been telling. Jeremy had been unable to disguise his revulsion at the very idea. Adam smiled.

"So, she is prepared to sail with us tomorrow?"

Relief flooded Jeremy's face. "I have every reason to believe that she will."

"Then, I shall expect the two of you at the docks at dawn. I'll take care of booking the extra passage for . . . what is her name?"

"Miss Olivia Marlowe," Jeremy replied.

Adam nodded. "Miss Marlowe," he repeated, committing the name to memory. He lifted his glass to Jeremy. "Well, my friend, tomorrow we embark on a new adventure. Welcome to Porterfield and Company."

Jeremy lifted his own glass and smiled. Adam couldn't help thinking that Jeremy looked as if he had just won a major victory as the two men sealed their business partnership with the last of their ale. He just hoped the young

Englishman would be as delighted six months from now as he appeared to be this evening.

Olivia paced the length of her room and back again, pausing at the open window to listen for the sound of Jeremy's carriage. She had remained dressed since leaving her stepfather and Sir Dudley. She wanted to be prepared to intercept Jeremy when he returned . . . *if* he returned.

What had he meant with his veiled hints of escaping the marriage? How could she possibly trust him? She must be mad . . . or desperate . . . or both. She continued to pace as she considered the possibilities, the small train of her orchid moiré dinner gown whipping into place behind her as she made each turn. She fingered the rope of large pearls that wound round her throat twice and then cascaded over her breasts. Someone seeing her might have thought that she was using the pearls almost as a rosary, but she was not counting prayers, she was ticking off the reasons why she must be completely out of her mind to even consider talking with Jeremy about whatever harebrained scheme he'd concocted.

Jeremy wasn't intentionally mean-spirited. He was a boy in a man's body, an only child who had been indulged all his life and had quickly learned to use his boyish charm to his advantage. She knew that he viewed her as far too rigid and rooted in the proprieties of life. She also knew that somehow he had uncovered the secret part of her that dreamed of a very different life, that longed for the kind of carefree embrace of life her mother had perfected. Otherwise, he never would have imagined that the mere mention of New York might get her attention.

The clock chimed two. Hours earlier she had heard Sir Dudley leave and her stepfather's heavy tread as he passed her room on his way to his. *What if Jeremy didn't return at all? What if he was even now entangled in the arms of a mistress with no thought of returning until dawn? What if . . . ?*

She heard the crunch of booted footsteps on gravel in the courtyard and raced to the window. The fog that had enshrouded the house earlier had lifted and the light from her window cast a spotlight onto the courtyard below.

"Jeremy," she called in a loud whisper.

"Ah, my lady fair," he replied in full voice.

"Sh-h-h," she commanded. He had been drinking as usual, but at least he was here. "Come to the library."

He swept off his hat and gave her a low bow. "At your pleasure, my lady," he replied, again making no attempt to lower his voice.

Her only recourse was to close the window before he woke the entire household. She crossed the room and carefully opened her bedroom door a crack. Seeing no one about, she hurried down the stairs and into the library.

"Ah, dear sister," Jeremy greeted her. He was already at his father's sideboard pouring a glass of brandy. "Will you join me?"

Olivia ignored the proffered snifter and closed the doors, checking first to be sure that none of the servants were around. "Haven't you had enough to drink for one night?"

He lifted his eyebrows and then the glass. "Possibly." Then he looked unbearably sad, so sad that she was taken aback. "And, possibly not," he said more to himself than to her. He seemed to study the amber liquid for a long moment before taking a swallow.

"Tell me what you meant earlier," Olivia said when it seemed that he might actually have forgotten she was in the room. *Mistake,* she thought instantly. *You're far too eager.*

Jeremy smiled. "How are the wedding plans coming?"

He took his time selecting a cigar from his father's humidor and bit off the end.

"You *know* the plans. Sir Dudley and I are to be married in the chapel on the grounds of his country estate with you and your father and Sir Dudley's sister in attendance."

"Ah, yes. That's still on for a week from tomorrow, is it?"

She might have to take some brandy herself to calm her nerves if he didn't stop toying with her, but she had long ago learned that the best way to deal with Jeremy was to refuse to rise to his bait.

"I leave tomorrow for the estate." She moved to a chair near the fire and took a seat, focusing all of her attention on the log that would not last much longer.

"And, I leave tomorrow for New York." He studied her for a moment and then smiled. "How would you like to come with me?" he asked in a casual tone as he turned to the French doors that led to the garden and peered out.

"You're completely mad," she chastised him.

"Am I? Let me think . . . a dank old country house that is no doubt badly in need of a woman's touch—or—New York." He raised one hand and then the other as if balancing a scale. "The next decades of my life spent with a man who bores me silly or the excitement of a city on the rise filled with eligible and successful men who might be charmed by my accent and oh-so-proper demeanor." He raised and lowered first one hand and then the other several more times as if trying to decide. "Not a difficult choice," he said turning back to her. "Perhaps you are the mad woman in this scenario . . . or you may be driven to it."

Olivia sat calmly and waited for him to finish speaking. Only her tightly clenched hands betrayed her frustration.

"To marry or flee, which shall it be, sister dear?" Jeremy added in a singsong tone.

"That's several times that you have mentioned New York this evening," she replied calmly. "You'll forgive me if I fail to understand what that city has to do with my future happiness, or, for that matter, why you, of all people, would concern yourself with that happiness at all."

Jeremy grinned. "It's a basic concept, really. You are about to tie yourself to a man you don't love and a life that will provide you no end of tribulation. I am offering you an alternative." He lit the cigar and drew on it.

She tried waiting him out, but he was a master at staging these little dramas. "I'm still waiting for the particulars, Jeremy. As we are both well aware, you are not in the habit of helping others unless there is something to be gained for your own interests." She fought to keep her tone light and only vaguely interested, but knew that her actions in waiting up for him had already told him everything he needed to know about her curiosity related to his plan.

He strolled past her and drew his finger along the pearls at the back of her neck. "Did I mention how lovely you look this evening, Olivia? Those pearls set off your gown to perfection. You do have the penchant for choosing rather drab colors for your wardrobe. Thank heavens, you have the proper jewels to lighten and brighten."

"If there was a compliment in there, Jeremy, I thank you for it."

"There was indeed. Your mother had the most exquisite taste, Olivia, and she was quite accomplished at acquiring a treasure trove of such objects."

"You need cash," Olivia said wearily. It was an old story. They were both heirs to considerable fortunes. In her case, she had acquired an impressive collection of jewelry following her mother's untimely death. Of course, everything else from her mother's estate remained under the control of Jeremy's father.

For his part, Jeremy stood to inherit the family title with all the real estate and wealth that attached when his father died. For now, he was provided with a sizable monthly allowance which he ran through quickly each month, spending lavishly on clothing for himself, gifts for his mistresses, the racetrack and nightly outings to the theater or the pubs with his friends.

"You want me to pay your way to New York and if I'll do that, you'll let me come with you. Is that the gist of it?" Olivia asked.

Jeremy smiled triumphantly. "Not at all. I need resources to establish myself in business in New York. I have made an important alliance with an American businessman. Part of the arrangement is that I shall go to New York to work with him. . . ."

Olivia couldn't help herself. She burst out laughing. "Jeremy, you have never worked a day in your life. You may show up at your father's offices when it suits you, but the very idea of you putting nose to the grindstone, as it were, is . . . well, it's ludicrous."

"You wound me, Olivia. I have many gifts—unorthodox perhaps, but attractive to an innovative businessman like Mr. Adam Porterfield, nevertheless."

"I'm going to bed," Olivia said and stood, knowing that her action would get Jeremy to come to the point.

"Would you not be willing to invest your mother's jewelry in the opportunity to escape marriage to Sir Dudley?"

"Jeremy, I am not going to just hand over my mother's jewels. You may be your father's pride and joy, but even you cannot change his feelings about the importance of this marriage for *his* estate. You know as well as I do that he views this union as a business arrangement. He will be rid of me and whatever expense I incur for him and he will be forming an invaluable alliance between two powerful families."

Jeremy frowned. "You and my father have one thing in common, dear Olivia. You both live in the past. We stand at the brink of a new century. The day of entitlement is over. The new age will require independent thinkers."

"Like you?"

"Like Adam Porterfield from whom I am sure to learn a great deal."

"Mr. Porterfield must be a fool if he has thrown in his lot with you."

Jeremy set down his glass and pulled a large ottoman close to Olivia's chair. "Olivia, I know who I am, but this is an opportunity for me to become my own man, to achieve something . . . build something on my own. Adam is someone who can teach me a great deal. I respect him enormously, and it is I and not Adam who stands to gain the most from our alliance. But, in order to present myself properly, I need some stake of my own. Unfortunately, I do not have the luxury of time. Adam sails tomorrow and I plan to go with him."

For the second time that evening, Olivia was taken aback. She almost believed that Jeremy was sincere . . . almost. She narrowed her eyes and studied him closely.

Suddenly, he smiled, and she recognized it as the smile he had perfected to charm women of all ages. "And all I need is a little investment to make it happen," he admitted. "Which is where you come into this . . . a collaboration so to speak."

Olivia laughed. "Jeremy, there is no collaboration when one person gets nothing from the bargain."

"What are you saying?" Jeremy pressed his hand to his chest as if shocked that she would even think of suggesting such a thing. "You go to America. You spend the rest of your life doing exactly as you please. You enter the new century as a fully independent woman. My stars, woman, it would seem to me that *you* are the one who stands to gain the most from our bargain."

"And you would be doing this for me for what altruistic reason?"

"I don't deny that I need funds for my own purposes. However, they are genuine business purposes. Surely, you can't expect me to start my business career without the proper accouterments—a house, furnishings, and such? We both stand to gain a great deal from this venture."

"Tell me why I couldn't simply take your idea—admittedly an intriguing one—and use my jewelry to purchase my own passage?"

Jeremy feigned shock. "And, travel alone—a lady of your standing? No lady's maid to attend you? My heavens, tongues would wag, my dear." He shook his head in mock censure. "And how would you get your trunks to the dock without alerting half the household? You would need a driver and carriage and . . . well, it's an ambitious project and you have less than four hours to arrange it."

He gave her a moment to consider and she knew that her face had revealed her realization that he was right. He pressed his advantage. "Admittedly my plan involves a bit of subterfuge. You'll be posing as a commoner—a lady's companion, actually. Mr. Porterfield's mother. . . ."

"Are you daft?" Olivia started to laugh, thinking he was trying to irritate her, but then she looked into his eyes. "My stars, you are serious," she gasped. "You actually expect me to hand over my mother's jewels and then further help you make an impression on your Mr. Porterfield by posing as some sort of household help?"

Jeremy shrugged. "I won't deny that I need your help in this, but make no mistake, I can manage on my own long enough to get to New York. If things fall apart then, well. . . ." He shrugged again and winked at her. "New

York is an incredibly large city—easy for one to lose oneself among the masses."

The silence stretched between them. The years stretched before her.

"Why can't I go as myself?" she asked finally.

"Ah, Livvy, think of it. Going as yourself, you're still tied to my father and even Sir Dudley. Your lineage follows you everywhere and the scandal you would commit in abandoning a man of Sir Dudley's stature—no pun intended—at the altar would not exactly enhance your entrée to society in America. The Americans can be a bit stuffy about lineage, my dear, having so little of it themselves. They delight in picking at the carcass of anyone they think has held a high position and fallen."

She turned away and stared out into the blackness of the pre-dawn. "Are you suggesting that I live out my days as someone's companion?"

"Absolutely not. I am suggesting that you use this as your opportunity to evaluate how best to make your mark in the New World. As stuffy as Americans are about fallen nobility, they have a rather charming trait—making heroines of those who have fallen and then risen again. I believe they refer to it as 'pulling oneself up by one's own boot straps.' "

Olivia did not respond. Her mind raced with the possibilities inherent in Jeremy's proposal. Perhaps she could use this as her opportunity to establish a life for herself free of the influence and patronage of some man. It was a delicious possibility, most intriguing.

"Think about it overnight," Jeremy urged. "If you wish to join this venture, we sail tomorrow on the *Cornucopia*—fitting, don't you think?" He kissed her cheek and headed for the door. "Oh, and Olivia, I would suggest packing only a few of your plainer costumes. One trunk will raise fewer suspicions among the staff and give us more time to get underway. Besides, that way, you'll look more the part of a proper English lady's companion."

She did not acknowledge this, but remained seated facing what was left of the fire.

Jeremy ignored her deliberate silence. "Yes, well. If you come, be sure you bring the jewels . . . all of them. We shall have considerable expense even before we arrive in New York. Ta, darling."

"I'll still need transportation to get to the docks," she said quietly and knew Jeremy had just smiled in triumph even though she was not facing him.

"And I shall provide it. Have your things packed—no one will suspect anything amiss since you are preparing to leave for Sir Dudley's, in any case. My man, Robert, will see that they are taken to the ship along with my own luggage."

Olivia glanced up at him and he smiled. "One has to trust someone, my dear. Robert will be handsomely rewarded for his discretion."

"With the money you raise by selling my mother's jewelry, no doubt," said Olivia.

He frowned. "I am not totally without means, Livvy. I shall pay Robert. Your jewels are an investment in the future . . . for both of us."

She paused for a long moment, knowing she was making perhaps the most momentous decision of her life. "Very well," she said softly.

Jeremy's sigh of relief was audible. "You need to be in the stables by six. Robert will drive, although I fear I must ask you to secret yourself, hiding under a blanket that will be left on the floor of the carriage. It simply wouldn't do for you to be seen. Father would have you off that ship before we could sail."

"You've never gone out at six in the morning in your life," Olivia challenged. "For that matter, you've never arisen before eleven. Won't your early morning escapade arouse suspicion?"

He reached into his coat pocket and produced an envelope. "I have thought of that. In this envelope is a note to Father telling him that I am taking a few days in the country and will meet him at Sir Dudley's in time for the wedding. I'm giving it to Father's valet to give to him in the morning . . . this morning. This way no one will be concerned with my early departure. Clever?"

"Brilliant," Olivia admitted softly. "You have indeed thought of everything."

"Why, Livvy, take care, else you display just the slightest hint of admiration for your dear stepbrother!"

She squared her shoulders. "Go to bed. I have a great deal to do." The clock chimed three, and as she thought of the fact that in just three hours she would launch a new life for herself . . . for better or for worse, she shuddered with nervous excitement. The life she had dreamed of as a girl was within her grasp. And then she hugged herself and smiled.

Adam paced the dock and checked his pocketwatch once again. Jeremy Barrington was late. Perhaps the woman was the problem. He frowned. Perhaps she had changed her mind. His mother would not be disappointed since she hadn't known of his intention, but he would be at a loss to know what else he might do to bring his mother some measure of comfort and pleasure.

He scanned the passing chaotic parade of drays loaded with luggage. As the dockworkers pushed their cargo along, their breath came out like steam in the cool spring morning. Passengers dressed in their finest traveling clothes gathered in small clusters to say their farewells and the occasional wagon filled with cargo for the hold lumbered along, forcing everyone to move out of its path. At last, he saw a carriage stop at the far end of the dock. Jeremy got out, glanced around and waved when he spotted Adam. He shouted something, but it was lost in the commotion of the scene so Adam simply nodded and waited. His disappointment was keen. Jeremy appeared to have arrived alone. There were no other passengers in the carriage.

Then, as the driver took care of unloading several pieces of luggage, Adam saw Jeremy wrestling with some sort of bundle wrapped in a horse blanket. A gloved hand appeared from the folds of the blanket and shoved Jeremy aside. Moving closer, he saw a slim ankle and lace petticoats revealed by skirts entangled in the blanket. Finally the covering was cast aside and a woman stood shaking out her skirts. She tugged the boxy outer jacket that matched her sapphire blue traveling costume into place and turned on Jeremy Barrington. She seemed to be positively enraged as she pulled what appeared to be a piece of straw from her upswept raven hair.

Adam could not suppress a smile as he watched her exchange heated words with Jeremy. This was no shrinking violet, to be sure. She reminded Adam of Miss Jessup, his first teacher. That woman had struck fear in the heart of every child and in most of their parents as well. This woman looked as if she were more than a match for Miss Jessup. He just hoped she was a match for his mother.

A blast from the ship's horn signaled passengers to board at once. Jeremy ignored the woman's ranting and spoke to his driver who nodded and walked quickly toward Adam. Jeremy took a firm grip on the woman's arm and led her in the opposite direction, perhaps to have a word with her. Adam decided to take this opportunity to observe them and to wait for Jeremy to bring the woman forward for a proper introduction.

"Will Sir Barrington be long?" Adam asked the driver as he approached.

"He asked me to tell you that he would just take care of getting Miss Marlowe settled and then he would meet you in your stateroom once you're underway, if that's agreeable, sir."

"I suppose," Adam replied. "Please inform him that I have taken the liberty of covering his passage as well as that of Miss Marlowe." He handed the driver the ticket folders.

"Very good, sir." The man retraced his steps and caught up with Jeremy.

Adam turned to board the ship, but not before he had glanced back at the woman. While Jeremy moved aside to speak in private with his driver, Miss Marlowe continued to pull bits of straw from a ridiculously small feathered hat. She was tall; while the shapeless outer jacket hid the details of her figure, she appeared slender. She was also younger than Adam would have thought from Jeremy's description of her. Jeremy had led him to believe the woman would be quite homely.

As Jeremy rejoined her she made one final attempt to properly adjust the hat before spearing it with a lethal-looking hatpin. For one moment, Adam thought she might actually use that hatpin on Jeremy as he once again attempted to take her arm. Instead she jerked her arm free of his touch and turned on him. Their conversation was intense for several minutes and then he saw the woman turn and glance over her shoulder. Whatever she saw made her abandon her debate with Jeremy. Instead, she turned on her heel and walked away from him toward the gangplank that led to the second class cabins. There was something elegant about the way she moved—the proud posture, the grace of her long, willful stride once she had freed herself of the unsightly blanket.

The blanket. What was the story behind that bit of vaudeville? Jeremy Barrington had potential, which was why Adam had offered him a position in his firm. But, the young man was not above some shenanigans when it came to making an impression. After all, Adam had only mentioned the business of finding a companion for his mother in casual conversation. Yet Jeremy had turned it into a mission. He was like an overeager younger brother—anxious to please, especially when he wanted something. And Adam knew that Jeremy wanted very much to move out from under his father's shadow and make his own mark. Still, Adam was having second thoughts about the wisdom of having allowed Jeremy to select a companion for his mother.

As he recalled the unorthodox arrival of Miss Marlowe and the way Jeremy had whisked her away without even attempting an introduction, he frowned. He had a few questions for his new business associate . . . and for Miss Marlowe as well.

Two

Olivia had spotted Jeremy's Mr. Porterfield almost at once. There was something about him that made one take note. Perhaps it was in the way he was dressed—a bit more informally than his English counterpart. He wore a suit of brown plaid accented by the pristine white of his wing collar and perfectly knotted black silk tie. The coat of the suit reached his knees and fitted him perfectly through the shoulders and waist. He carried brown leather gloves and a walking stick that appeared to have a carved knob of perhaps ivory. He was clean-shaven and his hair was hidden beneath a brown felt derby.

In short, he was perfectly dressed, perfectly groomed, and yet there was not the slightest doubt that he was not British. Perhaps it had been the fact that he was watching her with unabashed interest now as he had been watching her when she emerged from the carriage. More precisely, she had struggled out of the vehicle as she fought her way free of the foul-smelling horse blanket that Jeremy had so kindly provided and insisted she stay beneath for the duration of their journey to the docks.

The mere thought of her charming rascal of a stepbrother caused her temper to flare all over again. She must have been out of her mind to agree to this foolhardy plan of his. She had no doubt at all that he had somehow tricked the American into taking him on with the promise that Jeremy had great sums of money to invest. Who knew what story he had told the man about her?

She removed another bit of straw from her hair and pulled the jacket of her traveling costume firmly into place. Jeremy was speaking with Robert and they were both looking at the American. She followed their gaze and found the insolent man still watching her. And, was that the hint of a smile on his face? He was laughing at her. The point was that he thought that he *could* laugh at her—a thing even a rude American would never have dared to do had he realized her true position in society.

She jammed her bouclé muff firmly onto one forearm, turned on her heel and walked away. Jeremy hurried to her side, taking her elbow as if to guide her steps. She jerked her arm away.

"This is a mistake," she said tersely.

"Lower your voice, my dear," he said through a tight smile and a nod at a passing couple. "We have very little time and I need to fill you in on a few details."

She focused her attention on the rearrangement of her hat, considering the damage she might do to Jeremy's smiling face with her hatpin.

He reached up and pulled yet another piece of straw from the shoulder of her jacket. She shrugged him off. "What things?"

"The gentleman that Robert is speaking with is Mr. Adam Porterfield. It is his mother that you will. . . . That is, that he is expecting you to. . . ."

"I think that 'serve' is the word that seems stuck in your conniving throat, Jeremy," she said. "I am to masquerade as a servant, am I not?"

"A companion for his invalid mother. It's not as if you'll be scrubbing floors, Livvy. Mrs. Porterfield is English and misses the refinements of her English upbringing, especially now that Mr. Porterfield's father has passed on."

"Well, Mr. Porterfield, the Younger, must not think very much of his mother if he would hire a companion without even so much as meeting her face to face."

Jeremy grinned broadly. "I have given you a glowing reference, Olivia. There was no need for him to meet you prior to today once I had assured him of your sterling character and multiple talents."

"No doubt," Olivia replied dryly.

"Of course, he will expect to interview you in person once we are on board and have departed on the voyage. And, it is for that interview you must prepare—you must keep your wits about you and be very sure that you don't let anything slip that might raise his suspicions."

"I usually have my wits about me at all times, Jeremy. You are the one who seems at sixes and sevens much of the time." She stabbed the pin viciously into the hat, anchoring it to her upswept hair. "On the other hand, you may have a point. After all, I must have taken leave of my wits and senses and every gleam of intelligence when I agreed to take part in this plot of yours."

Jeremy's eyes widened, but he was looking past her. "Come this way," he ordered tersely and once again took her elbow.

"No." She resisted but he pulled her along.

"Well, stay if you will, but Father has just arrived on the scene and the manner in which he is scanning the docks would say that he is looking for someone—probably you, my dear."

Automatically, Olivia glanced over her shoulder. Her stepfather indeed was there, and he did not look pleased. He was speaking with a man who appeared to be part of the ship's crew.

"This way," Jeremy said, moving her quickly toward the

gangplank for second class passengers to board. "Let's get you aboard and out of sight while Father is otherwise engaged."

"What if he sees you . . . or Robert?"

"I'll take care of that. Just get on board . . . unless, of course, you've changed your mind and would like to return to your fiancé. He seems to have come along with Father."

Olivia felt panic as she spotted Sir Dudley who was hurrying back toward her stepfather. His face was very red and very angry. He was shouting at Lord Barrington, who was clearly trying to placate his old friend.

"The choice is yours," Jeremy said as he followed her gaze. "If you prefer to stay, I can say that we came to see off an old friend before leaving for Sir Dudley's estate." He smiled. "What I cannot do is return the investment you have made in our future in America, I'm afraid. On the other hand, I'm sure that Sir Dudley over time—and you shall certainly have plenty of that—will reward your fidelity with jewels of your own."

"Oh, do shut up and let me think," Olivia demanded. Her head was pounding. She had been up all night. She had made a decision that promised to change her life, but to what end? Perhaps it would be the wiser choice to stay with the familiar. Her life might not be all that she had hoped but she was a bit old for girlish dreams.

She looked once again at Sir Dudley and felt a combination of pity and revulsion. "This way?" she asked and did not wait for Jeremy as she thrust both hands into her muff and strode up the gangplank, confident that her stepfather and fiancé would never think of looking anywhere but among the first-class passengers for her. As she stepped aboard the ship, she looked back down at the dock and saw Adam Porterfield watching her. She could not resist the urge to straighten her spine and hold her head high. Mr. Porterfield might think he was getting a simple domestic to serve his mother, but even posing as a servant, she was and would always be a lady.

Jeremy watched her go and breathed a sigh of relief. For one horrible moment he had thought she would change her mind. When he had told her that the jewels would not be returning with her, he'd wondered if he'd gone too far. Her eyes had flashed but then he realized that she wasn't thinking about the jewelry. She was weighing her choices, testing her courage. He had to admire her mettle. In her shoes he would have taken the safe way and hoped for something or someone to come along and rescue him. Olivia was taking a greater risk. In electing to go forward she had effectively cut all ties to England. His father would certainly never welcome her back into his house. The members of their social circle would see her as having brought scandal to the family name. He would never have imagined that she would have the courage to follow his plan. He had hoped, but he had been trying desperately to come up with an alternative in case she'd told him he was completely out of his mind—as he'd expected her to do.

Once she was safely on board, Jeremy dodged his father and Sir Dudley by moving quickly through the throngs of people lingering to say their farewells. He reached the gangway for first-class and found Adam Porterfield waiting for him.

"I assume our young woman is aboard?"

Jeremy flashed a smile. "She's all settled in."

"I'll want to meet with her once we are underway. I've asked the steward to be sure that she is brought to me in the café. Miss Marlowe, I believe you said?"

"Yes." Jeremy hesitated, his mind racing with the logistics of how to get to Olivia and tell her what he had told Adam and what she needed to say and do. He had thought there would be more time.

He realized that Adam was watching him with a bemused expression. "It isn't a problem for you—my interviewing Miss Marlowe, is it, Jeremy?"

Jeremy realized that his sense of panic must have been revealed in his expression. Olivia had always said that she could read his face. He really needed to work on that. He smiled. "Heavens, no. She's in your hands—so to speak."

"Yes." Adam studied him for a moment longer.

To Jeremy's relief, the blast of the ship's horn alerted everyone to board or leave depending on their status as passenger or guest. "Yes, we'd best get on board or get left behind." He led the way onto the ship and handed his ticket to the purser.

"Welcome aboard, sir. The staterooms are in readiness." He nodded toward a steward who indicated that Jeremy and Adam should follow him.

As they moved quickly along the railing, Jeremy looked down in time to see his father and Sir Dudley hurrying along the side of the ship. He had been spotted.

"Jeremy!"

His father was waving madly and his lips were moving but Jeremy could not hear the words. It didn't really matter. His father's expression spoke volumes. As Jeremy felt the ship glide free of the dock, he looked directly at his father and waved farewell. He felt a pang of regret, but the fact was that his father's life was not his life. If he was ever to make his own place in the world, he had to free himself of his father's direct influence. Of course, it was to be hoped that in the not too distant future, his father would see the initiative in his move, forgive him and continue to fund him. Until then he had to rely on Olivia.

* * *

She was sitting in his stateroom when the steward ushered him in. The steward was obviously taken aback.

"Sir, I apologize. . . . Madam, I am afraid that you. . . ."

"I'll attend to this. Thank you for your assistance," Jeremy said placing a coin in the young man's palm and seeing him to the door.

"Very good, sir," the steward replied but he was clearly doubtful.

Jeremy closed the door and waited a moment to be sure the steward had left, then he turned. "Are you completely insane, Olivia?"

"I thought you wanted to talk—get our stories straight, so to speak. Shortly after I boarded, I received word that Mr. Adam Porterfield expects to meet with me later this morning. I thought you might want to discuss that." She sat on a small side chair and folded her hands primly, waiting for his response.

"I . . . yes, we do need to discuss strategy. However. . . ." He froze as other passengers could be heard moving down the passageway toward their staterooms. "However," he lowered his voice to a whisper, "we must be circumspect."

"I thought that I was being circumspect, Jeremy. No one observed my coming here. Other than the steward, no one knows I'm here and I am sure that the reward you gave him just now is incentive enough for him to keep our confidence."

"He probably thinks you are my mistress."

"Then he probably feels sorry for you," she observed quietly.

"All right. We do need to talk, but we must make this brief so listen very carefully." He paced the room. She had taken him by surprise and he had not yet had the time to form his thoughts. As a result, he made two or three false starts before she sighed and interrupted.

"Jeremy, just tell me what you have told the man and what he has told you."

"I told him that you were intelligent and capable."

"Thank you. What of my background? What stands behind my decision to do this so abruptly?"

He gave a bored sigh. "You're an orphan—without family. You have always dreamed of going to America. This was your opportunity."

"But what of my loyalty to your father?"

Jeremy shrugged. "The topic did not arise."

Olivia could see that it was going to be more difficult than she had thought to gather information from Jeremy. "Shall I offer to pay my passage?"

"Of course not," Jeremy snapped. "He assumes that expense as a part of your employment expenses."

"Then you have not paid for my passage? It has been handled by Mr. Porterfield?"

Clearly, she had caught Jeremy unawares. "I—that is, we—shall have any number of expenses, Olivia. I don't think we need quibble over the cost of your ticket," he replied.

"Very well. We can discuss the financial side of this venture later. For now, tell me everything you can about Mr. Porterfield and his family."

"But you would not know those things—if you slip and reveal something that there is no possible way you could know. . . ."

"Jeremy, I have trusted you thus far. It is time for you to trust me. I simply want to know as much as possible in order to think through answers to his questions that will make him confident that he has indeed selected—or more to the point permitted you to select—a suitable companion for his beloved mother. Now what is her condition and how does he wish me to assist her in regaining her health?"

"I don't know much. Adam has talked about his mother off and on in the course of our acquaintance. I believe the deceased father is at the root of her illness—deep mourning and all that. I take it that the elder Mr. Porterfield was quite devoted to her . . . probably indulged her shamelessly and now she misses that."

"But, are there no physical maladies?"

Jeremy shrugged. "I don't think she goes out much. Whether that is due to frailty or simple lack of interest, I cannot say."

Olivia stood, forcing him to give her his full attention. "Jeremy, you have placed us both in a difficult position. You do understand that any faux pas on my part affects your credibility with Mr. Porterfield as well. I cannot believe that I am saying this, but we do need to work together on this."

Jeremy was clearly surprised. "Why, Olivia, does this mean you've recovered from your earlier fit of pique?" He smiled and then turned serious. "You have a point. For now, however, I think that it is vital that you return to your quarters in the event that Adam sends for you."

She turned to collect the muff she'd left lying on the bed and then looked around his stateroom. "You've done quite well here, Jeremy. I trust that my jewels have already been of benefit."

He had the grace to color slightly. "I told you that I have some funds of my own, and one must make a good impression in business, my dear." He frowned. "Are your quarters . . . acceptable?"

"As with any second class accommodations, my cabin is clean and comfortable, if not as luxurious as yours. In spite of the fact that I share a watercloset down the hall,

I've no doubt that I shall survive the journey," she said with a wry smile. "I'll go now."

Olivia could not help but shake her head at the way Jeremy had insisted on checking the passageway to be sure that she would not be seen leaving his stateroom. She suspected that he was getting a bit of a thrill out of his scheme. She only hoped that he hadn't jeopardized both their futures.

"Hello, dearie."

Olivia had been so lost in thought that she had not noticed the petite woman coming down the second class passageway toward her. "You're the one traveling to New York with that lovely Mr. Porterfield, aren't you, love?"

"I—that is. . . ." Olivia was at a loss as to how to respond. In the first place, no one of her acquaintance would ever have been so bold as to ask a stranger outright about her plans. In the second place, she could not imagine how this woman could possibly know those plans.

"Oh, you're no doubt wondering how I know so much about you . . . Livvy, is it?"

"Olivia."

The woman gave her a curious smile. "Oh, a bit above it all, are we?"

"Not at all. Olivia is my name."

The smile was genuine again. "And, I'm Molly. I'm Mrs. Abigail Rutherford's maid. You know Mrs. Rutherford? No? Well, no doubt you will. She and Mr. Porterfield's mother used to be the very best of friends—giving parties in the other's honor, traveling together—their husbands too. Of course, then we lost poor Mr. Porterfield. A charmer, that one. His son appears to have inherited that trait in spades, if you get my meaning. Clever young man and completely devoted to his Mum."

Olivia was tempted to question the woman, but one didn't gossip with the help even to gather information.

Well, Jeremy probably did, but a woman in her position certainly would not.

"How come you decided to ditch it all and head for America?" Molly asked. "What did your family have to say?"

"I . . . I have no family."

Molly's face was flooded with sympathy. "Oh, dearie, I'm so sorry."

"Thank you," Olivia replied and realized that she was beginning to like the woman.

They had reached her cabin.

"Would you like to join me in a cup of tea?" Molly asked, indicating her own cabin next door.

"That would be lovely."

Molly beamed. "Oh, we're going to be the best of friends, Livvy. Just like my Mrs. R. and your Mrs. P."

Over tea with Molly, Olivia learned that the maid was not that much older than she was. She also learned that Adam Porterfield's mother had had something of a complete change in personality since the death of her husband two years earlier.

"She's not herself," Molly confided. "I can tell you that. Mr. Adam must be almost at his wit's end. He's tried just about everything and I expect you're his last hope."

"I can't imagine how he would think I could be of help," Olivia mused more to herself than to Molly.

"Oh, Livvy, you're so . . . so very English. Mrs. P. is gonna love you . . . well, perhaps not at first. She's got past appreciating much of anything." Molly lowered her voice and glanced toward the closed cabin door as if expecting someone to overhear. "Truth to tell, she's become quite the grouchy one. Never satisfied. The changeover in help in that house has been something to behold since the mister passed on. I expect your Mr. Adam Porterfield is hoping that bringing home an English woman like his Mum is just the ticket."

"Molly, he's not *my* Mr. Adam Porterfield," Olivia corrected gently.

Molly grinned. "Play your cards right and he could be." She studied Olivia's face closely. "You're not at all bad looking. Lovely skin and eyes. A bit of cosmetics could help and wearing things with a bit more color. You've got good assets, that's a fact and a man notices that right away."

Olivia blushed as she realized that Molly was referring to her bosom. "Molly, really." She wanted it to sound like a bit of a reprimand, but the fact was that the twinkle in Molly's eye was irresistible and she started to laugh instead.

The two of them were still laughing when there was a knock on the door. Molly immediately went still. Olivia was nearer and rose to answer the door.

"Yes?"

The steward frowned, clearly not liking her attitude. "I'm looking for Miss Marlowe. She is not in her cabin and I have a message for her."

"From whom?"

"The message is for Miss Marlowe, girlie. Do you know where she is?"

"She's standing before you," Molly announced, taking her place next to Olivia at the door. "Now, come off your high horse and give her the message."

Olivia bit back a smile and held out her hand for the envelope the young steward was tapping against one thigh. "Thank you," she said and closed the door.

"You can't let them think they can push you around, dearie," Molly instructed, eyeing the envelope with undisguised curiosity. "They're hired help just the same as us and there's no call to put on airs just because somebody dressed 'em up in a uniform."

"You've been very kind, Molly. Thank you so much for the tea. Perhaps I can return the favor tomorrow?" Olivia opened the door again and moved into the narrow passageway. She knew that Molly was disappointed that she was not going to share the contents of the note, but she couldn't take the risk that the message was from Jeremy; how would she explain that?

She closed the door of her own cabin, which was more crowded now that her trunk had been delivered. She studied the handwriting on the envelope. Her name was written in a large bold script that was not Jeremy's hand. She slid her thumbnail under the sealed flap, noticing the quality of the paper and its lined envelope as she removed the single sheet of paper.

Dear Miss Marlowe,

I trust that you are settling in and that you have received the message sent via the purser requesting a meeting. Please join me for lunch in the Palm Café at half after one.

Cordially,
Adam Porterfield

Not "would you join me," just *do* it. Olivia bristled. What if she were otherwise engaged? But, of course, Adam Porterfield had no interest in her calendar. She now worked for him. She was hired help.

Unconsciously, her hand went to her hair. She glanced around at her reflection in the mirror. And, what should she wear? Was her traveling costume appropriate? Her trunk stood unopened where the steward had left it. She took the key from her purse.

She struggled with the lock and opened the latches, then

slid the heavy thing open to reveal her clothes and the interior compartments that held her personal grooming items. By this time, her mood was as frayed as the two fingernails she had broken struggling with the unwieldy trunk in the cramped space.

She stared at the contents of her wardrobe and knew instantly that nothing was appropriate. "Molly," she whispered knowing that her newfound friend could advise her.

On Molly's advice, she wore her traveling suit without the outer jacket for the meeting. Molly helped her rearrange her hair and insisted that she apply at least a little lip rouge.

"You're pale as a ghost, Livvy, and it simply will not do for him to think he's hired someone not in the pink of health." To emphasize this last, she pinched both of Olivia's cheeks hard.

"Ouch!" Olivia protested.

But, Molly only smiled and stood back to survey her handiwork. "Gave those cheeks a bit of color is all. You look right smart, dearie, if I do say so myself. Now, a word to the wise. You keep those enormous green eyes of yours focused on Mr. Adam as if he's the only man in the room and I'll vouch you'll be naming your own terms." She giggled mischievously and Olivia found herself blushing yet again.

"Honestly, Molly. The things you say!" But she was smiling as Molly pushed her out the door and down the passageway. She glanced back once and Molly was still there, smiling and holding up her fingers crossed for luck.

Adam had deliberately selected a table at the far end of the café. He wanted the opportunity to observe Miss Marlowe as she crossed the long room. He had not let Jeremy know the exact time of the meeting. He didn't want

Jeremy there, for whatever had happened between the two of them that had caused that ruckus on the dock was not his concern at the moment. He had hired this young woman to care for his mother. How much should he tell her? What questions might he ask to get her to reveal her true motives for sailing to America? Worst of all, what if she was completely unsuitable?

He called the waiter over and ordered a light lunch for the two of them. He considered wine and decided against it. This was, after all, a simple business meeting, an interview of a prospective employee.

When he looked up, she was at the door of the café and he saw the steward point him out but stop short of escorting her to the table. Adam frowned in irritation at the man's act, which was clearly based on nothing more than his vanity that would not permit a man of his position to serve someone of a lesser station. Before Adam realized what he was doing, he had risen and walked halfway across the café to meet her.

"Miss Marlowe? I am Adam Porterfield. Thank you for coming." He started to offer her his arm and realized that it would not look right so he awkwardly gestured toward the table. "We're over here," he said lamely and led the way back to the table.

As they reached their places he caught the eye of the waiter who was sharp enough to come over and hold the chair for Miss Marlowe while Adam reclaimed his place across from her.

"I hope you don't mind. I took the liberty of ordering before you arrived. I do hope you have no objection to chicken."

"Chicken is fine. Thank you," she murmured.

He could not seem to stop looking into those large eyes of hers. Their color reminded him of the evergreens his father had planted at the back of the estate. He cleared his throat and spread his napkin over his lap. "Well then, shall we begin?"

She looked down at the empty place in front of her and back up. He was momentarily taken aback. Her eyes were wide with questions. They were quite mesmerizing. He shook off the fascination and smiled. "I meant the interview," he said gently. "The food should be here soon."

She continued to look directly at him, an unusual trait in someone of her position. "What is it you wish to know?" she asked.

"How do you know Sir Barrington?"

He could see that she was a bit surprised at the question. She lowered her eyes, hiding whatever expression they might have revealed with her impossibly long lashes, then looking up at him again.

"I managed the house of his father for a number of years."

"I see." Adam deliberately waited a beat. "And your relationship with the younger Sir Barrington?"

He was sure that he saw a flash of irritation before she composed herself and replied simply, "He lived in the house as well."

"And, why your sudden decision to leave the employ of Lord Barrington?"

She paused briefly. "I hope this won't give you cause to doubt my propriety, Mr. Porterfield, but perhaps you have already discovered that Sir Jeremy Barrington is quite . . . social." She glanced up to see how Adam was taking this line of conversation. "That is to say, he enjoys visiting with . . . well, just about anyone who happens to be in the room."

Adam could not help himself. He laughed, for this was a very polite but totally accurate description of Jeremy Barrington. "The man would talk to an empty chair if the room were unoccupied," he agreed and won for himself a slight smile from her.

"On one such recent occasion, he found himself talking to me as the sole occupant of a room. He told me of his plans for coming to America, and I do hope this won't cause you to think less of him, but he spoke most highly of you and the friendship the two of you have forged. He admires you a great deal. At any rate, on that day, I believe that I expressed an interest in someday coming to America myself."

It made perfect sense. Jeremy was impetuous enough to have tied that brief comment from household staff to Adam's lament that he had hoped to find a companion for his mother, and assume that he had the perfect solution. "You must have been surprised when he approached you."

"Heavens, yes," she replied. "It was all to be done in such haste. His father—that is, Lord Barrington—has kept his son on a rather tight leash for most of his life. I immediately understood his need to leave without warning."

The waiter brought their food, stopping the conversation momentarily. Adam could see that the young woman had relaxed, let down her guard a bit. He observed the manner in which she accepted the waiter's service as if it were her due. He supposed that someone who had held a high position in the household of a duke might indeed have learned to expect a certain level of service. He watched as she filled her fork and put the first bite into her mouth before continuing the interview.

"Yes, I suppose that I can understand why Sir Jeremy Barrington wished to leave without a great deal of fanfare. But, surely you had no such need, Miss Marlowe. Forgive me for inquiring, but your willingness to do so does raise a question of loyalty to your employer."

She swallowed her food unchewed and reached for her water goblet to wash it down. Her hand trembled slightly as she brought the crystal to her lips. He had interviewed enough people to know that she was taking the time she needed to shape her answer.

"Of course, you have every right to wonder," she began and for only the second time since the interview had begun, she did not meet his gaze. "I do not wish to go into detail. What I will say is that Lord Barrington can be extremely demanding and difficult. Sir Jeremy Barrington presented me with an opportunity, and I accepted it." She looked directly at him once again. "It is my hope that as a man who has made his own way in the world, you would understand that occasionally one must take a risk in order to achieve the next plateau."

"And, what will happen, Miss Marlowe, should you stumble across an equally enticing opportunity once you have been established in my household as my mother's companion?"

"I shall quite possibly take it," she answered with a candor that shocked and impressed him.

Then to his surprise she continued. "Mr. Porterfield, as you have no doubt surmised, I am past the age of marriage and family for myself. It is my sincere hope that I can be of service to your mother—and to you. But, it would be foolish of me to think you would believe that I would pledge my eternal devotion to your household. All I can say is that I am grateful for the opportunity. Once your mother meets me, she may not wish to retain me. After all, it is my understanding that you have hired me without her knowledge."

It was his turn to consider the best response. "I had no idea that Jeremy . . . that is to say. . . ."

She smiled. "I am afraid that people of my class are voracious gossips, Mr. Porterfield. I had hardly settled into my quarters before I was given information about my position that I had not learned from Sir Barrington."

Adam laughed. "I'll keep that in mind, Miss Marlowe. Frankly, I believe that if my mother does not take to you instantly, then I am at a loss as to how I might help her. You see, my mother has always been quite direct as well . . . at least, she was, until my father died."

"And now?"

Adam drew a deep breath and considered how much to tell her. "My mother's grief over my father's death has been far deeper and longer lasting than anyone might have expected. She has become more withdrawn with each passing month. She does not leave the house at all and has stopped even attempting to entertain at home."

"I'm so very sorry," Olivia replied.

The waiter interrupted to refill their water goblets. Even after he had left them alone again, the conversation did not resume. In fact, Olivia noticed that Mr. Porterfield seemed quite lost in thought. She even wondered if he had forgotten that she was sitting across from him. He concentrated on his food, which he consumed quickly and with zeal. Not knowing what might be the most appropriate comment, Olivia remained silent and took the opportunity to survey her surroundings.

The café was an informal dining room decorated to call to mind a tropical setting. Rattan furniture rested on thick Oriental carpets in a floral motif. All was set against a background of alcoves created by latticework trellises and giant palm trees and ferns. The effect was one of being a place for intimate tête-à-têtes. As she became aware of the other patrons in the café, she realized that she and Mr. Porterfield were drawing more than their fair share of curious glances. She saw one or two ladies whispering to each other behind their gloved hands.

She felt the color rise to her cheeks and focused her attention on her food. "How does your mother spend her days, Mr. Porterfield?"

Adam shrugged. "It's difficult to say. I am at my office for a great deal of the day. My father left a thriving business that demands my full attention. The truth is, Miss Marlowe, I am away from the house a great deal of the time. From what I can gather from the staff, Mother spends most of the morning in her room. On nice days she will sometimes take her lunch in the palm garden or on the terrace, but most afternoons and evenings are spent in my father's library, unless I am at home. Then, she seems to prefer to leave the library to me and spend the time in the drawing room."

"No doubt she feels close to your father in the library and perhaps when you are at home, the sound of you moving about in there is a comfort as well," Olivia said softly. She remembered how she would spend hours walking through the formal gardens at the Barrington estate because her mother had so loved to walk those paths. "Does your mother join you at dinner?"

"Sometimes. There are many occasions when I need to attend functions in the evening. When my father was living, my parents would entertain a great many guests at such gatherings in our home—at least two each week."

"I imagine that the occasions you must attend in the evenings were . . . are important to your business."

She saw that her comment had surprised and pleased him. "Exactly," he agreed, leaning forward. "And yet, they are difficult to enjoy because I am so worried about my mother."

"She does not accompany you? Ever?"

"In the beginning she made an effort, but it quickly became too much for her. Now, I go without her."

She wanted to inquire whether he might not go with a female companion, but knew that such curiosity was completely inappropriate for someone of her supposed station. "Obviously, your mother's malaise is taking a toll on your own social life as well," she said. "It occurs to me that—as a mother—she might be approached from that view. Surely, she has not lost interest in your happiness?"

Adam Porterfield was one of the most handsome men she had ever seen, but when he smiled, her heart threatened to stop altogether. She found that she could not bear to look at him, afraid that her expression might reveal her attraction. She looked away.

"Miss Marlowe, you have no idea. The one thing that my mother rallies herself for is the idea that I might settle down with some suitable—her word, not mine—young woman and present her with half a dozen grandchildren. Before Father died, she was always matchmaking. Her seating arrangements at our twice-weekly dinner parties were inspired. Usually, I found myself surrounded by two—or even three—candidates that my mother considered possibilities."

Caught up in the picture he painted, Olivia laughed. "Yet, none were acceptable?"

"That is the best part. My mother would observe said young ladies during the course of the dinner and by evening's end would have declared that not one of them was suitable for me."

"But, what of your feelings?"

He leaned back in his chair and signaled the waiter to bring coffee. "I was relieved. And then, after awhile, I have to admit that I pretended great interest in this candidate or that, knowing that Mother had already labeled her as not worthy. It was always great fun to see how Mother would approach me about those ladies." He sipped his coffee, momentarily lost in his reverie of happier days. "I would be very grateful to anyone who might bring back those days for my mother, Miss Marlowe."

Olivia thought of her own mother again. The young widow that she had been and how she had deeply mourned the passing of Olivia's father. Then after a time, she had focused her attention on Olivia and announced that while her husband had died, she had not, and she had responsibilities here on earth. Shortly after that she had met and married Lord Barrington and in so doing had secured a place in society for her daughter's future.

Of course, now Olivia had renounced all of that. It stung her deeply to think of how she had thrown aside the very sacrifice her mother had made to insure her security . . . if not her happiness. Her resolve to make a success of her decision to leave England wavered slightly.

"Miss Marlowe?"

She glanced up and found Adam Porterfield watching her. "Have I said something to upset you?"

She composed herself and shook off the memories and the newly discovered guilt. "Not at all, sir," she replied. Suddenly she wanted the interview to end. It was more difficult than she had imagined posing questions and responding in such a manner that he would not become suspicious.

"Please don't take this in the wrong way, but why have you never married, Miss Marlowe?"

Her first instinct was to curtly inform him that this was none of his business. The gall of these Americans! She could not disguise her shock at such a personal question.

Her distaste must have registered on her face, for he held up his hands as if to forestall a runaway carriage. "Really, I mean no offense. It's just that . . . well, quite frankly, you would not be the first woman of your . . . you would not be the first to come to New York in hopes of finding a husband."

"And, while that is not at all my intent, Mr. Porterfield, I fail to see what harm there could be if I should have that good fortune. Surely, my duties in service to your mother could be accomplished whether or not I marry."

He smiled again. "Good point, Miss Marlowe. Forgive my audacity, and it might interest you to know that my mother would have been equally shocked by my impudence."

He was a charmer all right—a different sort from Jeremy, to be sure. Still, he was clearly accustomed to using his smile and those devastating deep midnight-black eyes of his to get his way. She pushed her coffee cup away and laid her linen napkin on the table next to it. "Are there any other questions, sir?" she asked.

The smile disappeared. "Not at this time," he replied.

She stood. He pushed back his chair and stood as well. "Then I shall be getting back below." She fought the urge to offer him her hand, but settled instead on a curt bob of her head, and fled the room. She could not help but notice the disapproving glances of other first-class patrons as she passed. It struck her then that they looked on her as hired help and that by their raised eyebrows and whispered comments, they were letting her know that she did not belong on this deck, in this café.

Once she had reached the sanctity of her tiny cabin she closed the door and leaned against it as the tears she'd held at bay since leaving the café fell freely. "What have I done?" she whispered to herself as the full realization of how decisions she had made less than twelve hours earlier had changed her life forever.

Three

By the third day of their voyage, Olivia had settled into a routine of sorts. Every morning she would rise at first light to take a brisk walk on deck before the other passengers were up and about. She relished this time for it had replaced the solitary walks she had often enjoyed in the gardens of the Barrington estate.

After breakfast, and weather permitting, she would select a novel from the ship's library and seek out a lounge chair she had discovered in a little-used area of the ship. There she would wrap herself in a blanket against the increasingly cold air of the north Atlantic and read until lunch.

She had thought that more of her time might be taken up in meetings with Adam and discussion of his mother's needs. She was only just beginning to realize that the passage would be best used to adjust to her new circumstances and plan for how she would live her life once they arrived in America. The memory of her mother's sacrifice to assure a good life for Olivia had resolved itself in a determination to make something of this opportunity. Jeremy was right about one thing—her mother had not had choices, but Olivia was free to make her own life now.

That life would begin in the Porterfield household where she would have a safe, secure base from which to plan her next steps. The more Molly told her about Adam's mother, the less Olivia considered abandoning the lady from the outset. Perhaps she could be of help, offer a bit of sympathy, draw her out. Her more immediate concern for the remainder of the voyage was that she not call attention to herself while on board.

In order not to appear completely antisocial, she always tried to join Molly and her peers at lunch. Because they all had duties to perform for their employers throughout the day and into the evening, they seemed not to notice the vast amount of leisure time that Olivia enjoyed. She doubted that they suspected how very much she looked forward to lunching with them, for it gave her the opportunity to learn more about the goings-on in first class. The truth was she found their irreverent descriptions of their employers and their shenanigans extremely entertaining.

"Ripped her gown by catching it on the doorway, my arse," declared Molly to a spellbound audience of her peers one day. "More likely it was ripped for her, if you get my drift."

"Are you implying that her mister got a bit amorous?" asked a wide-eyed Irish girl.

Molly let out a derisive snort of laughter. "Her mister was in bed already . . . alone. Mrs. Armbruster was taking a bit of the night air with that Englishman . . . Sir Jeremy Barrington." She turned to Olivia. "You worked for him, didn't you, Livvy?"

"For his father," Olivia corrected.

"Either way, he's a charmer, that one. Wouldn't kick him out of me bed, I can tell you that."

"Sounds like Mrs. Armbruster agrees," laughed Chester Maplethorpe, a man Molly had introduced to Olivia as the Rutherfords' valet.

"Oh, she agrees, all right. Thinks nobody's noticed but it's there for the world to see."

"What is?" asked the Irish girl.

Molly sighed. "They don't even try to hide it. Why, Mickey told me that he passed right next to them and they never knew it."

Mickey was a member of the ship's crew who had taken a liking to Molly. Olivia knew of more than one evening when Molly had returned to her cabin only to slip out later to meet the young sailor.

Molly lowered her voice so that everyone had to lean in close to catch her words. "According to Mickey, Sir Jeremy had that gown plumb off her shoulders and one of his hands was up and under her skirt. Also, his mouth wasn't where it might have been, kissing her and all. He was sucking her. . . ."

"Molly!" The shocked exclamation escaped before Olivia could recall it. She felt her face flaming red at the image of Jeremy and the socialite caught in such a compromising position.

Molly glanced at her and shrugged. "It's the way of the world, Livvy. You've led too sheltered a life." She resumed eating her meal as did the others. "Anyway, *now,* she expects Sofia here to repair the gown—says it's her favorite and all. Wants Sofia to alter *all* her gowns a bit, she says. Scandalous, if you're asking me," she groused as she wrapped a comforting arm around Sofia.

Molly's sudden ill humor inflicted itself on the others and they all finished the meal quickly and in silence. But not long after Olivia had returned to her cabin, she heard a light tapping at the door and opened it to find Molly standing with Sofia, who was in tears.

Olivia immediately invited them both inside and closed the door. Sofia was wringing her hands and sniffling.

"I can't . . . I don't know how . . ." she sputtered, then finally wailed, "I can't sew worth a tinker's darn."

Molly took up the cause. "It's bloody ridiculous. The woman is asking far too much. How is Sofia supposed to fix that gown or the others?" She flailed about in the tiny cabin, finally coming to rest on the edge of the narrow bed where she spotted Olivia's needlework. "You sew. Livvy, you sew," she shouted, clutching at the handiwork. "We are saved. Thank you, Lord."

"Oh, Molly, I'm afraid that the little handwork I do to pass the time is a far cry from dressmaking. Why. . . ."

"Stay right here," Molly ordered and hurried from the room. In less than a minute, she was back, holding a gown of gold satin with an overlay of lace and beading. She presented it to Olivia.

"Molly, I . . ."

"Just look at it," she pleaded. "See, here's the tear. Try to tell me that came from catching the beading on a doorway," she huffed. "Sofia brought it to me, but there's no hope for it as far as I can see."

The gown was torn from the shoulder to the bodice. Olivia had the sudden image of Jeremy pushing the fabric out of his way so that he could . . . She closed her eyes to banish the image of her stepbrother making love to a married woman. She fingered the lace and beading.

"Please say you can repair it," Sofia begged.

Olivia held the gown up to the girl. "Are you and your mistress the same size?"

"She's a bit taller."

"Put this on," Olivia ordered and turned to get her sewing basket. "The only way to know if it can be salvaged is to see how we might rearrange the fabric or trim. . . ." She studied the gown as Molly helped Sofia slip it over her head.

"My lady wants the neckline to be lowered," Sofia said shyly. "She wants them all lower."

Molly gave a derisive snort. "The woman may have a boatload of money, but she's common as they come, if you ask me . . . wanting to go parading around like some tart."

Olivia considered her options, then went to work, pinning and basting and pinning again until she was satisfied. "There, see what you think," she said to Molly, turning the maid so that she could see herself in the small mirror behind the door. "I've had to change the neckline but. . . ."

Molly's eyes widened. "Oh, my stars in heaven, Livvy. That's beautiful and elegant and yet. . . ."

"My lady is going to love this," Sofia said in awe.

"Not to even mention that Sir Barrington is going to go out of his mind with wanting to have at her," Molly added. "I can take it from here, Livvy. Thanks, luv."

Sofia stood on tiptoe to kiss Olivia's cheek. "Oh thank you, Livvy. Thank you so much."

She changed back into her own clothes and carefully folded the gown over one arm. "I've got to get this back to her, as she wants to wear it this evening." She lowered her voice. "Truth be told, I think it's a signal she's worked out with Sir Barrington. I know that my mister plans to be part of a poker game tonight."

Molly's only comment was to raise her eyebrows in disapproval, and as she followed Sofia out the door, she squeezed Olivia's hand in gratitude.

Olivia waited until Molly and Sofia disappeared up the stairway to the first class staterooms and then quickly wrote a note to Jeremy.

We must meet. You are in danger. O.

Her stepbrother was playing a risky game. Normally she would not have concerned herself with his antics, but in this case, what he did could affect her future as well. He had many possibilities while she did not. She folded the note and considered how best to deliver it. She couldn't risk entrusting it to a crewmember. Now that she knew the level of shared gossip, she couldn't take the chance that there might be speculation about her own relationship with Jeremy. She decided to slip it under Jeremy's door herself.

Trusting that most passengers would be dressing for dinner and the crew would be otherwise occupied as well, she hurried along the passageway to Jeremy's stateroom. She planned to simply slip the message under his door and then wait for him to contact her.

She had just completed her mission when she turned and saw Adam Porterfield coming out of his room at the end of the hall. For a second she was mesmerized by the sheer beauty of the man dressed in full formal attire with the single imperfection of his tie held in one hand and the top button of his starched shirt open.

"Ah, Miss Marlowe, please tell me that you have the skill to tie one of these things. I sent my valet off on an errand, certain that I could manage alone, and frankly I overestimated my skill."

Before she could think of how she might refuse, he had placed the strip of fabric around his neck and anchored the top stud of his dress shirt.

"I'm afraid that I. . . ."

"Oh, please give it a shot, Miss Marlowe. Actually I was on my way to have Sir Barrington do the honor but then I recalled that he was going up to the bar. You didn't see him, did you?"

Olivia shook her head, her eyes riveted on his neck and jaw as he stretched both to accomplish the closing of the collar. "There," he said with a satisfied grunt. "And now with your assistance, I shall possibly make it to dinner on time." He grinned at her and bent slightly so that she could reach the tie.

Not knowing what else to do, she began the intricate process of forming the bow, making sure that it was straight and even. She almost had it done when he looked directly at her.

"What were you doing up here, Miss Marlowe?" There was no reprimand in the question, just simple curiosity. "Were you coming to see me about something?"

The carefully crafted bow came undone in her hands and she was forced to start over. "I . . . my friend, Sofia, is a maid to Mrs. Armbruster. I had helped her in the repair of a gown and I wanted to be sure that everything was all right. I must have made a wrong turn."

"Not at all. The Armbrusters have the staterooms there." He pointed to the rooms directly across the hall from Jeremy's stateroom.

"Oh." She focused all of her attention on completing the bow. "There," she said with a sigh of relief. "I do hope that will be all right, sir."

He fingered the tie but did not take his eyes from hers. "I'm sure it's fine, Miss Marlowe. Thank you." His voice had gone husky and soft, nearly a whisper and far too intimate for their circumstances of standing alone in a narrow, deserted passageway.

"You are very welcome, sir, and now if you'll excuse me." She turned to leave.

"Weren't you going to check with Mrs. Armbruster's maid?"

"I've reconsidered," Olivia replied, glancing back at him. "If Sofia needs my further assistance, she'll contact me. It would be presumptuous of me to impose myself on her or her mistress at this time. Good evening, sir."

"Good evening, Miss Marlowe."

Adam watched her retreat back down the stairway to the second class level. Absentmindedly he fingered his tie. He could still smell the unique scent of her . . . light as a spring breeze and floral, totally out of step with the very prim demeanor she presented. He wondered what one might discover if he could get beyond the carefully constructed armor that she presented to the world. While she'd been tying the bow tie, he'd been observing her. Lost in concentration, she had the most engaging habit of biting her tongue and he was quite certain that she was completely unaware of this, which, of course, made it all the more charming.

He smiled. There was no doubt in his mind that there was more to Miss Marlowe than one might expect. The woman intrigued him. She was obviously quite intelligent and he had a good feeling about how his mother might respond to her. Yes, he was going to have to thank Jeremy again for bringing Miss Marlowe to his attention.

Olivia made two wrong turns in the labyrinth of stateroom corridors and found herself walking down a hallway toward Mr. and Mrs. Armbruster who were obviously on their way to dinner.

"Jasper," Mrs. Armbruster was saying in a high-pitched babyish voice. "Must you play in that awful old poker game tonight?"

"It's business, my dearest. You know that."

"But, I shall miss you terribly."

They passed right by Olivia without acknowledging her. She doubted that they even saw her, so she stopped to watch them.

He laughed. "You won't miss me at all and you know it. You'll dance the night away as you do every night. Besides, I'm feeling lucky tonight. Perhaps I might even win enough to buy you another bauble for that perfect neck of yours."

"Oh, Jasper," she giggled and snuggled closer to her husband.

Her husband eyed the neckline of her gown and his

expression needed no interpretation. "Perhaps, my dear, I could postpone this evening's card game. You are looking especially tantalizing this evening."

"I have a better idea. You go play your game. Tomorrow we'll spend the entire day together . . . alone," she added seductively.

Suddenly Jeremy emerged from the entrance to the dining room. It was as if he'd been waiting for their arrival. Olivia saw the way his eyes drifted immediately to the exposed décolletage of Mrs. Armbruster's gown. "Good evening," he murmured, his eyes never leaving her.

"Barrington," Armbruster replied and Olivia knew by the man's use of the surname with no title that his opinion of Jeremy was not high. "Come my dear," he said as he took his wife's arm and guided her into the room before Jeremy could say anything more.

Instead of returning to the dining room Jeremy headed down the passage in the other direction, away from Olivia.

"Jeremy," she called in a loud whisper.

He turned, obviously startled. "Are you completely out of your mind, Olivia?" he demanded, hurrying to where she waited and ushering her onto the deck and into an alcove where they were unlikely to be seen.

"I might ask the same of you," she huffed, pulling her arm free of his clutch. "I left you a note."

"Yes, I received it. I was on my way to find you. What danger?"

"That danger," she replied, jerking her head in the general direction from which they'd come. "Mrs. Armbruster," she explained when he looked mystified.

Jeremy relaxed and grinned. "Ah, yes, Grace Armbruster. Didn't she look delicious?"

"I see that you received *that* message as well."

Jeremy actually looked shocked. "Why, Olivia, I do believe that your change in social standing has made you a bit coarse."

"Oh, really. So, wearing the gold gown is not a signal of her intention to meet you later for some illicit encounter?"

His shock was genuine. "How . . . that's not . . . you could not possibly. . . ."

"The people of my station, dear Jeremy, have one lovely advantage. The people of *your* station tend not to notice us even when one of us is standing not two feet from you when you are practically undressing the beautiful Grace."

"You were there? You saw?" His face flamed red with embarrassment.

"Blessedly, no. I did not. But others did . . . one of them closely associated with your precious Grace. I would strongly urge you to be more circumspect in your choice of companions, dear Jeremy. The lady is married, after all, and to a very powerful man from what I can gather."

"Grace has her own money," Jeremy sniffed.

"Well, I just wonder how Mr. Porterfield would react to his new associate romancing the wife of one of his colleagues. He strikes me as a man of honor who would not look kindly upon such a thing."

Jeremy sighed. "But you saw her. She's so . . . desirable . . . so inviting . . . so. . . ."

"Married," Olivia repeated softly. "Jeremy, there must be a dozen or more eligible young beauties on this ship, each of them dying for you to notice them."

She could see that he wasn't listening. "I shall handle this, Olivia. Now, please return to your cabin before we are seen talking and more rumors are begun."

Olivia frowned. "You will be careful?"

He grinned. "Why, my dearest Olivia, one might actually think you cared."

He was impossible. "Good night," she said and made her

way to a door that led out to the deck. From there she was certain that she could find her way back to her cabin.

" 'Evening, Olivia."

She had been so focused on the encounter with Jeremy that she hadn't even noticed Chester Maplethorpe.

"Good evening," she replied.

"I see you've been kept working late tonight as well as I have," he said in a light conversational tone as he fell into step with her.

"I . . . yes. Molly told me that you work for the Rutherfords?"

He chuckled. "Fine family, but the mister is a bit of a tightwad so he calls on me for double duty on trips like this one. On land, I'm his driver, but on the high seas, I'm his valet. Saves one passage, don't you know?"

There was no malice or bitterness in his tone.

"But that doesn't seem quite fair," she exclaimed. She was beginning to relax and appreciate the fact that he was leading the way through the labyrinth of storage lockers, ventilators, and stored lifeboats that crowded the second deck.

Chester shrugged. "He pays me a bit more, and he's an easy gent to please. Not like some."

She caught the change in his tone. "You've worked for other gentlemen, then, who have not been as appreciative?"

"Not meself. I've always been with the Rutherfords, but there's some like that right here on this ship. That Barrington chap for one."

Olivia was so surprised by his mention of Jeremy that she did not see the deck chair in her path and stumbled. Chester was immediately there to keep her from falling. "Are you all right?"

She nodded. "Just a bit clumsy, I'm afraid."

He took her hand and placed it firmly in the crook of

his arm. "Don't have your sea legs as yet, I'll wager." He covered her hand with his and walked on.

"You had mentioned Sir Barrington," she reminded him, hoping that she didn't sound too curious. "You don't care for him?"

"He's a bloody scoundrel, if you'll pardon my language. He's one of those with the fancy title and the rich father who's not worthy to polish the boots of men like my Mr. Rutherford or your Mr. Porterfield. Self-made men, them, with plenty of reason to puff out their chests and strut about."

"Perhaps Sir Barrington is just immature," she ventured.

"He's mature enough to go after other men's wives," he replied, and she could tell that his jaw had tightened in anger. "You'd best watch yourself around that one, miss. Pardon my saying so, but a woman like you who has a quick mind and is pretty to boot is just the kind he'll go after and never think twice about having his way, luring you to his stateroom on some silly pretense and then. . . ."

"Mr. Maplethorpe, I really don't think. . . ." Olivia was shocked by the realization that he was on the verge of painting a fairly graphic picture of his ideas of what Jeremy might do to her.

Chester stopped. "Oh, Livvy, I am sorry," he mumbled and ducked his head in shame.

"There's no harm," she assured him. "Thank you for seeing me safely back to my cabin. I'll say goodnight then?"

"I was wondering . . ." He glanced up and down the passageway as if checking to be sure they were alone. "It was a real pleasure walking with you, Olivia. Do you think that maybe we might do it again?"

"One never knows what happenstance may find us walking in the same direction, Chester," she replied lightly.

He frowned. "I was meaning something more intentional," he said. "I was thinking maybe tomorrow night . . . oh, never mind. Goodnight, Livvy." And with that, he practically fled back out onto the deck where the darkness swallowed him.

It was very late when she heard Molly's knock. "Livvy, are you awake?"

"Come in," Olivia invited, laying her book aside.

"I just couldn't keep this 'til morning," Molly bubbled. "You'll never guess what happened to Sofia's mistress tonight."

Jeremy, what have you done now? Olivia thought and her heart sank. She steeled herself against what Molly might reveal.

"Sir Jeremy never showed up after dinner. Oh, Sofia told me that Mrs. A. was furious, all right until my Mickey brought her a message."

"From Jer . . . Sir Jeremy?"

"The same. Apparently he'd been drawn into the very same poker game Mr. A. was playing in. If you ask me, Mr. A. arranged it all. The man isn't blind and he must have seen how Sir Jeremy and the missus had been making eyes at each other."

"So, she forgave him?" If the socialite were placated, perhaps she would not make trouble for Jeremy.

"She sure did, especially when he wrote that there would be a special reward for her patience and told her that the gift Mr. A. would bring her from his winnings at the game was actually a gift from Sir Jeremy. Oh, he is a rascal, that one."

"I don't understand," Olivia replied.

"Well, Mr. A. comes back to the stateroom just as Sofia was helping the missus get ready for bed and he gives her this velvet box and she opens it and there inside was the most smashing rope of pearls ever seen. Oh, she squealed out loud over it and Mr. A. thought she was happy with him, but . . ."

Olivia had stopped listening with the words "rope of pearls." There was no doubt in her mind that Jeremy had used her jewels for his gambling and that he had deliberately paid his losses with her mother's impressive strand of pearls just so that he could find favor with a woman.

"Livvy, dearie, are you all right? You're looking quite flushed all of a sudden. Perhaps opening the porthole a bit. . . ."

"No, no. I'm fine. Go on with your story."

"Nothing more to tell, but you can bet that Mrs. A. will be flaunting those pearls right under the mister's nose tomorrow, and you can also bet that Sir Jeremy will collect his reward."

"This is terrible," Olivia said more to herself than to Molly, but Molly only shrugged.

"It's the way of things. Rich folks have all these rules about how you're supposed to be, but in the end they do pretty much as they please. If you ask me, half the fun for them is breaking the rules and not getting caught." She touched the back of her hand to Olivia's forehead. "You're not looking at all well. Shall I call someone?"

Olivia smiled. "No, please don't trouble yourself. I just need some rest. I'll be fine in the morning."

"Very well. I'll leave you then, but if you get to feeling worse, just peck on the wall there and I'll come running."

As soon as Molly was gone, Olivia got up and dressed. How dare Jeremy use her pearls to entice some woman who had no business becoming involved with him at all? He had told her that the jewels were to be an investment in Mr. Porterfield's business. She was not going to stand by idly while he squandered away her property on gambling and loose women.

She slipped out of the cabin and up to the first class deck.

Unfortunately, there were two couples saying prolonged goodnights in the passageway that led to Jeremy's stateroom. Determined that she would have this out with him tonight, Olivia decided to walk the deck until the coast was clear. She pulled her shawl closer and wished she had taken the time to dress more warmly for the cold night air.

"Evening, ma'am. Can I be of service?" She had not even noticed the crew member approaching.

"No, thank you. Just getting a breath of air," she said.

"Well, there could come a change in the weather, Miss. It promises to get a mite stormy tonight. I'd advise you to get inside."

She smiled at him. "Just a short walk then," she said.

He tipped his hat and moved on.

Olivia heard laughter from the passageway. The two couples evidently were in no hurry to retire. She started to walk the perimeter of the deck where it was darkest, enjoying the wind and sea spray on her face as she walked. She had not taken the time to put her hair up and it blew around her shoulders and face like a cloak. The ship cutting its path through the sea, racing toward something it could not see out there in the darkness suddenly became an analogy for her own journey. As she closed her eyes and gave herself up to the motion of the ship, the full ramifications of her choice in being on her way to a completely new life hit her. It was as if she had escaped something far more significant than a boring marriage. She stood on the precipice of something far more exhilarating and profound than anything she ever could have imagined. As the force of the wind buffeted her skirts, she held to the railing and slowly swayed in rhythm with the ship's riding of the waves.

"Miss Marlowe?"

Olivia almost lost her balance and might have found

herself cast overboard were it not for the strong arms of Adam Porterfield catching her and holding her close.

"You startled me," she gasped, raising her voice in order to be heard above the raging wind.

He did not reply, nor did he release her except to raise one hand and capture her hair as the wind whipped it around his face.

Olivia knew that she should step away and yet she could not seem to move at all. Her eyes were riveted on his, blacker now than ever as a beam of light from the lit passageway cast his features in shadow.

"Miss Marlowe," he said again and this time his voice was husky. He drew her closer and she could feel the warmth of his breath on her face in sharp contrast to the chill of the wind and sea spray.

She turned away from him toward the sea and felt his lips skim her cheek. "I'm all right now," she said shakily and took one step back.

He loosened his hold but did not entirely let her go. "Come. You're freezing. Let's get you something to warm you."

He guided her toward the passageway—deserted now. "Please, Mr. Porterfield, this is quite inappropriate."

He smiled and tucked a wisp of her hair behind her ear. His gesture only served to remind her of how she must look, her hair loose and tangled around her shoulders.

"Surely, there is nothing improper in a cup of coffee or tea to warm you before you catch cold, Miss Marlowe. After all, now that you are in my employ, I have a responsibility to look after your welfare."

"Nevertheless," Olivia stated firmly.

"Nevertheless, Miss Marlowe, I'm afraid that I must insist." It was quite clear that he was not accustomed to debate when it came to his decisions.

Four

With only the slightest relief she saw that he was not leading her back to his stateroom as she had suspected but rather toward the café where they had shared lunch.

"I am quite sure that the ship's crew has retired for. . . ."

"Then I shall have to serve you myself," Adam replied, anticipating her every objection. He led her to a chair and waited for her to be seated. "Fortunately the staff keeps a pot of coffee brewing for the crew. The trick is to uncover the accessories."

As soon as his back was turned, Olivia made a useless attempt to tame her hair. She had to settle for gathering it in one hand, twisting it as if she were wringing out a wet cloth and pulling it over one shoulder.

"Are you inclined to take a midnight stroll on a regular basis, Miss Marlowe?" He was rummaging about in the service area, clanging metal containers, as he set silver spoon on china plate. "I'm not sure I can manage cream," he commented, his voice muffled as he continued his search and serving of the coffee.

"Really, this is not necessary," she insisted.

"We were discussing your midnight walks," he reminded her.

"I am not in the habit of strolling the decks past midnight," she replied.

"But you enjoy taking walks," he stated. "I've noticed you walking in the mornings. Quite determinedly at times."

"I believe that fresh air is a health advantage, sir."

He laughed. "As does my mother. There is a lovely park just across the street from our home in New York, Miss Marlowe. My parents used to take morning and evening strolls there together. Since my father died, my mother has not set foot in that park. I do hope you can persuade her to return to that habit." He set a mismatched china cup and saucer in front of her and another for himself across from her. Then he returned to the service area and brought the steaming coffeepot.

"Please allow me," she said, pulling his cup closer to her own and reaching to relieve him of the pot.

"It's very hot," he warned as he set it on the table and turned the handle toward her.

Expertly she poured coffee for each of them. "Sugar?" she asked.

"Three," he replied with a sheepish grin.

She plopped three cubes into his cup and passed it to him. His fingers brushed hers as he took it and for that instant their eyes met. She thought of the moment on deck when he had held her close, when his lips had brushed her cheek. She wondered if she had only imagined the attempt to kiss her or if she had brought on the action of his lips brushing her cheek through the act of turning her head so suddenly.

"It was very nice of you to think of this, sir," she said, concentrating on filling her own cup and setting the pot down without revealing how shaken she was by the mere memory of his touch. She warmed her hands on the sides of her cup.

He sipped his coffee, watching her over the rim. "Are you feeling better, Miss Marlowe?"

"I was not feeling ill," she replied without thinking.

He smiled. "Still, you'll forgive me for worrying about you. After all, I would like to get you to New York in fine health." He reached across the table as if to pat her hand.

"So you have said," she replied, withdrawing her hand to her lap as she took a sip of her own coffee. "Perhaps this would be a good time for you to explain exactly what my duties are to be, Mr. Porterfield." She hoped that her tone and her direct gaze left no question of what she was really asking. When he actually colored slightly, she knew that he had understood.

Adam felt his face flush and turned his attention to refilling his coffee cup. The woman was a complete enigma. She had an aura about her that was unlike any domestic he had ever met—even those who had achieved highest rank in a household. In his travels through England and the Continent, he had stayed in the homes of some of the wealthiest families, and not once had he met anyone like Miss Olivia Marlowe.

The best household staff held high standards for how they would interact with their employers and visitors to the home. The best of them were loyal and dedicated, viewing themselves as an extension of the overall reputation of their employer's family heritage. Even on those occasions when the employer was less than honorable or even morally bankrupt, it was not uncommon for the servants to be above reproach. Miss Marlowe appeared to have those qualities as well. But there was another dimension to her.

The woman had standards for *herself* and how she would permit others to treat her. That was the difference, and he had never before met a woman in whom he was immediately interested as he was in Miss Marlowe. It amazed him how much of his time since beginning this voyage had been taken up with thoughts of her.

Still, he could not help but be slightly offended that she had assumed he was hinting at something other than a purely business relationship. "Miss Marlowe, please be assured that I am not in the habit of . . . that is, I do not now, nor have I ever. . . ." He swallowed his coffee in two quick gulps, and stood up. Casting about for anything with which to occupy himself, he began clearing the table.

"That is a great relief to me, Mr. Porterfield," she replied in a calm and gentle voice. "And now, perhaps you would be so kind as to let me attend to clearing away our dishes while you retire to your stateroom. I'm sure that a man of your position must have important business that awaits you in the morning, and you need your rest in order to be at your best."

He stood looking at her for a long moment and then set the dishes back on the table. "Very well," he said. "Thank you, Miss Marlowe."

"Goodnight to you, sir," she said as he turned to leave the room.

"And to you," he replied without looking back.

On the way back to his stateroom, he mentally chastised himself for his fascination with this stranger. He had never been in the least attracted to any servant or employee before. Throughout his youth, the house had been filled with a variety of comely immigrants who started life in America by serving his parents. His friends as well as his father's business associates had ogled one young woman from France whose face and figure had turned heads whenever she walked down the street or entered a room. Further the young woman had made no secret of her attraction to him. But his parents had taught him early and well that living a life of privilege did not entitle him to take advantage of others . . . even if others seemed perfectly amenable.

What was it about the very prim, almost prudish Miss Marlowe that had him acting in a manner that went against the very core of his honor? Had she not resisted when he'd caught her in his arms on deck, he would have surrendered to the moment and kissed her. It was completely out of character for him. He forced himself to analyze the unusual predicament as he might a tricky business project.

Her intelligence was undeniable and along the way she had developed her own innate sense of good breeding and elegance. She carried herself with dignity and presented the picture of a woman of high social standing. He supposed it was the result of her years of service in managing the households of people like Lord Barrington. Yet, even knowing all of this, he'd been drawn to her from the moment he'd observed her arrival at the dock in Southampton. She was an enigma and as such, a hazard to his moral code.

Well, there was only one solution. If he was going to survive the remainder of this trip with his honor—not to mention hers—intact, he needed to take immediate action. The least obvious course was one of spending as much time with her as possible. On the surface it might seem the very antithesis of what was required and yet Adam believed that in spending time with her, getting to know her, he would recover from whatever spell she seemed to have cast over him. In this case familiarity would indeed breed contempt, at least for a relationship beyond that of employee and employer. Satisfied that he had solved the problem, he returned to his stateroom and sat down at his desk to compose a message to Miss Olivia Marlowe.

Olivia woke from a mostly sleepless night to discover that an envelope had been slipped under her door. She did not need to leave her bed to reach it in the narrow confines of the cabin. She recognized the bold scrawl as that of Adam Porterfield and drew a deep breath before sliding her nail beneath the sealed flap.

Dear Miss Marlowe,

It occurs to me that, while you are already in my employ, your duties as my mother's companion cannot begin until we reach New York some ten days from now. As my assistant did not join me on this trip, I would call upon you to assist me with the day-to-day tasks associated with various business matters during the remainder of our journey. I have been impressed with your obvious intelligence during our brief discussions, and I am sure that you could be of great assistance in managing such matters as my correspondence and similar secretarial tasks.

I shall expect you to report to my stateroom as soon as you have breakfasted this morning. I have requested a second desk in the parlor of my suite, which I am using as an office while on board. I believe that a schedule of two hours after breakfast each morning and four hours in the afternoon will still leave you ample time for your daily constitutional.

Cordially yours,
Adam Porterfield

Olivia read the note, then read it again. She mentally chastised herself for the rush of excitement that came over her at the thought of spending more time with Adam. What on earth was she thinking of? This was the worst possible event. Now, she would have to keep up the pretense that Jeremy had thrust upon her for hours every day. It was one thing to prepare herself to deceive a sick old woman, but Adam Porterfield was another matter altogether.

She sighed. Under other circumstances, any opportunity

to be in his presence would be thrilling because she would be his equal . . . if not his better. Then if he looked upon her with those deep-set obsidian eyes of his, she might actually consider that his interest ran deeper than the baser instincts of a man studying a woman. But to Adam, she was hired help and a man like that—even an American—surely did not seriously consider any sort of binding relationship with a servant. Would Jeremy for one instant consider a lasting relationship with any one of the barmaids or housemaids he had bedded through the years? Of course not. He would find the idea laughable . . . as would Adam Porterfield.

And, if he knew your true identity . . . your true position in society? she silently asked her reflection in the dresser mirror. Perhaps he might look her way if her estate or social standing might enhance his own, but men of his ilk did not base their choice of a wife on passion. Her mother had taught her that marriages were intended for the merger and enhancement of two powerful families to make them even more prestigious and powerful. That's why Lord Barrington had promoted her marriage to Sir Dudley. That's why her mother had married Jeremy's father, and it was even at the foundation of her marriage to Olivia's father. The fact that her parents had come to love each other, much in the way that Adam described the love of his own parents, was the exception, not the rule. No, love and passion had no place in a decision on marriage from what she had observed. Men of that class—*her* class—sought their pleasures in backstairs dalliances with the help or affairs with the wives of their associates. As often as not, they did so with the full knowledge and unspoken approval of their wives.

Well, if Mr. Adam Porterfield had gotten any such ideas of conducting an illicit affair with her during the long, tedious days of their crossing, he could think again. She had the advantage here without his knowing it. She did not need this position and she could certainly repay him many times over for his payment of her passage to America. One item from her mother's jewels should more than compensate him for the price of her ticket. On the other hand, it was too early to risk revealing her true identity. She must first get to New York and see how best to establish herself. The position in the Porterfield house gave her a measure of security and the time necessary to get her bearings and plan her future. Besides, if she could continue the pose of an employee and thwart any ideas he might have of a dalliance, then she might indeed be striking a small blow for others. Perhaps in watching her, Molly and her friends would see an example to follow, for she had no doubt that once they found out that she was spending her days in Mr. Porterfield's stateroom, they would assume the worst.

She threw aside her covers and dressed as quickly as possible. Yes, this might be an interesting project and one that would indeed hold her attention for the remainder of the trip. She had planned to find Jeremy and discuss the matter of the pearls, but that could wait. She cast off her nightclothes and laced on her corset, using the trick that Molly had shown her for lacing herself without assistance. She selected her green serge skirt and a white high-necked blouse with a lace bodice, piled her hair expertly into a no-nonsense topknot, armed herself with the small notebook she had been using as a journal and a pencil and headed off to breakfast.

"In his stateroom?" Molly asked again after Olivia had told the group at breakfast of her new duties. Olivia did not miss the glances that passed between others at the table. Chester Maplethorpe refused to raise his head, pretending an inordinate interest in his food. Molly simply rolled her eyes. "Oh, dearie, clearly you've caught his eye."

Olivia feigned both ignorance and alarm. "Why, whatever do you mean, Molly?"

"He fancies you," Chester replied bluntly and abruptly pushed back his chair and left the room.

"And, why not?" Molly replied defensively. "There's some who likes the smart ones."

Olivia blushed, well aware that Molly had not identified her as beautiful—or even pretty. "I'm sure you're mistaken," she said and sipped her tea.

"Not bloody likely," another lady's maid replied with a hoot of laughter. "Work in his stateroom indeed! It'll be you that's doing the work, love, of satisfying him."

"That won't happen," Olivia replied with a calm determination that got their immediate attention. She stood and picked up her notebook.

"Livvy," Molly reached over and detained her with a gentle hand on her arm. "If you're thinking that Mr. Porterfield is different from the others, don't be so sure. When it comes to—urges—he's a man, same as any other."

"Ah, but Molly, he has not yet had to deal with the likes of me," Olivia replied.

As she reached the door, she heard Mickey mutter under his breath, "Me money's on the gent. He'll have his hands inside that starched shirt before sundown and she'll be on her back before the week's out."

Olivia shut her eyes tight to block out the images his words created, then squared her shoulders and headed for the ship's library before continuing on to her appointment in Adam's stateroom.

"Good morning, sir," she announced when Adam himself answered her knock at his stateroom door. He was dressed in a navy blue double-breasted jacket and light gray trousers. His white shirt played against the darker tone of his skin and thick hair and his carefully knotted blue tie made his eyes sparkle like the ocean on a clear sunny afternoon. He took her breath away. It seemed as if every time she thought she was prepared to see him again, she was struck anew by his incredible good looks and something more . . . something she could only define as dangerous for the very fact that she could not put a name to it.

"I do hope you won't mind but I have taken the liberty of securing working space in the ship's library for us," she said. "The purser has assured me of a quiet corner where we can discuss the assignments you have for me and where I can then pursue them without interruption, leaving you the privacy and respite of your stateroom." She had practiced the speech repeatedly as she came down the hallway. She had concentrated so hard on getting the words out in just that order that she had failed to take a breath. As a result, she finished the statement and then gulped air.

Adam seemed amused. "I'm not going to compromise you, Miss Marlowe," he said and stood aside indicating that she should come inside.

Beyond him she could see the very proper parlor with the expected sitting area and desk and no hint of the bedroom and personal area that lay beyond. She stood her ground and remained in the hallway.

"I am not questioning your motives, sir. However, it's a small ship and I would not have people speculating about a man of your status. It would not be at all proper and could certainly jeopardize your standing with important clients or associates."

Now he frowned. "Some of my dealings are a matter of confidentiality, Miss Marlowe. I can hardly discuss them in a public venue."

"I have thought of that, sir. The area where we will work is quite removed from the general seating area of the library and when one speaks in low tones, it is quite impossible to hear what is being said."

"You've tested this?"

She nodded. "Quite frankly, sir, in my opinion you would have a far greater chance of having your conversation overheard by someone listening at this door than you would of being overheard there in the library."

"I see." Adam looked over toward the small table he had obviously planned to use as her desk. She took heart when she saw that indeed there seemed to be work waiting for her attention.

"Miss Marlowe, I am not in the habit. . . ."

"Oh, forgive me, sir, for being so presumptuous. It's just that in my management of Lord Barrington's affairs, I gained the habit of taking initiative to assure that his every need was being met while also looking out for his welfare. He was such a busy man—as are you—and well, frankly, sir, sometimes I know how things that seem of no import to you might in fact cause you problems down the road a bit." At this, she brushed past him and gathered up the pile of papers and letters that he had placed on the small table. "Besides, as I mentioned," she added brightly as she hurried past him back into the passageway, "with my working in the library, you'll have your privacy here for carrying on."

His eyebrows lifted and a smile played at the corners of his mouth. *"Carrying on,* Miss Marlowe?"

She blushed. "Oh, I didn't mean to imply . . . that is, sir . . . what I was trying to say was that when you want to hold private meetings and such. . . ."

Now he laughed aloud. "Thank you, Miss Marlowe. I can see that I have been right to place my confidence in your ability to attend to my best interests in terms of secretarial needs for the balance of our journey together." He stepped out into the hall and pulled the door to the stateroom closed behind him. "Lead on, Miss Marlowe, for I am embarrassed to say that I have not yet had the occasion to locate the ship's library." He gave her a slight bow and waited for her to lead the way.

When they reached the library, she discovered that he had indeed organized quite a stack of correspondence that needed attention. She began looking through the letters and other documents, taking in his scribbled notes.

"I am afraid that I am not very good at this," he told her. "I tend to be far too direct for many of my colleagues. Much of the time our correspondence calls for a gentler touch," he added with a wry smile. "Some of my clients are French, and there is one German, and it would appear that when it comes to dealing with an American, they have their own opinions about how things should be done."

"How do you handle that when you are in your office?"

"My secretary is adept at letting me tell her the gist of what I want to say and then putting it into words that are appropriate for the occasion."

"We could certainly give that a try and see how things go," she replied, never stopping to consider whether or not he might find it odd that someone supposedly untrained in secretarial skills might be a bit less confident about taking on the role. "I used to handle some of Lord Barrington's correspondence," she hurried to add.

"Then, let's begin," he said and selected a letter from the stack. "Ah, this one is routine and a response is overdue." He quickly read through the letter and then handed it to her. "Let him know that while I will be back in the city by said date, I am not available for a meeting for at least three weeks. Choose a date and state that I will expect to see him at eleven on that morning in my offices."

She scribbled notes in her notebook, nodding as the instructions rolled off his tongue. "You're not particularly interested in what this man has to offer?" she asked.

"Very astute, Miss Marlowe." He selected another letter, gave her similar brief notes and when she looked up expectantly, selected a third and kept going until an hour had passed and they were already more than halfway through the pile.

"Well," he said, glancing at his pocketwatch and standing, "I think we have given you quite a lot to complete on this your first day, Miss Marlowe. Perhaps I will stop back later this afternoon and we can review the drafts of your replies?"

"That would be fine, sir," Olivia replied. "And, thank you, sir, for this opportunity to be of service."

He nodded, gave her a tentative smile and seemed about to say something more. Instead he nodded and started for the door.

She watched him walk the length of the room, saw how the three other men and two women in the room glanced first at him and then at her and then returned to their reading or letter writing. She smiled at her little victory. There wasn't the slightest chance that anyone would mistake his relationship with her for anything more than employer and employee. She turned back to the work at hand with a satisfied smile.

"Oh, by the way, Miss Marlowe . . ."

He was standing all the way across the room at the double doors of the library when she turned. He spoke to her in a ridiculous pseudo-whisper that only served to attract more attention than he would have received had he spoken in a normal voice. "When we meet again, I shall provide tea and cakes with strawberries . . . the kitchen has the most wonderful strawberries." He gave her a little wave and left the room as five pairs of eyes followed his exit and then turned to observe her.

He was as much a rogue as Jeremy, no doubt enjoying the fact that he had lulled her into a false sense of being in control and then spoiled it all with his thinly veiled hint that in the afternoon their meeting would be far less formal.

By two she had completed every letter. The first two had been difficult, but then somehow she had gotten into the rhythm of his speech, remembering their conversations. If she did say so herself, she had done an admirable job. She sat back and stretched her tired back.

"Ah, Olivia, my dear, how goes the voyage?"

She had not been aware of Jeremy's presence in the now deserted library.

"I would have thought to see you anywhere but here, Jeremy," she replied and busied herself with reorganizing the correspondence so that she did not have to look at him. "Perhaps you have mistaken this for the card room?"

"I do not play cards at midday, Olivia. It's an evening sport."

"Shipboard gossip has it that you enjoy other *sport* in the evenings."

"Olivia, you shock me." It was clear that Jeremy was amused, not shocked.

"Let's be perfectly candid about one thing, Jeremy," Olivia said, dropping any pretense of banter. "I did not invest my mother's jewelry in this little venture so that you would be able to use it for your gambling or to assuage the hurt feelings of your paramours. Is that understood?"

"Why, Olivia, I am simply conducting business. My methods may be unorthodox, but never fear, my dearest sister, the results will be well worth the effort."

"I am *not* your sister any more than Mrs. Armbruster is a business associate."

"She and her husband are clients of the firm, Olivia. Of course, I am going to pay attention."

"Judging by the rope of pearls around her throat when

I saw her earlier this morning, you are paying her more than attention, Jeremy."

"Olivia. Olivia." He shook his head as if dealing with a small child. "I lost the pearls to him so that he would give them to her. I had shown them to her earlier and she had coveted them. Don't you see, by letting him win something of such magnificence, I endeared myself to him. He may not respect me, but he likes me."

"Why would he like you?"

"Because when he gave those pearls to his wife, it is my guess that she was extremely grateful."

"Don't be crude."

"At the same time," he continued without acknowledging her reprimand, "his lovely—and oh so grateful—wife, upon recognizing the pearls knew very well that they had been placed on the gambling table as a message . . . a gift of sorts from me to her."

Olivia was intrigued in spite of herself. "I do not follow you."

"Earlier that day when I showed Grace the pearls, I told her that I was going to see that she had them since she was clearly so fond of them."

"And, how did she respond?"

"She laughed, of course. What would you have done?"

"I would not have been party to such a conversation since the pearls already belong—belonged to me," she reminded him.

"Humor me," he said impatiently. "Think of it, Olivia, when Mr. A. walked into her stateroom and draped that very rope of pearls around her throat and regaled her with the tale of how he had outwitted me to gain them, she knew."

"Knew what?"

"Don't be obtuse, dear Olivia. She knew that I had kept my word."

Olivia could not believe that she was actually wasting her time listening to this. "Jeremy, the pearls are not the issue. Well, actually they are because they symbolize what I will not tolerate and that is the wanton dispersal of my valuables."

"Olivia, my dear, you seem to forget one important matter in all of this."

"And that is?"

"You 'invested' those jewels in return for saving you from marriage to Sir Dudley. Bluntly put, Olivia, your jewels were the price of your escape from a life of tedium, not to mention having to deal with Sir Dudley performing his husbandly duties. My plans for them are truly none of your affair."

Instinctively she raised her hand to him. He caught it easily and stopped the blow. "There, there, my dear," he said as he led her to a chair. "Why don't we sit down and discuss this calmly?"

"I have been a fool—all the more so because I know you so well and yet. . . ."

He shrugged. "Sometimes, desperation will lead us to act in ways we would not ordinarily think to act. If it's any consolation, I was stunned when you agreed to my plan."

"Nevertheless, you led me to believe that the jewels were to be our security once we arrived. It was my understanding that in the event things did not go as planned, we would have them to. . . ."

"Olivia, regardless of what you may think of me, I am not completely heartless. I will not leave you to flounder should the position in Adam's household not work out for you. I. . . ."

Her eyes widened in understanding. "You think that you have solved everything—rescued me from an unwanted wedding by placing me in the role of a domestic?"

It was clear that he was confused by her shock. "Well, haven't I?"

"Jeremy, would *you* be satisfied with that?"

"It's not the same thing at all. My needs are. . . ."

"Jeremy, I don't know the first thing about being a lady's companion. In spite of the fact that it seems to have escaped your memory, I have lived my entire life being served."

He blinked. "Well, yes, which puts you in a perfect position to know exactly what Adam's mother will expect. Don't you see, dear Olivia, you are going to amaze her and Adam and *that* shall be your entrée to great success in America. Titled ladies and gents are everywhere in New York—hardly worth noticing. Believe me, we have set for ourselves a path that will permit us to distinguish ourselves from the pack. We shall be the toast of the town within a year."

"I must have been completely mad to have put my faith in you," she murmured as she covered her face with both hands.

Jeremy seemed at a loss and actually patted her shoulder in an awkward attempt to comfort her. "Livvy, please. This will work. It will," he promised. "It has to," he added more to himself than to her.

She looked up at him. He was staring out the stained glass windows of the library, and it was clear to her that he was thinking of the future—*his* future.

"Jeremy, I want my jewels back."

His attention was immediately back on her. "I can't do that, Livvy. And, should you be thinking that you will create a scandal here on board, rest assured that it will be your word against my own—unless, of course, you wish to bring Father into it. In that case, you shall win, but at what cost?" All evidence of the comfort he had offered was gone and in its place was the Jeremy she knew best—

the man who was determined to make his mark regardless of the cost.

"Miss Marlowe?"

She turned at the sound of Adam Porterfield's voice. "Yes sir," she replied as she turned her back on Jeremy and picked up the portfolio of letters. "I have completed your correspondence, sir."

"Very good, Miss Marlowe. Then shall we review the work over tea and strawberries?"

Jeremy's eyebrows shot up in surprise.

"We'd ask you to join us, Jeremy, but I believe that you were planning to join the archduke in the smoking lounge?"

"Yes . . . of course," Jeremy stammered and Olivia could see that it was the tantalizing mention of strawberries that had piqued his curiosity. He gave her a questioning look, which she ignored. Let the man wonder. Let his vivid imagination deal with the idea that perhaps she had the ear of his mentor and business associate, and that two could play his game of power.

She gathered her work and swept past Jeremy. "Very good, sir," she said and had the childish urge to stick out her tongue at her stepbrother as she left the room with Adam.

Five

"Was Sir Barrington bothering you, Miss Marlowe?" He held open the door for her and donned his derby as he took his place at her side once they were on deck.

"Bothering, sir?"

"You know that you do not have to accept . . . that is. . . ."

She found his attempt to shield her quite endearing. "I was upset," she replied evenly. "There had been a slight misunderstanding between us."

Adam looked down at her with concern, then out at the endless sea as they walked together along the deck. "Sir Barrington has a way with the ladies, Miss Marlowe. I'm sure that having lived in his household. . . ."

"His father's house," she corrected for what reason she could not fathom.

Adam nodded and continued. "At any rate, he can be quite charming when he sets his mind to it. The thing you must keep in mind is that what may seem like serious intent is really nothing more than flattery."

Olivia glanced up at him and saw how seriously he was taking the little paternal lecture he was delivering. She stifled a laugh. "I appreciate your concern, sir, but I am well aware of Sir Barrington's affinity for the ladies. I take a certain amount of pride in not having succumbed to his considerable charms."

She heard a breath of what could only be described as relief escape his lips. She could not imagine why this should matter to him one way or another. "Mr. Porterfield," she continued, "I know that you have taken Sir Barrington into your business. I honestly don't believe that he would make the mistake of incurring your disapproval by making advances to me or anyone else on your staff."

Adam grinned. "Ah, but my dear Miss Marlowe, should I then have to worry that he might incur my disapproval by making advances to others?"

She did not return his smile as her mind immediately shifted to the notorious pearls and Jeremy's brazen affair with Mrs. Armbruster. "I wouldn't know about such matters, sir," she muttered as they reached the café and she turned to enter.

"Actually, Miss Marlowe, I arranged for our tea and strawberries to be served in another location," he said. "I hope you won't mind."

"It depends on the location," she blurted and then thought of how inappropriate that response would be coming from ordinary hired help. She sighed with exasperation. The actual duties associated with her position had been no problem. It was the protocol that eluded her and threatened to expose her if she made a mistake.

To her relief, he laughed. "Ah, Miss Marlowe, you are such a breath of fresh air. Quite frankly I had despaired of ever meeting any English person who was less than completely proper on all occasions no matter how that person might be distressed inside. Then you come along and out pops the first thing that comes to mind. As I believe I have mentioned, my mother is like that, Miss Marlowe. I think that she may find her match in you."

"Perhaps that will not be wise," Olivia replied. "After

all, they say that it is opposites who are attracted to one another. If I am so like your mother, perhaps she will not take to me at all."

"In the beginning that may well be the case. I expect there will be some fireworks, but that is precisely what is called for at this stage. Something, or more to the point, *someone* needs to agitate my mother enough that she will shake off her malaise and come back to us. She is quite the most delightful woman." He indicated that Olivia should precede him up a short stairway. "I miss that very much," he added as she passed him and she had the inclination to stroke his cheek and assure him that his mother would indeed recover.

The stairway led to a small private deck shielded from lower decks by potted plants and polished wood paneled railings. In the center of the space was a small table, covered with a pristine white linen cloth and set for tea. Two cast iron fan-backed chairs faced each other across the small diameter of the table. Adam indicated that she should sit and as soon as she did, a uniformed waiter appeared to serve them.

"This is quite. . . ." *Romantic* was the word that sprang to mind and she bit it back.

He grinned. "Yes, isn't it? Money has its privileges, Miss Marlowe, and as my father used to say, What good is the stuff if you don't occasionally use it for fun? I'm just pleased that the weather has decided to cooperate."

The waiter brought scones and strawberries and a bowl of clotted cream. He filled her cup and offered a silver tray stocked with sugar, lemon, and cream. She selected lemon and watched in amusement as Adam dropped three cubes of sugar into his cup.

"My father used to filter his tea through a sugar cube by holding the sugar in his teeth and then sipping the tea," she said and could not for her life imagine why she shared that with him.

He grinned. "Waiter, leave the sugar, please," he asked.

"Very good, sir." The sugar was replaced on the table and the waiter disappeared from sight.

Adam selected the largest cube and anchored it firmly in his front teeth. "Like this?" he asked, his speech distorted as he tried to speak and hold the cube in place.

He looked so ridiculous that Olivia just nodded. It wouldn't do to laugh outright at one's employer.

"You do it too," he said.

"Oh, I couldn't, sir."

"Well, of course, you can and I'll not be the only one playing the fool here." His voice was stern but his eyes crinkled mischievously.

"Very well," she replied and placed a cube between her own teeth. "You mustn't bite down too hard or you'll crush it," she explained.

He concentrated on rearranging the sugar cube and nodded. "Now what?"

"Sip your tea." She picked up her cup and watched him over the rim.

He did the same but waited. She had no idea what came over her but she slurped the tea noisily just as her father had when she was a child. The result was the same as hers had been with her father. Adam Porterfield burst into laughter.

She had made an utter fool of herself, but she would do it again just to hear the magic of his laughter. The next thing she knew, she was laughing as well. They were on top of the world, steaming across a vast endless expanse of blue skies and calm waters and for the first time since leaving England, Olivia felt alive and normal.

"Okay, show me how this clotted cream business

works," he said when they had composed themselves and returned to sipping their tea in the normal manner.

"You'll just tease me about that as well," she accused lightly.

"Not at all. Here, let me see if I can guess." He selected a small dark strawberry and dipped it into the bowl of cream, twisting it so that the cream clung to the sides of the berry. Then he leaned forward and placed it next to her lips.

"Mr. Porterfield, I. . . ."

The minute she opened her mouth, he slid the berry inside and she had no choice but to bite down on it. She could feel a dab of the cream on her chin, feel the gush of the sweet juice staining her lips, but her eyes were locked on his. He was not laughing now, as he used his linen napkin to catch the bit of juice that had escaped the corner of her mouth.

Determined to regain some control of her own emotions, she reached for her napkin and briskly cleaned her face and chin of any trace of the berries. "You must try it with a little less cream," she commented. "Perhaps a bit of marmalade on a scone would suit you better."

He leaned back in his chair and she could feel him studying her. She could not read his expression, in shadow now that the late afternoon sun had gone behind the cabin behind them, and his sudden silence after the laughter just earlier was disquieting. "Here," she suggested, pushing a plate of scones and the marmalade a bit closer to his side of the table. "I think this might be more to your liking."

He frowned and pushed the plates away as he bent to retrieve the papers she had prepared for him. "Perhaps we should review this work," he said.

For the next several minutes, there was perfect quiet as he drank his tea and read through each letter, sometimes rereading the letter that had precipitated the correspondence in the first place and then returning to her reply. The waiter came and cleared the table and disappeared again. Olivia sat stiffly on the edge of her chair awaiting some sign, some comment that would let her know that she had not failed in the task he had asked of her. For some reason it was enormously important to her that he approve of her work . . . and of her.

Finally, he laid the stack of correspondence aside and sighed deeply. "It appears that I have made a grave error, Miss Marlowe," he said as he stood and wandered the short distance to the railing.

Olivia thought she might burst into tears. She had done her best, but she was not trained in . . . well, the truth of the matter was, she wasn't trained in anything. What could she have been thinking? Now he was going to tell her that he had been mistaken to hire her at all. She was not intelligent enough for his dear mother, she would not. . . .

"I should have found another companion for my mother," he continued then turned to look directly at her for the first time since the incident of the strawberry. "I should have hired you myself . . . as my secretary."

She thought she had misunderstood, but then he smiled. "The letters are quite wonderful, Miss Marlowe. You have managed to capture exactly the right tone for each occasion. You have delivered my thoughts better than I could have myself and with much greater tact in most cases, I might add."

The relief that flooded through her left her breathless. "Thank you, sir," she said and it came out a whisper.

"Tomorrow, I shall present you with something more challenging if that is agreeable to you?"

"Perfectly agreeable, sir."

"Then. . . ." He glanced around as if expecting to see something more. "I suppose I should let you retire to your cabin. You've had a long day. No doubt, I've given you no time for your usual constitutional."

"I can walk after supper," she replied and stood up, realizing that it was her place to stand in his presence. "Shall I come directly to the library after breakfast tomorrow?"

"Yes."

"Then, I'll wish you a good evening, sir." She headed for the stairway.

"Miss Marlowe?"

She turned. The setting sun was behind him and she could not see him clearly so she raised one hand to shield her eyes. "Yes, sir."

He hesitated. "Take care on that walk. There's foul weather predicted for this evening."

"I'll be careful. Thank you, sir."

Later that evening as Adam scanned the main dining room, he could not understand why, but he also could not deny that he was hoping Olivia might be there. Of course, the thought was laughable, and yet, he seemed incapable of entering a room these days without looking for her. It had become increasingly apparent that his idea that seeing her on a daily basis would lessen his fascination with her was not working. He forced himself to put her out of his mind and enjoy the evening.

The Captain's Ball was the social event of the crossing. Every first-class passenger was there for the occasion. The room was a blur of color as women in the latest designer ballgowns spun around the dance floor in the arms of men in the prescribed formal uniform of white tie and tails. The orchestra played from a small stage at one end of the room. The dance floor was surrounded by round tables for six or eight, bolted to the floor to steady them against the normal shifting of the vessel. They were covered with gold cloths and furnished with the finest English china and silver. In the center of each table was an impressive flower arrangement. The petals of the blossoms stirred as if caught in a breeze, but Adam knew that they moved in response to the oncoming storm and the roll and pitch of the ship in the increasingly turbulent seas.

He accepted a glass of champagne offered by a passing waiter and made his way across the crowded room to where Jeremy Barrington was regaling the Armbrusters with some misadventure or another. He noticed Grace Armbruster's diamond brooch strategically placed at the center of her daring neckline and wondered if Jeremy had once again managed to "lose" the jewel to Jasper Armbruster in a card game.

"Ah, here he is," Jasper bellowed as Adam approached the table.

Adam did not miss the way Grace looked at him nor did he miss the way Jeremy immediately drew her attention back to himself.

"My dear Grace, I have been admiring your gown. As always you are not only the loveliest creature here, but the most fashionable. I do believe that you are the envy of every woman in the room," said Jeremy.

"Not to mention the object of every gentleman's admiration," Jasper added with an appreciative glance at his wife.

"I have discovered treasure on this voyage," she replied with a gay little laugh. She fingered the intricate beading of her gown, calling Adam's attention to the fact that it had been specifically designed to highlight the perfection of her alabaster shoulders.

"A treasure?" Jeremy exclaimed. "You're being deliberately obscure."

"Not at all. I believe that Adam knows the young

woman. It seems that she will have less time to spend on making my gowns now that he has abducted her to handle his so-called business correspondence."

"Miss Marlowe is your seamstress?"

"In a manner of speaking. She seems to have quite a talent for lace and beading and other arts of the needle." She glanced at Jeremy. "Why, Jeremy, you look quite taken aback. Oh, that's right. You know Miss Marlowe, don't you? Quiet little mouse. Can't get a word from her."

"No doubt she knows her place," Jeremy mumbled.

"You're certainly being secretive about Miss Marlowe, Adam," Grace continued.

"As you have already demonstrated, my dear lady, she is an excellent worker—whether with a needle or a pen." He smiled and raised his glass in her direction.

She frowned. "I feel like dancing. Darling?"

Jasper laughed heartily. "Adam and I have business to discuss, my love. Perhaps, Jeremy, you would be so kind?"

"It would be my pleasure," Jeremy replied as he stood and offered his hand to Grace.

Adam and Jasper watched them go.

"I'm not the fool you are thinking, Adam," the older man said after a moment. "I know my wife."

"I will speak to Jeremy, Jasper," Adam promised.

"That isn't necessary. Grace knows how much I will tolerate. She loves my money and in the end, that means that she loves me. She's young and she's never known anything other than total indulgence of her every whim. Jeremy is a dalliance . . . nothing more."

Adam subdued a shudder. If this was marriage, he wanted no part of it. "As you wish," he said and gratefully turned their conversation to business.

By the time Jeremy and Grace Armbruster returned to the table, dinner was being served. The captain joined their table, a testament to the power gathered there. He invited a widow and her daughter as his guests. They were charming enough, but Adam found that he kept glancing around the room.

"Are you expecting someone, Mr. Porterfield?" the young woman asked.

"Not really, but I am being rude. Will you forgive me, please?" Adam stood. "I'm afraid I have a number of things on my mind." Without further explanation, he bowed to the ladies and left the room.

He was relieved to have escaped the festivities, but he did not feel like returning to his stateroom. He could hear the music from the ballroom accompanied by the laughter of the partygoers. The wind and spray outdoors were a welcome relief from the stuffiness of the room. There were no stars, no moon and the night was as black as any he could recall. He adapted his footing to the pitch and roll of the ship. He heard the groans of protest as the rising waves beat the ship relentlessly. The truth was, the storm matched his mood. Not wanting to take the chance of meeting any of his fellow first-class passengers and having to socialize, he moved down to the second deck, which was blessedly deserted. He removed his coat so as not to call attention to himself and placed it on a chair.

The deck was far less spacious than the one he'd left and he understood why Miss Marlowe preferred taking her walks on the first-class deck. He frowned at the thought of her. She had a way of invading his thoughts at the most unusual times. At the moment he needed to give his attention to matters of business—more specifically, the wisdom of bringing Jeremy into his business.

He was having second thoughts about the young Englishman. It struck him that Jasper's description of his wife might also apply to Jeremy. The man had been indulged throughout his life. Perhaps it had been a mistake to encourage him to come to New York. Of course, there was no denying that his presence would be an asset in expanding the operations more quickly than Adam could do on his own. On top of that, Jeremy had the unique ability to attract investors who might not have ordinarily shown an interest. His title and English accent held an undeniable attraction for several tycoons traveling on this voyage. Besides that, the man amused him. He was a charming traveling companion and showed an unexpected streak of compassion from time to time that Adam found appealing. In the final analysis, he might bear watching, but there was no arguing the point that he was an asset on many fronts.

Adam felt a relaxation of some of the tension he had endured earlier and turned his attention back to his more immediate surroundings. The wind had begun to howl and the first spatter of rain beaded on the highly polished railing. He should return to the salon or his stateroom and yet he was enjoying the energy of the storm. Like a dancer, the ship swayed as the seas heaved and buckled and the challenge became one of keeping his balance against the elements. Adam unfastened his tie and the top two studs on his shirt, now limp from the damp air. He turned to face the thunder and lightning and closed his eyes as he stood at the railing, legs spread wide for balance, arms braced, as he gripped the railing and prepared to ride out the storm.

Suddenly the door to the passageway behind him was thrown open and a woman ran to the railing and leaned far over it, retching into the foam below.

"Miss Marlowe?"

She glanced at him only briefly and her expression, caught in the dim light from the open door of the passageway, was one of surprise and horror. But she had little time to compose herself before the next wave of seasickness hit.

Not knowing what else to do, Adam put his arms around her to steady her as she draped herself over the railing. With one arm firmly around her waist, he used the other hand to gather her loosened hair and hold it away from her face. As her heaves subsided, he felt them replaced by shudders that racked her slim body.

"Come over here," he ordered, half dragging, half carrying her to the deck chair where he had left his jacket. He steadied her with one arm and draped the coat around her. Then he bent down so that he could see her face. "Are you. . . ."

With both hands, she pushed him aside and raced for the railing. Again, he steadied her and let the attack run its course. She half turned and he realized that she was trying to say something.

"What is it?" he shouted above the noise of the wind and raging sea.

"I'm all right," she replied, raising her voice only enough to be heard. She shrugged off his coat and handed it to him. "Thank you," she mouthed and turned to go.

When her knees buckled, he caught her and scooped her up into his arms. "Which is your cabin?" he asked in a more normal subdued voice as he carried her into the passageway, then saw the open door. "Never mind," he added as he strode toward it.

"Mr. . . ."

"Hush," he ordered as he turned sideways to get himself and her through the narrow doorway. "For once in your life, stop worrying about how things might look, Miss Marlowe. You are ill and as your employer I intend to see that you have the proper medical attention."

"It is a simple case of seasickness," she said weakly. "I shall be quite fine by morning."

"You're soaked to the skin and it's freezing in here." He cast his eye about the cramped space for some solution.

Spotting her flannel nightgown neatly folded at the end of her bed, he picked it up and handed it to her.

"I am going to get you some seltzer and crackers to help settle your stomach and while I am gone, I want you to remove those wet clothes and put this on." He ignored the defiant flash of her eyes. "It's that or have me remove your clothing and dry you myself, Miss Marlowe," he informed her and took some pleasure in the way her eyes widened in shock. "Ah, well, I see you have made the wiser choice. I shall be right back and I expect you to be under the covers."

"And what if I . . . what if. . . ."

He took the bowl from the washstand in the corner. "Use this if you feel the need to be sick again, although I doubt there is anything left."

"A fact that you intend to remedy with your seltzer and crackers," she muttered as she set the bowl on the bed and clutched her nightgown to her soaked bosom. "I do wish you would stop trying to feed me at every turn," she said irritably.

He grinned. "This is an old family remedy from my Irish grandmother," he assured her. "Works every time. Now, get changed," he ordered once more before stepping back into the hall and pulling her door gently closed behind him.

She considered throwing the latch, but what if he returned and started knocking. Adam Porterfield was a man clearly used to giving commands and having them obeyed. He would not take kindly to her locking him out. She clutched her tender stomach as she considered her options. Finally, she decided that, as he had already surmised, she had better do as he had ordered and change into her nightgown.

By the time she got back into bed, she was shivering violently and with each pitch of the ship, she felt her insides tighten in protest. She pulled the blankets to her chin and curled up facing the wall.

She could not have said if it was only minutes or an hour later that she felt the wet cloth cool against her face as he stroked her forehead and cheek.

"Try to sip a little of this," he said gently as he offered her a glass half-filled with seltzer. He had rolled back the sleeves of his shirt, exposing surprisingly muscular forearms.

She tried not to stare and did as he asked, then collapsed once again against the pillow . . . pillows, she realized. Somehow he had brought an extra pillow and more blankets in addition to the soda water and crackers. He was sitting on the side of the bed looking down at her with a worried frown.

"I'm quite certain that it's not terminal," she assured him and tried to accompany that with a little smile.

He smiled. "Perhaps at the moment, you might prefer that it were?"

She tried to laugh but her throat was raw and her stomach rebelled against any tightening of the muscles. The laugh became a grimace and he was immediately attentive, offering her the bowl.

She shook her head in refusal and closed her eyes. How humiliating this was going to be in the morning when she reported for her duties in the library.

"Mr. Porter—"

"I have been thinking," he interrupted, "and it would seem to me that under the circumstances we might be on a first name basis, Miss Marlowe. Would that be agreeable?"

Her eyes flew open.

"Oh, not at work, of course, but frankly, at times such as this, it does seem a little unusual to remain so formal."

"It is my sincere hope that we have endured the last of times such as this, Mr. Porterfield."

"That's not my wish at all, Miss. . . . Olivia. Not that I wish you ill, of course, but I rather enjoy your company and conversation and I would hope that we might establish a sort of friendship, especially once my mother takes on the role of your employer."

She did not know what to say. "I . . . that is. . . ."

"My given name is Adam, Olivia," he said softly as he resumed his ministration with the cool cloth.

She became aware of the stillness of their surroundings. The storm had abated. The ship had set itself on a more even course. Everyone was sleeping. For an instant it was as if they were the only two people in the world. She saw the way he was looking at her and knew what he was thinking only because she was thinking the same. It would be so easy to reach up and stroke his cheek as he was stroking hers. And, from there?

She reached for the cloth and took it from him. "Thank you . . . Mr. Porterfield, for your care and concern. I believe that the worst has passed and I shall be able to sleep now."

He studied her for a long moment but did not protest. "Then I'll say goodnight." He stood at the door. "Perhaps you should take tomorrow to recuperate, Olivia."

"That won't be necessary," she replied. "Goodnight, sir."

She lay very still listening for his footsteps as they faded away. Then she put the cloth to her face and inhaled the scent of him that clung to it like faint cologne.

By the time Adam reached his cabin, he had resolved that he must do whatever it took to remove thoughts of Olivia Marlowe from his mind. He told himself that it was the traveling, the business, the lack of time to develop their relationship. It was clear that it could not be limited to simple friendship . . . at least from his point of view. When he was with her he found it next to impossible to treat her as he did his other employees, with whom he considered himself to have a very appropriate form of fellowship in addition to their business dealings. There was something about Miss Marlowe that went beyond what could be considered suitable between an employer and a member of his staff. In the first place, every time he was with her, he thought about touching her. He noticed things—her hair, her hands, her perfume. He heard things in her tone and tried without success to decipher them. He found himself watching her, cataloguing her mannerisms to savor once she had left him.

Seeing her every day would not work. Rarely did he miscalculate the appropriate solution to his problems. However, it was clear that the decision to see her every day had been a mistake. If he were to maintain his honor—not to mention his sanity—that would have to cease immediately. There was no reason to have so much direct contact with her. He could just as easily prepare the work to be done and leave her the notes. She had proven herself capable. Clearly he had underestimated her ability to mesmerize . . . not that it was deliberate. In fact, the very innocence of it was what made it so damned appealing.

The truth of the matter was that his mother was not the only one who had pulled away from friends and associates following the death of his father. Adam had buried himself in work, telling himself that his priority must be the business, proving himself worthy of the confidence of longtime clients his father had spent years cultivating. Lately, he had indeed begun to think of his life in terms of marriage and a family of his own. Olivia brought those thoughts to the forefront with a vengeance. She was obviously not the appropriate choice for a wife, which only served to emphasize the fact that it was past time to give attention to his social life.

This was the answer. His attraction to Olivia was nothing more than an infatuation with the idea of a romance, of rediscovering his natural passion. Circumstances had thrown them together in this artificial environment that encouraged a courtship, but Olivia was not the one. In spite of the fact that her every move was of interest to him, she was an employee and nothing more. Getting involved with her would be a serious breach of his moral code. No, he would put a stop to this at once.

He did not come to the library at all the following day. She found the usual stack of documents awaiting her attention and a note advising her that he was otherwise engaged. On the day after that, the stack of work was smaller and came accompanied by a message thanking her for her assistance and indicating that his need for her secretarial services would be far less for the remainder of the voyage. He thanked her for her devotion and praised her skill. In the future, she need only check with the purser to see if he had left work for her to complete. If not, her days were once again her own.

Fortunately, she had little time to ruminate on the disappointment she felt at his sudden decision to keep his distance. Word had spread of her talent with the needle and several of the maids had come to her with messages from their mistresses requesting that she come to their staterooms to advise them on the fit or cut of a gown. She fetched a gown she was altering for the wife of the Archduke of Luxembourg from her cabin and went to the salon to work on it.

Having left behind her own wardrobe of fancy dress, Olivia took some pleasure in handling the beautiful fabrics and exquisite workmanship of the gowns of the other passengers. She found that she was quite good at changing a detail here and there to make a gown particularly becoming to its owner, and she was delighted to pass the time in such a pleasant manner. It even amused her to accept the sometimes quite generous gratuities the American women insisted on giving her for her work.

She took their money and smiled. If they only knew. . . .

"Olivia, my dear."

Olivia turned at the sound of Jeremy's greeting. "Jeremy," acknowledging him and turning her attention back to her work.

He sat on the chair next to hers and pulled it closer. "We need to talk." His tone was unusually subdued.

"We are talking, Jeremy."

"It's the jewels . . . your mother's jewels."

He had her instant attention. "Yes."

"They're fakes . . . excellent fakes, but fakes, nevertheless."

She started to laugh. "Jeremy, this will not work. I agreed to invest my jewels in this venture, but once we arrive in America and you have established. . . ."

"I have proof, Olivia. They're copies."

She looked at him closely and could detect no hint of duplicity or insincerity. "But. . . ."

He pulled a paper from his pocket and laid it on the table, smoothing the wrinkles from it as if he was trying to make the words disappear.

It was a cable. "This came last night from Father," he said softly.

Jeremy, my son, I do not know how your stepsister convinced you to partake of her folly but it may interest you both to know that the jewels she has taken are not the actual collection that her mother accumulated and left to her after her untimely death. That collection is still quite safe here in the mansion. The jewels Olivia has in her possession are excellent copies of the originals. If you doubt my word, it is quite a simple task to have the pearls appraised. I am quite certain that there is someone on board capable of that.

You may wish to advise your stepsister of her folly and counsel her to come to her senses and return here where Sir Dudley has decided to forgive her youthful impetuosity and wed her as planned. I shall await your reply, once you have put the arrangements into place.
Father.

Olivia read it and read it again. "Appraised. . . ."

"They're fakes, Olivia, the pearls and no doubt the rest as well. I retrieved the pearls from Grace on the pretense of having the clasp repaired and had them appraised by a jeweler I met in the smoking lounge. Grace is going to. . . ."

Olivia gripped his hand. "Jeremy, Grace Armbruster is hardly our greatest problem at the moment. We have—you have—misrepresented yourself, unknowingly to be sure, but. . . . Good heavens, Jeremy, if Mr. Porterfield should discover that you have no resources. . . ."

"Don't panic," he said, looking wild-eyed and totally panicked himself. "Let me think."

Olivia reached across the table and touched his arm. "Jeremy," she said softly, surprised at her instinct to comfort him.

He raised his face to her and she saw such anguish there that she tightened her grip on his arm.

"I can't go back," he said miserably. "If I return, Father will never let me . . ." He swallowed and shook his head.

"Olivia, all I ever wanted out of this was the chance to be my own man for a change . . . to show him that I could succeed."

"All right, Jeremy, all right," she said softly, her grip on his arm having softened to a gentle pressure.

"What shall we do? I mean, you don't want to return, do you?"

Olivia felt a sudden rush of panic. Of course, she didn't want to return to the life she would face as the wife of Sir Dudley. On the other hand, she could not deny a longing for England. Everything had been so much simpler there. She stared out the window for a long moment. Behind them lay England . . . and a host of problems for each of them. But, what lay ahead? Who really knew?

"Now listen to me, Jeremy," she said returning her attention to her stepbrother. "Other than the pearls you 'lost' to Mr. Armbruster, neither of us can be accused of duplicity or fraud. Mr. Porterfield has paid for our passage and we have few additional expenses on board here." She was calculating their destiny. "Therefore, we have a bit of time."

"But, once we reach New York . . ." Jeremy reminded her.

"Well, fortunately we both have positions which presumably will produce some income."

"Fine for you. You have lodging and food as a part of your position while I. . . ."

"May have to forego some of life's luxuries for at least a period of time, Jeremy," Olivia reminded him sternly.

He gave her a woebegone look. "I'm not sure that I know how."

Olivia could not help herself so she covered her smile. "Well, necessity is a wonderful teacher, my dear Jeremy, and you are nothing if not resourceful. If you keep your wits about you, I suspect you can endure even this, assuming that you are sincere in wanting to cut the ties to your father."

"Oh, I am sincere, Olivia. I've never been more sincere about anything in my life."

"He has given you this one chance to return, Jeremy. Once you have openly defied him, there will be no going back," she warned. "At least until you have proven that you are quite capable on your own."

"I know," Jeremy replied and it came out as a hushed whisper. "I know." He looked up at her. "Once we reach New York, I shall need your help, Olivia."

She felt a compassion for him that she would have thought impossible even a week earlier. She was actually tempted to tell him of the small amount of cash she had saved through her needlework, but decided it would be wiser to keep that to herself. "We shall work this through together, Jeremy," she assured him. "Now, I must leave you. I must deliver this gown to the duchess."

Jeremy clung to her hand. "Thank you, Olivia," he said standing so that he was looking directly at her. "I don't deserve such kindness from you."

Olivia sighed. "No, you probably don't, but, we find ourselves walking a common road. Keep your wits about you, Jeremy, and all will be well."

On her way back from delivering the altered gown to the duchess' maid, Olivia saw Chester Maplethorpe coming toward her in the passageway. Throughout the journey she had discouraged or refused his offer to walk with her in the evening. It occurred to her that she had responded to him as she would have to any servant in her role as the English lady. But now circumstances had changed not only her social position, but her need for a circle of friends and acquaintances. With all her ties to her past cut, the task before her was, in effect, to construct a completely new life. Although she was unsure of his reasons, it was clear that Adam had decided to distance himself from her. She certainly was in no position to rebuff the few friends she'd made in the course of this crossing.

"Good afternoon, Mr. Maplethorpe," she murmured as he came nearer.

He seemed surprised by her gentle tone. "Miss Marlowe," he replied with a nod of his head.

She knew that he stood watching her as she continued down the corridor. She smiled to herself as she climbed the stairway that led to first class and could not resist looking back just before taking the last step.

He was still watching her. She smiled at him and gave him a little wave. "Will I see you at dinner, Mr. Maplethorpe?" she called.

He grinned happily. "Yes! Yes, indeed."

Olivia walked to the library with a lighter step. She felt an impressive sense of her own power. The difference between life in England and life in America would lie in her freedom to choose what she would and would not do in her life. That was a risk well worth taking.

She was surprised to see Adam Porterfield in the library. Ever since he had adopted the habit of leaving what little correspondence there was with the purser, she had barely seen him. He was deep in conversation with Mr. Armbruster when she entered the room. She wasn't even sure that he had noticed her and she felt a pang of disappointment at that. She took her position at the writing table across the room and opened the leather folder he had left for her. She tried to concentrate but snatches of the conversation between the two men floated across the quiet room.

". . . is a fool, Adam. It isn't like you to suffer fools."

"Jeremy is young," Adam replied and Olivia's senses became alert. "He has a great deal of potential. Besides, if men like you hadn't given me my chance, where would I be?"

"The pearls he lost to me in that poker game are fakes . . . excellent fakes, but fakes."

"I thought they appeared too large to be real," Adam said and then chuckled. "I was wondering if you had noticed."

"I suspected as much that same evening. The point is . . . I don't think Barrington realized it."

Again, Adam laughed. "Ah, my friend, you said yourself that they were excellent reproductions. After all, Barrington probably thought they were an entitlement—part of the fortune he'll come into when he inherits his father's estate some day. He has a certain talent for the dramatic and that is exactly what makes him of value to my business."

Olivia did not believe what she was hearing. Adam knew Jeremy's failings. He knew about the fake jewels and still. . . .

Now, it was Jasper Armbruster who laughed. He also stood up. "Well, you were always very savvy when it came to your instincts for people, Adam. I'll take your word for the fact that this Barrington fellow has potential."

Adam also stood. He shook hands with the older man and watched him leave the room. "Do you agree with my assessment, Miss Marlowe?" he asked without turning to look at her.

"Sir?"

"My assessment of Sir Barrington. Would you agree?" Now he walked the short distance to where she sat.

"I really couldn't say, sir." She kept her eyes on her work.

"Really?" He walked behind her. She could sense him looking over her shoulder. "You have a very lovely handwriting, Miss Marlowe."

"Thank you, sir." He was far too close. She was much

too aware of the fabric of his sleeve, the scent of his cologne, the mere inches that separated them.

"You lived in the same household as Sir Barrington for several years, did you not?"

"I worked for Lord Barrington, not his son."

"Yet, even so, you were both in residence in the same house. You must have noticed things."

She paused—her pen in midair. "Sir Jeremy Barrington is . . . as you noted . . . a bit immature, Mr. Porterfield. He's younger than his years in some ways." She turned and looked up at him. "And, that, sir, is all I will say on the subject."

Adam smiled, but his eyes were serious, even troubled. He was near enough to touch her and she realized that she wanted him to do just that. She turned her attention back to her work. She was lonely and a little apprehensive of what the future might bring. Her reaction to Adam Porterfield arose from that—she was certain of it. Perhaps if she focused on someone else . . . perhaps Chester.

"Miss Marlowe, I. . . ."

She stood and presented him with the completed work. "I really must be going, Mr. Porterfield. Will you need me tomorrow?"

He hesitated, then accepted the leather folder. "Why, Miss Marlowe, tomorrow, we arrive in New York."

Six

The sound was what woke her. A low murmuring filled with excitement, building with each passing moment. She pulled her shawl around her and moved to the porthole. It was barely light and from her vantage point, the view was the same as it had been for the past twelve days . . . fog that obliterated the sky and water . . . endless water.

"Livvy? Oh, Livvy, do wake up! We must get on deck to see the lady." Molly knocked repeatedly at Olivia's cabin door.

"I'm coming," Olivia called back, hastily putting on her clothes. "I'm coming."

By the time she opened the door, Molly was all the way down the corridor. "Come on," she called excitedly, "or we shall miss her."

Olivia hurried through the long hallway. Above her she could hear other footsteps as well. Surely the ship would tip if everyone ran to the same place, she thought. As she got closer to the deck, the murmur grew louder, more intense.

When she stepped on deck, she couldn't see beyond the throng of passengers. One thing was certain, they were all straining to see something through the mist and fog of the early morning. She worked her way through the crowd and squeezed into a small space next to Chester Maplethorpe at the railing.

And there she was.

It's a statue, Olivia told herself and yet she could not take her eyes from the woman holding one arm high with a torch. Olivia could not really see the eyes and yet the lady seemed to be looking directly at her.

Her own eyes welled with tears and she felt herself leaning toward the lady in the harbor, the very symbol of freedom and independence. Olivia's freedom from a life she had not wanted and yet had never thought to change. Her independence to choose her own path, to make her own life. She looked around and knew that for many of the others, the Statue of Liberty symbolized far more. In some cases they had escaped from a persecution she blessedly had never known. For them, freedom meant freedom from poverty, insecurity, and fear. Olivia's eyes welled with tears.

"Look at their faces," Chester said, nodding toward the immigrants who had crowded onto the deck from steerage and who now pressed forward for a better look at the statue. "They look at that statue and believe that their struggle is over."

"You sound as if you think they will be disappointed," Olivia replied.

Chester shrugged. "Many of them—most of them—will never achieve what they dream of at this moment. It will not be as easy as they want to think."

Olivia looked back at the excited faces and shining eyes of the other passengers and knew that he was right. She wondered if he might really intend to warn her. Had he seen that look on her face—that look filled with naked longing for something more? "You are very cynical, Chester," she replied, deliberately keeping her tone light.

His eyes went dark and he did not smile. She could

feel his body pressed to hers as more and more passengers pushed forward to glimpse the skyline of New York.

"I, too, have hopes, Olivia," he said and she saw that he wanted very much to kiss her. Not some chaste beginning kiss, but something filled with all the passion of the moment. He satisfied his longing by touching her cheek, his palm rough against her skin.

"Chester," she said and looked away, over his shoulder and up to where Adam Porterfield was standing on his private balcony. He seemed to be looking directly at her.

The moment was broken by the announcement that all first-class and second-class passengers should report to their respective dining rooms for customs processing. Those in steerage would be left at Ellis Island.

"I don't understand," Olivia said.

Chester was guiding her toward the stairs that led to their dining room, his hand at her waist as he made a path for them through the crush of other passengers.

"The ship will stop at Ellis Island to let those in steerage off and then continue on to the docks over there." He nodded toward the skyline of the city. "Have you your passport and papers?"

"I . . ." Panic gripped her as she realized that Jeremy had never mentioned such matters. She had simply assumed. . . .

"Ah, Miss Marlowe." Adam Porterfield waved to her from across the large second-class dining room.

"My employer," Olivia explained and made her way across the room, leaving Chester waiting in the long line that had already formed.

"I thought you might need these," Adam said, handing her a packet of papers. "Don't look so startled, Olivia," he added with a smile. "Sir Barrington gave them to me along with your references. I should have delivered them back to you long before now but it slipped my mind."

References? What references could Jeremy possibly have concocted? she wondered, but accepted the papers. "Thank you."

"Shall I wait with you? Sometimes, the first time through customs can be confusing and a little unnerving."

"No. That won't be necessary." She certainly did not want to run the risk of making a mistake in front of him. What if they asked some question and she couldn't think of an answer or what if something in her papers revealed her true identity? She was so focused on the papers that she failed to notice that Adam was still standing there, watching her.

"This *is* your first passage to America, is it not?"

"Yes. Of course," she replied.

"And yet you seem unperturbed by all of the confusion and regulations." This was said more to himself than to her. He continued to study her closely.

"I appreciate your offer of assistance, Mr. Porterfield, but you really mustn't concern yourself with me. I have others here who have traveled back and forth any number of times. There's Mrs. Rutherford's maid and Mr. Rutherford's chauffeur." She glanced back at Chester and waved.

Adam's gaze followed hers and for an instant the eyes of the two men locked. Then Chester nodded politely and looked away. "I'll leave you to your friends, then, Miss Marlowe," Adam said. "I shall send my driver to collect your things when we dock and show you the way."

"Thank you, sir," Olivia replied as he turned and left the room.

By the time she had passed through the customs inspection and returned to her cabin to finish packing, the ship had ceased to move. Assured by the steward that her trunk would be delivered to the docks, where Mr. Porterfield's driver would collect it, she followed the other passengers on deck and toward the gangplank.

The scene that greeted her there was one she knew she would never forget. If Southampton had been noisy and crowded, it was nothing compared with the chaos of the docks in New York. The harbor itself was so crowded with traffic that she feared an accident at any moment. Ocean liners vied with ferries and tugboats and barges for space, their horns bellowing out their right to move ahead of others. Below, thousands of pieces of luggage and cargo were stacked in teetering piles on the docks themselves. Hundreds of people threaded their way through the maze of the luggage and every person seemed to be talking at once. Her eyes widened as she saw how quickly everyone moved and how little patience they obviously had with those foolish enough to linger. The potpourri of smells enveloped her and she raised her white lace handkerchief to her face to cover her nose from the potent and distasteful odors.

She felt like covering her ears as well for the noise was deafening. Men shouted—some of them raising their voices in obscenities when things did not go as planned. Vendors screamed to be heard above their competitors. Children were crying hysterically as their mothers herded them along the docks. Everyone seemed to be moving with no particular course in mind, and the buzz of a dozen languages only added to the general feeling of chaos.

"This way, miss," a man said, taking hold of her elbow as she stepped off the gangplank.

"You there, stop!" Chester hurried forward and the man immediately dropped his hold on Olivia and ran off into the crowd.

"He has my purse," Olivia cried, but immediately saw the futility of anyone trying to find the man.

"Stay close to me," Chester ordered tersely as he took hold of Olivia's elbow and looked back to be sure that Molly was still at his other side.

"Did you have much in the purse?" Molly asked sympathetically.

"No. Thankfully I had followed your advice and secreted my valuables . . . elsewhere," Olivia replied.

Molly grinned. "Good girl."

"There's the boss," Chester announced and turned suddenly in the direction of Mr. Rutherford.

"I don't see. . . ."

"Mr. Porterfield's there with him along with that Sir Barrington," Molly assured her. "Come on."

Olivia had never moved so fast in her life, nor had she ever felt more out of control. She looked up to see Jeremy smoking a cigar and laughing at some story Mr. Rutherford was telling. He looked as if he didn't have a care in the world while the rude Americans—all of whom seemed to have no time to spare for even the most rudimentary rules of etiquette—were crowding her on all sides.

"Miss Marlowe," Adam said when Chester and Molly had at last delivered her safely. "Shall we go?" He indicated a carriage waiting at the end of a gauntlet of luggage carts, scrambling dockworkers, and confused travelers.

"Yes, sir," Olivia replied as she prepared to endure yet another onslaught. She squared her shoulders and narrowed her eyes, focusing all of her concentration on attaining the safe refuge of the carriage.

It was then that she felt the gentle guiding hand of Adam Porterfield on her elbow. "It really is a lovely city," he assured her as he allowed the Rutherfords and Jeremy to move ahead of them for a moment. "Please, don't judge us by these first impressions."

With him at her side, Olivia could not help but notice how the way opened up for them. Dockworkers, who had thought nothing of buffeting her about when she was with Chester and Molly, nodded politely and waited for Adam to pass. Some even touched grimy fingers to well-worn caps as they passed.

"Quite different from Southampton, isn't it, Jeremy?" Adam remarked as the Rutherfords said their goodbyes and headed for their own carriage and Jeremy dropped back to walk with Adam.

Olivia noticed that Jeremy's eyes were glittering with excitement. He was looking at everything around them. "It's magnificent," he replied with a touch of awe. "Simply magnificent."

"And, do you find it magnificent as well, Miss Marlowe?" Adam asked.

"It is certainly lively," Olivia replied and felt the now familiar rush of pure pleasure when her comment made Adam Porterfield laugh out loud.

Sylvia Porterfield paced restlessly, pausing only to glance out the windows of her spacious bedroom whenever she heard a carriage turn onto their street. Adam's cable had promised a surprise. Her son was well aware that Sylvia did not like surprises. Not since her husband, Clay, had died. It was as if he had taken any joy she might have found in life with him . . . excepting Adam, of course.

The sound of horses' hooves on cobblestone brought her hurrying back to the window. Her heart quickened as she recognized their family carriage. She strained to see the occupants but the light April mist and cool air meant the carriage was closed against the elements. All she could see were three occupants, one of whom was a woman.

"Martha," she called out. "My son is arriving."

The parlormaid hurried into the room. "Yes, ma'am. Shall I have him come up as soon as he's inside?"

"No," Sylvia snapped impatiently. "Help me with my

hair so that I can receive him properly in the drawing room."

"Yes, ma'am," Martha replied meekly and made an unnecessary inspection of her lady's perfect coiffure, then opened the door and stood aside while Sylvia selected a silver-headed cane from her collection and moved slowly toward the grand stairway.

"Martha, go downstairs and find out who my son has brought home with him and bring me word before he comes to the drawing room."

"Yes, ma'am." Martha scurried past her and down the back stairway.

Sylvia was tapping her fingers impatiently on the table when Martha appeared, breathless and only steps ahead of the sound of Adam greeting the servants as he moved through the house.

"Well?"

"He's brought a young woman and young man with him. Sir Barrington is. . . ."

"Never mind the gentleman. What of the woman?"

"Mr. Adam told the cook that she was to be a surprise for you . . . nothing more."

He has married, Sylvia thought and felt her heart race with panic. *How could he?* In an instant she saw herself alone in the mansion, for surely the young woman would want her own place. She prepared to dislike her on sight and turned toward the door to await her son.

"That will be all, Martha," she said tersely and gripped the handle of her cane until her bony knuckles turned white. "Adam? Is that you, dear?" she called as she settled herself in one of a matched set of high-backed petit point chairs with deeply carved mahogany arms and legs. As a boy, Adam had called them the *thrones*.

"Hello, Mother," Adam said as he hurried forward and kissed her cheek. "I've missed you."

"And I, you," she replied as she took advantage of his kiss to study the woman who lingered at the door. The woman was tall and not as young as Sylvia would have thought. She looked directly at Sylvia and smiled. "Was your trip a success?" Sylvia asked Adam, turning her attention away from the woman.

"Very much so." He returned to the doorway, but instead of bringing the woman into the room, he presented a young man who moved toward Sylvia with a grace and elegance that could only mean he was English. Sylvia relaxed slightly.

"Mother, may I present Sir Jeremy Barrington? He has come to New York to join the business."

Jeremy made Sylvia a formal bow and then smiled. "Perhaps you know my father, Mrs. Porterfield—Lord Barrington?"

"I am afraid that I have been away from England for some time, Sir Barrington, and my memory is not what it once was." She gave him a coy smile, hoping he would engage her in further conversation. It was delightful to hear a proper British accent again. Besides, conversation with him would delay the inevitable introduction of the woman. "Is your family's country home near Windsor, by chance?"

"Exactly right, my dear lady."

He continued to regale her with stories of her beloved England and he was so charming that Sylvia almost forgot about the young woman still standing about in the hall.

"And, Mother, I have someone else for you to meet."

Sylvia tightened her grip on her cane and any trace of a smile disappeared as her forehead wrinkled. "Well?" she said, looking at the woman, taking in her well-appointed but slightly mussed traveling costume at a glance.

"This is Miss Olivia Marlowe, Mother. I have retained her to serve you as your companion and social secretary."

Sylvia could not put her finger on it at the moment, but she caught something in the way that Adam spoke of the woman. Miss Marlowe started to say something but Sylvia cut her off. "I wasn't aware that I was in need of further staff," she said, and as if to prove her point, rang the small silver bell next to her chair. "Martha, you may ask Winston to bring tea," she said when Martha appeared almost instantly, "and you may stop listening at doorways or take your leave," she added.

"Yes, ma'am," Martha replied humbly and immediately left the room.

"Sir Barrington, I do hope that we can prevail upon you to be our guest at least until you are properly settled in a place of your own," she said, deliberately turning her attention away from Olivia.

"Why, that would be very generous of you, Mrs. Porterfield. If it suits Adam, of course." He leaned closer to the older lady. "He is my employer, after all," he told her in a stage whisper that made her color slightly with pleasure.

"Yes," she returned in a similar stage whisper, "but this is *my* house."

Jeremy laughed and the sound of it filled the room as the butler brought the silver tea service and placed it on the table in front of Sylvia. "Perhaps Miss Marlowe would do us the honor of pouring?" Sylvia swung her attention back to the woman and did not miss the fact that her comment was unexpected. "You do know how to serve tea, do you not?"

To her delight, the young woman actually bristled. It was subtle but unmistakable and she saw that not only Adam, but the charming Sir Barrington sent her a warning glance.

"Yes, ma'am," she said softly and moved to the tea table. Everything about her performance was impeccable.

"That will be all," Sylvia said dismissing her as soon

as she had handed Adam a cup of tea. She took some pleasure in the fact that Miss Marlowe seemed at a loss as to what she should reply or where she might go. Sylvia saw her glance around the room and then back at Adam.

"I'll just wait in the hall," she said to no one in particular, and as she headed for the door, she almost ran right into Winston.

"Winston, please escort Sir Barrington here to the gold room and have his luggage brought there as well. He will be staying with us for a few days."

"Very good, madam. And the young lady?" he asked as he reached the door.

"See that she waits in the hall. My son will be with her momentarily."

"This way, sir," Winston said with a slight bow to Jeremy. The look he gave Olivia spoke volumes and she obeyed his unspoken command that she follow behind.

The room was silent for several minutes as mother and son sipped their tea and waited for the other one to speak.

"It isn't like you to be ungracious," Adam said finally.

"I thought I was most gracious. I invited the man to stay, didn't I?"

"We are not discussing Jeremy, Mother."

"I am not in the habit of fawning over the servants, Adam."

"But, you were always kind and welcoming. You and Father both. . . ."

"Please do not bring your father into this, Adam. You know as well as I that he would not have disapproved and he certainly would never have reprimanded me on the subject."

"I am concerned, Mother. We are all concerned."

Sylvia looked out the window, hardly taking in the fact that it had started to rain in earnest. "What could you *have thought, going behind my back,* choosing someone without even . . ."

"I have brought others for you to interview and consider," he reminded her. "You rejected them all for one reason or another—mostly because they were not English. Miss Marlowe is."

"And, you think that simply because you have dragged this woman across an entire ocean I will not reject her?"

"I hope that you will accept her on her merits," Adam replied. "As you observed, her skill in serving tea is impeccable."

Sylvia sniffed in derision. "They could all pour tea, Adam."

"Ah, but they weren't English," he said, reemphasizing the one thing that made Olivia Marlowe different and therefore, worth considering.

"I don't need a companion and I don't socialize so what exactly is the point of a social secretary?"

"The point is that it is high time you did socialize. However, even should you choose not to do so at this time, Miss Marlowe will make fine company for you on rainy afternoons such as this. She can entertain you on those long evenings when I have a business dinner or charity function."

"I do not need a nanny," Sylvia replied testily.

Adam laughed and it was so much his father's laugh that Sylvia felt overwhelmed by a sense of utter grief. Her hand shook uncontrollably as she placed the cup and saucer on the tray.

Immediately, Adam was at her side, offering his white linen handkerchief as he knelt on one knee next to her chair and wrapped a comforting arm around her. "Mother, please see this for what it is. I am worried about you as Father would be if he could see how after all these months, you've become a recluse."

Sylvia tried unsuccessfully to stem the flow of her tears. She had never permitted herself to cry in front of Adam or the servants. She had held her grief inside as something so private that it was impossible to share—even with her only son.

"I am asking that you give this a chance, Mother," Adam pleaded. "I want so desperately to do something, but I honestly have no idea what else I might try if you reject even this."

Sylvia gave herself a moment to regain her composure then reached up to stroke her son's thick chestnut hair. "And if I don't care for her?"

"I only ask that you keep her on staff for three months. If she doesn't suit, then I will personally assist her in finding a new position."

Sylvia was surprised. "That would hardly be your responsibility, Adam."

"I have brought her here, Mother, away from everyone and everything she has known in her life. You and Father have always taught me that people are not conveniences that we can abandon once they have served us."

Sylvia smiled as she returned his handkerchief to him. "It is unfair of you to invoke my teachings in your cause," she said. Then she straightened herself in the chair and nodded toward the door. "Very well, bring her in and I'll interview her."

Adam rushed toward the door, then turned. "Three months, Mother. Do we have a bargain?"

"I am your mother, not one of your business associates, son."

Adam frowned.

"Very well," Sylvia replied with a sigh of resignation. "Three months . . . assuming she is capable."

* * *

Olivia could hear them talking in low tones as she sat in the large hall and waited. There was no need to hear the actual words. It was clear that Mrs. Porterfield was not going to accept her presence. The task for Olivia was to devise a plan for taking care of herself once she had been dismissed.

She clutched the small purse that she had pinned inside the waist of her skirt. It held the gratuities that she had acquired through her needlework on the crossing. How that pittance had amused her until the day that Jeremy had told her that the jewels were copies and had no value. Suddenly that bit of money became everything. She wondered what the conversion rate might be—what she might be able to afford in the way of a place to stay until she had found some other employment.

As she considered the possibilities, she glanced at her surroundings. The hall was quite opulent, setting a tone for the rest of the house. The walls were wood-paneled and supported a high ceiling of ornamental plaster. The marble floor shone. She was seated on a tufted bench upholstered in deep chocolate brown velvet. To her left, a wide staircase accented by an ironwork railing in a floral pattern wound its way to a second and third floor. At each landing light spilled in through tall stained glass windows, again in a floral motif.

At the end of the hall were carved double doors, open now to afford her a view of an impressively long gallery. She had learned that Adam's parents had been avid collectors of paintings and other objets d'art and that they had traveled extensively to add to their collection. Adam had apparently inherited his parents' love of art for before leaving the docks, he had supervised the very careful loading of a large wrapped parcel into a closed delivery tram that also carried their luggage.

"Miss Marlowe?"

Olivia brought her attention back to the open drawing room door and Adam. She stood and waited to be dismissed.

"If you would be so kind as to come in, my mother will interview you now." He stood to one side while she entered the room, then softly closed the door, leaving her alone with Mrs. Porterfield.

"My son tells me that you are English," Mrs. Porterfield said after spending several minutes staring out the window and ignoring Olivia.

"Yes, ma'am."

"And, you've done this sort of work there?"

Olivia wasn't certain how best to answer that. "I have managed the household of a gentleman for the past several years."

"My butler manages the household," the older woman stated flatly.

"I believe that your son had other duties in mind for me," Olivia said softly and then blushed, wondering if she might have put that badly.

Sylvia turned her clear, cold blue eyes on Olivia and looked her up and down. "You have potential," she said, deliberately misinterpreting the response. "Not a beauty, but I can see where he might be . . . intrigued."

Olivia blushed deeply. "I did not mean to imply. . . ."

"You don't behave as a domestic would, Miss Marlowe," Sylvia interrupted her. "Your speech, your posture, even your clothing—plain as it is—speaks of quality and breeding."

Olivia swallowed around the knot in her throat and waited.

"You must have had good training."

"Yes, ma'am," Olivia murmured and shifted slightly as her back began to ache, protesting the fact that she'd been standing at attention since entering the room. She saw herself reflected in the large gilded mirror over the white marble fireplace. She was positive that the vases at either end of the mantle were Chinese porcelain. If she had had any doubts about the extent of wealth represented by Adam Porterfield, there was no doubt now that she had seen the house and its furnishings. The Porterfield fortune was substantial, and it was clear that Sylvia Porterfield was a great deal more refined and sophisticated than any of the Americans that Olivia had seen on the voyage.

"Well, come sit down and let us discuss this ridiculous idea that my son has to provide me with a nursemaid—albeit, an English nursemaid with obvious good breeding."

She nodded toward the chair opposite her own and then turned her attention to pouring tea for the two of them. "Lemon or milk?"

Olivia sat perched on the edge of the chair. "Lemon, please."

"My son and I have struck a bargain, Miss Marlowe. Three months."

Olivia accepted the china cup and saucer and willed her hand to remain steady. "I don't understand," she said.

"I have agreed that you may stay—and do whatever it is you do—for three months." She took a sip of her own tea, her eyes never blinking or leaving Olivia's face. "I would strongly urge you to use that time wisely in order to secure a position for yourself when that ends. Should you secure such a position prior to that, please do not hesitate to say so. The shorter our forced acquaintance, the better for each of us."

"I. . . ." Olivia had never heard anyone speak so directly—especially not a lady.

"Clearly, I have shocked you, Miss Marlowe." Sylvia waved a hand as if the entire matter was exhausting for her. "I suppose that living over here in the colonies for so long has taken its toll."

"What is it that you wish me to do for you?"

The piercing blue eyes were back on her in an instant. "I wish for you to find ways to occupy yourself in some manner that will be of benefit to me and make sense of the salary my son will pay you. This activity is to be conducted throughout the day within close proximity to me without involving me in those activities. I wish you to join us for dinner on those evenings when my son is at home and to sit with us after dinner until I announce my intention to retire. You shall have Saturday afternoons to yourself and on those evenings when my son is not at home, you may spend your time as you see fit here in the residence. I don't suppose that you have had time to form acquaintances, but in time. . . ."

"I became acquainted with the maid and driver of your friends, the Rutherfords, on the crossing," Olivia said, hardly aware that she had interrupted until the deed was done. "Sorry," she mumbled.

The older woman paused and for an instant she looked almost wistful. "How are they?" she asked in a voice that was barely audible. "The Rutherfords."

"They seemed quite well," Olivia replied, her own voice softening sympathetically. "Mrs. Rutherford's maid mentioned that Mrs. Rutherford misses her visits with you."

There was no response. Sylvia moved to the window again and stared out. "The garden has become quite overgrown," she said more to herself than to Olivia.

"I couldn't help but take note of the floral themes repeated throughout the entrance, as I was waiting. They really are a lovely and somewhat unexpected touch in a home as substantial as this one appears from the exterior."

Sylvia glanced at her with a surprised look. "Yes, that was the intent when Clay and I . . . when the house was originally designed." She continued to look at Olivia for a moment, but her expression was not as stern as it had been earlier. "Are you a garden enthusiast, Miss Marlowe?"

"Yes, ma'am. My mother was quite talented when it came to coaxing things into bloom that by rights should never have appeared in any garden in London."

"I see." She turned her attention back to watching the falling rain. "Perhaps when the weather has improved a bit, you would enjoy walking through our garden on your free afternoons."

"I would enjoy that immensely. Thank you, ma'am."

The silence between them lengthened. Olivia finished her tea and waited.

"Do you sew, Miss Marlowe?"

"Yes, ma'am."

"Ah well, there's our solution. In addition to the gardener, I also dismissed the seamstress shortly after Adam left for England. There is quite a stockpile of mending to be done." She turned to Olivia. "Of course, my son is to know nothing of these duties that are not related to what he has determined are to be your responsibilities. You do understand that, do you not?"

"I understand," Olivia replied evenly.

Mrs. Porterfield nodded once and turned away.

Not knowing what else to do and feeling that the interview had come to an end, Olivia stood. "Shall I clear?" she asked when Mrs. Porterfield continued to be lost in her own reverie at the window. "That won't be necessary," Sylvia replied and walked slowly back to the table where she rang the small silver bell. "Let's get you settled in, Miss Marlowe. I daresay my son will make it his purpose to be on the premises for dinner this evening. He'll be checking up on me to be sure I am keeping to our bargain." She sighed dramatically and then turned to the butler who had appeared at the door. "Winston, Miss Marlowe here will be staying in the house and assisting me for the next several weeks. Would you be so good as to show her to the tower room?"

"Very good, ma'am," Winston replied as he lifted the silver tray and then led the way through a small service door toward the backstairs of the house. "I shall just stop by the kitchen, miss."

"Of course," she replied and not knowing what else to do, she followed him.

"Oh, and Winston, please acquaint Miss Marlowe with the sewing room. She'll be attending to some mending while she's with us."

"Very good, ma'am." Winston wordlessly led Olivia down a short hallway and through a swinging door into a pantry where he set down the tea service. "This way, miss," he announced as if she had intruded on sacred ground. Once again he set the pace, leading the way up the back stairway to the second floor. "The tower room is just here," he instructed as he opened a door to reveal another even narrower stairway.

"The tower room—it sounds a bit ominous," she commented in an attempt at conversation.

"I believe that you will find the room quite comfortable, miss. It overlooks the garden."

"Yes, I'm sure I shall be very content here," she assured him as he opened the door on a small, stuffy bedroom with a narrow bed, a small dresser, and one chair.

"There is a bath down the hall, there."

She looked in the direction he indicated and saw a number of other doors. "There are other servants on this floor then?"

"No, miss. Everyone else is quartered in the west wing or elsewhere. I suspect Mrs. Porterfield has chosen this accommodation for you because it is quite close to her own suite of rooms as well as to the sewing room, there—second door to the left." He pointed to a bell near the door. "The mistress will ring for you when she requires your attendance. In the meantime, you will find the accumulated mending in the sewing room."

"I see. Thank you, Winston." She saw one eyebrow rise slightly and wondered if she had breached some sort of domestic's etiquette by using his given name. "I am Olivia," she added with a smile.

"You'll want to meet the others," he announced as he moved around the small space with amazing alacrity, opening the window, checking for dust.

"I expect that they are curious to meet me," she replied.

Winston turned away before she could be certain but she was fairly sure that he had smiled. "I shall ask Mrs. Porterfield if I might take you on a tour of the house and introduce you before dinner," he replied. "Until then, I shall leave you to unpack and get settled."

"Thank you again, Winston. You have been most kind."

He nodded and left the room, closing the door behind him.

Olivia collapsed onto the bed. She felt as if she had been standing at attention the entire day. Her shoulders and neck ached. She closed her eyes. She had barely slept the night before. It seemed like days instead of hours since the ship had sailed past the Statue of Liberty and she had felt that rush of freedom calling out to her. She opened her eyes and stared up at the plain ceiling.

What had she done, she wondered? *How could she have been so stupid as to have thrown aside a perfectly secure life to come here to . . . what? How could she have thought for one single minute that she might actually be able to pull off this charade?*

Seven

"Winston," Adam called out from the library where he and Jeremy were enjoying their cigars.

"Yes, sir."

"Has my mother finished her conversation with Miss Marlowe?"

"Yes, sir. I have just shown the young miss to the tower room."

"Well, I was just about to give our guest, Sir Barrington, here, the grand tour and I thought that perhaps Miss Marlowe might wish to become acquainted with the house since she'll be staying here for some time."

"There is no need to trouble yourself with that, sir. I can show her around or have one of the others. . . ."

"Nonsense. Let's kill two birds with a single stone, as the saying goes. Please ask Miss Marlowe to join us as soon as possible."

"Very good, sir," Winston replied, but it was clear by the rigid set of his face that he saw nothing good about the idea at all.

"Winston considers me far too liberal when it comes to the help," Adam confided to Jeremy with a wink.

"Well, he has a point, Adam. After all, Miss Marlowe is part of the household staff. As such she should probably not receive any special consideration. You'll only make it difficult for her in the long run."

Adam considered that for a moment as he drew on his cigar and slowly blew out the smoke. "Perhaps. On the other hand, if she is to engage my mother in activity and encourage her to return to her former full routine of social interaction and interests, she needs to see the house and know its history as it reflects my mother. I doubt that even Winston could provide that sort of insight."

"It's your decision, of course," Jeremy replied. "However, for myself, I am afraid I shall have to beg off for the grand tour. I have an appointment with Jasper Armbruster at four o'clock and it is nearly two now. By the time I dress and. . . ." He checked the clock on the marble mantel, then turned and smiled at his host. "Not knowing the city, I am assuming that it will take some time to get there?"

"You didn't mention an appointment," Adam said, studying the younger man through the haze of smoke that encircled him.

"Didn't I? My apologies. It came about quite spontaneously as we were docking this morning. I believe that he wishes to discuss a possible real estate transaction."

"Or perhaps he wishes to discuss the fake pearls you lost to him in that poker game," Adam said quietly and was not surprised to see Jeremy flush a deep red.

"Adam, I assure you that I was as duped as he was by those pearls. I had purchased them in good faith for a lady friend."

"Yet, you did not give them to her."

Jeremy shrugged and smiled. "We had a bit of a falling out over my decision to come here to New York. When I saw that the pearls would have no effect in softening her ire, I decided not to give them."

"I see. Nevertheless. . . ."

"Adam, I have been less than forthright with you. The truth is that having discovered my error—one that I unwittingly passed along to Jasper—I must go to him and make my apologies. He is a valuable client and now that I am associated with you, it is only fitting that I clear up any possible misunderstandings. I fully intend to make good on the wager that I used the pearls to cover. It is for this reason that I am going to his house today."

"So, there is no pre-arranged meeting."

Jeremy shook his head, and for the first time since they had met, Adam saw that the man's confidence had been shaken.

"I have one cardinal rule for my business associates, Jeremy—do not lie to me. I will tolerate and forgive honest mistakes, but I must be able to trust you."

"I understand," Jeremy replied and he was so contrite that Adam had no recourse but to believe that he could not fake such sincere regret.

"That includes lies of omission, Jeremy."

There was the slightest hesitation. "Yes, of course. I do apologize for getting us off to a bad start now that I am finally here."

"Very well. We won't speak of it again."

"Thank you, Adam," Jeremy gushed with relief as he crossed the room in two strides and took Adam's hand between both his own. "You won't regret the faith you have placed in me."

"You should get going. The Armbrusters live on Fifth Avenue across from Central Park. That is quite some distance from here and you don't want to interrupt their dinner hour. I'll ask our driver to take you there."

"Of course," Jeremy agreed and moved quickly toward the door. "Thank you, Adam . . . for everything."

"Jeremy? One more thing."

Jeremy smiled and paused at the open door.

"The city is filled with eligible young women who will be only too delighted to make your acquaintance. Stay away from married women—especially Grace Armbruster." He saw that his warning, although it had been delivered in a lighthearted manner, had had the desired effect. Jeremy now knew that Adam had been aware of everything the younger man had done on the crossing. It was unlikely that he would be so foolish as to slip up again. He was far too bright and ambitious for that.

Jeremy simply nodded and left the room as Adam turned back to the fireplace and the portrait of his father above it. He stared at the portrait as he often did when he was in this room. He wondered if his father would approve of how he was managing the business and how he was trying to care for his mother.

"I'm doing my best," he said softly, stubbing out his cigar in a large crystal ashtray. "I just hope that it's enough." When he looked up, Olivia Marlowe was standing at the open door. She was dressed in an orchid brown tea gown of a fine woolen fabric with a lace inset that covered her throat and accented the length of her neck. The cocoa brown sash was cinched tight in the fashion of the day. The sleeves puffed at her narrow shoulders and then closely fitted her arms all the way to their lace cuffs just above her delicate wrists. He brought his gaze back to her face.

She had arranged her hair into a no-nonsense chignon at the base of her neck. It would have set off her face far better had she piled it high on her head. On the other hand, he remembered it to be absolutely ravishing when she permitted it to fall unfettered to her waist. He took a moment to savor the image. She stood waiting and said nothing and yet as always, there was not a single ounce of servitude about her.

"Well, Miss Marlowe, I understand that my mother has moved you into a room. That's progress. Come in, please."

She stepped fully into the room and looked around.

"This was my father's study and library—his favorite room, other than the gallery. The servants tell me that Mother spends some time in here when I am absent from the house, as I mentioned before."

She ventured closer to the shelves lined with books. "These bookcases are rather unusual," she commented, running her hand over the leather surface of the waist-high shelves.

"Yes. Father thought that one should be able to take a book from the shelf and open it flat right there—perhaps several books at a time."

"He was a scholar then?"

"An avid collector of knowledge would be more accurate. He enjoyed learning new things. Mother as well."

"They seem to have been quite suited to one another," Olivia observed as she continued to observe the details of the room. "Sometimes when two people are so devoted, they cut themselves off from others. Then when one of them is gone. . . ."

"That was never the case with my parents, Olivia. They were devoted, but they had a great many friends—dear friends. The Rutherfords, for example, live just across the way. They were in this house so often that when I was growing up I thought they were family. I even called them Uncle and Auntie."

"And yet, from what I gathered in conversations with Mrs. Rutherford's maid, it has been some time since your mother has visited her . . . or accepted her card when she called here."

"I hope that you might inspire a change in that." He watched her carefully. "What happened during your interview?"

He thought that he saw the hint of a smile, but when she turned to face him, her expression was one of complete composure.

"Mrs. Porterfield and I discussed our . . . my duties."

"Which are?"

There was a long pause and then she looked directly at him. "Mr. Porterfield, forgive me if this seems disrespectful, but it is my belief that if I am to be in the employ of your mother, then any conversation between your mother and me should remain between us . . . unless, of course, *she* chooses to discuss the matter with you."

Adam laughed. "Well stated, Olivia, but for one minor detail."

Her eyebrows lifted in question.

"I believe that it was I who employed you," he reminded her.

Her forehead wrinkled slightly with disapproval or consternation—he couldn't be sure which. "Of course. Forgive me," she replied demurely.

Her decision not to debate the issue further was disappointing. He had come to enjoy their exchanges. "Well, then, are you ready for the grand tour?" he asked with a heartiness he did not feel.

"As you wish," she replied and moved closer to the door. "It is certainly an impressive home."

He was more aware of her than he would have anticipated as he walked with her through the spacious reception hall toward the gallery. Perhaps if they had been walking in close quarters he might have anticipated awareness, but this was a large open space and yet he was conscious of her every move. She had a way of observing the details of her surroundings without a hint of gawking or staring. She seemed to like what she saw without being overly impressed by any of it. The expressions that played briefly across her face before disappearing behind that carefully composed mask reminded him of fireflies' lights on a summer's night—there one minute and gone the next.

He told himself that it was that damnable English reserve of hers . . . that sense that what was presented on the face of it was a far cry from what was going on beneath the surface. It gave him more pleasure than he would have admitted when she could not stifle an involuntary gasp as they entered the gallery.

She stood in the doorway at one end of the long, sparsely furnished room as if needing to stand still in order to take it all in. The room was impressive, filled as it was with light and the large art collection hung, one painting above another, on walls that soared up to the vaulted ceiling. Slowly she moved forward, walking down the center of the room, oblivious to the equally impressive collection of sixteenth and seventeenth century handwoven Oriental rugs under her feet. Her eyes fairly danced from one painting to the next and her face softened as she took in the beauty of the collection.

"As I mentioned, my parents have always been avid collectors," he explained. "When they designed this house, it began with this room. They were determined to have a proper showcase for their treasures. In addition to this large gallery, there are two smaller ones there at the far end. Father built them to house Mother's collections of Staffordshire china and Lalique crystal."

"The skylight is . . ."

"A fake," he finished. Following her gaze up to the leaded and beveled glass apparition. "Yes, Father was concerned about the effect that natural light might have on the paintings, and yet, Mother has always inclined toward bringing the outside inside."

They had walked the length of the gallery and halfway back. She had taken note of every painting as they passed, and he sensed that she recognized the work of every artist aside from the few that were unknown except to his parents and a small group of art lovers in New York. He directed her toward a side door.

"The music room," he stated, opening the door to a smaller octagonal room that featured a small performance stage and a grand piano. "Do you play, Olivia?"

"A little," she admitted as she permitted her fingers to brush the polished ebony of the instrument. "Does your mother play?"

"She sings. She and Father used to entertain guests with their music—he would play and she would sing." Adam smiled at a sudden memory. "He once persuaded her to sing a set of rather bawdy tavern songs when the guests were old and dear friends." He shook his head and chuckled. "Believe me, Olivia, you would not have thought it possible even in those days that my mother would permit herself to do such a thing."

"I do find it hard to imagine," Olivia admitted, recalling the stern-faced unbending woman who had interviewed her earlier.

"She even danced," Adam reported as he continued the tour by opening a door cleverly disguised as a part of the wall and revealed a beautiful oasis. "Father created this palm garden for her and in here, the skylight is indeed real."

He saw her eyes light as they moved into the interior palm garden that boasted a view of the sky over a pond filled with waterlilies and several very fat goldfish. The only sound was the splashing of a fountain that cascaded into a small waterfall. Orchids bloomed among the palms and ferns, and the room was furnished with ornately carved black wrought iron settees, chairs and café tables set discreetly around the pond amidst the foliage.

"Oh, how perfectly lovely," Olivia sighed. "I can see why your mother would love this room so."

"Yes, well, she did," he said and then aware that perhaps he had permitted himself to show too much emotion, added, "Are you an admirer of flowers, Olivia?"

Her gentle laugh seemed in perfect harmony with the cascading water. She looked completely relaxed and at home for the first time that day. "I'm afraid we English do have a fondness for our gardens," she admitted as she examined a small orchid blossom more closely.

"I'm pleased to hear that. I do hope that you'll be able to rekindle that interest in my mother. I'm afraid that while Winston manages to keep this indoor garden thriving, the outdoor version has not fared as well."

"We have the advantage that it is just coming on April, Mr. Porterfield, and the start of a new growing season. Your mother and I discussed the garden briefly during our interview."

He felt a flicker of hope. "Did you?"

"She invited me to make use of it in my free time if I wished."

"How did the subject come up?"

"I believe that I mentioned my own mother's love of gardening." She released the blossom and the mask that revealed little returned. She stood perfectly straight and still, as if awaiting his instructions.

"I'll be interested to hear your assessment of the work to be done then." He indicated that she should precede him into the dining room where the table had been set for two. "Winston, we'll need a place for Miss Marlowe and Sir Barrington. Is my mother not down yet?"

"His grace sends his regrets, sir. He did not think that he would return in time for dinner. Your mother is not feeling well and has asked that her dinner be brought to her in her room."

Adam frowned. "I'll take it up to her, Winston," he said. "Perhaps you would be so kind as to introduce Miss Marlowe to the rest of the staff and see that she is properly fed."

Olivia did not miss the look of stark disappointment and concern that crossed his face, but by the time he had delivered his instructions, all hint of ill-temper had disappeared. "Miss Marlowe, I hope that you will make yourself at home," he said with a slight bow before leaving her alone with Winston.

In the days immediately following Adam's return from London, Olivia could not help but notice that he was away from the house more often than he was there. When he was there, his mother put on quite a performance. After that first night, she did not miss another meal. She smiled and encouraged conversation about his day and the business in general. She laughed at Jeremy's humor and treated both men as if they were the guests of honor at some large party. Basically, she ignored Olivia.

After dinner, she would encourage the men to go off to the library for cigars and brandy and announce that she and Olivia were retiring to do some reading and needlework. Olivia knew that Adam assumed that this meant the two women would sit in Sylvia's room sewing and talking or reading aloud to each other. But when the two of them reached the upstairs hallway out of sight of Adam, Sylvia would sweep into her room and close the door without another word to Olivia.

Once, Olivia had suggested that perhaps Sylvia would prefer that Olivia take her evening meal with the rest of the staff in the kitchen. The older woman had looked directly at her for the first time since that first day's interview and snapped, "Do not cross me, young woman. You will be at table as ordered and conduct yourself in the most pleasant yet non-intrusive manner. Is that clear?"

Before Olivia realized it, three weeks had passed, and though she had made little progress in her relationship with Mrs. Porterfield, she had begun to settle into a routine of sorts. She took her breakfast with the rest of the staff and had ingratiated herself with all of them with her avid curiosity about their families and their lives outside of the mansion. She endured their good-natured teasing about Chester Maplethorpe's obvious fascination with her, and listened intently to their gossip about the goings-on in the households of the rich and powerful. She spent the morning and part of the afternoon attending to the necessary repairs to household linens and clothing.

Occasionally, there would be an item of clothing that she knew could only belong to Adam. On those occasions, she found herself taking particular care, knowing that he would never notice the repaired button or the mended fray, but nevertheless taking pleasure in the task.

In the evenings, she appeared at Mrs. Porterfield's room at the appointed hour and accompanied her downstairs to the family dining room where Adam and Jeremy joined them. During these meals, she listened with interest to the discussion of the latest business deals and alliances. She was pleased to see that Jeremy seemed to have a real affinity for the business and that he was an eager student as Adam explained the ways of business in America.

The real surprise was Sylvia Porterfield's interest and knowledge of such matters. It soon became clear to Olivia that this was no ordinary woman and that she could teach Olivia a great deal about making her own way in New York. Once she realized this, Olivia intensified her efforts to win the woman's respect, for there was no doubt that in less than three months she was going to be on the street and she needed to learn everything she could about how she might survive then.

One evening Jeremy suggested a game of charades after

dinner. Olivia was certain that Jeremy was only being polite and that Mrs. Porterfield would refuse. But to her astonishment, Jeremy persisted and Sylvia allowed him to persuade her to take part in the parlor game. Further, she accepted his idea that the two of them should form a team against Adam and Olivia. Jeremy was a master at the game and Sylvia took great delight in their victory as she tallied the final score.

"Sir Barrington, it has been some time since I enjoyed myself as I have this evening. Thank you."

Jeremy smiled. "It is the first of many adventures you and I shall share, dear lady, for, you see, I am quite captivated by your charm and wit. I also suspect that beneath that very proper exterior lies the heart of an adventuress."

Sylvia actually blushed, but she looked extremely pleased. "Really, your grace. . . ."

"Ah, you protest, but I can see that I am right, my lady."

"Jeremy, you are incorrigible," she replied and smiled again.

"Incorrigible perhaps, but charmingly so, I hope."

Olivia observed all of this with as much interest in Jeremy as in the elderly lady. It dawned on her that Jeremy had grown genuinely fond of Adam's mother and that something about her state of melancholy had inspired him to show her some special attention. The most surprising thing of all was the realization that his intentions were pure and not colored by any desire to flatter Sylvia or impress Adam. She had never seen this side of Jeremy. She wondered if perhaps Sylvia had somehow brought back memories of his own mother and it was this that lay behind his kindness.

Later that evening, after Jeremy had persuaded Sylvia to join them in a sherry before retiring for the night, she urged Adam to introduce Jeremy to an old family friend who owned an apartment building near Central Park.

"A handsome young bachelor needs rooms of his own," she said, flirting a bit as she looked over at Jeremy. "I suspect he will become quite popular with the eligible young socialites of the city . . . if he hasn't already."

"You flatter me, my lady, but perhaps it *is* time for me to establish a place of my own. After all, I cannot impose on your hospitality indefinitely."

"Then it's settled." Sylvia nodded at Olivia, indicating her desire to retire. She said her goodnights and walked between the two men out into the hall where they left her with Olivia at the foot of the grand staircase.

"Goodnight, fair lady," Jeremy murmured as he bent and kissed her hand. "I shall look forward to our next adventure."

Sylvia smiled. "Go along . . . the two of you . . . and have your cigars and your brandy while you tackle the problems of the world."

Adam kissed his mother's cheek and Olivia could see that he was enormously pleased with the progress he thought had been made during the evening. "Goodnight, Mother . . . Olivia."

As soon as the men had closed the door to the library, Sylvia turned to Olivia and said, "Miss Marlowe, if you have any thought that there exists the remotest possibility of a relationship with my son, I would advise you to think otherwise. There is no question that he finds you amusing and mildly intriguing, but that will come to nothing. Good evening, Miss Marlowe." Without waiting for any response from Olivia, she slowly climbed the stairs to her room.

Eight

A few days later, Jeremy moved uptown to rooms in the recently completed Dakota apartment building across from Central Park. Once he was gone, the house seemed to lapse back into the malaise of those first days when Jeremy and Olivia had first arrived. Adam's time was increasingly taken up with social events and business meetings and he was rarely at home, believing that his mother had made enough progress that he could give his full attention to business.

Olivia spent her days in the sewing room or walking the tangled overgrown paths of the garden, making notes about changes that the gardener—once hired—might undertake. As the weather warmed and the days lengthened, she would sometimes sit at the far end of the garden to complete some mending that was impossible to manage on the machine. Frequently, she would use the time to attend to the alteration sewing work she continued to accept from the maids she had met on the voyage. Occasionally she would look up at the bedroom window where Sylvia spent her days and see the curtain move. She knew she was being watched, but she also knew that Sylvia would say nothing. A month had passed and with only two months to go before she would be out on her own, Olivia was determined to use her free time to her best advantage. Still, she could not help wishing that there were something she could do for Adam's mother . . . not just because he expected it, but because underneath the gruff exterior, it was clear that Sylvia was in pain.

The others on the staff were kind, but treated Olivia with polite distance. Clearly, they believed she was not long for this household. For that reason and the fact that her duties set her apart from the work of the others, they made little effort to include her in their off-duty activities. Fortunately, Molly was the exception and continued to be her friend. Occasionally, on their days off, they would meet under the arch at Washington Park, and head off from there for some shopping or other pleasant activity.

When Mickey had shore leave, he and Chester would join them, and on those occasions, Molly and Mickey would soon disappear into the heavier foliage of the park or head off for a nearby tavern. Chester had made some effort to further his own pursuit of Olivia, but she had maintained her distance in spite of what she could see was his growing frustration.

One evening as he walked her back to the servants' entrance of the Porterfield house, she sensed that his mood was blacker than usual. He seemed to have reached a decision and she was certain that it was not one she would like. She steeled herself for an argument. As they reached the cobbled yard between the back of the house and the coachhouse, he suddenly caught her arm and pulled her into the stables.

He said nothing, but pushed her against the cool stone wall and pressed himself against her.

"Chester, no!"

His mouth was on hers, his tongue thick and wet against her face. She felt the heat of his hands moving over her back and around to her breasts. She found that she could not move for he was large and strong and determined.

"Kiss me, Livvy," he ordered, his mouth again on hers, one hand a steel clamp on her jaw to hold her still under his assault. "Open it, damn you," he said squeezing her jaw and cheek until she cried out in protest and her mouth indeed opened to him.

"This is what we could have, Livvy." He was speaking rapidly between plundering kisses that left her feeling as if she might be sick. "You have passion, woman. I can see it in your eyes, in the way you move. You know what that does to a man and you use it to advantage."

"Chester, please, I. . . ."

He thrust his hips at her and she froze, her eyes meeting his as he began slowly grinding his hips against her. "Feel what you do to me, woman."

She was so terrified that all ability to think had escaped her. She felt tears roll down her cheeks. She felt Chester's hand bunching her skirt until he found a way under the hem. His eyes reflected triumph and he groaned and bent to cover her breast with his open mouth.

"Someone is coming," she said as she continued her futile struggle against him. She prayed it might be so, but the carriage only paused, then continued on its way down the narrow alley.

"Chester, please don't do this," she begged, crying in earnest now.

And then, quite suddenly, she was free. It happened so unexpectedly that she slid to the floor, and it was from that vantage point that she saw Adam Porterfield rear back and strike the stunned and disoriented Chester one powerful blow that sent him sprawling.

"Good heavens, I think you have killed him," she managed to squeak out as she scrambled across the floor to where Chester lay.

"I doubt it. Are you all right? Did he . . . are you all right?"

He bent down next to her, his hands hovering but not touching her.

"I'm fine, Mr. Porterfield. My friend had just. . . ."

"He's a friend of yours?"

"Yes. We met on the passage over and we have. . . ."

"Been keeping company," Adam said more to himself than to her. "I'm sorry, Olivia. I thought . . . well, never mind what I thought. I had no idea that you were seeing someone. Please be assured that your young man will come around in a minute and while he'll have a bit of a bruised jaw, I think he'll recover in a few days. Goodnight, Miss Marlowe."

And, to her astonishment, he left her there on the floor next to the now-moaning Chester Maplethorpe. He walked across the courtyard and into the house without so much as a glance back. If he had not come along she might have been ravaged and yet, here he was leaving her with the very culprit. . . .

Oh, my heavens, she thought. *He thinks that Chester and I . . . he thinks I was a willing . . . he thinks. . . .*

"Livvy," Chester moaned and reached for her hand. "I'm sorry, Livvy, truly I am. Can you forgive me?"

"Oh, do shut up," she snapped and stood up herself, pacing the stables and rearranging her clothing to some semblance of proper dress.

"Livvy, I would never do anything to hurt you. I love you, Livvy."

She wheeled on him. "Well, I do not love you, Chester Maplethorpe. You are a perfectly nice person when you are not in this state, and I have appreciated your friendship, but what happened here this evening will *never* happen again or anything remotely similar. Do I make myself clear?"

He nodded miserably.

"You could have gotten us both sacked," she continued.

"I don't know about your circumstances, but at the moment mine are directly tied to maintaining my employment in this household. Do you understand that I will do nothing to jeopardize that nor will I allow you to do anything that might endanger my position in this house?"

He stared up at her as if she were speaking in tongues. "Oh, do get up and make yourself presentable," she ordered and turned away from him. She stood in the doorway of the stables and looked up at the house. The lights were on in the library and she could see Adam moving around in there, pacing, to be exact. She shuddered to think what he might be considering.

"Livvy?" Chester was at her shoulder.

"If you lay one finger on me, Chester, I shall scream bloody murder and have you carted off by the police," she said in a low, dangerous voice.

He moved past her, out into the courtyard and on to the street without another word.

Olivia took a long moment to repair her appearance, making do with the few hairpins that remained entangled in her hair to pile it atop her head and anchor it there. She used her handkerchief to wipe her face, then glanced at the library window once more and took a deep breath. Then, with a determined stride she crossed the yard and entered the house.

Adam could not imagine what had come over him. Of course, she would have developed relationships with other servants from the neighborhoods. He recalled that during their sessions in the ship's library, she had from time to time referred to her friendship with the Rutherfords' maid. Now that he thought of it, she had been with the man he'd just assaulted the day they had docked.

Still, the very idea of this man's—of any man's—hands

on her was intolerable. In the weeks that he had known her, he had come to appreciate and admire her refinement. She had a quality about her that garnered respect. Surely, she would never. . . .

A firm knock at the library door interrupted his reverie.

"Come in," Adam snapped impatiently.

Anticipating Winston, he was surprised to see Olivia open the door and enter the room. He looked at her closely enough to see that she had done what she could to straighten her clothing and hair, but she had come straight from the stables without bothering to stop to refresh herself in her room first. "Is there something you need, Miss Marlowe?" He kept his tone deliberately cool and impersonal.

He saw her assurance falter slightly, then she lifted her chin a fraction and straightened to her full height. "I came to apologize and to assure you that I have taken measures to make certain that nothing of that nature ever happens again."

Adam smiled ruefully at her. "Why, Miss Marlowe, *never* again seems a bit over the top. Have you no interest in being courted . . . no interest in romance?" He had no explanation for the fact that he was directing his anger at her with his sarcastic comment.

"There was nothing romantic about. . . ." She stopped herself and bit her lip. "What I mean to say, sir, is that I would not wish you to think that what you may have thought you observed is. . . ."

"Miss Marlowe, I believe that what you choose to do on your time off is your affair . . . business. It was my mistake in forgetting that you are an eligible and attractive young woman and your options for pursuing a courtship are not quite as. . . ."

"Will you please stop referring to my association with

that man as a courtship . . . sir," she added hastily. "We are acquaintances . . . nothing more."

"You may wish to explain that to the young man. He appeared to have other ideas." Adam turned away and took a swallow of his brandy. He found that he could not look at her without seeing her swollen lips and imagining that man's mouth on hers, his hands on her . . . "The subject is closed, Miss Marlowe. We'll have no more discussion of this matter," he said coldly. "Good evening."

He heard nothing for a long moment and knew that she was still standing there. *Go,* he thought. The pocket doors of the library slid open and then were shut tight. He let out the breath he'd been holding since the moment she'd walked into the room. He set down his brandy glass and rubbed his tender knuckles. It had been years since he'd used his fists to settle any matter, but when he'd heard her small cry and walked into the stables to see who might be there, his need to protect her had been instant and his rage had been overpowering. He would have happily ripped the man apart, had one punch not sent him sprawling. He had wanted a fight, wanted to show the bastard that Olivia was not to be handled like some common. . . .

He slumped into a chair and stared into the fire. For the first time since he first saw her pulling bits of straw from her hair on that dock in Southhampton, he realized that his attraction to Olivia Marlowe went well beyond simple curiosity. He wanted her in all the ways that a man wants a woman he finds mysterious and desirable. He glanced up at the portrait of his father. He reminded himself that Clayton Porterfield had had one cardinal rule for running his business and his household—no dalliance with the staff. It always led to heartbreak and misery for both parties.

I'll keep my distance, he promised the benevolent image of his father and drained the last of his brandy. "Although

I may have to move out of the house to make good on that promise," he muttered to himself as he extinguished the lights and headed for bed.

On his way up the stairs, he walked the length of the hallway past his mother's room to the entrance to the third floor and looked up. A thin beam of light showed beneath her door. Unable to stop himself he climbed the stairs, knowing since childhood how to navigate every staircase in the house without making a sound.

He stood outside her door for a long moment. He could hear her moving around on the other side of the door and nothing seemed unusual about her movements. What had he expected? That she would be sobbing uncontrollably? That she would be packing her trunk, preparing to leave? He knew her better than that. She had a pride that would permit neither tears nor flight. She would stay and do her job . . . at least until she found a better option. Olivia was nothing, if not pragmatic. She was also the most alluring woman he'd ever known. He turned and walked away. After all, he was the master of this house. She was merely an employee. He could handle this.

The following morning he was up and out of the house before any of the servants were stirring. He was still thinking about Olivia when he arrived at the office. She had refused to look at him when she had first entered the library and he had hated her sudden servitude. Seeing that man kissing her had triggered weeks of fantasy and had been far more distressing than he could have imagined. He had often thought that perhaps if she had a beau, it might make her seem less intriguing. He could not have been more mistaken. Never had his instincts failed him so. Suddenly, he seemed incapable of thinking of anything but his own mouth on hers.

"Do you have a minute?" Jeremy Barrington tapped

lightly on Adam's office door and opened it just enough to show his face.

"Come in," Adam urged as he got up from his desk and took one of the high-backed leather chairs in a seating area near his files. "Sit down."

Jeremy smiled and accepted the invitation.

"We haven't seen much of you these last weeks," Adam continued, "but clearly New York agrees with you."

Jeremy chuckled. "More than I could have imagined. The food, the theater. . . ."

"The women?" Adam asked with a wry smile.

"Yes. The *eligible* ones," Jeremy said with emphasis.

It was Adam's turn to laugh. "You haven't come to the house lately. Mother misses your visits. She was quite disappointed that you could not join us last week."

"Then I shall have to make amends at once," Jeremy readily agreed.

"Good."

"How is Miss Marlowe working out?" Jeremy asked.

"Mother seems to have taken to her lately."

"Ah, then your plan is working? Your mother is feeling better?"

"She has shown some improvement."

"Clearly your decision to employ a British companion for your mother has been a success. How is Miss Marlowe herself—settling in, is she?"

Adam paused in the act of pouring them each a cup of coffee from the service at the sideboard. Jeremy's question was perfectly natural, but had he imagined that it was just a bit too studied in its offhand delivery?

"She seems well and content. A difficult person to read, but then perhaps that is a British trait?"

Jeremy laughed as he accepted the coffee and stirred in sugar and cream. "Hardly. One could never say that I am difficult to read, I should think."

Adam relaxed. "No, one could never say that." He sat down and sipped his coffee. "So, to what do I owe the pleasure of this visit?"

Jeremy's eyes lit with excitement. "I have a prospect—I cannot say who at this time—but I can assure you that it is a real estate transaction that could expand this year's business in that arena by half."

"Impressive. What is the property?"

"Properties . . . plural," Jeremy explained. "Again, I am not yet at liberty to provide details but, Adam, this is a massive opportunity, and one that, if we do not act quickly, will slip through our fingers."

"Why the rush?" Adam kept his tone cool and calm.

"The client has experienced a series of reversals in his overseas business. Obviously, he is reluctant to permit news of these reversals to reach the States and affect his business here as well. His plan is to seek a buyer for several diverse properties and business holdings—properties that would not draw any particular notice were he to dispose of them, but properties that, nevertheless, have value in their own right, and in combination have immense potential."

"I see. And, he has come to you because . . . ?"

"We met a few weeks ago and found that we had much in common. Some mutual friends . . . each of us coming to New York from other places . . . similar philosophies and hobbies. During the time we have spent together, he began to confide in me."

"Not to belittle your friend or your own ability to judge character, Jeremy, but such a ruse is not uncommon in the business world."

Rather than take offense, Jeremy nodded soberly. "I thought of that. I have made it my personal business to look into his story. You have not seen me here at the office for the past weeks because I have been traveling about, looking over his businesses and properties, and I assure you, Adam, they are legitimate opportunities."

"You have seen the books? The ledgers?"

"Not all of them, but the client himself has indicated his certainty that any buyer would need to look closely at every record." Jeremy sat forward and looked intently Adam. "These are sound investments, Adam. His failures lie in the investments that he has made overseas. He has overextended himself, and if there is anything that I know well, it is that. He needs an immediate infusion of cash in order to save himself from complete ruin and preserve his good name and reputation."

"And, would I recognize this name?"

"No, I don't believe you would."

"Are you asking me to make this investment on blind faith, Jeremy?"

"Of course not. I am asking if you would be interested."

"What is the sum we are discussing here?"

Jeremy removed a paper from the inside pocket of his suit coat and spread it on the table. "I have taken the liberty to develop this chart. It shows the individual and sum value of the properties and businesses concerned as compared to the sum of the advance. As you can readily see, our client is seeking only a small percentage of their true worth."

"It is still a great deal of money, Jeremy."

"But easily redeemed through the revenues from these businesses and sale of properties. *And,* it opens the door to expansion of the firm beyond our present East coast holdings."

Adam studied the chart. He could not help but be impressed with Jeremy's thorough presentation of the opportunity, at least to the degree that he was at liberty to identify specifics. He had labeled the properties and businesses by state and location and indeed, on paper, they did present an opportunity to expand from New York to Chicago, to Denver, and beyond. "I must insist that you tell me the general field of interests represented here, Jeremy. Manufacturing? Raw goods? What?"

"Entertainment," Jeremy replied with a grin. "And hospitality," he rushed to add. "Think of it, Adam, as people continue to gather in larger metropolitan areas, what do they need? Places to spend their leisure. Restaurants, hotels, theater."

"All extremely risky ventures, my friend, influenced by whims of the people, not to mention the ups and downs of the economy."

"Yes, of course, and this is what keeps *most* investors from taking full advantage of the opportunity they represent. Look at it this way, Adam, you already hold several of the finer theater properties here in New York. If you expanded those holdings to reach across the country, think of the empire you could build, thus spreading your risk over a broader area than a possibility of a downturn here in New York!"

"The few entertainment holdings we own were my father's folly, Jeremy. I continue to hold them for the sentimental value they represent. I have no interest in expanding that particular branch of our holdings."

Jeremy frowned. "You will not consider the idea, then?"

Adam looked at Jeremy. The younger man had clearly spent a great deal of time and energy on preparing to bring him this idea. Perhaps rejecting it out of hand was unfair. "I'll not reject any opportunity without careful consideration, Jeremy. I am willing to meet with your client and consider the full details of his offer—in the strictest of confidence, of course."

Jeremy relaxed visibly and drank the rest of his coffee. "You won't regret this, Adam," he promised as he stood and pumped Adam's hand vigorously before heading for the door.

"Come to the house at six for dinner and we can discuss this further."

Jeremy grinned happily and waved as he left the office. Adam saw that he'd left the carefully prepared chart lying on the table. He picked it up and considered it. It was an intriguing possibility to be sure, and perhaps just the project he needed to take his attention away from the charms of Olivia and bring them back to business where they belonged.

It was following the disastrous evening in the stables that Olivia decided that she must take matters into her own hands. The weeks of enduring the continued refusal of Sylvia Porterfield to permit her to do anything for her unless Adam was in the house were at an end. Even though she had yielded on the issue of the garden and actually begun to take interest in its progress, she still maintained her distance with Olivia.

When Olivia heard that neither Adam nor Jeremy would be in for dinner the following evening, she went to the kitchen and told the cook that she would take a tray up to Mrs. Porterfield and join her for the meal.

Winston looked up from his newspaper in surprise. "Mrs. Porterfield requested that you do this?"

"No, but it is part of my agreement with Mr. Porterfield that I help his mother, and I intend to do whatever I can to fulfill that . . . even if it means losing my position here," she added when she saw Winston's skeptical expression.

Olivia took some pleasure in the fact that she had clearly begun to earn Winston's respect in the weeks of her tenure, and she hoped that her decision to take a tray up to Mrs. Porterfield would please him.

"Oh, bless you, my child," the cook, whose name was Bertha, gushed as she bustled about setting up a tray. "You do understand that she's not been herself since the mister passed, and we're all worried to distraction about it, especially young Mr. Adam. That boy is devoted to his mother, not like some I could name." She cast a critical eye in the direction of her own son, Willy, the family's driver.

"That's what I'd hope to have from me own son there, miss, should the day ever come. But, given the way he treats his old mum . . ." She permitted the thought to hang there, punctuating it with a shrug.

Willy grinned at his mother and she returned the smile. Olivia fully understood that they were devoted to each other and there was not the slightest question of disloyalty between them.

"I've put an extra plate there for you, dearie," Bertha said as she handed the tray to her son. "Here, take this up the stairs there for the young miss and mind you come straight back."

"Thank you," Olivia said to Bertha. Bertha put a comforting hand on her arm. "Are you sure that this is wise, Livvy? She doesn't take to folks forcing her hand."

"I was retained as a companion," Olivia reminded her. "That means that I am expected to spend time with her. There will be no more meals taken alone . . . even if she wants to eat in her room. Whether we dine there or in the dining room, we will dine together."

She did not miss the way that Willy rolled his eyes or the way Winston and Bertha exchanged nervous glances.

"Just don't you mind Mrs. P.'s little tempers, dearie," Bertha advised. "Just keep remembering that she's had trouble adjusting. The mister was just the dearest man and how he adored her. 'Twould be hard for any woman, I'd wager."

The service bell jangled and they all jumped. "That'd be herself ringing to see where her supper is," Bertha continued. "Go along now," she urged her son and Olivia hesitated, wondering if perhaps she was about to make yet another huge mistake.

She knocked lightly at Sylvia's door and then took the tray from Bertha's son. "Good evening, Mrs. Porterfield, I've brought our dinner tray," she announced as she entered the room and kicked the door lightly with one foot so that it closed with a click.

The room was large, with windows on either side of the carved headboard of the bed. At one end of the room was a chaise longue and two chairs upholstered in yellow silk brocade, in front of the fireplace. The dressing table was furnished with an array of items, all precisely arranged. Sylvia Porterfield reclined on the chaise near the lit fire, the only source of light in the room. She was wearing a blue satin wrapper and she looked up at Olivia with an expression of surprise and disgruntlement.

"Winston was to bring that."

"Yes, I know. But it seemed more appropriate that I bring it, given my post as your companion . . . at least for the next several weeks. Mr. Porterfield would be quite disappointed to know you still take meals in your room when he cannot be here. He would also disapprove of the fact that I don't keep you company." Olivia continued talking as she arranged the dishes on a small table near the chaise.

She waited for Sylvia to speak and when she didn't, Olivia introduced a topic that she thought might gain her employer's attention. "On the passage over, your son asked me to assist him with some of his business correspondence. From what I observed then and what he has told us all at dinner since, it would appear that his trip to London was quite a success. He certainly has been busy since his return. Meetings here and there, dinners, charity balls."

Sylvia frowned as Olivia presented her with one of two starched linen napkins, took the second for herself, and pulled a chair close to the opposite side of the table.

"You have your cheek, young woman," Sylvia said irritably.

Olivia looked directly at her for the first time since entering the room. "Why, Mrs. Porterfield, I am simply following your instructions. I know that Mr. Adam is out, but he might return at any time and what would he think to find you dining alone?"

"I meant when we are all at dinner in the dining room and you know that very well. You are impudent, but not stupid."

"Thank you," Olivia replied and placed a plate filled with slices of roast beef, roasted vegetables, a spiced apple, cheese and a rye roll in front of Sylvia. She tried introducing another topic. "Bertha is an excellent cook, isn't she?" She served herself. "And, a lovely person as well. Devoted to you, of course. How long has she been in your service?"

"Miss Marlowe, you may force me to endure your company in order to appease my son, but I do not require your conversation, is that clear?"

"As you wish," Olivia replied and continued cutting her meat and taking stock of the room.

Sylvia poked at her food, moving it around the plate without eating more than a bite or two. She glanced at Olivia from time to time and then away. Olivia pretended not to notice, but ate slowly and settled her own gaze on the fire.

"That dress you're wearing," Sylvia said when the silence in the room had become almost palpable.

Olivia immediately turned her attention to Sylvia. "Yes?"

"Well, I can't help but note that it is of a quality that is unusual for one of your . . . position. The same can be said for all of your clothing."

Olivia fingered the fabric and smiled. "It is lovely, isn't it?" she replied and resumed eating.

"May I ask where you acquired such a gown?"

Olivia pretended not to understand the question. "Do you mean the fabric? It came from a little shop in. . . ."

"Not the fabric, you stupid girl, the gown itself. It must have cost you a month's wages."

"Not at all. It was my. . . ." Olivia almost slipped and said that the gown had belonged to her mother as it indeed had, but caught herself just in time. "The dress belonged originally to Lord Barrington's wife. It was given to me . . . along with other of her costumes following her untimely death."

She could see that Sylvia was intrigued on several levels but struggling to maintain her distance. "I see." She took a bite of her food and held out her wineglass to be refilled.

Olivia permitted her eyes to wander to the open door that led to the dressing room of the suite. "I imagine that you have some truly lovely gowns—a woman of your social position must attend any number of functions in the course of a year."

"I am in mourning," Sylvia replied pointedly. "The rest of my wardrobe does not interest me."

"And yet, your son tells me that Mr. Porterfield died over two years ago. Surely . . ."

Sylvia half rose from the chaise longue. "We shall not discuss Mr. Porterfield," she ordered in a low but emotional voice. "Is that understood?"

Olivia nodded, lowering her eyes. "I am sorry," she said

in a near whisper. There was no response, but Sylvia sat back in her chair and picked at her food.

The rest of the meal was taken in silence. Sylvia ate very little, pushing her plate away and leaving the newly poured wine untouched.

After a few moments, Olivia rose to clear and load the tray. "May I get you anything else, Mrs. Porterfield?"

A dismissive wave of her employer's hand was her only response.

"Very well then, I shall bid you good night and see you in the morning."

"I won't come down for breakfast," Sylvia announced when Olivia had nearly reached the door.

"Then perhaps I shall see you after breakfast in the library." She opened the door and turned to pick up the tray. "I thought we would discuss some ideas that I found for revival of the garden," she added and was pleased to see a flicker of interest from the woman who looked very old and shrunken, huddled as she was into the corner of the chaise.

"Good night, ma'am," Olivia said and closed the door.

Sylvia sat very still for a long moment after the woman had left the room. There was something about her. *She reminds me of myself,* she thought. *She is every bit as independent and forthright as I was at her age. Still, with my background, such a thing was considered charming. She should know her place.*

Yet she could not help admiring Olivia's pluck. She wandered over to the window and looked out at the garden. Clayton had worked so very hard to have everything just so. Perhaps it was time to revive it as a tribute to him, if nothing more. She went to her writing desk and began making notes.

Later, there was a soft knock at her door. "Yes, come

in," she answered irritably and turned, expecting to see her maid.

"Are you feeling better, Mother?" Adam asked as he walked to her side and stood looking down at her.

"I was a bit tired," she said, not meeting his gaze. "I thought you had gone out."

"The meeting was canceled at the last minute. I stopped at the club for a bite to eat before coming home."

Sylvia wondered if Olivia had been perceptive enough to have gotten this information in advance or was just lucky. She indicated the chaise. "Sit with me for a moment. You've never really told me about your most recent trip to London . . . aside from your new habit of picking up stray English people and bringing them home," she said. "Miss Marlowe seems to be of the impression that your visit was inordinately well-timed. I am wondering if that extended to areas other than just business."

"England was quite successful . . . quite profitable. The contacts that I made in London are beginning. . . ."

"Oh, you know I don't want to hear about business," Sylvia chastised him. "Did you meet anyone of the fairer sex in London?"

"I met a great many people—some of them female. I brought two of them back with me. You certainly seem quite taken with Jeremy Barrington—he is quite the charmer."

"So I noticed."

"And Miss Marlowe is quite capable."

Sylvia frowned. "She told me that you had her handling your correspondence on the crossing. Do you think that was wise? You know what a gossip the Armbruster woman is and I understand that she was on board."

Adam chuckled. "For someone who stays in your room day and night, you are always extremely well-informed, Mother."

Sylvia shrugged. "Nevertheless, having that young woman assist you in. . . ."

"She was not in my stateroom, Mother. We worked in the ship's library at her suggestion."

"Really?" She could not help but be impressed. After all, Adam was both handsome and wealthy. Any young woman would not have been blamed if she had taken such an opportunity to get to know him more intimately. Not that Adam would permit such a thing. He was like his father in that way—a man of the highest principles. Perhaps she had misjudged Olivia. "What do you know of the Marlowe woman's background . . . her previous employment? Why did she leave?"

Adam evaded the question. "Why does anyone leave? She wanted something more challenging. Her parents are both dead and she has no siblings. Her decision lies partly in a certain spirit of adventure, I'd say."

Sylvia gave a derisive sniff. "Then, no doubt, she will not be here long. She'll find something more exciting than playing nursemaid to an old woman."

"I wasn't aware that she had been retained as a nursemaid, and who, pray tell, is this old woman?"

"Don't try to get around me, Adam. You know that I'm right."

"I know nothing of the sort. She seems determined to fulfill the duties you have outlined for her."

"She's a nuisance," Sylvia huffed.

"On the other hand, you and I have a bargain," Adam reminded her. "You may as well let her attend you while she's here or accept the fact that you are paying her a handsome salary to live in your house and dine on Bertha's scrumptious meals."

Sylvia started to protest and saw that Adam had set out to provoke her. He knew full well how she felt about employees earning their pay. Idle hands and all of that had always been her motto. Clay had been far too easy on the help and Adam showed the same inclination. Someone in this household had to make sure the staff knew what was expected.

"She's planning the garden," she blurted and immediately wished she hadn't.

Adam frowned. "I don't know, Mother. Can you entrust such a project to a mere nursemaid?" Then he grinned. It was Clay's grin—and it broke her heart.

"Go to bed," she snapped.

He stood and bent to kiss her forehead. "I love you, Mother," he said softly and left the room.

She sat looking at the closed door, his words echoing in her head. He did love her and she knew that Olivia Marlowe was his attempt to demonstrate that. Perhaps she had misread the looks she had seen Adam giving the woman when he thought no one was watching. Perhaps his focus on her was simply surprise at what she had been able to accomplish and her obvious intelligence. Sylvia could not help being attracted to the woman's pluck and wit herself. Perhaps she owed it to Adam to give at least a semblance of accepting this representation of his care and affection. Perhaps she would see what Olivia Marlowe had planned for the garden.

The following morning, Adam heard voices from the library as he came downstairs. He paused at the door and overheard Olivia talking to his mother.

"I discovered the original plans for the garden in this botany book, Mrs. Porterfield," Olivia said. "Let me lay them out here so that you can see them more clearly."

"I know the plans, Olivia," his mother replied testily. "There, that is the fern garden and there, the herbs and there. . . ."

"Do you want everything restored as it was?"

"Precisely as it was. If this is to serve as a fitting tribute to my late husband, then I want it to be exact, down to the smallest detail."

"Yes, ma'am."

Adam decided that he could do without the papers he had intended to retrieve from his desk in the library. He did not want to risk interrupting what promised to be an important first step in his mother's recovery. He wondered how Olivia had managed to interest his mother in the project.

He left the office early and stopped at a florist on his way home. He had to rely on the shop's owner to advise him on a selection, but he was delighted with the result.

"Good evening, sir," Winston greeted him with his usual cordiality, but was clearly mystified by the plants that he and Willy were unloading from the carriage.

"Winston, would you be so kind as to help Willy place these on the terrace?" he asked as they unloaded several potted ferns, a large gardenia plant in full bloom, and something that looked as if it might actually grow into a tree.

"Of course, but. . . ."

"I want my mother to be surprised when she comes down in the morning." Adam frowned. "Do you think it's still too cool for them to be outside overnight? Perhaps we should cover them somehow."

"I am quite sure that they will survive the night, sir. However, your mother and Miss Marlowe are still in the garden. Shall I find somewhere to put these until they have come inside?"

"They're still out there?"

"Yes sir. They took a brief respite for lunch and then later this afternoon for tea. However, Mrs. Porterfield seems quite intent on completing drawings and notes to-day."

"Really?" Adam could not have been more pleased if Winston had told him that his mother had gone out dancing. "How wonderful!"

He hurried down the hallway and into the drawing room where he could observe his mother and Olivia from the window without their knowing he was there.

His mother was wearing her straw gardening hat and flat shoes. She was gesturing here and there from her position on a bench near the terrace. Olivia nodded and took rapid notes, then used wooden stakes to mark out designs that his mother had obviously dictated. Both women looked exhausted.

"Well, Mother, what is all this?" he asked as he stepped out onto the terrace.

His mother was clearly surprised to see him, but she smiled. "It would appear that Miss Marlowe has an interest in gardening."

"I see." He looked up and saw Olivia standing a little away from them, unsure of how to respond.

"Well, she could not have found a better teacher than you, Mother. I brought home a few things that might be of help as you plan the renovation."

"How lovely. Olivia, did you hear?"

"Yes, ma'am."

"We'll have to see what you've brought and incorporate them into our plan."

"Not this evening. Frankly, you two ladies are looking quite exhausted. I think you've done enough for one day. After all, it took months for the garden to get into this condition . . . it cannot be set right in a single afternoon."

Sylvia laughed and got slowly to her feet. "I *am* quite weary," she said. "It's been some time since I exerted myself so. Would you mind terribly, dear, if Miss Marlowe and I excused ourselves from dinner?"

Adam hesitated. He very much wanted to ask Olivia how she had managed to get his mother outside and actually involved in a project of this magnitude. On the other hand, what did it matter? All that mattered was that she had succeeded and that his mother was clearly taken with her.

"You two go along. I'll ask Bertha to have dinner for you and Miss Marlowe sent up in an hour, Mother."

"Thank you, dear." Sylvia said. "Olivia? Coming?"

"Yes, ma'am."

Olivia closed her notebook and hurried after Sylvia. Adam had never seen her so passive. Perhaps it was the secret to her success in getting through to his mother. Whatever she had decided to do, it did not matter whether or not he liked the change in her. The important thing was the change in his mother.

"Thank you, Olivia," he said softly as she hurried past him.

She paused for only an instant and glanced at him. "I've done nothing," she murmured and continued on her way to escort Sylvia to her room.

Adam remained on the terrace for a few moments, looking out over the garden where only the small wooden stakes spoke of what it might become. His thoughts turned to Olivia. What would become of her now she had come into their lives? What would she come to mean to his mother? To him?

A few days later, Olivia heard Adam say goodnight to his mother, heard the tenderness in the way he spoke to her and wondered why his tone moved her nearly to tears. The thought occurred to her that she might never know such caring, such tenderness. She heard the latch click as he closed Sylvia's door and his footsteps retreating toward the main staircase. A few minutes later, she heard Winston welcome Jeremy to the house and escort him to the smoking room where he and Adam would enjoy a night of billiards or cards. The laughter of the two men floated back up the stairs and found its way up the narrow staircase that led to her room, and then all was silent.

She sat on the edge of the narrow bed and stared out the window into the blackness of the night. When the jewels had first been revealed as copies, she had believed that she had nothing but the small savings of cash she had earned on the ship. Over the last weeks she had added to that savings and she had developed the habit of counting her funds and counting the days until the three-month agreement between Adam and his mother was at an end.

She had no doubt that in spite of the fact that she had made some small inroads with Sylvia, when the three-month term had expired, she would be asked to leave. She had to be ready, and this was why she had started to seek as much additional work as she could manage. Every dime counted. Her options had narrowed in a way that was completely unsettling for her. She believed that Adam would be as glad as his mother would to see her leave.

She counted the money once again. Of course, nothing had changed. As one accustomed to having her own way, doing what she chose where she chose without a thought for the costs, she felt trapped in a situation over which she had absolutely no control. Where would she go? What would she do once her tenure with the Porterfields had ended?

In the weeks of her employment, she had begun to understand that things could be far worse than she might have imagined. Once, on her Saturday off, she and Molly had made the journey down to Hester Street to visit

Molly's family. Olivia had been appalled at the conditions under which they lived. Three rooms, each one much smaller than her own quarters at the Porterfield mansion. One served as kitchen and dining room, the second as bedroom for Molly's parents, and the third as a combination factory and parlor.

In order to make ends meet, Molly's mother and three sisters took in additional piecework from a nearby factory where they all worked during the day. Her younger brothers hauled the finished work back to the factory in bundles so huge that they were bent double under the weight of them. Molly's father worked two jobs, yet they were barely able to meet their expenses. Molly was especially happy to hear news that they were expecting two cousins from Ireland to join them by the end of the month. The cousins would pay a small rent—money that would permit Molly's parents to keep the tiny apartment.

"They will live with your parents?" Olivia asked as she and Molly made their way past pushcarts thronged with women haggling for a better price. She dodged children running from angry shopkeepers accusing them of theft in several different languages, and she had to shout to be heard above the general chaos of the street.

"Of course—at least until they marry. Anna is coming to work for the Rutherfords, so she'll have a room there," Molly replied. "Watch out!" she added as she dodged around a man of indeterminate age pushing a rack of clothes straight toward them.

He didn't even make an apology for his rudeness as he brushed past them. Indeed, had Olivia not stepped off the curb and into muck up to the ankles of her high-topped shoes, the man would have run right into her and blamed her for the accident. But, that wasn't the worst of what she had seen that day. She had seen women her own age who looked decades older. She had seen men huddled in doorways begging for something to eat. She had seen abject poverty, and Molly had walked past it all as if it were the most normal thing in the world.

"Doesn't it bother you?" Olivia had asked when they had finally stepped off the streetcar near Washington Park and were saying their farewells before heading in opposite directions to their respective mansions.

Molly had shrugged. "As the saying goes . . . there, but for the grace of the Rutherfords go I!" she had replied. "Gotta go. Mickey's in port and I'm to meet him at the tavern."

Olivia had thought of that day often and of Molly's flippant response to her question. *There but for the grace of . . . Adam Porterfield* . . . she thought.

She could not imagine how she would manage, but she was far too proud to go to Jeremy for help . . . not that he had help to offer. The way he usually spent every penny the moment it came to hand, he was probably as panic-stricken as she was. The ruse that had formed the basis of their escape from life at Barrington Manor had become reality for each of them. She saw that Jeremy had come to idolize Adam. Adam was independent and self-assured. He had the respect of his peers, his clients, and his employees. Jeremy would do almost anything to impress him. Jeremy and she were both dependent on the employment and generosity of Adam Porterfield and his mother. Apparently, Jeremy was receiving an allowance from his father and earning enough to meet his expenses and enjoy an active social life, while she—Olivia Marlowe, the daughter of a duke—was hired help.

It had occurred to her more than once that now that she had arrived in New York, there really was no reason to maintain the secret of her identity. But she had heard the way the servants on the ship talked about those passengers of lesser nobility who were a bit down on their luck. Their discussion of such passengers had run the gamut from scorn to pity and she would have neither judgment foisted upon her. Better to bide her time until she could establish herself properly . . . perhaps a shop of her own someday.

She counted the meager funds one last time and recorded the figure in her journal. There had to be something more that she could do, some way she could find to avert this potential disaster.

The bell above her door jangled, startling her so that she leapt to her feet. She stared at the bell and it jangled again, dancing impatiently on its bracket. In all the time she had been here, this was the first time that Sylvia Porterfield had called for her. She quickly slid the folded bills into a drawer of the small dresser and checked her hair in the mirror before hurrying to answer her lady's call.

"Yes, ma'am?" she asked once she had knocked and received a curt command to enter the room. Her eyes widened in surprise.

Every surface of the room was covered with clothing—gorgeous gowns in a rainbow of colors, the finest silks, and wool so finely woven that it draped like silk. There were tea gowns, walking costumes, traveling costumes, and the most exquisite ball gowns.

"I have been looking through my wardrobe," Sylvia announced. "It occurs to me that these gowns are terribly outdated. I haven't worn them since . . . I haven't worn them in years."

"They are very lovely," Olivia replied, wondering what could possibly lie behind Sylvia's sudden decision to review her wardrobe.

"Yes, they are practically new . . . some of them are unworn and yet . . . well, see for yourself how dated they are."

"Even so, with a bit work, they would be perfectly fine."

Sylvia eyed her. "It occurred to me that if I am to assist you in developing some options for making your way once you leave my employment, I might as well get something in the bargain."

Olivia remained silent, resisting the urge to remind her of the piles of linens Olivia had mended, not to mention the draperies she had completed for the dining room, the ones that the dismissed seamstress had left only half finished.

"You sew . . . more than simple mending, do you not? I have seen you sitting out there in the garden working on things. My maid, Martha, says that all around the park here, my neighbors are abuzz about you and your talent with a needle."

"I did a few alterations for some of the ladies on the voyage here," Olivia said. "They have continued to seek my services. Since you seemed to have no interest in how I spend my time off, I thought that there would be no harm in taking on a bit of alteration work." Her heart hammered. If Sylvia ordered her to stop, how would she earn the money she would need to sustain herself once her position here was terminated?

"Precisely. Winston tells me that you have caught up with the backlog of mending. I have also asked that he hire a gardener capable of reviving the gardens according to the plans we discussed. Therefore, you'll have time now to spend on some personal sewing for me. We'll begin with this one. Here, take it along and I'll expect your ideas in the morning." She pulled a gown from the pile on the chaise and tossed it in Olivia's direction.

Olivia could see that it was a gown at least twenty years old—actually nearer thirty. The fabric was a pale rose-colored moiré taffeta embroidered with tiny pink roses, stiff with age. The trim was worn. Olivia saw it for what it was—a test.

"Is there anything else?" she asked politely.

"Yes." She rummaged through another pile and produced a hand-crocheted wrap in deep burgundy chenille. "This goes with it. Go along. Cut it apart and put it back together again in some form that is respectable for this day and age. Then we shall discuss your future." Olivia took the garment. "I'll expect you at nine in the drawing room and we shall see what kind of talent you have for the needle arts."

Olivia nodded and left the room. In one way she felt excited to finally have something definitive to do. But then as she examined the gown more closely, she saw the hopelessness of the situation. She laid the gown out on her bed and stood back to look at it. After turning it this way and that, considering and rejecting half a dozen ideas, she sighed with frustration. There was so much fabric in the thing—yards and yards of it bundled to form the hideous bustle that had been the fashion in the seventies. She was determined to find a solution, even if it took her all night.

She stared at the dress and had the oddest feeling that she had seen it before, and then it struck her. A painting in the gallery came to mind . . . not a portrait exactly, but she was positive a gown the same color as this with that distinctive chenille wrap. Could it be the same gown?

She slipped out of the room and down the stairs, intent on reaching the gallery. The clock in the main hall chimed half past the hour. Everyone was asleep. The main rooms of the house were all dark, but a dim light glowed from the gallery. She slowed her steps and approached the room with caution.

Adam Porterfield was sitting on a small sofa at the far end of the long room. He was looking at a large cityscape painted by the French artist François Boucher. He seemed completely enthralled with the painting as if seeing it for the first time. Trying to escape back to her room, Olivia turned too quickly and banged her knee into the doorframe.

"Ouch," she squeaked involuntarily.

"Olivia? Come in. What on earth are you doing wandering the house at this hour? It's half past two."

"Is it? I . . . was working on something for your mother and lost track of time."

"Really?" His eyes lit with hope. "She gave you some new project to do?"

"It's just a small dressmaking project," she stammered, not wanting to get his hopes too high.

"And, why are you here in the gallery?"

He would think her ridiculous. "Inspiration?" she replied, not intending it to come out as a question.

He smiled at her for the first time since that horrible night in the stables. "Well, then let's illuminate the subject." He turned a switch and lights came on around the perimeter of the false skylight. "More?"

"That is fine, thank you," she said with a weak smile as she eased toward the painting she had come to see.

"That one?" He seemed surprised. "That's a joke."

"I beg your pardon. It may not be up to the standards of Boucher, but. . . ."

"No, seriously, Father had it done as a joke. See? There's my mother frolicking in the meadow."

"Oh, my good gracious, it *is*." Olivia covered her mouth with one hand and stared at the painting in shock. "Why would your father *do* such a thing?"

"It was done in jest, Olivia. Don't people play pranks on each other in England?"

"And your mother found this . . . amusing?"

"Winston once told me that she laughed until tears rolled down her face." He looked at the painting with a fond smile. "Father could always make her laugh." He pointed to the driver of the cart waiting for the woman in the painting to complete her dance. "That's him there."

"Are you in the painting as well?"

He grinned. "In a manner of speaking." He pointed to the figure of his mother.

She moved closer and squinted at the canvas and then colored to the roots of her hair. "Oh my," she whispered.

Sylvia Porterfield was extremely pregnant in the painting.

"Why Miss Marlowe, I do believe that we Porterfields have managed to ruffle that British reserve of yours."

He was leaning against the sofa, one ankle crossed over the other and his arms folded across his chest. The man was laughing at her.

"Really, Mr. Porterfield, I hardly think. . . ."

"Oh, come on, Olivia, it's all right to smile!" He reached out and touched the corner of her mouth with one finger. "Truly it is, and you have to admit that the painting is at least mildly amusing."

"It's . . ." She felt a bubble of laughter, improbable as that was. She cleared her throat. "Really, Mr. Porterfield . . ."

"I thought we had agreed to first names at times like this, remember?"

"Nevertheless . . ." She turned deliberately away from the painting. "Nevertheless, that *is* your mother."

"That, Olivia, is my very pregnant mother frolicking in a meadow. It's amusing. No, it's hilarious. Why aren't you laughing?" He had taken hold of her shoulders and turned her around so that she was facing the painting once again. The lighting seemed to accent Sylvia's extended stomach.

"Mr. Porterfield, this is not at all . . . ," Olivia tried a stern no-nonsense voice and the bubble of laughter escaped.

She tried to push it back inside, but he started to laugh as well, and it became contagious. Before she knew what was happening, they were giggling together like a couple of schoolchildren on summer holiday.

His grip tightened on her shoulders as she held her sides and almost lost her balance. In the next moment they had both collapsed onto the sofa and their faces were close. She ducked her head to dodge his laughing face, to try and regain some semblance of decorum. And, then she looked up at him, aware that he had stopped laughing, that his face—his mouth—was close to hers.

"Well," he said huskily, his breath fanning a tendril of her hair that had escaped her tightly wound bun. "Now, you know the deep dark secret of the Porterfield house." He pushed her hair behind her ear, his eyes avoiding hers. "Olivia, I. . . ."

She moved away from him and stood up. "It's very late, Adam, and your mother is expecting me to present her with a finished project in just a few hours. If you'll excuse me."

"Goodnight, Olivia," he said as she turned and fled the room. He decided not to comment on the fact that she had finally called him by his given name.

Nine

"Well, Olivia, what have you to show me this morning?" Sylvia asked, with an air of confidence that indeed she could anticipate only minimal results.

Olivia nodded toward Winston who brought in the dress form for the altered dress. She had wrapped the form in a sheet to protect her work. She saw Sylvia's eyes flicker with interest.

"Where on earth did you find that?" she asked.

"It was in one of the storage rooms next to the sewing room. I discovered it several days ago when I was searching for dressmaker pins." She nodded her thanks to Winston, who came as close to openly smiling at her in his mistress' presence as she'd ever witnessed.

"Well, uncover the thing so I can see," Sylvia ordered.

"In a moment." Olivia poured coffee for the woman and presented it to her. "I thought that perhaps we might come to an agreement."

Sylvia accepted the coffee and held the cup and saucer close to her lips as she watched Olivia suspiciously. "I am hardly in the habit of bargaining with the help."

"I believe that you have entrusted me with a garment that means a great deal to you. Assuming that I have not damaged that trust in what I have created, I am asking you to do something in return."

"What?"

"Wear the gown when you have tea with Mrs. Rutherford."

Sylvia turned away and fixed her gaze on the window. "I have explained to you that my days of entertaining visitors are over."

"That may be, but Mrs. Rutherford is far more than simply a visitor. She is the godmother of your only child and her husband is his godfather. Surely, that makes them more than mere visitors in this house."

Sylvia's head snapped around and she pinned Olivia with a steely gaze. "Uncover the mannequin, if you please."

Olivia opened the sheet and stood to one side as she permitted it to fall away, revealing the gown she had spent the rest of the night redesigning. When Sylvia gasped, set the coffee cup aside, stood and crossed the room for a closer inspection, Olivia knew that she had succeeded.

"It is quite . . . how did you manage . . . ? Why that is the wrap you have used as trim. . . ." The older woman moved around the mannequin checking every detail, fingering the fabric, examining the design.

"Take care," Olivia warned. "I'm afraid that it is only roughly basted at this stage and there may yet be several pins in the seams."

Sylvia stepped around the short train of the gown and lifted one of the sleeves to view the detail of it. Then she bent to examine the way the skirt was folded and tucked so that when she walked, the deeper color of the trim would appear from the deeply inverted pleats. "It's quite astonishing," she whispered and Olivia knew that she was unaware that she had spoken aloud.

"Mrs. Porterfield, you are a woman of impeccable taste and style. Even in your state of mourning, your pride in appearance is evident. I expect that this is in part a tribute to Mr. Porterfield. The servants tell me that his pride in your beauty knew no bounds."

Sylvia's eyes glistened with tears and for the first time, she did not reprimand Olivia for invoking the name of her late husband. But all too soon, she caught herself and her back straightened as she returned to her chair and picked up her coffee.

"I assume that you had help," she said.

Olivia was just about to deny the accusation when Adam entered the room. "Good morning, Mother," he said cheerfully. "You're looking well." He bent and kissed her cheek and then turned and spotted the gown. "Well, well, well, what have we here?" he said in a voice that left no doubt as to how impressed he was.

"Apparently Miss Marlowe has some talent for the needle arts beyond simple alterations," Sylvia replied, feigning disinterest.

"Why Mother, this is your gown from the painting . . . you know, the one that Father. . . ."

"I *know* which painting, Adam," Sylvia interrupted, her cheeks scarlet with embarrassment.

Adam continued to walk around the dress form, admiring the dress. "Where will you wear it?"

"I won't," Sylvia huffed. "It was an exercise for Miss Marlowe, nothing more."

Adam raised his eyebrows and grinned. "Really?" He stood behind the form, positioning his own face at the head and creating a ridiculous and comical image of wearing the gown himself. "Then I guess I'll just have to find the right occasion."

Olivia could not repress a smile and quickly covered her mouth with one hand. Sylvia tried to remain stern. "You are being quite silly." A smile broke across her face, and she was transformed.

"Oh, Mrs. Porterfield," Olivia said before she even knew the words were out. "You really are quite beautiful."

Sylvia seemed not to know how to respond to that. "Has it happened that everyone of your age has become foolish, Adam?" she asked her son, turning away so that Olivia could not see her expression.

"She is right, Mother," Adam replied. "You are still one of the most beautiful women I know."

"Pshaw," Sylvia huffed. "No wonder you are as yet unwed."

"I was suggesting that perhaps your mother might wear the gown for tea with her friend, Mrs. Rutherford," Olivia commented and ignored the scathing look Sylvia cast her way.

"That's wonderful news, Mother. Shall I invite her? Better yet, why not have both my godparents here for dinner on Sunday? We can all go to church and then have dinner here the way we did when I was a boy. Winston!" He moved to the door and bellowed out the butler's name.

"Do not shout, son," Sylvia instructed.

He turned to Olivia. "Can you have the gown completed by Sunday? It looks a bit . . . fragile at the moment."

"It can be done," she assured him.

"Mother? You will not disappoint me?"

"Really, Adam, I. . . ." She paused and looked at him, and in that moment, Olivia knew that Sylvia saw in her son all of the hope and eagerness of the small boy she had raised. She would not disappoint him. "I will be at Sunday dinner," she agreed with a sigh.

"And church," he stated and it was not a question. He glanced at the gown again. "She'll need a hat," he said to Olivia as he reached into his pocket and thrust a handful of bills at her. "Have Winston arrange for you to purchase whatever you need to make one to match the gown."

"Adam, really, just because Miss Marlowe is mildly talented with a needle does not mean that she is a milliner. That takes special talent."

"Your mother is right, sir," Olivia replied, handing the bills back to him.

He refused to take them. "Then, take her out or bring the milliner here. She cannot be in church without a hat." He crossed the room again and kissed his mother's cheek. "I'll invite Jeremy as well, all right?"

On his way out the door he looked directly at Olivia and winked. She could feel the color flood her cheeks, yet it was accompanied by the queerest sensation of pleasure of a nature she had never before experienced. When she turned back toward Sylvia, she saw that the older woman was regarding her with interest.

"Well now," Sylvia said as if she'd just uncovered a surprise, but she said no more as she poured herself a second cup of coffee.

"Miss Marlowe," she said finally. "I do believe that we may have discovered your calling." She stood and walked over to the windows.

"I beg your pardon, ma'am."

"Your calling, my dear—your employment—once we have endured our enforced time together. With your skills with the needle, there is no doubt that you will easily find work in a fine shop. In fact, I will do everything I can to make certain that your work is noticed." She examined the gown once more and Olivia saw a faraway look in her eyes, a look that said she was remembering happier days.

But, her heart sank as Sylvia regained control of her emotions and turned to face her with a frown. As she had worked on the gown through the night, Olivia had dared to hope that Sylvia might see something in the work—in her—worth cultivating. She had thought that this might actually gain her additional time in the household. Sylvia's agreement to attend church and invite the Rutherfords to Sunday dinner had seemed like a personal victory for her as well as Adam. Now it was clear that nothing had changed in Sylvia's perspective. She still expected Olivia to leave—the sooner, the better. It surprised her to realize that she would not only miss seeing Adam every day, she would miss seeing Sylvia and the staff. "I don't understand," she said softly, hoping that indeed, she had misread the moment.

"Of course you do," Sylvia replied. "You may be many things, but you are an intelligent young woman, uncommonly so. Very little has changed here, Olivia. The wearing of a gown . . . attending church . . . seeing my dear friend. . . ." She shrugged.

"If that has all come so easily, then why have you not managed it before?"

Sylvia flinched slightly and then shrugged. "It did not suit me."

"And, suddenly it does?"

"It serves my purpose."

"Which is?"

Sylvia faced her and looked at her with hard gray eyes. "Which is, my dear Miss Marlowe, to be delivered from the likes of you and to be left alone to mourn in my own way, in my own time." Without waiting for further response, she swept past Olivia and spent the rest of the day in her room.

By Sunday, Adam could hardly contain his excitement. His mother was actually leaving the house for the first time in months. Furthermore, she was entertaining their old and dear friends at Sunday dinner, and for the first time since his father's death, she was wearing a gown that was not black. The wonder was that Olivia Marlowe seemed not to take the slightest pleasure in her triumph. She could have been forgiven for gloating a bit, for swaggering or whatever it was women did that paralleled a man's proud strut in the face of success. Instead, she remained, as always, on the fringes. She was attentive but aloof, her expression revealing nothing at all.

He paced the hall awaiting the appearance of his mother at the top of the stairs.

"Mother? The carriage is here," he called impatiently.

"Well, the carriage is our own so I trust that it runs on our time schedule not one of its own," Sylvia fumed as she appeared at the top of the broad curved staircase. "Well?" She waited for him to come to meet her on the stairs and escort her down.

"Oh, Mother, you look . . . you are. . . ." His voice choked slightly and he cleared his throat. "Thank you for doing this, Mother," he said softly as he took the steps two at a time to reach her side. "I have never been more honored to be your son."

Indeed she was a vision. The silk of the gown rustled as they made their way down the stairs. She held her head high under the black plumed hat with a veil that seemed to accentuate the flawlessness of her skin.

When he glanced up, he saw Olivia standing at the railing, watching their descent. Her eyes brimmed with emotion . . . pride in her accomplishment, surely, and yet there seemed to be something more.

"Coming, Miss Marlowe?" he asked, pausing so that his mother also looked up at her.

"Of course, she's coming," Sylvia replied. "Of what use is a companion if she doesn't accompany one here and there? Get your cloak and hat, Olivia, and come along. The carriage awaits, as my son is so fond of reminding me."

Adam glanced back at Olivia as he and his mother reached the bottom of the stairs. She had hesitated and he had the oddest notion that she was about to refuse his mother's order. Then she turned and he heard her climb the stairs to her own room.

By the time he had settled his mother in the carriage, Olivia was at the door. She had put on her hat and a fitted jacket that matched her skirt. It was the same skirt she had worn when he'd seen her that first morning in Southampton, and he had a momentary thought to check for any stray bits of straw still caught in the velvet band and feathers that decorated her hat. He retraced his steps up to the front entrance and offered her his arm.

"You look quite lovely this morning, Olivia. That color of blue suits you well."

"Thank you," she murmured and he noticed that she hesitated a moment before permitting herself to place her hand very lightly in the crook of his arm. When she stepped into the carriage, he could not help but take note of her slender form, her elegant grace in movement. She took her place next to his mother, while he sat opposite the two of them and pulled the door of the carriage shut. He tapped his walking stick on the ceiling of the closed carriage to let Willy know that they were ready to go. Aware that he risked irritating his mother if he made too much of this first outing, he remained silent, seeming to focus his attention on the passing scene when, in fact, he was observing Olivia.

He could not have been more conscious of her in every detail if she had intentionally tried to gain his attention. She sat perfectly still, her gloved hands folded in her lap. His mother became more agitated the closer they came to the church, but Olivia remained composed. Yet, there was something about her that reminded him of an animal about to spring—someone bent upon escape at the first opportunity. She kept her eyes on her folded hands, although he saw her glance over at his mother from time to time. It occurred to him that she wanted very much to place her own hand over his mother's in a gesture of reassurance.

"Mother," he said quietly, reaching across the narrow distance separating them to take his mother's hand between his own. "I know how difficult this is for you. I believe that Father would be very pleased that you have taken this step."

Sylvia grew as still as Olivia had been throughout the journey. She nodded once and sat back against the tufted leather seat, staring out the window as if lost in memory. Adam continued to hold her hand but his eyes sought Olivia.

She was looking directly at him now and a shadow of a smile flickered across her face. "We are here," she said softly as the driver brought the horses to a halt.

"How do I look?" Sylvia asked, but her question was directed to Olivia.

Olivia straightened an errant feather on the older woman's hat. "Quite lovely," she assured her.

Sylvia's hand tightened on the sterling silver knob of her walking stick and she took a deep breath. "Then, let us try to get through this without creating too great a spectacle," she instructed Adam.

It was impossible not to notice the surprised reaction of the parishioners as he led his mother down the aisle to their family pew. After all, it had been months since anyone had sat there. Olivia followed them down the long aisle and took her seat in the pew just behind them. For the whole of the service, Adam was aware of nothing save Olivia Marlowe, the low throaty murmur of her accented voice reading responsively with the congregation, in contrast with the lilting sound of her singing. When the benediction had been delivered and the postlude begun, she waited for Adam to lead his mother back toward the church doors before following a few steps behind.

Once outside, there was a joyous reunion with the Rutherfords . . . or rather it was joyous on their part. His mother maintained the reserve she had adopted ever since his father's death. Adam stood next to Olivia off to one side, and allowed Abigail Rutherford to work her magic.

"And, how do you think the morning has gone so far, Olivia?" Adam asked.

"I think that your mother has missed church more than she realized."

"Yes, I do believe that is true."

They stood in silence for a moment, observing the exchange of conversation between old friends. The minister made a special point of talking to Sylvia for several minutes.

"I should like to be excused from dinner, sir," Olivia announced suddenly.

"Why on earth would you want to do that?" Adam asked and knew that he had allowed his surprise at her request to color his tone.

"I would be an intruder. This is a time for you and your mother to rekindle old acquaintances, old routines."

"Nevertheless, had it not been for you, we would not have reached this moment."

"May I assume that you are grateful?"

"I am in your debt," he agreed.

"Then, please excuse me from the dinner."

"What shall I tell my mother?"

She smiled and glanced at Sylvia. "I doubt that she will mind. She seems quite caught up in Mrs. Rutherford's stories."

A thought crossed his mind and he stiffened. "I apologize, Olivia. It is, after all, your day off. Perhaps you have an engagement with the Rutherfords' driver?"

Her eyes flashed angrily. "That is none. . . . Perhaps," she replied.

"Very well." He signaled for their carriage.

It was late afternoon when he saw her sitting at the far end of the garden. The Rutherfords had come and gone. Jeremy had sent word that he had been unable to attend church, but that he would be stopping by later in the week for a long visit to make amends.

The dinner with the Rutherfords had been a success by anyone's measure, and his mother, exhausted with the excitement and exertion of the day, had retired to her room to rest. Adam was in the library, trying to concentrate on some contracts that he had brought home from the office. However, his mind kept wandering back to Olivia. Throughout the long afternoon of conversation and dining, he had found himself thinking of her, wondering if indeed she was with that man . . . that driver who had handled her so commonly that day in the stables.

When he spotted her, she was seated on one of the wicker settees, a parasol shading her as she read from a slim volume. She was wearing a white blouse and the skirt of the suit she had worn to church—the blue one that set off her eyes so perfectly. Her hair was piled high. She looked as if she might have been there for some time, enjoying the warm sunshine of the late May afternoon. As he watched, the book slipped to her lap and he realized that she was dozing. He smiled to himself and, taking his suit coat from the back of the desk chair, headed out to the garden.

Olivia felt the shift in the wind and stirred, aware that with the setting sun, it would soon be time to return to the house . . . to the small, closed room that at least for the time being was her home. Reluctantly, she opened her eyes, regretting the need to abandon her dreams and the peace and fragrance of the garden.

She shivered slightly and rubbed her hands over the thin batiste of her blouse as she looked around for the book of poetry she had borrowed from the library. It had landed in the path, and she gave a little cry of alarm as she reached for it, fearful that it might have become soiled or damaged. Before she could retrieve it, Adam Porterfield stepped forward and bent to pick it up.

"I'm sorry," she said as she accepted the volume and hastily glanced through it, searching for any damage. "I'm afraid that I dozed off and the book fell . . ."

"There's no harm, Olivia," he assured her, taking the book from her and examining it himself. "Even if there were, it's only a book." He slipped it inside his coat pocket. "Have you been sitting out here long?"

"Most of the afternoon, it seems. I didn't realize how late it had gotten. Has Mrs. Porterfield sent for me?"

"No. Mother retired to her room about an hour ago. I expect that she, too, was in need of a nap. It was quite a full day for her, especially after so many weeks of little activity."

"And, what of Jere . . . Sir Barrington?"

"He sent word that he had been detained and would make amends with a long visit later this week. It will give Mother something to look forward to and yet another reason to have you work your magic on one of her gowns, I'll wager."

Olivia could not help wondering what really lay behind Jeremy's last minute cancellation. More than likely he had been out carousing until the early morning.

"I came out here to thank you, Olivia," Adam said, drawing her attention away from concerns about Jeremy. "Not only for myself, but for my mother as well."

"I am glad for her . . . and for you." She turned and picked up her parasol, closing it with a snap.

"It might also interest you to know that, according to Mrs. Rutherford, your talent with the needle is quite the topic of conversation among my mother's friends and their daughters. This did not go unnoticed by my mother who was singing your praises at dinner."

Olivia did not know how to respond to that so she changed the subject. "Excuse me, I should go in."

"You sound reluctant to see the end of such a lovely spring afternoon. Perhaps you would do me the honor of joining me in a walk. I'd like to hear you describe the plans for reviving the gardens. Winston tells me that you have made copious notes on the project beyond the ones Mother dictated."

She hesitated, but saw no reason to refuse. "Very well."

"So, how shall the work begin?"

"The work has already begun. I should expect that the new gardener will make quick work of the plan," she said and gave in to the urge to fold her arms across her chest for warmth.

"Here," he said as he removed his jacket and placed it around her shoulders. "You are far too valuable to me—to us—to risk illness," he added, and when she made a gesture of refusal, he left his hands on her shoulders for a moment longer.

She felt the warmth of his touch more than that of the coat. "Thank you."

"And now that we have hired a gardener . . . what next?" He walked beside her, his hands clasped behind his back, his bare head bent in concentration.

"There are a good many perennials that will thrive with a bit of attention." She touched a lilac branch filled with buds at its crown. "Some judicious pruning here and there. The tulips and daffodils will need dividing now that they have bloomed."

He reached up and pulled a partially opened lilac blossom to his nose and sniffed it. "This is the scent that you wear, Olivia." He offered it for her to inhale as well. "What is this bush?"

"Lilac."

"Lilac," he repeated and took another sniff of the blossom. "It's quite intoxicating."

Olivia moved further along the path. "There is lily of the valley in abundance. It makes a lovely border."

"Olivia?"

She was aware that he had stopped and was waiting for her to turn around. The shadows of an overgrown forsythia in full riotous golden blossom stretched across the path, shielding them from the house and anyone who might look out at the setting sun.

"Olivia?" He moved a step closer. "I did not come out here to survey the garden."

She felt as if everything had become perfectly still—the songs of the birds, the rustle of the breeze. He took another step and now he was close enough for her to feel his breath against her temple.

She did not move and yet she knew that every fiber of her being was leaning toward him, longing for his touch beyond the whisper of his breath. She closed her eyes and savored his knuckles stroking her cheek and then his finger was under her chin, urging her to look up at him, and, when she did, he whispered her name.

"Olivia." It hung in the air between them like the flutter of a butterfly's wings. Hesitantly she touched his face, and as if that were all the assurance he needed, he swept her into his arms and kissed her with a force that left her senses reeling.

Instinctively she knew that all that was necessary was the slightest resistance—a hand pushing against his chest, a step backward, the merest turn of her face away from his. But she did none of that for she wanted the kiss to go on forever, to continue its magic of transporting her from the humdrum life she had come to accept to the possibility of something far greater, far more thrilling.

She heard sounds as his mouth moved over hers, when his tongue swept across her lower lip and beyond. It took her by surprise to realize that the sounds were coming from her—murmurs of ecstasy, moans of desire.

She felt his hand flattened against her waist urging her closer. His other hand became entangled in her hair and she was aware of the soft metallic ting of hairpins dropping onto the stones that lined the path.

"Olivia. Olivia," he chanted, following each calling of her name with a kiss. Now on her temple, now on her throat, now the word breathed into her ear.

Somehow she found the sanity she needed to resist further advances. "Adam." She punctuated his name with a step away from him.

She saw that his actions had stunned him as they had her, although she doubted it was in the same way. She bent to retrieve her parasol and a few of the hairpins she could see.

When she finally faced him, he reached out and took a lock of her hair between his fingers. "Your hair was one of the first things I noticed about you," he said. "I have often found myself wanting to relive that moment on the ship when I first touched it." He glanced at her for the first time since kissing her. "I seem to have gotten my wish." He laid the curl gently on her shoulder and stepped away from her. "Are you all right, Olivia?"

"Yes, of course." She busied herself repairing her hair and did not look at him.

"Shall I apologize?"

"No." She picked up her parasol again and wished that she could open it but the shadows were far too long for any protection against the sun.

"Good," he said softly. "Because it would be a false apology."

She looked up at him in alarm.

"Well, at least that got your attention," he said and smiled.

She knew she should not return that smile and yet she seemed incapable of stopping herself. "You are hopeless."

"So my mother tells me." He took her arm and began

walking back along the path toward the house. "Have you had anything to eat today, Miss Marlowe?"

As much as she wanted to fall into the pattern he was clearly prepared to establish, she could not permit herself to do so. Someone had to maintain a sense of propriety here. She pulled her hand free of his arm and widened the distance between them. "Yes, thank you. Bertha is like a mother hen when it comes to making sure that I eat properly."

They had almost reached the house and the mood between them had shifted. "Olivia, I. . . ."

"Please," she whispered, closing her eyes to blot out his handsome face looking down at her with such unabashed longing. "Good evening, Mr. Porterfield." She hurried inside the house and did not look back until she had reached the back stairs. She had made the right decision, of that there was no doubt. Becoming romantically involved with her employer could only bring trouble, and Adam would regret it in the end.

But when she reached her room, she could not resist looking out the window and down on the garden. She closed her eyes and inhaled the heady fragrance of the lilac as she recalled his kiss and knew that she would never spend a single moment in that place again without remembering . . . reliving the moment. The tears rolled down her cheeks, wetting her neck where he had kissed her as well. She rested her fingers where his lips had been and felt even now the hammering of her pulse.

Impossible, she thought, opening her eyes and brushing away the tears with the back of her hand. *You are lonely and frightened and the least kindness would be your undoing at this moment.*

As was her ritual, she took out her small accumulation of bills and began to count, but before she had gotten halfway through the small stack, her attention drifted. *How would she deal with future encounters with Adam now that they had kissed? How could she continue to sit across from him at meals and pretend to feel nothing? What if he expected her to attend church every Sunday with his mother and him . . . as he surely would now that he thought the day had been such a success? And now with the fair weather and longer days, he would sit with his mother on the veranda and expect her to join them.*

She took down the calendar that she had hung on the back of her door. When she had put it up, the intent had been to remind herself that she needed to find some way to please Mrs. Porterfield after the ninety days stated in her bargain with her son. Now, the remaining days loomed like years of torture to be endured under the same roof as Adam Porterfield.

Olivia replaced the calendar on its hook and then went to the window and pulled the curtains shut with a snap. Jeremy's plan might have brought her out of a disastrous engagement, but she would have to rely on herself to make sure that she did not escape the frying pan only to land in the fire, as her friend, Molly, might say.

Elsewhere in the house, Sylvia paced the length of her room and back again. Earlier she had glanced out the window in time to see Olivia and Adam walking toward the house from the garden. She had thought little of it until she saw Olivia run into the house as if she were upset. *What could have happened to upset her? What had Adam done?* She was shocked to find herself instinctively taking the girl's side.

Try as she might, the facts were undeniable. Olivia and Adam were a good match. It was an impossible one to be sure, and that was exactly why she needed to take appropriate steps to secure a future for Olivia that did not include Adam.

Ten

"Good morning, Mrs. Porterfield." Olivia greeted her employer as usual the following morning. "I trust that you slept well."

"Good morning, Olivia. Do sit down."

Sylvia did not miss Olivia's startled reaction to her blunt invitation. She saw that Olivia was nervous, and why shouldn't she be? "Olivia, these past few weeks, there have been times when I have treated you with less than fairness. I would like you to know that this is not my usual way. It seems that in the grip of my grief for my late husband, I have become . . . that is to say. . . ."

"It is perfectly understandable, ma'am," Olivia assured her.

"Perhaps. But nevertheless, Clayton would be appalled. I am a bit appalled myself, to tell the truth."

Olivia certainly did not know how to comment on that statement so she remained quiet.

"Perhaps you are not aware of the stir your concept of my gown caused at church," Sylvia continued. "Abigail Rutherford sent word this morning that she has had at least half a dozen inquiries about it."

"I am certain that it was your appearance in the gown, Mrs. Porterfield. You have a style and elegance that would be the envy of any woman."

"Why, Olivia . . . flattery? This is not like you at all."

Olivia poured tea and handed cup and saucer to Sylvia.

Sylvia took a sip of her tea and made a face. "Oh, for heaven's sake, is there no one who can make a proper cup of tea?"

"Perhaps if you would permit me to prepare your tea instead of insisting that Winston do it," Olivia replied evenly.

"Winston has been in my service for twenty-five years."

"Then, if it is a question of loyalty. . . ."

"Don't be impertinent." She poured the rest of her tea into a nearby potted fern. "Very well. While you are here, you shall prepare the tea and perhaps you might teach the others in the process. Now, where was I?"

Olivia took a deep breath. "You were speaking of Mrs. Rutherford."

"Ah, yes. Olivia, you have a gift—unusual for one of your circumstances, to be sure. It is my belief that talent should be encouraged. How would you like to build a business as a successful design house here in the city?"

Olivia clearly could not have been more surprised if Sylvia had suggested that she ride naked through Central Park.

"Well?" Sylvia prompted, when Olivia did not respond immediately.

"I . . . that is, I don't know how to reply to such a question."

Sylvia permitted herself a smile. "At last, I seem to have stumped you, Olivia. Believe me, it has not been for the lack of trying these past few weeks. Nevertheless, I am quite serious and, to be frank, I would enjoy the opportunity to bring your talent to the attention of people who might well be able to assist you in building a proper business for yourself."

Olivia's head was swimming with possibilities. Certainly

she enjoyed dress designing, but it had never occurred to her that she might actually be able to make a living at it. Alterations, certainly. But, her own creations?

"I am speechless, Mrs. Porterfield."

"Yes, I can see that. Fortunately, when you are struck dumb, your face is most expressive. You are even now trying to calculate exactly why I might do this for you."

"Yes, ma'am."

"In the early years of the business, Clayton . . . Mr. Porterfield . . . and I worked as a team. We discussed everything and I was quite involved in the establishment of the business . . . albeit behind the scenes. Those were exciting times, Olivia, for we were building a future and at the same time enhancing the future for others. The truth is, I miss that."

"But I have seen how Adam . . . how your son relies on you as a sounding board for his ideas and business dealings," Olivia assured her.

"Nevertheless, it is his business now. Quite frankly, while I enjoy hearing of his dealings, I am no longer as engaged as I once was, and therein lies the intriguing idea that came to me last night. Olivia, how would you like me to become your patron?"

"I . . . I. . . ."

"We shall begin with one or two additional clients. Abigail was hinting broadly earlier this morning. The woman is a dear, but subtlety is not among her talents."

"Mrs. Porterfield, I truly do not know how to properly thank you for such a generous offer."

"Of course, we shall need to approach this in a manner entirely different from the usual alterations or seamstress approach," Sylvia continued as if Olivia had not spoken. She seemed to be thinking out loud rather than speaking to Olivia, so Olivia remained silent and let her think. "We shall need some assistance." She walked across the room to the small French desk and took out a single sheet of paper and an envelope. When she had written two sentences and signed her name with a flourish, she rang the bell and her maid appeared instantly as if she had been waiting for the call.

"Have this delivered at once and tell the boy not to wait for a reply," she said.

The maid took the note, made a half curtsy and disappeared.

"Mrs. Porterfield?" Olivia said softly when the older woman had gone into her dressing room and stayed there for several minutes.

"Well, come here, Olivia. We need to select the most promising of the lot." She was going through her collection of gowns.

"Mother?"

Both women froze where they were. To Olivia's surprise, Sylvia put a finger to her lips and shook her head. "In here, dear," she replied and thrust one of her many plain black gowns at Olivia as they returned to her bedroom. "Olivia is assisting me this morning."

Olivia turned away and focused all her attention on preparing the gown, but she was aware of Adam's every move, every word.

"I see." He poured himself a cup of tea and seemed inclined to tarry.

"Was there something you wanted to discuss, Adam?" Sylvia asked. Olivia did not miss the hint of impatience in the older woman's voice.

"Trying to get rid of me, Mother?" He moved closer to the bed where Olivia was working. She knew he wanted her to look at him, knew that she was at least part of the reason for his visit.

"Don't you need to be at the office or have I completely

lost track of the days and it is Sunday instead of Monday?"

"I just wanted to see if the glow of yesterday's outing and afternoon with the Rutherfords had worn away."

"Do not press, Adam," Sylvia said in a warning tone that made Olivia turn around. She found herself facing Adam Porterfield who seemed oblivious to his mother's admonition. His eyes went instantly to her mouth and she unconsciously licked her lips, gone suddenly dry. His eyes darkened and she knew that her reaction had seemed provocative. She moved past him.

"I'll just clear these tea things," she said softly, "so you and your son can talk, ma'am."

"Stay," Sylvia commanded. "It is Adam who is leaving, aren't you, dear?"

Adam smiled. "Apparently so." He bent and kissed his mother's cheek. "I'll be home for dinner."

"Lovely," Sylvia replied dryly, but then she reached up and patted his cheek. "You're looking quite exhausted, son. Are you not sleeping?"

His eyes flickered to Olivia and back again. He smiled. "I have things on my mind."

"Well, see that you attend to it. Your father would have. . . ."

This time Adam laughed. "Well, that's a good sign. If you start invoking the name of my father, I can stop worrying so much about you."

Sylvia gave him a gentle shove, but it was obvious that she was touched. "Go to work," she said. "And tell our young duke that if he ever stands me up again, I shall be quite cross with him."

He left the room then came back. "Mother, I was thinking that you might enjoy the theater. We have tickets for Thursday night."

"Perhaps. Now go." She actually shooed him out of the

room and closed the door behind him. "Now, where were we?" She spotted the black gown Olivia had laid out on the bed. "Put that away and bring the blue. If Adam is bent on the theater then you'll have to start with the blue."

"Might I ask why you did not want Mr. Porterfield to know what you were planning?"

Sylvia smiled. "If you are to be in the world of business, Olivia, there is one lesson above all that you must learn. Men—even those with the best of intentions—will be convinced that you cannot possibly succeed without their direct help. They can get in the way if one lets them."

The rest of Olivia's day was taken up with the physical work of taking Sylvia's gown apart and putting it back together again, and the mind-boggling task of considering a future for herself that included an actual career. Not far from her thoughts throughout the day was the idea that, as an independent business woman, might she not be able to meet Adam on a more even ground? And given that, could there be a possibility of a future for them?

"If we're to appear at the theater, you must have a gown for yourself as well," Sylvia told Olivia as she fitted the gray crêpe de chine gown upon Sylvia's small frame late the following afternoon.

"I have something suitable," Olivia assured her.

"I doubt that very much. Martha, go there to the closet and bring me my green satin," Sylvia instructed. "And, then go and see what is keeping Mrs. Rutherford. She was due an hour ago."

"Yes, ma'am," Martha said as she scurried to bring the requested gown and then hurried from the room.

"Squirrels, all of them," Sylvia muttered.

"I beg your pardon, ma'am?" Olivia asked politely, speaking around a mouth filled with pins.

"They all scurry about like squirrels . . . except for you and Winston. Am I so intimidating, Olivia?"

"They wish only to please you."

"Well, it pleases me to have people move at a normal pace, not as if they cannot wait to escape."

"Then you may wish to lighten your tone with them," Olivia replied, her attention focused on a difficult revision of the drape of the gown rather than on what she was saying. It was only Sylvia's complete silence that brought her back to awareness. "I do apologize," she said. ". . . that was completely. . . ."

"Honest and forthright," Sylvia replied and then she laughed. "You know, Olivia, there is something about you that reminds me of myself at your age. Frankly, it was the very trait that caught Mr. Porterfield's attention. I shocked him."

Olivia smiled and resumed her work. "Really, ma'am?"

"Yes. We were at a ball and he stepped in front of me . . . unknowingly to be sure . . . but nevertheless, I found it quite rude. He was very handsome and full of himself that evening. He was the guest of honor following his graduation from college."

"What happened?"

"I informed him in no uncertain terms that he might have received his degree in business but clearly they had neglected to teach him proper manners."

Olivia laughed and Sylvia laughed with her. "What did he reply?"

"Well, he was speechless as were most of the people around us. I was several years younger than he was, and the young beauties vying for his attention—including my own cousin—were mortified. They immediately apologized on my behalf, but I was having none of it. I had grown so tired of not being seen just because of my age and I told him so. I said, 'If you are given to treating people you don't need to impress in the manner in which you have treated me, sir, than you are a poor excuse for a gentleman.' And with that I walked away."

"Oh, my. What happened next?" Olivia touched her shoulders and turned Sylvia a little on the platform that Winston had provided for the fittings so that she could work on the sleeves of the gown. It was the first ordinary conversation she had had with the woman, and she was determined not to break the mood.

Sylvia's voice softened, but did not falter. "He pursued me across the room and insisted that I permit him to make amends by doing him the honor of dancing with him. Well, I wasn't entirely immune to his charms and the very idea that I—rather than any of the young beauties who had been collected for his inspection—should have the honor of that first dance was quite heady stuff for a girl of seventeen."

"How romantic!"

"Oh, it was very romantic, for you see, my dear, he danced with no one else. We created a bit of a scandal that evening for his attentions were totally given to me. The others were furious, of course, not to mention their mothers who had hoped him to be a good catch for their offspring. He proposed to me that very night." Her voice trailed off dreamily.

"He didn't," Olivia said with surprise and delight.

"Oh, but he did. We walked in the garden and by the time we returned to the ballroom, we were promised . . . in more ways than one." She glanced down at Olivia who was on her knees completing the cuffs of the gown. "Have I managed to shock you again, Olivia?"

"Were you trying to do so?"

Sylvia smiled. "Perhaps a little."

"Then you have . . . a little." Olivia stood and gently

turned Sylvia again so that she could see herself in the mirror.

"Oh, my dear," Sylvia said as she looked at herself arrayed in a long gray silk gown with lace overlay that covered her from her chin to her finger tips and yet showed off her elegant shape and beauty to perfection. "You were right to reject the blue. This is stunning."

"Thank you. It is a simple task when one has such beautiful materials and such an elegant mannequin."

"Then should you ever attempt anything for Abigail, you shall have more of a challenge," Sylvia commented and both women broke into giggles as Martha came to report that the very short, very portly Abigail Rutherford had arrived and was waiting in the downstairs drawing room.

Olivia could not help but feel a rush of excitement as she dressed for the theater. Since coming to New York, she had occasionally attended a music hall performance with Molly, but this was different. She dressed with great care. Practiced now in the art of arranging her own hair, she allowed her mind to drift to the evening ahead as she expertly pinned the curls into an elegant chignon. The green satin gown that Sylvia had insisted she remodel for herself set off her eyes and pale creamy skin to perfection. She felt beautiful and she was looking forward to the evening. As always, when she permitted herself the luxury of thinking of things other than her work, other than survival, she thought of Adam.

It was foolish, of course, but she wanted his eyes on her tonight. She wanted him to look at her the way he had looked at her that afternoon in the garden, his eyes black diamonds of desire.

"You foolish woman," she chastised her image in the

mirror. "To what purpose? What is the point? He thinks you are a servant . . . a domestic in his pay." The small cloisonné clock on her dressing table chimed the dinner hour. She stood and took a long look at herself in the mirror. "I am a lady," she reminded herself softly, "and no one can change that because it is who I am."

Her reverie was interrupted by the unusual sound of a motor car on the drive. She looked out the window in time to see Jeremy pulling up to the front of the house in an open-air vehicle. From the look of things, he had managed to startle horses and infuriate carriage drivers up and down the street, but he seemed oblivious to the chaos in his wake. He hopped out of the car, ripping off a cap and goggles and stuffing them into the pocket of a voluminous duster as he ran up the front stairs. Typically, Jeremy had made a most dramatic entrance.

Olivia checked her appearance one last time in the mirror and then left her room. She tapped lightly at Sylvia's door. "Mrs. Porterfield?"

"Nearly ready," Sylvia replied. "Go see what that horrible clamor was about."

"Yes, ma'am."

From the top of the stairway, Olivia observed Jeremy talking excitedly to Adam in the hall below. Clearly he was describing the monstrosity he had left parked in front of the house. She also saw that Winston had lingered after taking Jeremy's coat to hear the details. What was it that fascinated men these days about a noisy pile of metal?

"Leave it to Jeremy to upstage Sylvia on this night," she murmured to herself and, as she started down the stairs, she forced herself to smile pleasantly.

When Adam turned, expecting to see his mother descending the stairs, his breath escaped in a rush. "Olivia," he whispered and was halfway up the stairs to meet her before he realized what he was doing.

"Well, well, well," Jeremy exclaimed and began to applaud. "Look at you, Miss Marlowe!"

"Good evening, your grace," she murmured with a slight nod of her head. "It's been some time since we had the pleasure of your company."

Jeremy grinned as Adam and Olivia reached the bottom of the stairs. He held out his hand to her. "May I escort you in to dinner, my dear?"

Adam had no choice but to bow and let Jeremy take his place. He had not missed the fact that she had refused to meet his eyes and now he saw her look past him back up the staircase. He followed her gaze and for the second time had his breath taken away.

His mother stood at the top of the stairs, her white hair swept high and caught with pearls, her gown a cascade of white lace over gray silk. He wished that his father could see her in this moment. She smiled at him and her eyes were alive with excitement.

Adam felt a definite lump in his throat. "You are radiant, Mother," he said, leading her down the stairs.

"She will be the loveliest woman in the theater," Jeremy agreed and turned to Olivia. "My dear, I do hope you understand, but I have always made it a habit to be in the company of the most beautiful woman in the room."

Olivia could not help smiling as he released her hand and crossed the room to offer his arm to Sylvia. "Madam, would you do me the honor?"

Sylvia blushed and laughed and she did indeed look years younger. Olivia saw Winston discreetly wipe a tear from the corner of his eye as he stepped forward to announce that dinner was served. With Jeremy and Sylvia in the lead, Adam offered Olivia his arm and escorted her in to dinner.

"Tell me what that terrible racket was about earlier, Adam," Sylvia said as they began a first course of clear consommé.

"I am afraid that I must take the blame for that disturbance, dear lady. I thought that it would add to the festivities if we all went to the theater in an automobile."

Sylvia looked at him with alarm. "Are you actually suggesting that we get into one of those machines in our finest clothes, your grace?"

"I have brought along dusters for all and the trip is really not that far. We'll be there before you know it," Jeremy assured her.

"You have purchased this car?" Olivia could not help asking and she hoped that her tone revealed only mild conversational interest and not the dismay that she truly felt. She knew that Adam paid Jeremy well in addition to the small monthly stipend that he received from Lord Barrington. Still, such a contraption must be terribly expensive.

"A client has lent it to me." He glanced at Adam. "He is a gentleman Mr. Porterfield and I are considering as a possible partnership."

"And, he has lent you his vehicle?"

"I am trying it out. One of his businesses is a distributorship for these automobiles. He thought that perhaps this evening might be an excellent time to experience the comfort and convenience of this particular mode of travel."

"It is the future now," Adam agreed. "Well, Mother, what do you say? Will you risk your life with Sir Jeremy or shall I ask Winston to order the carriage brought round?"

All eyes turned to Sylvia.

"I think . . ." she said slowly as she looked first at Jeremy, then Adam. "I think that we might indulge his grace, however it would be wise to have our carriage follow us . . . just in case there are any problems."

Both men laughed and looked quite pleased with themselves. Sylvia smiled and nodded at Winston who instructed the maid to serve the main course.

Olivia could not understood why everyone was taking this ridiculous idea so seriously. After all, Jeremy had never so much as driven a *carriage.* Were they really willing to entrust him with their lives in a vehicle capable of going over twenty miles per hour?

"Why Miss Marlowe, you're looking quite pale," Jeremy commented. "Perhaps you would prefer to ride with the driver in the carriage?"

"I wouldn't dream of missing this opportunity, your grace," Olivia replied. She would get through it and do so with a smile on her face so that Jeremy wouldn't have the pleasure of marking her as a coward.

Yet when the time came to board the automobile, Olivia began to have second thoughts. Jeremy insisted that Sylvia ride in the front seat with him, leaving Adam and Olivia to squeeze into the more confined quarters of the rear seat. She felt utterly ridiculous in the duster coat and piece of veiling that Jeremy provided to protect the ladies' gowns and coiffures, but she was happy to have both once Jeremy had fired the noisy engine and pulled somewhat jerkily away from the curb.

"Hold on," he shouted as he hit the accelerator and the car seemed to take off like a racehorse headed for a close finish. Olivia uttered a little shriek and instinctively reached out for something to hang onto. That turned out to be Adam's knee.

When she realized this, she was horrified at her action but seemed incapable of letting go. Adam gently pried her fingers free and held her hand in his for the remainder of the trip.

Once they had started up Broadway toward the theater, Olivia actually began to relax and take in the passing scene. It was quite exhilarating to be racing along and watching people and buildings flashing past in an instant. She started to smile with delight and then she was laughing.

"It's quite wonderful really," she said aloud, raising her voice to be heard above the motor.

"Yes, quite wonderful," Adam agreed, but he was looking at her, not the passing scene.

She became captivated by that gaze and lost all sense of movement or speed or noise as she saw that he was thinking of their kiss . . . as was she. And, when she realized that she desperately wanted him to kiss her again, she tried to pull her hand free of his, but he held her fast.

When they arrived at the theater, there was a great stir as people pressed forward to examine the automobile. Jeremy thoroughly enjoyed his place as the center of attention and used the opportunity to assist Sylvia in the removal of her duster and veil so that the crowd of theatergoers turned their attention to her instead of the machine.

"My lady," Jeremy said after he had turned the car over to a young man who had obviously been instructed to meet them at the theater. Grandly, he led Sylvia into the lobby and up the curved stairway to the Porterfield box. Adam and Olivia followed, creating far less of a stir.

When they were settled in their seats, the Rutherfords, who had seats in the next box, stopped to visit with Sylvia and Adam. Jeremy took this opportunity to turn to Olivia.

"How are things going?" he asked in the same tone he might have used to discuss the weather.

"I'm managing," she replied. "Apparently you are doing quite well."

"I'm managing," he replied with a smile and then he turned the full force of his charm on Abigail Rutherford.

There was no time to pursue the discussion further. The theater lights dimmed and everyone reclaimed their seats as the curtain rose on the first act.

Olivia was immediately captivated by the play. She had always enjoyed the theater and only now did she realize how very much she missed the times when she had the luxury of attending plays and concerts whenever she pleased.

The play was one of Ibsen's latest works, always one of her favorites, and she was so caught up in the story that the intermission seemed to come much sooner than she had expected.

"I'm happy to see that you are enjoying yourself, Olivia," Adam said as soon as the lights came up. "As is my mother. We must do this more often."

"I'm sure your mother would like that, sir," Olivia replied demurely.

Jeremy excused himself to visit someone he had seen in a box across the way. In fact, Olivia had noticed that his opera glasses were focused on the woman in that box throughout much of the first act.

Adam was the next to leave their box. "Mother, forgive me, but the Armbrusters are here this evening and I have news for Jasper that cannot wait."

"Give them my regards," Sylvia said, then turned her attention back to the audience. She was clearly looking for someone and she seemed to have forgotten that Olivia was still sitting there just behind her.

"Are you enjoying the performance, Mrs. Porterfield?" Olivia asked.

"It's interesting," Sylvia replied absently as she trained her opera glasses on a man who was standing in the third row and who glanced up at their box. To Olivia's utter amazement, Sylvia signaled him to come up to the box.

He was about forty years old and quite handsome and Olivia could not help but be intrigued.

"Now, Olivia," Sylvia said in a low instructional tone, "the man to whom I am about to introduce you can be of great assistance to you if you are serious about pursuing a career in fashion. He is the son of an old friend and the owner of one of the most prestigious design houses in New York. Do be nice, won't you?"

Do be nice? When had she failed to be anything other than . . . ? Olivia had a protest half out of her mouth when the man pushed the curtains of their box aside. "Good evening, Mrs. Porterfield. How wonderful it is to see you out and about again . . . and looking so well!"

Olivia saw the man take the measure of Sylvia's gown with the eye of a professional critic. "Have you been shopping in Paris again, my dear?" he asked, but there was no humor in the question.

"This old frock?" Sylvia protested. "Heavens, Trevor, don't you recognize the work of your own designers?"

"The fabric is familiar as are certain aspects of the cut, however. . . ." He frowned and Sylvia laughed.

"Allow me to introduce Miss Olivia Marlowe, Trevor. Olivia, this is Baron Trevor von Dorfman. Miss Marlowe was kind enough to assist me in freshening the gown for tonight's engagement since I had little time to order a new one."

"*You* did this?" The designer's total attention was riveted on Olivia. He surveyed her from head to toe and seemed incredulous that she might actually have managed such a feat.

"She also did the gown she's wearing—another of yours from a few years ago."

"Stand," Trevor ordered.

Olivia was so startled that she did as he asked.

"Turn," he commanded, taking the seat that Adam had

vacated and crossing his long legs as he surveyed every inch of her.

"Really, sir . . ."

"Turn," Sylvia commanded, and Olivia turned.

"You studied with Madame Boulivar in Paris?"

"I studied with no one," Olivia replied haughtily, incensed at his tone and his treatment of her.

"You're English?" The way the Baron said it in an accent that Olivia could not quite place, he made it sound as if nothing artistic could possibly come out of England.

"I am."

"Miss Marlowe came here to serve as my assistant for a brief time until she can get her bearings and establish a salon of her own, isn't that right, dear?" Sylvia patted the chair, indicating that Olivia should sit.

The designer seemed alarmed at this news. "You plan to open a salon of your own?"

"Perhaps . . . someday."

"And, you are planning to sponsor her in this venture?" His tone was incredulous as he turned his attention back to Sylvia.

"Perhaps . . . someday." Sylvia replied and her mouth twitched with the suppressed urge to smile. "Unless, of course, someone is smart enough to sponsor her himself."

Trevor blinked, started to say something, and then blinked again. "Do you not think that a time of apprenticeship is indicated, my dear lady?"

"Possibly, but that is a matter we shall have to discuss another time, dear Trevor," Sylvia said airily. "The second act is about to begin. So lovely to see you. Do think about our little conversation, won't you?" Sylvia snapped open her fan, a clear signal that the meeting had ended.

"Miss Marlowe," the Baron said with a slight bow as he left the box to return to his seat.

Seconds later Adam returned. "What was von Dorfman doing here?" he asked his mother.

"Admiring my gown," Sylvia replied and turned her attention to the stage. "Sh-h-h. The second act is beginning."

Jeremy slipped into his seat a few minutes after the curtain went up and leaned over to whisper something to Sylvia that made her smile.

"Have you met Trevor von Dorfman before?" Adam whispered to Olivia.

"No," she replied.

"Sh-h-h," Jeremy and Sylvia said, in tandem.

Adam didn't like this turn of events at all. Trevor was a businessman first and always. If he had made the trip up to the Porterfield box, it had not been a social call. And what had that business been with Olivia—preening and posing for him? She must have met him before. Perhaps his mother was matchmaking again. That would be a positive thing, of course . . . if it weren't for the fact that it was Olivia.

He observed her watching the play. Her concentration was complete. He could almost describe the action by watching the expressions that flickered across her lovely face. For the first time all evening, she had forgotten about disguising her feelings, her true thoughts. He observed a single tear coursing its way down her cheek and knew that something in a character's soliloquy had touched her deeply.

He fought the urge to reach over and catch that tear before it could fall and stain her gown. He thought about the moment when she had appeared at the top of the stairs. He'd turned because of Jeremy's sudden silence after his explosion of excitement over the automobile. Jeremy had been staring up at her as if he'd seen a vision, and indeed she was a vision as she descended the stairs with all the grace and elegance of a woman born to wealth and power.

The cut of her gown was modest by fashion's standards and yet it managed to accent her beauty in a manner that was stunning. The bodice of the gown fit her as closely as the long silk gloves that covered her arms from her fingertips to well above the elbow. A simple satin ribbon accented her tiny waist. The same ribbon formed the wide straps of the gown—straps that allowed a tantalizing view of her shoulders. The skirt was perfectly plain except for the drape of the slight train at the back—a detail that he'd had occasion to notice as he had followed her up the grand stairway to their box. She'd swept her hair into some sort of intricate arrangement of curls and twists that he could not help but imagine undoing . . . *slowly as his mouth followed the length of her neck down to her shoulder where the strap would. . . .*

The explosion of applause startled him back to reality. The curtain had come down on the second act. Olivia brushed the tear from her cheek as the lights came up.

As soon as they did, an usher parted the curtains of their box and handed Sylvia a folded piece of paper. Adam followed the glance of the usher toward the place where Trevor was sitting and saw the businessman watching his mother carefully.

"What is it, Mother?" Adam asked.

Sylvia quickly folded the paper and slipped it into the small evening bag that hung from her wrist. "Nothing of consequence, Adam," she replied. "Are you enjoying the play, dear?"

By the time the third act had concluded, Adam had become determined to find out just what his mother was up to with Trevor von Dorfman. The man had tried several times to get Adam to invest, but Adam did not care for the man's business ethics. He was known to run some of the most notorious sweatshops in the city in order to produce gowns cheaply that he then sold for a great deal of money to the high society matrons of New York. Word had it that he was trying to raise funds to expand his business, having recognized the need to appeal to a younger clientele. If Adam's mother wasn't going to tell him what was going on, he would ask Olivia. After all she had been in the box the entire time that the man had sat there. She must have some idea of what he was trying to do.

"You seem a bit grim after so lovely an evening, Adam," Sylvia commented after they had said their farewells to Jeremy and gotten into their own carriage for the ride home.

Adam smiled. "I'm glad you enjoyed yourself, Mother. I hope this means that you plan to do more of this sort of thing."

Sylvia gave a shrug.

"And you, Miss Marlowe," Adam continued. "Did you also find the evening enjoyable?"

"Oh yes. Thank you so much for including me. The play was quite touching, don't you think?"

"Did you attend the theater often in London?" Adam asked.

"Whenever I could," she replied.

Damn, Adam thought. *Can the woman never offer a straight answer? I've spent hours with her over a period of several weeks and I still know virtually nothing about her.*

For the remainder of the ride, they were both silent, each lost in thought until the carriage pulled up to the house. Winston immediately appeared to escort Sylvia up the stairs and into the house. Adam helped Olivia from the carriage, then followed her into the house.

"Well, goodnight, Adam," Sylvia said as she presented her cheek for him to kiss. "It was indeed a lovely evening. Thank you for arranging it."

She started up the stairs with Olivia following.

"Miss Marlowe, I wonder if I might have a word with you," Adam said and did not wait for a response as he strode into the library.

Olivia had little choice but to follow him.

"Close the door, Olivia," he said quietly.

She hesitated but did as she was told, then stood waiting for him to speak again.

He ran his hand through his thick hair and let out a sigh of exasperation. "Do you know von Dorfman?"

"I have already told you. Your mother introduced me to the Baron this evening."

"The *Baron?"* He scoffed. "Trevor von Dorfman is no baron, Olivia. It's a title he has awarded himself and is as phony as that accent. Trevor von Dorfman grew up in the Bronx as Tommy Dormanski. Why on earth Mother would introduce you to that . . . what was she thinking?"

"I expect that as always she was being polite. Mr. Von Dorfman stopped by the box and your mother made the introductions. It would have been awkward not to do so."

Adam seemed unconvinced. "Then what was all of that business with the pirouetting and preening?"

Olivia stiffened her spine. She was not in the habit of explaining her actions to anyone. "Did you think I was playing the coquette?" she replied with a lightness that she was far from feeling.

"Were you?"

She met his gaze directly and knew that her eyes were blazing with indignation. It was not her finest performance as a domestic, but he had no right to accuse her of anything. "The baron is a designer, I believe. He was admiring your mother's gown and mine."

Adam blinked and she saw that he was reconsidering his accusation. "Oh," he said and turned back to the window.

"Oh? You have accused me of. . . . Oh?" She was furious, and without thinking, she advanced on him, determined to make him turn and face her fury. "I may be in your employ, Mr. Porterfield, but I have never had to endure such insulting accusations, and the worst of it is. . . ."

He wheeled around and before she could complete her sentence his mouth was on hers. The kiss that began as combat between his frustration and her fury soon dissolved into pure passion on both their parts. He wrapped his arms around her, pressing her to the length of his body and still she sought to be closer. He kissed her eyelids, her cheeks, her throat and her bare shoulder. Slowly he pushed one long glove down her arm, following its path with a series of kisses. She felt the heat of those kisses to the very core of her being. The only sound was the rush of her own breath coming in gasps and whimpers.

"Adam," she whispered.

He looked at her for a long moment and then gently lowered the strap of her gown and began a fresh trail of kisses along her collarbone and back to her mouth where she welcomed him with barely restrained passion.

"I want you so," he whispered against her ear. "God forgive me, Olivia, I think of nothing but having you."

His words were both thrilling and alarming. She knew that she should stop him, that he would regret his actions in the hard light of day, but she had never known anything like this feeling. She might never know it again . . . a moment . . . just one more moment of ecstasy. She closed her eyes and gave in to the passion of his kiss, his whispered endearments, his hands moving over her, enchanting her with an awareness of her own body.

She thrust her fingers into his hair, knowing that doing so only encouraged him. He groaned and moved his hands over her breasts. "Beautiful," he murmured as he kissed her shoulders, her arms, the insides of her elbows. "So beautiful." He dragged his eyes away from her exposed skin and back to her face. A single lamp on his desk and the glow of the fire lighted the room.

"Olivia?"

Her heart was beating so fast that she thought she might explode. The image of his undressing her was not to be denied. She wanted him with a need and a desire that was shameless. She wanted him with a madness that she had never experienced and could not explain.

"Kiss me," she said huskily. "Please."

She did not have to ask again. Their open mouths met with a mutual hunger that defied satisfaction. He pressed her hips to his and she did not resist.

Neither of them could have said what might have happened had they not been interrupted by Winston's discreet knock at the library door. Adam motioned for her to remain silent and then went to the door. He spoke briefly with Winston and then closed the door.

Olivia was seated on the settee facing the fire. "Olivia," he said, "I have to go out. It's business that cannot wait. Will you be all right?"

"Of course," she replied and touched a hand to her disheveled hair.

He hesitated, then came and knelt on one knee at her side. "Olivia, I'm. . . ."

She looked at him and saw regret. She laid a finger on his lips to silence him. She could not bear it if he apologized. "Just go," she said softly.

He nodded and got up again, but she knew that he paused at the door for a long moment. She did not turn to look at him for that would surely have been her undoing.

Eleven

Adam was not at breakfast the following morning and Olivia heard Sylvia tell Winston that her son would be away on business for several days, possibly even a few weeks. Olivia's heart plummeted. Could she be the cause? She knew of Adam's ingrained moral principle that it was improper to become involved with the help. Had he left because of her, because of what had happened in the library?

"Well, Olivia, you were quite the belle of the ball last night. It would appear that you shall have more than one offer of employment once you leave my service."

"I believe that it was you who were the focal point of the evening, ma'am," Olivia replied.

"Nevertheless, the Baron will be calling on you this afternoon, Olivia. He will offer you a position in his design house. You are to take nothing less than a position as a designer, is that clear?"

"Yes, ma'am, but your son does not seem to approve of the Baron—nor do you, for that matter. Why do you want me to become his employee if both you and Mr. Porterfield do not respect him?"

"Because he is a master at his craft and you can learn a great deal from him. Clayton always said that the opportunity to learn was the opportunity to grow."

"I see. But, if the Baron's reputation is not above reproach. . . ."

Sylvia waved a dismissive hand. "In the world of business, Olivia, one learns to work with such people or one does not prosper."

"You seem to have learned a great deal from observing your husband, Mrs. Porterfield."

"And my son. Make no mistake, my dear, Adam may appear to be mild-mannered, but when it comes to protecting and perpetuating the family business, he is relentless."

Olivia saw the flash of pride in the older woman's eyes, and once again realized that if she had been born in more modern times, Sylvia might have run a successful business on her own.

"So, you are suggesting that I accept the Baron's offer—should he make such an offer—to work for him?"

Sylvia buttered a scone and spooned on strawberry jam, spreading it slowly and thoughtfully. "In the first place, Olivia, the offer has already been made. In the second, you are the person who must decide whether or not to accept it."

"But you would advise that I do?"

"The question is whether or not this is something you want to do. I believe that you understand the risks and the benefits."

"Then I think the wisest choice would be to accept the offer," Olivia replied quietly. It would get her out of the Porterfield house, away from Adam, and relieve him of any guilt he might feel after last night.

"Good. Adam's travels could not have come at a better time. We will have the house to ourselves and can concentrate fully on planning your strategy . . . three months with Trevor will do it, I should think. You are a quick study and there's no reason to waste precious time. You must take full advantage of the sensation you have created these past few days. From there, you can move into your own salon. You'll need investors, of course, and a proper location." She ticked off the items on her fingers. "There is a great deal of work in starting a career of one's own, Olivia, especially when one is a woman. We shall begin our strategic planning in the drawing room at eleven." She swept from the room, leaving Olivia open-mouthed at the table.

"Yes, ma'am."

"Miss Marlowe?" Winston stood just inside the dining room door. "This message is for you." He handed her the envelope.

"Thank you, Winston."

Livvy, I must see you as soon as possible. Make some excuse. I'm in the park to the right of the monument. J.

It was a glorious spring day. The flower beds in the park were in full bloom. The vibrant and delicate bleeding heart plants reminded her of yesterday, for surely her heart had suffered a wound when she had asked Adam for another kiss, which, clearly, he had regretted giving.

Once she entered the park, she was tempted to linger. It had been a confusing and exhausting time. Adam . . . Mrs. Porterfield's thinly veiled message of support for her to begin a career of her own . . . and now this mysterious message from Jeremy. She sighed and looked around.

The park was fairly deserted, not unusual for a weekday morning. A few nannies and nursemaids with their charges, and a man walking toward her . . . overdressed for the season in a coat with an upturned collar and a cap pulled low over his eyes.

"Thank you for coming," he said quietly as he came up to her and began to walk with her.

Olivia walked quickly, hoping to put some distance between herself and the man, but he kept pace. "I beg your pardon, sir, but. . . . Jeremy? What on earth?"

He looked around nervously. "Keep your voice down, please." He indicated a bench half hidden among the trees.

"You're being quite mysterious—I must be back at the house before eleven—I would suggest that you tell me what this is all about."

"I am ruined," he said miserably as he slumped onto the bench, oblivious to the fact that she was still standing.

Jeremy had many faults but he had always been a perfect gentleman. Forgetting himself and sitting in the presence of a lady was a lapse that only served to demonstrate the depth of his woe.

"What has happened?" She sat next to him and took his hand in hers. He was shaking. "You have me worried, now."

For a long moment Jeremy simply stared into space shaking his head. "I don't know what I was thinking of . . . how I could have been so duped . . . so foolish. I thought. . . ." He did not finish the sentence, just continued to stare at nothing and slowly shake his head.

"Jeremy," Olivia said sharply.

He turned and looked at her as if he had forgotten she was there. Then he looked down at her hands clasping his. "Ah, Livvy, how is it possible that you are truly concerned? How could I have misjudged you for so many years?"

"Please tell me what has happened."

"I met a man who told me that he owned a great deal of property—real estate, businesses—that he purported to need to sell. I spoke with Adam about the possibility. . . . he showed some interest but clearly had his doubts."

"He's quite experienced in these matters."

"Yes, well, I thought that if I could make the deal anyway—surprise him, so to speak—then Adam would be impressed and he would. . . ."

"Jeremy, tell me what you have done."

"I agreed to the deal and then planned to recoup the investment through the sale of some of the properties. In order to raise the cash the seller demanded, I borrowed from the account of one of Adam's clients."

"And, you are unable to repay that?"

"The properties were a sham . . . they never belonged to the man. There is nothing to sell, and I have no funds of my own."

"What of the man? He has tricked you . . . surely he holds some responsibility. You could threaten to call the police."

"He took the money and left for Europe last night while we were at the theater. I have to leave immediately as well . . . before Adam discovers what I have done."

"Jeremy, you can't just walk away from this. You have robbed someone of funds. That is every bit as criminal as what was done to you. We must find a way to repay that debt."

"We?" He gave her a sardonic smile.

"Perhaps I can speak with Adam," she said and knew by the look he gave her that he was certain that her influence with Adam would not be of use.

"I can't bear it, Livvy. He is everything I ever wanted to be. He has been my mentor, my friend . . . the older brother I never had. How can I possibly face him?"

"What will you do? You must take steps to make amends."

"I could return to London, ask father for help and then send the money to replace the funds."

Olivia thought of what it would cost her emotionally if

she ever had to return to London, ever had to place herself at the mercy of her stepfather. She could imagine what Jeremy would face if he returned. "There must be another way," she said.

"I pray that you are right for I don't want to go back, Livvy. Father would. . . ." He shook his head miserably. "I would never again have the chance . . ."

"Then you must find a way . . . *we* must find a way."

Jeremy actually shuddered. Then, once again, he was lost in thought.

"Jeremy," Olivia said gently. "I must go. Mrs. Porterfield expects me. Promise me that you will not do anything rash. Give me a day or so to think this through. Promise me."

"All right. I promise."

"I will speak with Adam."

Jeremy shook his head. "He is away . . . on business. His secretary said he would be gone for several days. Besides, what would he think of your coming to him on my behalf?" Then his eyes lit with excitement. "Livvy, if we could find a way to replace the money while Adam is gone, then he need never know!"

"How much money are we speaking of?" Olivia asked, mentally counting her savings from her alteration work hidden in her dresser.

"Fifteen thousand."

Olivia thought she surely must have misheard him. "You are not serious!" she exclaimed in spite of her intention to remain positive and calm.

Jeremy nodded. "It's quite hopeless, my dear," he said in a tone that showed that he was already resigned to that fact.

Olivia swallowed and glanced over at the mansion. If she did not leave immediately she would be late, and what would she tell Mrs. Porterfield? "Jeremy, listen to me, I am going in but we must discuss this further. Please do nothing until we have that opportunity."

Jeremy nodded. "Can you get away for dinner?"

"Come here for dinner. Mrs. Porterfield will be delighted to have the company with Adam away, and she is fond of you. Stop by around six to see Adam and then she'll invite you to stay."

"All right." He stood up and grasped her shoulders. "Livvy, thank you. I do not deserve your kindness or support, but I am relieved to have it." He reached into his pocket and drew out a velvet bag. "I thought you should have these."

She peered into the bag and gasped. "Mother's jewels," she whispered.

"Well, representations of her jewels to be sure, but I thought that perhaps you might like to have them to remind you of . . . happier times."

She kissed him lightly on his cheek and then impulsively hugged him. "It is a lovely gesture, Jeremy. Thank you." Then, she ran out of the park and back to the house.

Jeremy stood, cap in hand, watching her go. He had come to her because he had no one else. For all his girlfriends and associates, Jeremy had only her friendship. She looked back and gave him an encouraging smile before crossing the street and disappearing into the grand mansion. He pulled his cap back on and walked slowly out of the park. He doubted that Olivia could do anything to help the state of affairs in which he found himself, but it was comforting to know that she wanted to help him. He was glad that he had brought her the jewels, even if they were only imitations of what her mother had acquired and his father had kept from her. At least she would have the memories.

He walked up the avenue across the street from Adam's house. He noticed the drapery in the parlor move slightly and wondered if it was Olivia watching to be sure that he was all right or someone else from the household. He pulled his cap low once again and turned up his collar in case it was the latter.

It was late that evening before she had the opportunity to open the velvet bag that Jeremy had handed her in the park. Inside was a note.

> *Livvy, I know they aren't as good as the real thing, but I thought perhaps having these would remind you of your mother—and of the decision we each made to carve out new lives for ourselves here in the "colonies." Please know that I sincerely wish you well. Jeremy*

He had carefully wrapped each piece in crisp white tissue. One by one she opened the small packages, reveling in the memory of those times when her mother had worn them. She fingered the clasp on a brooch and smiled, recalling how it had caught on her father's shirt once when the two of them had been dancing. The brooch had twisted and bent before they could free it, and her mother had always claimed it was too fragile to be repaired.

Olivia fingered the clasp and then examined it more closely. The pin was bent and did not precisely fit the holder. The prongs holding the center stone were askew. She turned the piece over and over, examining it from every angle. *Could it be possible?*

She picked up a necklace . . . a garnet choker and found the place where her mother had hastily restrung the beads when the thread broke just before a ball to celebrate her engagement to Lord Barrington. She had been unable to match the black thread and had substituted a deep navy. With trembling fingers, Olivia separated the beads to reveal the thread, then laid it against a black skirt from her closet. The thread used to string the beads was navy.

The jewels were her mother's originals. They were authentic.

Her stepfather had tried to trick them into returning to London by sending that cable. *But, what of the pearls that Jeremy gave to Grace Armbruster?* Olivia thought. And then she remembered, and the memory made her smile. The pearls had been Lord Barrington's gift to her mother on their wedding day. It would have been totally in character for someone as frugal as he was to purchase something less than the finest.

Searching her memory, she recalled the exact words on the cable that Jeremy had shown her. *If you don't believe me, have the pearls appraised,* he had written. He *knew* that the pearls were false and he also knew that impulsive and easily agitated Jeremy would not bother to check the rest of the collection.

She spread the collection out on her dressing table. The jewels were real, and she was rich. She did not need investors. She did not need the Baron. The fortune represented by the dozen pieces lying before her would be more than enough to establish herself in New York.

She turned and picked up the tissue paper and the velvet bag. There was still one item in the bag. She opened it and there lay the faux pearls. Molly had told her that Grace Armbruster had sent the pearls back and broken things off with Jeremy. Apparently, she had found someone new. She closed her eyes. *Jeremy,* she thought, *I may be saved, but what is to become of Jeremy?*

She needed time to think and to plan. She would do nothing in haste. She would begin work with the Baron as they had discussed that very afternoon at tea. She would learn everything she could in as short a time as possible. In the meantime, she would find some way of ascertaining the true value of the jewels were she to sell them. She knew no one to ask about such a thing, but she would make some inquiries. Finally, she would not let Jeremy know that he had held the answer to all of his problems in the palm of his hand. She would help him, but she would not risk her entire future to make amends for his mistake.

Adam stayed away for nearly a month. He had meant to stay longer. He had visited clients up and down the eastern seaboard, not because they had requested it but because he needed to be anywhere other than in the same house . . . the same city . . . as Olivia. He had tried to think how he might rationalize his fascination with her with his moral code. Since their first kiss, the need that could only be filled by being in her presence had intensified into something very close to an obsession. One kiss had only brought on the desire for another. One touch and he had been lost, powerless to control the urge to be near her, shameless in his intent to have her . . . all of her.

He found himself thinking of her at the oddest times. One day he was walking along the beach and saw a shell among the hundreds of others that was perfectly shaped and a soft pink. In the instant it took him to bend and pick up the shell, he saw her face, her eyes alight with pleasure at the discovery. He heard her laughter in the waves and the whisper of her breath in the wind. But, it was not just her physical presence that haunted him. As he sat in meetings with clients and potential clients, he thought of her—how she might react to what they were saying. She had an incredibly good instinct for judging people, Baron Trevor von Dorfman notwithstanding.

But it was the afternoon that he was hurrying back to his hotel in a light rainfall that he saw the sight which caused him to leave for New York the same evening. For there, in the middle of a deserted street were two people—lovers, clearly—who were dancing, oblivious to the rain, kissing, touching, cherishing. The woman's hair fell to her waist and swung wide behind her whenever the man turned her. He bent her back over his arm and kissed her throat and Adam thought of Olivia. The woman pulled herself upright, buried her fingers in his hair and pulled him to her and they were so close that they made a single silhouette on the wet pavement.

By the time the train reached Penn Station, it was late. Adam had passed the journey fantasizing about Olivia. He had imagined her there waiting for him . . . at breakfast—in the library with only the fire to light the room—in his bed. The closer the train came to New York, the more he admonished himself to get control of his emotions. While he had almost come to terms with his passion for her, there was still the question of what she might feel for him. Even if he were willing to abandon his own code of honor in order to have her, how would he know if she would do the same? Olivia was a woman of principle—uncommonly so, for her station in life.

No, he must proceed with care. He would see her at breakfast and take the measure of her mood then. In order to hold himself to his plan, he decided the best course would be to stop at his office first, delaying his arrival at the house until he was quite certain that she would have retired. He would not risk the possibility of finding her alone again. Had Winston not interrupted them that night in the library, he had no doubt of what would have happened. The next time he kissed her, it would be to celebrate the fact that she had accepted his proposal of marriage . . . or at the very least agreed to let him begin an open courtship.

It was well after closing when he reached the building

his father had built from the profits of the business. As he strode through the hallway that led to his office, he noticed the single light that burned at the opposite end of the hallway in the office of his bookkeeper. Puzzled, he retraced his steps and pushed the door open.

"Bertram?"

The wiry older man looked up and blinked rapidly several times over the tops of his half glasses. "Oh, good evening, sir. How was your trip?"

"Fine. Have you been here all this time, Bertram?" He looked at the wall clock above the bookkeeper's desk. "It's nearly ten-thirty."

"Yes sir. I was doing the quarterly report earlier today and well, frankly, sir, some of the numbers did not tally as they should have. Oh, overall, there seems to be no problem, but there were individual entries that were puzzling. I thought that if I worked on it after the others had left . . . in the quiet. . . ."

"Have you found something?" Adam kept his voice calm, but Bertram Sanders had been with the firm since before Adam's father died. He was dedicated and meticulous. If he had suspicions, they were likely well-founded.

"Yes, sir." Bertram stepped around the desk more quickly than Adam had ever seen him move. He gathered two thick ledgers in his gangly arms and brought them to the desk where he had been working on yet another ledger. "It's this entry here, sir."

Adam followed his finger. "That's a rather large withdrawal. An unlikely sum for Jasper Armbruster to have taken without discussing it with me first."

"And, now this . . ." Bertram pointed to an entry in the second ledger. "And this. . . ." He pointed to the third.

The evidence was irrefutable. Someone had moved funds from the Armbruster account through what appeared to be a legitimate cost center and on to the third account where the funds had been deposited earlier in the month. The third account was one he had never seen. "Are there other entries for this third account, Bertram?"

"Yes, sir." Silently, Bertram displayed the evidence that Adam had requested. He said nothing while Adam studied the columns and entries. "He's young, sir, and ambitious. I don't think it was meant to. . . ."

"I'll handle this, Bertram. Thank you for alerting me to the problem. I know I can count on your discretion."

"Without question, sir," Bertram assured him earnestly.

"Go home now and take the day tomorrow as well."

"Thank you, sir."

Adam barely heard the man gather his belongings and leave. His complete concentration was on the ledger entries before him.

Jeremy.

Adam slumped into a chair and buried his face in his hands. He was beginning to rue the day he had met Jeremy Barrington. Not only had the man now betrayed him, he had brought into Adam's life the one woman he desired, the one woman he was in danger of breaking his own code of honor to have. Furthermore, in this his hour of torment, the one person he wanted to confide in, seek comfort from was Olivia. He must be completely out of his mind.

He rechecked the accounts twice again. When there was no possibility that the bookkeeper had made a mistake, he left the office and headed for home.

Twelve

The mansion was dark except for the light in the library. He entered the house by the back entrance where he left his luggage and hat. He hoped that the light might have been left on inadvertently as he made his way into the front hallway. He did not know what might happen if he went into the library and found Olivia there.

He paused at the open door and looked in, telling himself that if it were Olivia, he would retrace his steps and go up to his room. He was not ready to see her yet, not now that Jeremy had betrayed him. However thin the connection between Jeremy and Olivia, it existed and he was not yet prepared to test it. He could not restrain the rush of relief that he felt when he saw that it was his mother sitting by the fire, and not Olivia.

"Hello, Mother."

She glanced up, startled but not alarmed and then she smiled. "Ah, Adam, how wonderful to have you home."

He returned her smile and bent to kiss her cheek before taking the chair opposite hers. "How have things been in my absence?"

"Quite fascinating, actually," Sylvia replied and Adam felt his spirits lifted by the excitement in her voice and the light in her eyes. "I have something to tell you . . . that is, if you aren't too tired." She studied his face and her expression turned to worry. "You look quite done in, son. Perhaps we should postpone this until the morning when you've had a good night's sleep."

Adam almost laughed at the thought. He hadn't had a decent night's sleep since that night with Olivia in the library. He had failed completely in his attempt to banish the memory of her kisses, the feeling of holding her in his arms. Now, he had returned to find that Jeremy had betrayed him. He seriously doubted that he would sleep tonight either, so he smiled. "I'm fine, Mother, and you're obviously bursting with news." He got up and poured himself some brandy in a snifter, offering his mother one which she declined with a wave of her hand.

When he sat down again, he smiled. "Now, what has you so excited that you are up well past your usual bedtime?"

She actually sat forward on the edge of her chair. "As we both know, your purpose in bringing Olivia into the house was to coax me out of my malaise."

"That was a part of it, though I would hardly view it as her task. It was my hope that your interaction with her might . . ."

"Oh, do stop rationalizing, Adam. The fact is that I have become an admirer of Miss Marlowe. She is most intelligent and enterprising . . . a bit too willful at times, but nevertheless, she has qualities worth encouraging."

Adam smiled. "I see. Is that why you introduced her to Trevor?"

"She is talented but not yet ready to strike out on her own, I think. She can learn from Trevor and she is self-possessed enough not to permit him to take advantage of her."

"Are you saying that you are going to ask him to take her on when her term here is finished?"

"Actually she has already started her work for him. I

have relieved her of further duties here." She waved away Adam's protest. "I know that we agreed to three months but we said nothing of what was to happen if my health and spirits improved sooner. There is ample evidence that they have and there is no reason why Olivia should not move forward with her life. I should think that you would applaud that."

"I . . . will she be leaving us, then?"

"Well, I should think so once she has found suitable lodging. Trevor is paying her a designer's wage, which is not to say that she will be wealthy but certainly she will have the means to live comfortably. Besides . . ."

Clearly, she had started to say something and thought better of it. "Besides what, Mother?"

"Never mind."

"No, there is something you are not telling me—something that, judging by the expression on your face, you find quite delightful."

"She has a beau," Sylvia said in a near whisper, her eyes sparkling.

Immediately, Adam thought of the servant he had discovered kissing her in the stables. Surely, Olivia had not turned for solace to that brute. "Not the Rutherfords' driver?"

Sylvia looked shocked. "Heavens no. Olivia is too refined to be drawn to a man like that. Actually I had thought that it was you who had caught her eye, but I couldn't have been more mistaken. No, it is his grace—Sir Jeremy Barrington—whose heart she appears to have captured."

Adam felt as if someone had punched him hard in the stomach. He couldn't seem to get his breath. He certainly couldn't speak.

"I know," Sylvia said with barely contained delight. "It came as a total surprise to me as well, but I saw them together one day in the park. They met secretly and it was all so very romantic. Then, that very evening, he pretended to stop by to see you but I knew that he had come to see her. She was quite nervous in his presence and he kept casting his gaze at her, and seemed incapable of focusing on the conversation at all. So, after we had dined, I pretended a headache so that the two of them could be alone. They walked in the garden." She sighed. "I found the whole thing quite romantic. Olivia will be an excellent influence upon Jeremy."

While Sylvia prattled on about the details of young love, Adam fought to maintain his poise. His mind raced with thoughts of how back in London Jeremy had dismissed the very idea that he might ever be attracted to Olivia. His mother must be mistaken.

"Have they seen each other since?'

"Oh heavens, yes. He pretends to come to call upon me—bringing me flowers and other tokens, but it is clear that his purpose is to be with her."

Adam examined every minute the two of them had been together in his presence—at numerous dinners, in the car, at the theater. Oh, how clever they had been in disguising their love. He thought of Jeremy kissing Olivia and his hand tightened into a clenched fist.

"Why, Adam, are you not well?" His mother peered at him with concern.

"Just a bit tired, Mother. I think I will go up after all. Will you excuse me?"

"Of course, dear. Sleep well."

When Adam reached the top of the stairs, he looked toward the end of the hall where the stairs led up again. He started toward them, then stopped and turned abruptly back to his own wing of the house.

* * *

Olivia had adopted the practice of examining the jewels every night much in the same way that she had once counted the small savings she had collected from her sewing. It had become a ritual and usually it gave her a great deal of comfort, but not tonight.

Jeremy had sent her an urgent message that afternoon and right after dinner, she had feigned illness and received Sylvia's permission to retire for the night. Then she had slipped out of the house and met Jeremy in the park. He had been more than usually agitated. In the weeks since he had first confided in her, she had urged him to continue to attend to his work in the normal way. Jeremy had agreed and gradually settled into a routine that had provided him with a false sense of security that he would not be discovered and everything would be all right.

At her insistence, he dutifully handed over his pay to her each week. She sorted it into envelopes—one for repaying the Armbruster account and a smaller one for paying his rent and other necessities. She suspected that one of the reasons he made it his business to call at the mansion so often was so that he could eat there and have funds for the pleasures she had firmly told him he could not afford.

Initially their plan had been to build as large an account as possible that he could present to Adam as evidence of his remorse and intent to repay every penny of the debt with interest. Adam certainly paid Jeremy well enough and the bank account was already growing nicely. Given enough time, they would have been able to repay the debt, but, now, clearly something had gone wrong.

"Jeremy, calm yourself and tell me what happened today that has you so agitated?" she had said as they walked together in the park.

"I happened to stop by the office of Bertram Sanders this afternoon before leaving for the day. It was the old man's birthday today and everyone was making a fuss so I wanted to be sure to add my good wishes."

"He has come to the house once or twice to bring papers for Adam," she had replied. "He is a sweet old gentleman."

"He's also relentless when it comes to making sure that every account tallies to the penny."

In that instant, Olivia had understood. "He knows?"

"I think he does. The ledgers he was working with were the ones concerned and he gave me a look when I stopped by."

"Nervous? As if you had caught him at something?"

Jeremy's laugh had been brief and bitter. "No, dear Livvy, just the opposite. It was a look of disappointment as if he had caught *me*."

The rest of their walk had been unproductive. In the face of Jeremy's abject panic Olivia was forced to face the fact that there was no possibility that Jeremy would have the opportunity to come forward with his confession before Adam learned of his deed from others. She had thought of the jewels and known in that instant that she was going to use them to help Jeremy.

After assuring Jeremy that all was not lost, she had returned to her room and her nightly ritual. As she studied each piece, her eyes filled with tears. Her tears were not for the sacrifice of the jewels themselves—they were but a representation of memories and memories could be savored without the tangible goods. The truth was that ever since she had discovered the treasure, she had dared to dream of her own future.

She shut her eyes and felt the closeness of the unusually warm May night closing in on her in the cramped little room. Hastily, she returned the jewels to their pouch and slipped down the back stairway and out into the garden. She needed to think and the night air and sanctuary of the garden would help her find the answers she needed. Perhaps there was some way that she could save Jeremy without completely abandoning herself.

After retiring to his room, Adam buried himself in work, catching up with correspondence that had accumulated during his absence, responding to social invitations, charitable requests. He moved through them one by one, making notes for his secretary, answering those that required a personal response. He worked by rote for his mind was on one thing—Olivia. Could his mother have misunderstood? But then why a secret meeting in the park? Why the gift? The embrace? The kiss? The repeated visits in his absence, knowing that they could be alone?

And, what of his mother? She had come to like both Olivia and Jeremy. The change in her since the two of them had come from England into her life had been remarkable and far more of an improvement than Adam had ever hoped to see. Earlier, when he had heard her come upstairs and go to her room for the night, Sylvia had been humming to herself as she passed his door. He could not recall the last time he had heard that.

He pushed the papers on his desk aside and stood up. He had come home filled with anger and disappointment over Jeremy's betrayal, but the minute his mother had told him of her observation of Jeremy and Olivia in the park and Jeremy's visits to the house in his absence, he had been incapable of concentrating on anything but her. He would have no peace until he spoke with her, heard it all from her own lips. In spite of the hour and his own exhaustion, he was determined to have answers tonight.

When he reached her room, the door was slightly ajar and a single light glowed. He knocked at the door and pushed it open.

"Olivia?"

There was no sign of her. Her bed was untouched except for the small velvet bag lying at one end. He caught a glimpse of gold spilling from the bag and sat on the bed to examine its contents.

The jewels were exquisite. More to the point, they seemed to prove his mother's theory. It was exactly the gesture Jeremy would make once he had accumulated a sum of cash. Adam placed the brooch, the gold chain, and garnet choker with matching earrings back inside the bag with other pieces and drew the satin string closed.

With all that had happened in just a few hours, he felt as if he could not catch his breath and moved to the open window. Her room overlooked the garden and he thought he caught a movement below. He peered out, allowing his eyes to become accustomed to the change in light and saw her. She was pacing back and forth, her hands clasped behind her back, her head lowered in concentration. *Was she waiting to meet Jeremy?* He wondered.

Like a moth drawn to a flame, he headed for the garden. His emotions roiled with a mixture of anger and disappointment and passion and desire, for whatever she had done, Adam could not deny that he was in love with her. It was this above all else that made it impossible for him to think clearly.

She was unaware of his approach, which afforded him the opportunity to observe her. She had opened several buttons of her shirtwaist, no doubt to cool herself. She had also removed her shoes and stockings and paced barefoot through the dew-covered grass. That endearing fact touched him deeply in spite of his fury at her part in Jeremy's betrayal of his trust.

He stood at the entrance to the arbor, watching her, until she turned and saw him. Her eyes widened in surprise and then, without a word, she came toward him. Her face was in shadow and he could not read her expression. She seemed about to speak, but he did not want to have the moment spoiled by her words. In the next moment he had pulled her into his arms and in an instant they were lost in a kiss so fiery that there could be no possibility of reason on his part or calculation on hers. He moved her further into the shadows of the arbor and he knew as he deepened the kiss that he was lost. Whatever she and Jeremy were to each other, whatever lay behind her coming to him so freely just now, she was as drawn to him as he was to her. Just this once she would be his.

He pressed her against the post of the arbor's arch and continued kissing her as he opened the remaining buttons on her blouse. Whenever she tried to speak, he silenced her with yet another kiss, his tongue plunging into her mouth until she moaned her surrender. He pulled the blouse free of her skirt and pushed it off her shoulders. Her breath came in heaves beneath the lace camisole. She wore no corset. He stood motionless looking at her, undressing her with that look until she reached for him.

"Adam." In that single word, he heard her need for him.

He kissed her throat, her collarbone, her shoulder. He untied the ribbon lacing on the front of her camisole, spreading it until he could taste her skin, her breast. When he opened his mouth over one nipple, she cried out softly and grasped fistfuls of his hair, and he thought of the couple in the street—in the rain. He half-expected that she would try to break free, but she held him there. In that single moment, he stopped trying to avenge his rage on her and surrendered to the desire he had felt for her for weeks. If she asked him to stop, he would do so, but he would always know that whatever she might have with Jeremy, in this moment, she felt the same passion for Adam that he felt for her. In another time, under other circumstances, they might have become lovers. If tonight was all they would ever have, then it would be a night neither of them would ever forget. But, it would be up to her.

He pulled the edges of her camisole back together and raised her chin so that she was looking at him. "Olivia," he whispered, "if you are going to stop me, it must be now."

There was a moment of hesitation—of decision—and then without looking away for even an instant, she reached up and hooked her fingers under his braces. She pushed them off his shoulders until they fell free to his sides. Then she began to unbutton his shirt, pulling it free of his trousers as she went. When it was fully open she pushed the fabric aside and flattened her palms on his bare skin.

Adam groaned and swept her into his arms so that her nearly naked breasts were pressed against his bare skin. Wildly they exchanged kisses, her lips on his eyelids, his tongue circling her ear, her head thrown back to invite his open mouth to roam the length of her neck, her hands massaging the muscles of his chest, his back, his shoulders—touching him as if she could never have enough of touching him.

As one, they sank to their knees. He undressed her to her waist, then shrugged out of his shirt. She made no attempt to cover herself although he could see that she was trembling—whether from the chill night air or from anticipation, he could not have said. He covered her breasts with his palms, felt the hard points of her nipples soften and swell under the warmth of his massage. Her eyes were closed and she seemed to be lost in the sensations he was creating. He eased her back onto damp, cool grass and knelt next to her, lifting her skirts and kissing her bare feet, her calves. Her soft moans and trembling hands only fed his desire. When he started to remove her undergarment, she went absolutely still, and she did not stop him.

He moved again so that he was next to her, one hand tracing a pattern up and down her inner thigh until she was writhing with need. A thin sliver of moonlight found its way through the thick canopy of the arbor vitae above them to highlight her features—her hair free of all restraints, her lips swollen by his kisses, her eyes afire with excitement.

Slowly he began stroking her with his fingers. He felt her arch in anticipation of his touch. She closed her eyes and swallowed. Her shallow breath came in little gasps as he increased the pace and when he saw that she was nearly to the edge of pleasure he withdrew.

Her eyes flew open, but she said nothing. He stood and finished undressing. He lay on his back next to her and brought her hand to the flat of his stomach. "Touch me," he said.

Slowly she moved her hand over his naked body, touching his chest and stomach and thighs until he thought he would not be able to control himself one more instant. Then she was touching him, stroking him, driving him as close to the edge as he had taken her.

"You're certain," he asked once again, forcing her to meet his gaze.

"I want you," she said.

He pulled her on top of him, spreading her skirts so that they partially covered them both but left her open to him. He lifted her and eased himself into her.

She tightened convulsively and pulled away, then slowly began lowering herself onto him, taking him inside herself, her hands braced against his chest for balance as she sank ever more deeply onto him. For an instant he thought that this indeed might be her first experience, but that was impossible. Jeremy would not have allowed such a thing.

He forced the image of Jeremy from his mind and along with it any idea that Olivia might be pure.

He stroked her breasts as slowly he began the dance that he knew without doubt each of them would remember for the rest of their lives. Deeper and deeper he took her until she was setting the pace herself, matching him with every thrust, urging more and more and more until suddenly, she arched and stilled.

Knowing the moment was at hand, he pulled her to him and kissed her, taking her cry of release as well as his own into his throat so that they would not be heard or discovered.

Afterwards, they lay entangled in each other's arms for several long moments. He knew that she was waiting for him to say something, to ease the awkwardness in the afterglow of their lovemaking. But, with release came reality and the reality was that she belonged to Jeremy and the two of them had betrayed him. His anger diffused, replaced only by disappointment and hurt.

"You should go in," he said gently, rousing her. "Bertha will be up to start the baking before too much longer."

She raised herself only enough to look at him. She was smiling and her hair fell across his chest like a shawl. He curled a lock around his fingers and then moved his hand to the back of her neck urging her down for one last kiss—a kiss that he knew would have to last him a lifetime.

"We must go," he insisted when she began returning his kisses and rousing his passion all over again. He was sorely tempted to surrender to the moment, but knew he would regret it. "Get dressed," he urged and rolled away from her to collect his own clothes.

When they were both dressed, she stood looking at him with a confused and puzzled expression. "I. . . ."

He could not bear to hear her lies after what they had shared so he kissed her one last time and pushed her gently toward the entrance of the arbor. "Go," he ordered but his voice was husky. "Please," he added.

She did as she was told, running toward the darkened mansion, her shoes and stockings in one hand as she gathered her skirts in the other. Adam stood watching her until she had disappeared inside the house. He knew what he had to do but no one would deny him this last hour of savoring what might have been. *How could he have been such an utter fool?*

Because he wasn't prepared to face Olivia, Adam decided that he would begin with Jeremy. As soon as he arrived at the office, he called for the Englishman.

"Good morning, Adam, I do hope that your trip was. . . ." Jeremy stopped speaking the minute that Adam turned away from the window to face him.

"Please sit down, Jeremy," he said, indicating a place on the opposite side of the desk from his own high-backed swivel chair. He took his time, opening the report from the bookkeeper, then opening each of the three ledgers Bertram had shown him. He was aware of Jeremy watching every deliberate move. "Is there anything you would like to tell me, Jeremy?"

"I. . . ." He slumped deeper into his precisely tailored suit and looked at his folded hands. "Adam, there is little that I can offer in the way of an excuse."

"Then you know what has been found in these three accounts?"

Jeremy nodded, refusing to look at Adam.

"And you admit that it was your doing?"

"Yes."

Adam had been prepared for excuses, bravado, anything but this passive, submissive beaten man. Any posturing would have enraged him further, but now, looking at

Jeremy sitting there like a recalcitrant schoolboy, he was at a loss. "What could you have been thinking, Jeremy?" he asked finally.

There was a long pause, followed by several false starts. Then Jeremy said, "I wanted to make an impression, to show you that I could be an asset. I worked so hard . . . harder than I've ever worked on anything in my life." Jeremy risked a look directly at Adam and actually smiled. "The amazing part of it was how much I enjoyed it." Then, as if realizing anew what he had done, he sank back into the chair.

In the silence that followed his confession, Adam knew that each of them mourned bygone days when they had laughed and plotted together and lifted their glasses in toasts to a future that they would build . . . together.

"Well, there will be consequences," Adam said and realized that he was thinking aloud. This was not going at all the way he had thought it would. For one thing, as he studied the morose Jeremy, he found himself wondering what the devil Olivia saw in the Englishman.

"I'll do whatever it takes to win back your respect, Adam."

Adam caught himself just short of believing the man who had not only betrayed him in business but who had joined forces with Olivia to betray him in love. With that in mind he rediscovered his rage. "You are suspended, Jeremy," he said coldly. "Please do not bother going back to your office. I shall have your personal items sent to your apartment later today." He rang for his assistant and when she appeared at the door, said, "Please see that Mr. Barrington leaves the premises."

"Adam, I . . ." Jeremy began but when Adam looked at him, he stopped, swallowed, and turned to go. "I will find a way to set this right, Adam," he said quietly just before he left the office.

* * *

That morning, Olivia took the trolley to her job in the design room of Baron von Dorfman. She was glad not to have had to face Adam's mother or any of the rest of the staff. She had heard Adam leave for his office early. She wondered if he was feeling as confused as she about their encounter the night before.

She did not know what had come over her. It was as if when she'd looked up and seen him standing there that she had moved without thought. Certainly she could not say that it was all his doing. She had been his willing accomplice. She had wanted his touch, his kiss, and in the end, she had wanted his lovemaking. Repeatedly he had given her the opportunity to reconsider, yet she had not turned back. Even as she had instantly counted the probable costs of her actions, she had refused to turn back. She had no regrets, but she wondered if perhaps Adam did. When she'd left him in the pre-dawn hour, he'd seemed thoughtful, almost pensive. If only she'd had the opportunity to speak with him, to have that first encounter following *the* encounter. But reality had come with the dawn and each of them had responsibilities.

Olivia forced herself to concentrate on the work ahead of her. She was determined to learn everything that the Baron had to teach her as quickly as she could. Of course, the Baron took it for granted that she would be in his employ for years to come. The Baron was unaware of the jewels—*everyone* was unaware of the jewels except for herself.

She fingered the small velvet pouch she had pinned inside the waistband of her skirt. Inside was the amber set—pendant, filigreed chain, earrings, and bracelet. They were the most beautiful pieces in her mother's collection and the ones that held no memory for her except for the fact that her father had given the set the day before his death and her mother had never worn them. Selling them would cause her not one moment's regret.

"Baron," she said later that morning as they worked together on a gown for one of his private customers. "I have a friend who has some jewelry she would like to sell. She is in need of funds and the piece is an heirloom."

He studied her with a knowing smile. "Essinger's," he said as he pulled the basting from a drape she had created and then draped it one way and then another and finally back to exactly the way she had done it the first time.

"Yes?" she said.

"Essinger's Jewelers on Fifth Avenue and 38th Street. Sylvia is a regular customer there. I'm surprised she did not advise your *friend*."

Olivia felt herself flush. "Mrs. Porterfield was not asked," she replied, then added a soft, "Thank you."

"You're welcome. Just remember the date and time, my dear. I am not given to kindness on a regular basis."

"I'll keep that in mind."

About ten minutes later, the Baron stood back and considered the gown. "It is quite good, no?"

Olivia smiled for the first time all morning. "It is very good, yes."

The Baron lifted the glass of wine that was his constant companion in a toast to her. "You are gifted, child. Suppose I do you a favor?"

She smiled. For all of his bluster, she had discovered that in spite of his reputation, Trevor could be quite charming . . . even gracious, when it suited him. "I have learned from the master," she replied. "What more could I ask?"

"Let me make the deal for your friend's jewelry. If you go, you will be far too eager. Essinger knows me . . . he doesn't like me, and therefore, I will get more for your . . . friend."

Olivia was moved almost to tears by his generous offer. "I don't know what to say," she whispered huskily.

"Say nothing, my dear, for there will come a day of repayment, I assure you."

Olivia insisted on going with Trevor when he called on the jeweler, an action she saw that Trevor clearly did not appreciate.

"Do you not trust me?" he asked in an offended tone.

"Frankly, no, but please do not take offense. I am at a point where I find it best to place my trust only in myself."

She did not miss the way the eyes of both Trevor and Mr. Essinger widened when she spilled the contents of the velvet pouch onto the velvet tray the jeweler had provided.

The set brought a staggering amount of money. Olivia found it quite difficult to comprehend the value of a few stones set in gold. Trevor immediately argued for more and the jeweler readily agreed. As they walked back to the salon, Trevor offered to place the cash in his safe or at the very least escort Olivia home where she could secure the money, but she refused. She had an errand to do after work, she told him, and the cash would be quite safe on her person until then.

She was aware that Trevor watched from the window to see which way she went as she left the salon later that day. For that reason she hired a carriage at the corner and asked the driver to travel for several blocks in the opposite direction of her destination before heading downtown. By the time she reached Adam's office, most of his staff had left for the day. She was relieved at that. A charwoman pointed out his office at the end of a long hall. Olivia paused, squared her shoulders, and walked resolutely down the hall. Her heels sounded a cadence on the freshly scrubbed and polished tile floor.

"Good evening, Adam," she said. He was standing behind his desk staring out the window into the setting sun.

He turned slowly at the sound of her voice but with the light behind him, she could not read his expression. She smiled and moved further into the office. "Do you mind?" she asked as she turned to close the door.

He still had not spoken. He had not come forward to greet her with an embrace. He stood behind the massive carved desk and stared at her.

"Why have you come?" he asked and she noted that his voice seemed tense, unlike any time she had ever heard him speak.

"Adam—I . . ."

He clenched his fists and brought them down onto the surface of the desk. "Was it to plead your lover's case?" he asked. And, now she heard the bitterness that coated each word like bile.

Confused, she took a step back. "I . . . Adam, are you unwell?" He was not himself. Something had happened and he thought she was someone else perhaps. In the shadows of the dim office he had not seen her clearly. "It is I—Olivia," she said and stretched out her hand to him.

"Did he send you then? Is he so spineless as to send a woman?" Adam practically spat the words at her. "How could you love such a man, Olivia? A man who is not worthy to so much as touch your hand?"

Olivia was unaccustomed to being accused unjustly. To have Adam, of all people, do it after what they had shared was unthinkable. She felt her own anger begin to simmer. "I have no idea what you are talking about, Adam. I have come to you with. . . ."

"You're denying it?" He was incredulous. "I saw the jewels. My mother saw you in the park with Jeremy, saw the embrace, the gift. The man is stealing from me in order to buy expensive trinkets for you?"

"Now, see here," Olivia demanded, raising herself to her full height which was still a head shorter than his. "In the first place, Jeremy bought me nothing. The jewels are mine. In the second, he may have many faults but he idolizes you and would never do anything knowingly to jeopardize that. He was absolutely heartsick when he realized that he had been duped. He stole nothing . . . he merely. . . ."

"Took funds from a client's account without that client's authorization and moved them—not directly to another account but through a third account so that he could cover his tracks. I have no idea how the English view that but, trust me, here in New York, that is grand larceny."

"In the first place, he intended to repay the first account immediately. If he attempted to cover the transaction, it was to give himself a little time to repay the funds." She placed an envelope on his desk. It contained the money she had gotten from the jeweler plus the money she had accumulated from Jeremy's weekly pay. "This is a first payment. Jeremy will bring you the rest by the end of the week."

She waited while he opened the envelope and counted the bills. "Where did you get this?" he asked.

"That is none of your business," she replied archly.

"The jewels," he said. "You sold them?"

"I sold *some* of them," she replied. "I will convert the remainder to cash by the end of the week and Jeremy's debt will be cleared." In a moment of blind fury, the decision was made. The jewels would be used to help Jeremy.

Suddenly Adam looked sad and haggard. "Then it's true," he whispered huskily. "You and Jeremy are. . . ."

"Family," she replied. "Jeremy is my stepbrother. Perhaps if you and I had banked the fire of our mutual passion and taken the time to know each other better, you would have discovered that. At the same time I might have discovered that while you are given to jumping to unreasonable assumptions, it does not deter you from taking your pleasure from a woman you so clearly detest. Good evening, Mr. Porterfield."

She turned and left the office, nearly running down the dimly lit hall, past the charwoman and down the stairs to the street. Almost automatically, she hailed a passing carriage for hire and gave him Jeremy's address.

Adam remained standing where she'd left him, dumbfounded by her news. *Jeremy was her stepbrother, not her lover! Then why the subterfuge to get her here? Why not openly board the ship as siblings? Why hide behind a story of being hired help once she arrived?* And always, in the midst of every question, the pounding of his heart with joy at the news that she was not bound to any man . . . that she had come to him willingly . . . freely.

His relief was enormous, as if a great weight had suddenly dissolved into liquid and run off him, cleansing him with the clarity that comes with finally solving a puzzle. Oh, he had no doubt that her fury had been genuine and he could hardly blame her for that. Still, that could all be worked through, once they had had the opportunity to sit calmly and discuss the matter rationally, once she had the time to regain control of her emotions. She would forgive his accusations. Once she realized that he was willing to accept Jeremy's atonement and take him back into the firm . . .

He placed the envelope in the wall safe of his office and turned the dial. He would not permit her to pawn her jewels for the rest of it. He would replace the money in the Armbruster account himself and work out some sort of regular payment schedule with Jeremy. As he walked down the hall toward the staircase, he felt a lightheartedness that he had not felt in weeks.

"Good evening," he said genially to the woman scrubbing the floors.

"And to you, sir," she replied with a wide smile that

exposed her bad teeth and yet improved her appearance considerably.

Outside, he took the trolley to Washington Square and walked through the park on his way home. A flower vendor at the entrance to the park was just closing up for the night. "I'll take the balance of your stock," Adam announced, gathering up the three remaining bunches of mixed spring flowers in a rainbow of colors and scents that made him smile. Olivia would love these. They would be his peace offering.

He paid the vendor, tipping him handsomely, and continued up the avenue toward the mansion.

"She's not here, sir," Winston told him. "She telephoned to say that she had found another place to stay and that she would send for her things tomorrow. I was to tell Mrs. Porterfield that she would stop by later in the week to say a proper goodbye. Your mother was quite curious about this sudden turn of events, not that it wasn't expected now that Olivia is working with the Baron. Still . . ."

"She's gone?" Adam stood holding the ridiculously large bundle of flowers.

"Shall I place those in a vase for you, sir?"

He glanced at them as if realizing for the first time that he still had them. "Yes. Take them up to my mother's room. Tell her I had to go out for a bit and not to wait up."

"Very good, sir."

Adam could not be certain but he could have sworn that Winston was smiling as he turned away.

Thirteen

As soon as Jeremy opened the door to his apartment, Olivia brushed past him, tore off her hat and gloves, threw them onto a chair, and burst into tears.

"Oh dear girl, you've been sacked, haven't you? And it's all my doing."

"Worse," she blubbered and launched into a fresh onslaught of sobbing.

Jeremy cast about for something he might do to stem the tidal wave of her anguish. He poured brandy into a tumbler and handed it to her. "Sip this," he urged.

To his surprise she did as he suggested. Things must be quite out of order if Olivia was taking instruction without question. She considered the glass, seemed about to reject it, and then took it from him and downed the amber liquid in one dose. The only sign of any effect was that when she handed the glass back to him and said "Thank you," her voice cracked.

He was unaccustomed to the role of sympathizer and hovered uneasily near where she sat. "You're welcome. Now, tell me what has happened."

"Oh, do sit, Jeremy. I'm not going to do anything desperate," she snapped.

This was more like it. With a sigh of relief, Jeremy

pulled the ottoman closer to her chair and sat. "Now, tell me," he asked again.

She hiccoughed and released a shuddering breath that he sincerely hoped marked the end of her wailing. Twice she tried to say something, her eyes tearing up again, then regained control, and took another deep breath as if about to plunge into uncharted waters.

"There is so much to tell that I hardly know where to begin," she managed finally.

"Has the Baron let you go?"

"Oh heavens, no. He has been most kind."

"The Porterfields?" He could not imagine it but, of course, there was always the possibility that Adam had decided that since Jeremy had suggested her, she could not possibly be a fit companion for Sylvia.

"I left the Porterfields."

"I see." He saw nothing, but it seemed the wisest course to appear to understand for the moment until she could gather her thoughts and talk sensibly.

"All right, here it is—I had not intended to tell you all of this but you may as well know the whole of it."

He waited and tried not to notice the fear that what she was about to say might change his life as surely as she had changed her own.

"The first of it is—the jewels are real. The Baron assisted me in selling some of them so that I could then go to Adam to plead your case and, by combining it with the money we've accumulated, make a partial repayment of the funds. My intent was to use the balance of cash I could raise from the sale of the rest of the collection to set myself up in business once I leave the Baron's employ . . . which, actually, now that I cannot possibly continue to live in the Porterfield house . . . may come sooner rather than later. I went to Adam's office. He accused me of unspeakable things. I left the money and told him he would have the balance by the week's end. I could hardly go back to the mansion, so, not knowing what else to do, I came here."

Jeremy was still dealing with *the jewels are real.* "The jewels real? That's impossible . . . Father cabled. . . ."

She released a sardonic laugh. "Yes, and how he must have delighted in that. You see, he must have known that once he mentioned the pearls, you would have those appraised and that would indeed prove the truth of his message. He counted on the fact that you would go no further. The pearls are indeed inferior—*he* gave those to my mother. But, all of the other pieces are quite genuine, I assure you."

As the reality of what she had told him sank in, Jeremy looked at her, shocked. "You are saying that you sold your birthright to pay a debt owed by me?"

She waved him away impatiently. "Don't be so dramatic, Jeremy. I sold one set, the amber set—one that meant little to me. I paid only one small part of your debt."

"But, why would you do that?"

"Because, like it or not, we are linked . . . especially in the minds of Adam and his mother and now that I have told him the truth of our relationship, we are more joined than ever."

"You told Adam that we are siblings?"

"Well, what would you have me do? The man thought we were lovers. Tell me what was I to do?" Her indignation matched his and they both burst into laughter.

"Lovers?" Jeremy crowed. "Oh, that is rich. How did he take that news?"

"I did not stay there long enough to find out," she replied in a tone that told Jeremy that pursuing this particular topic was not a good idea.

"Olivia, I hardly know what to say. I am genuinely

touched by your actions, but I cannot allow you to do this."

"It is done," she replied.

"Not all of it. I will not allow you to use your inheritance on my behalf when I have squandered my own shamelessly." The look of surprise and respect she gave him inspired him. "I shall go to Adam and plead my own case for reinstatement and the opportunity to make amends."

"And, what if he refuses?"

"Then I shall do whatever work I can find—even if it means sweeping streets—until I have repaid every penny of the debt," he announced as he stood and strode about the room.

For the second time, the two of them looked at each other and started to laugh as they each tried and failed to envision Jeremy as a common laborer.

"But, first," Jeremy added, "we must dine. Go, wash your face and make yourself presentable. I have a bit of cash, and I am taking you out, Livvy dear. Tonight, we dine as Sir Jeremy Barrington and Lady Olivia Marlowe. Let New York society chew on *that* for a while." To his relief, her smile was genuine, not forced laughter and not a gesture of simple politeness. He had expected scolding that he could not afford the barest necessity at the moment, but instead, she stood and looked toward a hallway.

"Down here?" she asked.

"Second door to the left," he replied. "Just past my room where I insist you stay the night. I shall take the couch out here." He watched her go and felt a general lifting of his spirits. Things were not nearly so dreary as they had seemed before Olivia arrived. No, he did not know in what way but had no doubt that there was still the possibility that all would work out for the best . . . for each of them.

* * *

It was not until the following day that Adam finally tracked Olivia to the von Dorfman salon. He had gone to Jeremy's the evening before but received no response to his constant knocking. The doorman had told him that Jeremy had left with a young lady not half an hour earlier. Recognizing the futility of trying to find them and not particularly wanting to add Jeremy to the mix of trying to talk with Olivia, Adam had gone home. In the light of a new day, he had decided that perhaps an indirect approach would be a better idea.

"I have a message for a Miss Olivia Marlowe," the boy announced the following morning when he showed up at Trevor's salon.

"I'll take it," Trevor replied.

But the boy snatched it away. "The gent said I was to deliver it to herself."

Trevor rolled his eyes and indicated Olivia with a sweep of his arm. "Now, will you please leave? We are attempting to work here, young man."

"I'm to wait for a reply, miss," the boy said addressing Olivia directly and ignoring Trevor.

"Of all the impudent. . . ."

"Please wait outside," Olivia replied gently. "I'll prepare my reply and you may deliver it as you were charged."

The boy turned on his heel and left the salon.

Olivia studied the handwriting on the envelope. It was Adam's. She suddenly recalled that first note that he had sent just after she'd boarded ship to come to New York. She hesitated, not wanting to open it in the presence of the others. The truth was that even with Jeremy's improbable kindness of the evening before, she was still feeling a bit fragile.

Trevor clapped his hands loudly. "Back to work," he

commanded. "We have orders to fill." He glanced at Olivia as he herded the others away from her and back to the work.

Olivia slipped her thumbnail under the sealed flap. She did not know what she was expecting but it was not what she found.

Olivia, Mother and I request your presence at our home this evening at eight o'clock. The favor of an immediate response is requested. If, for any reason, you cannot make this evening's engagement, we will anticipate knowing a day when you will be free. Adam

There was no question in her mind that this was no ordinary invitation. It was a command to appear as surely as the first message had been. There was little point in refusing to go. He would just continue to send messages. One last meeting was inevitable and she might as well get it over with, but she was determined that it would be the last meeting and she would control the agenda. She took a piece of stationery from Trevor's desk and hastily scribbled her reply.

I shall be there at eight this evening.

No signature. None seemed required.

In the afternoon, she pretended illness and left the salon. First, she went to the Porterfield mansion using the back entrance, and collected a few of her things, including the rest of the jewels. Then, she walked to Essinger's Jewelers, wanting to give herself time enough to consider and reconsider the decision she had just made.

She was shown to his office, and seated in an easy chair in front of his desk. Momentarily Mr. Essinger walked in, greeted her, sat at his desk, and gazed at the jewels in the tray before him.

Mr. Essinger made her an offer, then glanced at her over the rims of his half glasses and increased the offer by a tenth. She made as if to take the jewels and he increased it again. The final payment was more than twice his original offer. Olivia felt a rueful pride in her skill in getting a great deal more for the jewels than she had imagined. With careful management, there would be enough for her to live in simple comfort after repaying the balance of Jeremy's debt. She hurried back to the apartment to change and learned that Jeremy also had received an invitation from the Porterfields.

"Well, of course, we should arrive together!" she said testily when he suggested that perhaps they should take separate transportation. "The need for subterfuge ended yesterday, Jeremy. There is little left but to clear up the details."

As it turned out, the discussion was moot. At precisely seven-thirty, the doorman rang to announce the arrival of the Porterfield carriage. The driver—Bertha's son, Willy—was waiting for them at the curb.

"He's taking no chances," Jeremy said tensely as he pulled on his gloves.

Olivia fastened her short cape. "Let us go," she replied and her voice was equally as tense. The carriage set off at a fast pace.

The mansion was ablaze with lights. "One would think the Porterfields were entertaining on a grand scale," Jeremy said as Willy pulled the carriage up to the portico.

" 'Tis just you two," he assured them. "Mum said she was told it would be just a light supper for the mister, his mum, and the two of you." The young man was obviously quite pleased that he could provide this information.

Winston opened the front door and took their coats.

"Very good to see you, Miss Marlowe," he said softly as he assisted her with her wrap.

"I have missed you and the others," she assured him. "It seems like a long time since I was last here and yet. . . ." She looked around the familiar hall—one she had grown used to seeing as a member of the household rather than as a guest.

She glanced up and saw Sylvia coming down the grand staircase.

"Well, well, well, Olivia . . . or shall I say, *Lady* Marlowe? You have given us all quite a surprise!"

Olivia hurried to meet her former employer at the foot of the stairs. "I would like to apologize, Mrs. Porterfield, for any. . . ."

Sylvia took both of Olivia's hands in hers. "Nonsense, my dear. You have become quite the talk of the town. Everyone is wondering if the Baron will appreciate the opportunity that he has to enhance his salon by permitting you to create your own label. And, Jeremy, my dear, what a naughty boy you have been. Keeping secrets like this!" she scolded gently. "Shall we go in?" She led the way to the drawing room. "Adam, our guests have arrived."

Olivia had been certain that the very sight of him would rekindle her fury at him. She fingered the envelope in her pocket. In the envelope was a bank order for the balance of the debt that Jeremy owed. Her intent was to pay the whole of it and be rid of Adam Porterfield. Yet when he turned as they entered the room, she saw immediately the deep shadows under his eyes, saw the lines that drew down either side of his mouth, saw that he was as wary as she was. She wanted only to go to him. Her heart sank. In spite of everything, she could not deny her feelings for him.

When they were all seated and Martha had served canapés and left the room, Sylvia set her sherry glass on the silver tray and cleared her throat. "Well, shall we get to it, then?"

Jeremy and Olivia exchanged wary looks.

"There are some pieces of your stories that do not make complete sense," Adam said in a low voice. "We have asked you here in order to clarify our questions."

"All right," Olivia said and then waited. Adam and his mother had called this meeting. She would not make it easy for them.

"Well, then let us begin at the beginning, I should think," Sylvia said.

"Why did you pretend?" Adam turned to Jeremy. "Why not simply say that you were bringing your stepsister with you to America? Did you think that I would object to that?"

Jeremy and Olivia exchanged a look. She could see that they were equally confused by the focus of the conversation on her rather than Jeremy's theft.

"Please allow me to explain," Olivia replied evenly, directing her explanation to Sylvia. "I was to be married to a gentleman in England. It was something of a. . . ." Olivia faltered when Adam turned his gaze on her.

"My father had arranged the marriage with an unpleasant old man as a business merger," Jeremy interrupted. "Livvy would have been completely miserable. This seemed the opportunity for both of us to escape a future that neither of us had had any role in planning."

"Ah, I see," Sylvia murmured.

"Well, I don't." Adam stood and began to pace the length of the room.

"If I had tried to leave openly, my stepfather would have had no choice but to stop me," Olivia explained. "The marriage was as much a business alliance for Lord Barrington as a betrothal. Surely you can understand that. It was Jeremy who offered the escape route. It was I who chose to take advantage of it."

"But surely, once you had arrived safely here in New York, there was no longer any cause to fear consequences," Sylvia reasoned.

Jeremy took up the story. "My father had sent us a transatlantic cable to say that the jewels that Olivia had brought with her—indeed, as a stake for both of us to make a success of our decision—were only paste copies. He claimed that he has the originals."

"If we agreed to return, all would have been forgiven," Olivia added. "Neither of us could abide such a thing. Therefore, the choice to maintain the ruse seemed obvious . . . to both of us." She turned to Sylvia. "It had always been my intent to tell you this once I was safely here in New York. However, thinking that the jewels were counterfeit, I realized that I *needed* the position your son had offered me. I was grateful to have that and everything that came with it."

Sylvia nodded sympathetically. "You must have been quite beside yourself. And you, Jeremy. I cannot imagine that your father was particularly pleased that you were still determined to defy him."

Jeremy smiled weakly. "He cut me off with just a small stipend—enough to assure a roof over my head and other necessities. Just enough to make sure that I remained tied to the family funds. If it had not been for Adam. . . ."

Olivia observed a slight softening of Adam's demeanor, but he quickly hid it. "Nevertheless, neither of you can deny the violation of the trust I . . . my mother and I had placed in you both," said Adam.

"I have told you . . ." Olivia began.

"I intend to repay every . . ." Jeremy said, but Adam cut him short.

"How does one repay such acts of kindness as my mother has lavished on each of you?"

Once again Olivia observed an exchange of messages

through the flicker of his eyes. He was warning them about something.

"Oh, don't be so dramatic, Adam," Sylvia said. "They have explained why it was necessary to tell certain untruths about their relationship. The important thing is that they are now forthcoming and no longer need to hide behind false identities. I, for one, think this is splendid news on ever so many fronts."

In that moment, Olivia understood. *Adam had not told Sylvia of Jeremy's stealing from the company. He had told her only that she and Jeremy were related by their parents' marriage and that they were not lovers.*

She sincerely hoped that Jeremy would not launch into his "I'll sweep streets" speech, and to prevent that, she moved to the serving table behind Sylvia. She caught Jeremy's eye, pointed to Sylvia and mouthed, *She does not know about the money.*

To her relief, Jeremy seemed to get the message. He turned to Adam. "I know that I have been a disappointment to you both. However, nothing has changed about my determination to prove myself worthy of the trust you placed in me several months ago."

"Actually, one of the reasons I wanted you to accompany your stepsister here this evening was that we might discuss a rather interesting new project that I have recently taken on," Adam replied. "Perhaps you would join me in the library and we can do so. I know that Mother is anxious to talk further with Lady Marlowe." Once again, it was not a courtesy as Adam opened the door to the hall and indicated that Jeremy should precede him out of the room.

"I'll make this short, Jeremy," Adam said as soon as he had closed the pocket doors of the library. "I could have you jailed for what you've done. Should Jasper Armbruster ever find out, the possibility of scandal alone would assure his insistence that you go to prison and repay the debt. On top of that, there is no doubt that we would lose his business and that of others once the news was out. You have endangered my business beyond anything that I should be willing to forgive."

Jeremy did not look away. "I am well aware that I have committed a terrible wrong, Adam. I would do anything to make it right again. I was a fool."

"Yes, you were. On the other hand, I can see that you did not do this for personal gain. You did what you thought might be good for the company. I won't ignore that. Nevertheless, I'm sure that you can understand that there must be consequences to your mistake."

"I expected there would be."

"As you are no doubt aware, Olivia has already made a generous contribution toward repaying the financial debt. Why she would do this, I have no idea, but apparently she holds you in some esteem. As I respect her judgment, I must assume that there are reasons to give you the opportunity to make amends."

Jeremy's heart pounded with relief but he remained silent.

"Here is what I'm willing to offer. An old friend of my father's, Harry Conroy, has recently fallen upon hard times. His business is failing, as is his health. He is justly proud of the business and views it the same way my father viewed this company—as his legacy to his only child. I am offering you the opportunity to bring that business back to life so that when my father's friend dies, he will do so knowing that his heir has inherited something of worth."

"What is the business?" Jeremy asked, intrigued at the possibility of making his mark.

"It's a small family circus."

Jeremy thought he must have misheard. "A *circus?*"

Adam nodded and lit a cigar. "In Wisconsin."

Jeremy swallowed, trying to dislodge the lump of dread that seemed to block both normal breathing and speech. Jeremy could see that Adam was enjoying this. He fought to keep his tone even and to suppress the hysteria he was beginning to feel. "Where, pray tell, is Wisconsin?" he said.

"Here," Adam replied, pointing to a tiny speck on the globe by his desk.

"It's in Canada?"

"No, just inside the border here, see?"

"Still, it is halfway across the continent. You cannot be seriously suggesting that I might actually go there?" Jeremy was imagining some sort of crude covered wagon like the ones he'd seen pictured in magazine articles about America's expansion to the West in the earlier part of the century.

"I'm suggesting that Wisconsin will be your home base for the foreseeable future. Of course, the length of your stay there is entirely in your hands. Once you have the business back on a profitable footing and can find a reliable manager, I would welcome you back here. The minute I saw it, I thought of you," Adam said jovially. "The circus . . . entertainment. It's an area of business you seem to enjoy and you said yourself that you thought it offered great promise for the future."

"Yes, but. . . ." Jeremy gathered his composure. "Is there an alternative?"

"Yes," Adam replied, as he rolled the cigar between his fingers and studied it for a long moment. "There are actually several alternatives. One would be, you return to England and seek your father's forgiveness and go into his firm. I'm sure that he would advance you the funds to repay your debt to me. Another is, you take your chances on being hired by some competing firm here in New York. Should you do that and should they seek a reference from me—as they surely would—I should be obliged to tell them that there was ample cause for your leaving." He paused and waited until he had Jeremy's full attention. "The third is the least attractive—you could go to jail."

"And, if I fail to make a success of this . . . this enterprise?"

Adam studied Jeremy for a long moment. "Then, my friend, I shall be most disappointed, because I will have to admit that you are not the man I thought you were when we first met."

"But, you have said yourself that the business . . . this circus. . . ."

"Has suffered from neglect and lack of proper management, neither of which are terminal at this stage. There are resources: Although, to be sure, they may be neither as great nor as obvious as you would wish them to be. This will take initiative and hard work, Jeremy. As I have pointed out, there are easier paths."

Jeremy glanced down at the speck on the globe, then back at Adam, and it dawned on him that in spite of every mistake he had made, Adam wanted very much to believe in him. "I can do this," he said more to himself than to Adam.

Adam grinned broadly and stubbed out his cigar in a large crystal ashtray. He took Jeremy's hand and pumped it heartily. "I knew you would rise to the challenge. I've made all the arrangements. You leave at the end of the month."

"Well, my dear Olivia, you certainly have turned things topsy-turvy for a great many people in a very short period of time," Sylvia said as soon as the men had left the room.

"I do apologize," Olivia replied, suddenly overwhelmed with the desire for Sylvia to understand why she had acted as she had. "My stepfather—Jeremy's father—very much wanted me to marry for the good of both families."

"You did not care for his choice, I take it."

"Sir Dudley is . . . quite decent and, of course, extremely wealthy. I would have wanted for nothing."

"Except happiness," Sylvia said softly.

"Precisely," Olivia agreed.

"So, you made a decision—a very rash decision and one that it would appear has escalated the situation into something far more complex than you had anticipated."

Olivia smiled weakly. "It would seem so."

Sylvia took a sip of her sherry and studied Olivia for some moments. "And where, exactly, does my son fit into all of this?"

"I beg your pardon?" Olivia was not being impudent. She honestly thought she must have misheard the woman.

"Adam. I don't know why I didn't notice it before this evening. I am usually quite acute when it comes to matters of the heart—especially when it relates to my only son."

Olivia swallowed. "I believe that your powers have indeed failed you, ma'am."

"Don't 'ma'am' me like some servant, Olivia," Sylvia snapped impatiently. "He has been miserable for days and I could not understand why, but the moment you entered this room tonight, I had my answer. He is in love with *you*. The only question is whether or not you love my son."

"I . . . we . . . yes, ma'am," Olivia replied instantly, slipping with ease into her role as lady's companion.

Sylvia smiled. "Then we must devise a way to smooth out whatever seems to have happened between the two of you and permit you to move forward."

Olivia felt a sense of quiet panic. On one hand, she would very much like to pour her heart out to Sylvia and seek her advice. But on the other, how could she now confide in her without also telling her what Jeremy had done? How could she tell her that Adam could not possibly love her or he would never have taken her in the garden like some common barmaid? Regardless of her own feelings, the idea of anything beyond a casual affair with Adam was out of the question. Adam had thought that she had betrayed him, yet that had not deterred him from having his way with her. Any feelings he might have for her surely were based in lust, nothing like the deep and abiding love that she had for him.

Just as Olivia started to form a response, the doors to the drawing room opened and Adam entered the room, with Jeremy following. Olivia took one look and knew that whatever offer Adam had made had devastated Jeremy.

"Mother, may I escort you in for supper?" Adam asked. "I'm sure that Sir Barrington and his stepsister will be along in just a moment."

Sylvia looked as if she were about to protest, but when she saw Jeremy's pale face, she changed her mind. "Of course, dear," she said quietly and took her son's arm and the two of them left the room.

The minute Adam had closed the doors, Jeremy slumped into the nearest chair. He held his head in his hands and did not say a word.

"He sacked you," Olivia guessed and prepared to offer comfort and advice.

"Worse," Jeremy mumbled from behind closed hands.

What could possibly be worse? Olivia racked her brain.

"I've been banished."

"He's forcing you to go back to England?"

"Worse," Jeremy said again, but this time he looked up at her. His expression was one of pure desperation. "Banished to Wisconsin," he whispered.

"Wisconsin? I don't understand. . . ."

"It's a . . . place out there somewhere." He gestured wildly toward the windows. "Adam showed me a map. It's somewhere at the far end of the earth. I doubt they have even heard of civilization as we know it." He glanced around as if someone might overhear. "I truly suspect that they may be constantly under the threat of attacks by savages." He actually shuddered.

"But, why? Is this some type of prison?"

"Oh no, prison might actually be preferable. Nevertheless, for some strange reason Adam is of the impression that he is doing me a great favor. He points out that he could have me arrested, put on trial, and sent away for a very long time. Instead, he is giving me a second chance to prove my worth . . . to use his words."

"But, Jeremy, that is wonderful news!"

Jeremy looked at her as if she had not heard a word he'd spoken. "Wisconsin, Livvy. And that is not the worst of it."

"I find it difficult to believe that Adam—Mr. Porterfield—would maliciously. . . ."

"I am to manage a circus," Jeremy announced, as if to prove the depths of Adam's maliciousness.

Olivia could not keep herself from smiling. The idea of Jeremy even attending a circus was completely ludicrous. She composed herself. "Perhaps he thought that giving you a business opportunity away from New York . . . from certain . . . temptations. . . ."

"Yes, but a circus? And, in Wisconsin? Have you ever *heard* of Wisconsin?"

"Well, no, actually. I believe that it lies somewhere near the Canadian border, does it not?"

"Yes, it's no doubt part of the same vast frozen tundra. Oh, Livvy, perhaps I *should* return to London, beg Father's forgiveness. . . ."

"No." Olivia actually stood. "You have made a mistake, but it is rectifiable. I am quite certain that once the debt has been repaid, Adam will lift the banishment and. . . ."

"I'm afraid that does not fit with terms to which Jeremy has agreed," Adam said quietly and they both turned to find him standing in the open doorway. "I was just telling Mother about Jeremy's new venture. Won't the two of you join us?"

It was perhaps the strangest meal Olivia had ever had. In the midst of crystal, silver, and china, they dined on a common meal of cold meats, cheeses, and Bertha's rye bread and cider. For some reason, Adam thought the menu an appropriate way to celebrate Jeremy's new *opportunity,* as he called it.

"I think this is quite splendid, Jeremy," Sylvia said. "I have been telling Adam that we should expand the investments of the firm beyond New York . . . Clayton always meant investments outside of the city to be part of the company's growth. And Harry Conroy will be so relieved . . . and delighted. He's a wonderful man, Jeremy. He's been such a comfort to me since Clayton died. Until you came along, his letters were the only communication I had that brought some measure of laughter into my life."

Olivia could see that Jeremy was trying to put a brave face on things for Sylvia's sake. She also could not help being impressed with Adam. He could have been taking a sort of malicious pleasure in his plan to send Jeremy to the outer edge of civilization, and yet, he remained focused on the advantages of the venture for the overall good of the company.

"Yes, Mother is absolutely right," he said. "And I have to give Jeremy the credit for coming up with the idea for the expansion . . . the entertainment industry is perhaps not the venue I would have selected, but I cannot deny that it has a certain appeal."

Sylvia smiled wistfully. "Oh, Clayton would be so pleased. He always did so love the idea that one day he might be able to add to his holdings in that field." She covered Jeremy's hand with her own. "This is truly wonderful, Jeremy, truly. Thank you in advance, for I know that you are going to make the last days of my dear friend extremely happy."

Olivia watched as Jeremy's face was transformed. It was as if he realized that he had the chance now to make a tangible change for the better in Sylvia's life, and in that realization lay the strength he needed to see his punishment through. She had never been more proud of him.

"I have every confidence that Jeremy will make this venture a great success," she said and looked directly at Adam.

To her surprise, he raised his glass. "To Jeremy, then."

She raised her glass as well. "To Jeremy," she replied heartily, challenging Adam's sincerity.

He smiled and clinked his glass to hers and then to Jeremy's and drank. His eyes, however, remained on her and his smile disappeared.

Sylvia went upstairs shortly after supper, and Jeremy and Olivia prepared to take their leave.

"Lady Marlowe, I wonder if I could prevail upon you to stay. I had the opportunity to discuss business with your stepbrother, but I believe that we have some unfinished business to discuss as well."

Olivia bristled. *How dare he speak innuendo especially in front of others?* Clearly, he understood, for he flushed and raised a hand to forestall her anger.

"I assure you, Olivia, that this is purely a professional matter. It has to do with your mother's jewels."

"That won't be necessary," she said quietly, taking the envelope from her pocket and handing it to him. "I believe this will settle everything and leave us with nothing further to discuss. Please thank your mother for the lovely evening, and thank you as well for giving Jeremy this new opportunity. Goodnight." She accepted her wrap from Winston and took Jeremy's arm as together they left the mansion.

Fourteen

In the days following the evening at the Porterfield mansion, Olivia's life settled into a routine that she found somehow comforting after the emotional trauma of the last several weeks. She worked every day at the salon. In the evening, she shared a quiet supper with Jeremy and then retired to her room to complete the design assignments that Trevor had given her. The truth was she found great personal satisfaction in the work. She was good at this and it gave her immense pleasure to watch something beautiful come to life under her guiding hands.

When time permitted, she sketched designs of her own and took them in to Trevor to request his appraisal. His reaction was always the same. He would barely glance at the drawing, then toss it casually aside and promise to look at it later. She understood that he was pressed to create his own designs for the coming fall social season. Even so she spent long hours trying to draw something so fabulous that he would not be able to ignore the sketch when she placed it before him.

She spent hours working on the actual construction of her best design, deliberately not showing that one to Trevor until she could also show him the finished product. In addition, when time permitted, she continued to alter gowns for Sylvia and her friends. She was glad to add these tasks for it gave her the chance to visit the mansion when Adam was not there. On these occasions she would enjoy tea with Sylvia and visits with Winston, and Bertha, and the others.

For his part, Jeremy continued to work as well. In order to prepare him for his assignment in Wisconsin, Adam had established a schedule of meetings with some of the more experienced staff in the firm. And, while he saw little of Adam, Jeremy reported to Olivia that it was clear that, other than Adam and Bertram Sanders, no one knew of his larceny. His admiration and affection for Adam were completely restored and he worked long hours in an attempt to regain the respect of his employer.

On the weekends, Olivia and Jeremy would take long walks or go to an art exhibit and occasionally they would meet her friends, Molly and Mickey, for an inexpensive evening out at one of the downtown taverns or music halls. Jeremy's friends seemed to have other things to do once it became clear that he did not have the funds to entertain them as he had in the past. Olivia was sorry for Jeremy's social loss, but happy that they were not likely to be able to afford to go anywhere that there was any chance of running into Adam.

One of the reasons that Olivia worked as hard as she did was because it kept her from dwelling on her feelings for Adam. The other was that once she had come to the decision to repay the whole of Jeremy's debt, she had depleted her own funds. She wanted to build her savings until she had enough to leave the Baron and go into business for herself. After all, hadn't she left England for that very purpose? Hadn't she abandoned the opportunity to have complete financial security for the rest of her days because the sacrifice of the right to make her own choices was too dear a price to pay?

* * *

When Jeremy left for Wisconsin at the end of the month, she would have the whole apartment and all of its expenses to herself. She went to the train to see him off, and was surprised when Sylvia and Adam showed up as well. It was still obvious that Adam had not revealed the true extent of Jeremy's crime to his mother and for that Olivia was grateful. Jeremy and Sylvia were genuinely fond of one another and it was a testimony to Adam's love for his mother that he had made the decision not to spoil that. When Sylvia pulled Jeremy aside—no doubt to give him some motherly advice—Olivia found herself alone with Adam on the nearly deserted platform.

"You haven't answered my messages," he said tightly. He had tried contacting her several times by sending messages to the salon or leaving them with the doorman of her apartment building. Once he had even used Jeremy as a courier. Olivia had not responded because she simply did not know what to say. She knew that he found her desirable . . . that much had been proven. She needed more, and as much as she wanted to be with him, she would not stoop to take him at any cost.

"I don't see the point," she replied, not daring to look at him, knowing she would forgive anything if he looked at her with the same longing he had exhibited that night in the garden.

He released a sigh of exasperation. "There is every reason, Olivia, and you know that as well as I do. I will not permit you to. . . ."

"Please, do not make a scene," she said, barely controlling her own anger that he would think he had the right to permit or not permit anything that had to do with her.

He took a moment to compose himself. "At least let me help you to get your own business started."

"No. Thank you, but no."

"You are going to regret getting involved with von

Dorfman," he said in a tight, quiet voice that spoke volumes about his dislike of the man.

"I am not *involved* with anyone," she said and risked a glance at him through the patterned veil of her summer straw hat. She could not deny that her own anger had risen to the bait he had set before her.

"That's not the context and you know it," he said. "He is not someone you can rely upon for honest counsel when it comes to your business dealings."

"I am well aware of the Baron's faults," she said primly.

He waited a beat. They heard Jeremy laugh. "Where will you live?"

"I am settled at Jeremy's and will maintain his apartment until he returns from Wisconsin."

"Do not make your plans based on Jeremy, Olivia," he said warningly.

She sighed wearily. "I will remain at Jeremy's because it suits me to do so. I will stay with the Baron for as long as I feel that I can learn from being there. I do need to earn a living, after all. You and Jeremy are more alike than you know. Both of you seem to think that I am incapable of making a single decision or proper move without the counsel of a man."

"Perhaps that is because we both care for you," he replied.

The train whistle blasted a shrill warning. Jeremy glanced nervously toward the short stairway that led to his train. Sylvia took his arm, talking softly to him with each step, and walked him back to where Olivia and Adam waited. Olivia saw Jeremy smile and then heard his laugh. All at once he was walking with his traditional confident swagger. "And in this ring . . ." he announced grandly, with a sweep of his hand to include Olivia and Adam, "we have the business tycoon and the lady."

His voice cracked and he disguised it by turning to kiss

Olivia's cheek. Not wanting him to see how upset she was at his leaving, she hugged him tight and felt his answering embrace.

"You can do this," she said softly, speaking into his ear as she continued to hold him. "You can make Adam believe in you again."

He chuckled. "Would you believe that the single most important person that I want to impress and prove worthy of is you, dear Olivia? Thank you for everything you did and tried to do on my behalf. These last few weeks I have come to admire you . . . love you as a true sister. Most of all thank you. . . ." His voice faded and she felt his cheek wet with tears next to her own. He cleared his throat and continued. "Thank you for believing in me when I didn't truly believe in myself."

She choked on her own tears and could not find her voice to answer him so she simply hugged him more tightly.

"All aboard," shouted the conductor.

"You must go," Olivia said, pushing him away enough to be able to wipe away his tears with the thumb of her cotton glove. "You are going to be magnificent at this, Jeremy. After all, did not the circus have its start in England? Who better to show them how it is done?"

She was aware that Adam was watching them and turned, expecting to see an expression of doubt or skepticism. Instead, she saw that he was noticeably moved by their farewell. When Jeremy turned, Adam thrust out his hand, and when Jeremy straightened and prepared to return the handshake, Adam pulled the younger man into his arms and hugged him. "We shall all miss you, my friend," he said huskily.

Jeremy seemed surprised but encouraged by the gesture. He picked up his small valise and boarded the train, swinging out from the step as the train began to slowly pull away from the station. "I shall see you in the fall," he shouted.

"Yes, do come for Thanksgiving," Sylvia called back, waving her white lace handkerchief fiercely.

Olivia stood quietly watching Jeremy until the train was so far down the track that he was little more than a speck. She recalled how he had bemoaned the fact that Wisconsin was little more than a speck on the globe and her tears flowed more freely.

"May I see you home, Olivia?" Adam asked in the suddenly quiet station.

"That isn't necessary. I must return to the salon," she replied and turned to Sylvia. "Thank you for coming. You have no idea how much it meant to Jeremy."

"He'll get his bearings, Olivia," Sylvia assured her. "He's a fine young man . . . just needs a bit of direction, I should think." She turned her attention to Adam. "Suddenly I am quite exhausted, dear. Call for the carriage, please."

Adam waved their driver over to where they stood. "You go along, Mother. I have a client to see uptown." He turned back to Olivia. "Perhaps Lady Marlowe and I might share a hansom?"

Not wanting to cause Sylvia any distress or involve her in their quarrel, Olivia turned her face to his and smiled. "How kind," she replied. "Thank you again, Mrs. Porterfield, on behalf of my brother and myself."

"I shall expect you for tea later this week, Olivia," Sylvia said as their driver escorted her to their carriage. "We have business to discuss."

"I shall be delighted," Olivia replied and stood with Adam until the Porterfield carriage had pulled away.

"Shall we?" Adam put out his hand to hail a hackney.

"It's quite a lovely day," Olivia observed. "I believe a walk might do me some good." She held out her gloved hand to him. "Thank you again for your kindness to Jeremy today."

To her chagrin, he took her hand in his and tucked it into the crook of his arm. "You're absolutely right. It's a lovely day for a walk."

Before she could stop him, they were walking together out of Penn Station and toward Fifth Avenue. He took a deep breath and released it. "It's been far too long since I took the time to truly appreciate the city, Olivia. Much of the time, I am hurrying to or from work or a meeting with a client. My thoughts are elsewhere. I miss all of this."

She stopped and extricated her hand from his arm. "Adam, I can't do this," she said. "Just a short time ago you thought that I had betrayed you with a man you had taken into your business, and yet. . . ."

"Olivia, that night . . . I. . . ."

People were passing and giving them curious looks as they stood facing each other in the middle of the street. Adam was either oblivious to the interest of passersby or he simply did not care.

"I will not discuss this with you in public," she said in a low voice.

He took her arm again and steered her toward a nearby drug store. "Then you'll do so over an ice cream soda," he replied and tipped his hat to two ladies leaving the shop.

Inside a ceiling fan circled lazily and a young soda jerk wiped the marble counter with zeal. He looked up at them and grinned broadly.

"Come on in, folks. What can I get for you?"

"Two ice cream sodas . . . vanilla," Adam ordered. Then he selected a table near the window and slightly removed from the other tables, all of which were unoccupied. "Is this private enough?"

Olivia sat at the small round table and lifted her veil.

"Really, Adam," she began just as the boy arrived with the sodas.

"You folks been married long?" he asked, then he blushed. "I only ask because I'm getting married myself next week and I've been making something of an unscientific study. I'd say the two of you . . . what? Five years?"

"Not quite," Adam replied and paid the boy, including a large tip. "For your honeymoon," he said with a wink.

"Thanks, sir. Thanks very much."

Olivia focused her attention on the passing parade of New Yorkers outside the window. It was maddening the way he kept doing these really lovely things . . . openly embracing Jeremy at the station, tipping the young bridegroom-to-be. How was she supposed to stay angry with him? How was she supposed to remember that he had thought she was in love with Jeremy and that had not prevented him from . . . from. . . .

"You've not tasted your soda," Adam observed.

She took the straw between her lips and drew on it. The cool ice cream soda was refreshing and she felt herself relaxing slightly. Then she looked up and saw Adam watching her, saw how his eyes had darkened, saw that he wanted her. She pushed the glass aside. "What is it you want to say to me?" she asked.

"I know that I have hurt you. I want the opportunity to make amends. I want to begin by helping you with your business . . . as an investor, as an advisor."

She toyed with her straw as she considered her response. "Adam, when I left England I did so for a single reason. I wanted to be free for the first time in my life to make my own choices. All of my life had been lived at the pleasure of a man—my father, Lord Barrington, almost Sir Dudley . . . even Jeremy. I saw the opportunity to discover myself, to discover a world I had only read about in novels."

"And, so you have," Adam said, leaning forward, his expression filled with hope.

"No. I have made a start to be sure, and for that I owe a great debt of gratitude to you and to your mother. But, in these last weeks, I have begun to understand that I do have it within me to make a life on my own . . . to be happy and fulfilled, not by a man, but by myself."

"Do you want to be alone then?"

"I want to know that I am capable of that—of being content and fulfilled if I should find myself alone."

"But if someone loved you?"

Her heart quickened and then went still. "Your pride was wounded, Adam, when you thought I had given myself to another. Do not mistake that for love."

It was his turn to consider his words. "I don't think you understand how devastating it was for me to think of you with any other man, and when I thought of you and Jeremy, I. . . ."

"I suppose that I should be flattered by that, but the truth is, I am disappointed. You had my heart with that first kiss. To think that you could so cavalierly discount that in the face of some circumstantial evidence of a possible relationship with Jeremy . . . that, Adam, is what *I* find devastating!"

He looked at her for a long moment and when she turned her head to the window, he reached across the table and turned her face back to his. "Do you love me, Olivia?"

She considered her answer carefully. "Oh, Adam, don't you see? I shall never be free to love anyone until I can do so without obligation. I don't want to love out of gratitude or duty. I want to love and to *be* loved out of . . . out of. . . ." She felt her face flush as the memory of his lovemaking flooded over her. She swallowed hard. "I cannot love you or any man as long as that person holds some power over my very existence. Your mother has shown me that true love comes when there is equality. That is what she had with your father. That is what my own parents had. Why would I settle for less?"

She could see that he did not know how to respond, so she stood up. "I must go," she said as she once again lowered the cream-colored netting of her veil. "The Baron is presenting sketches for the fall season to the staff this afternoon."

He stood as well, and she was relieved to see that he did so as a gesture of courtesy rather than a further attempt to stop her. "If I must prove myself worthy of you, Olivia, then I will try to do so on your terms," he said. "If you need my help—for any reason—you have but to ask."

In spite of her determination to forestall any gesture that might send the wrong message, she cupped his jaw tenderly with her gloved hand and then turned quickly and fled before she could change her mind.

Adam continued to sit at the table for nearly half an hour. He was aware of the young soda jerk's curious stares, but he ignored them. Finally, the boy wandered over on the excuse of clearing the table.

"Everything okay, sir?"

Adam considered him for a long moment. "Tell me, son, is your young lady a modern woman?"

The boy looked confused. "I'm not sure."

Adam pushed back his chair and stood. "Be sure," he said. "Chances are that she is and if you don't recognize that, it could be hard for you both."

He patted the boy's shoulder and then left the shop. He paused for a moment looking up and down the street, as if unsure of which way he wanted to go. He was a man used to being in full control of every situation that affected him. In the end, he headed downtown to the one place where he still felt as if he had some semblance of understanding of the ways of the world. He went back to work.

Once she reached the salon, Olivia quickly put her encounter with Adam out of her mind. The meeting had already begun and she could not help but notice the way the other employees avoided her eyes as she eased her way into the small room that served as Trevor's studio.

"And, we shall start with this one to be worn by Mrs. Jasper Armbruster at the art ball later this month." He placed a color sketch of a gown on the easel and everyone leaned forward for a closer look.

Olivia looked as well and then looked again. On the easel was a copy of the gown she had done for Sylvia Porterfield's theater night. The fabric was changed and the color. The neckline had also been lowered, but there was no doubt about the cut and style. She moved around the outer perimeter of the employee circle, studying the other sketches that Trevor had already presented. Each had been labeled with the name of a wealthy client. A name on the sketch meant that the lady had approved it. Other than changes in fabric and color and making new sketches in his own hand, there wasn't even an attempt to disguise her work as his own. These were pure copies of the sketches she had brought him day after day, hoping for some word of praise or encouragement.

Trevor faltered slightly when he saw her pick up several of the sketches, but then continued amusing his charges with lighthearted banter and gossip about their famous clients. Finally when he had given assignments and the room had cleared, Olivia lingered.

"Was there something you wanted to ask about your assignment, Olivia?"

"What I want to ask is why have you stolen my designs?" she replied without turning to look at him. "You virtually ignored them when I brought them to you over these past several weeks."

Trevor chuckled. "Please, my dear, let's not get carried away. I will admit that you had some mildly interesting ideas and it's possible that one or two of them have crept into my work. Nevertheless. . . ."

"One or two!" she countered, whirling around to face him and wave one of the designs at him. "This is an identical copy. You did not even bother to change the pose of the mannequin."

He smiled. "A copy? Of what?"

She moved from his drawing board to his desk. She rummaged through the piles of sketches. Hers were nowhere to be found.

"You may have failed to observe, Olivia, that I always make a duplicate of my work," he said calmly, "and I always sign it so that there can be no question of its origin. You may wish to remember that in future. Things can get misplaced so easily."

The warning he had given her earlier when he had escorted her to the jeweler's came back to her. *There will be a price.* He had stolen her designs but she had foolishly handed him the opportunity.

She had not thought about how she might support herself after leaving the salon that day. She only knew that she would not return. Her meager resources would now require more careful management than ever. Needing a quiet place to think, she walked to Washington Square. It occurred to her that had she still been at the Porterfield mansion she would have walked in the garden, but times had changed—and she had changed them. The park would have to do.

One by one, she reviewed her options. Using the money from the sale of the jewels to repay Jeremy's debt in full had been another rash decision, founded in her anger at Adam's presumptive attitude rather than reason. At the same time, the revelation that she was not a commoner, but a member of society—even by American standards—had changed her position. News of her title had already traveled through the social circles of New York's finest homes. Once her true identity had become known, her relationship with the members of the household staff whom she had treasured as friends had undergone a subtle but unmistakable change. Even her relationship with Molly had been affected. Still, she had always been able to count on Molly's help in the past, hadn't she? She glanced across the Park to the Rutherford mansion. It was worth a try.

Chester Maplethorpe was polishing a carriage in the courtyard when Olivia came around to the servants' entrance. She had not seen him except at a distance since that day in the stables.

He tipped his cap. "Olivia," he said by way of greeting. It was clear that he had been equally content to stay away from her. Molly had told her that he was deeply embarrassed by his actions. She had heard that recently he had started keeping company with Molly's cousin.

"Hello, Chester. Do you know if Molly is in?"

"She's there in the kitchen." He nodded toward the house, then looked directly at her. "It's good seeing you, Livvy."

"And, you, Chester," Olivia replied softly. She smiled and was relieved when he smiled in return.

"We were all surprised to hear your news," he continued.

Olivia did not know exactly how to respond. "Yes, well. . . ." She shrugged.

"I'm glad for you, Livvy. We all are proud to know you."

She was deeply touched by his obvious sincerity and in

that moment she realized that she had gained a great deal more from knowing them than they ever could have from knowing her. "Thank you, Chester." She hurried inside the house before he could see how his words had moved her.

"Livvy!" Molly looked up from her lunch with obvious surprise and delight. Immediately she came forward and hugged Olivia. "What a surprise to have you pop in on us like this, you being a lady and all," she said and punctuated her teasing with a curtsy.

"Stop that," Olivia replied, laughing.

"So, you've left the Baron's," Molly said as soon as Livvy had joined the others at the long kitchen table and accepted a bowl of stew from the Rutherfords' cook.

"Yes."

"Oh, heavens, Livvy, you know how news travels backstairs around here. Cook's sister works for the Baron doing piecework. She says that everyone's glad you did it. The Baron is hopping mad though."

"There's a pure devil behind that smile," the cook said disgustedly. "Works people to the bone and hardly pays them nothing for their efforts. Just always wanting more for less, that one."

"So, what are you going to do, Livvy? Heavens above, you do lead such an exciting life. It's hard to keep up with all the things you've got going on. We all heard about Mr. Jeremy, going off to Wisconsin of all places. Word is that you used your fortune to bail him out of a jam and. . . ."

Olivia could see that everyone hoped that she might add to the gossip they had collected. She changed the subject. "I plan to start my own salon," she said and saw that her announcement had had an effect. "I'll need workers—seamstresses, finishers, drapers. And, of course, equipment and dry goods and supplies. Not everything at once, but certainly a good machine and at least one talented seamstress."

"I know where you could get a good used sewing machine," Chester said, having come into the kitchen in time to hear this last.

"That would be wonderful," Olivia said. "I thought that perhaps some of you might know of immigrants coming recently who might be looking for work?"

Again, the cook gave a disgusted snort. "My guess is that you could get any one of those who've had the 'privilege' of working for the Baron to come work for you at half the price."

"They won't," Chester said quietly.

"And, I'd like to know why not," the cook argued.

"Because they'll stay with what they know. They can't take a chance. Livvy's right. She needs fresh off the boat."

"Two more cousins arrived last week," Molly said. "Kathleen is young but brilliant with a needle, and her little sister is a good worker . . . could be trained, I'll wager."

Olivia's spirits began to rise. "I can't pay a great deal in the beginning," she warned.

Molly shrugged. "Something's better than nothing."

"Thank you," Olivia murmured as she wrote out the address of the apartment for Molly to give to her cousin. "Thank you all," she said and made no attempt to keep her deep emotion from showing.

"Ah, Livvy, that's one of the best parts of being American—folks do for each other," Chester commented. "I'll have the sewing machine delivered on Saturday if that suits?"

Olivia thought about Chester's words as she walked back uptown to her apartment. Clearly, they all thought of themselves as Americans, even though some of them had accents that were every bit as thick as Olivia's. Certainly the opportunities available to her here in America were far greater than anything they might have found in Europe. As she walked, she began to really consider her surroundings. . . . the people, the shops, the sounds, the traffic. All so very different from anything she had known back in England.

She smiled at a dustman who lifted his cap as he passed her. She paused to admire the goods in a millinery shop, and waved back when the owner looked up from her work and smiled. She stood at a busy corner and considered the bustle of the city, and realized that after only a few short months, she had changed dramatically from the passive person she had been back in the confines of Lord Barrington's mansion. There she had contented herself with a routine which she rarely varied. It had been safe. It had also been numbingly boring.

Then Jeremy had opened a door and she had walked . . . no, run . . . through it. Suddenly she had found herself here in this enormous city with its complex mix of ethnic communities living and working side by side. Even though there was a class system of sorts, it was a long way from what she had known back in England. And over time, she had crossed back and forth, moving freely among the backstairs staff one day and the upper crust the next. In the process—almost without realizing it—she had discovered work at which she excelled, an artistry that gave her joy, and an innate spirit of independence that seemed perfectly in tune with this new land. She felt . . . at home.

However, when she reached her building, she dreaded facing the empty apartment. She already missed Jeremy terribly. She could not deny that it was going to take every bit of her willpower to keep from going to Adam and pouring out her anger and frustration over what Trevor had done. There was but one thing left to do. She must handle the situation herself.

"Ah, Miss Marlowe," the doorman greeted her as soon as she entered the foyer. "These arrived for you earlier."

He presented her with a florist's box. "Have a good evening, miss." He held the elevator door for her and she stepped inside and nodded to the older man who operated the elevator. As the machine labored its way to her floor, she opened the small white envelope slipped under the wide grosgrain ribbon on the box.

I am here . . . remember that. Adam

"Fourth floor, miss," the operator said and she realized that he had opened the cagelike door and was waiting for her to exit.

"Yes, thank you. Good evening," she said as she hurried down the hall fumbling for the key she was having trouble seeing through the mist of unshed tears.

. .

True to his word, Adam did not try to contact Olivia again. It was agony not to do so and more than once, he found himself in the neighborhood of Jeremy's apartment, but he did not try to see her. Soon after Jeremy left, Adam heard through his mother that she had left Trevor. It made him unreasonably happy to hear the news, but immediately he wondered how she was supporting herself. It was harder than he would have thought to wait her out, to remain true to his word not to contact her again. Instead, he sent her daily reminders—flowers and baubles he hoped would make her smile. Once he sent her a new hat, another time a beautiful silver fan. He knew that she received the gifts, but heard nothing in return.

"Adam, have you forgotten that we have tickets for the museum ball this evening?" Sylvia asked when he was late coming home after an especially difficult day at the office. He had indeed forgotten and he could think of nothing he would rather do less than attend some charity benefit where he would be expected to dance and make small talk.

"Mother, I. . . ."

"The Rutherfords are calling for us at eight. It's going to be quite an evening. The latest gossip is that a number of the women will be wearing gowns created especially for them by Trevor. It's his latest attempt to increase his clientele. Word has it that he stole the designs from Olivia. It seems that this was the reason she left him . . . a rash move, given her circumstances, but perfectly understandable, to be sure."

Adam's interest picked up at the mention of Olivia. "Has she spoken to you of this?"

"I haven't seen the woman since that day at the station. She promises to come for tea and then begs off because of so much work to be done. She continues to do exceptional work on anything I send her way. Martha took her one of my gowns to renovate for tonight. As always, her work is inspired."

"But, you have not seen her."

"No. I think her English pride may have gotten in her way. It would be awkward for her with my having been the one to arrange for her to work for Trevor. However, I anticipate that she will be there this evening and I intend to have a word with her."

As do I, Adam thought and went upstairs to change.

Fifteen

They arrived fashionably late. Most of the guests were already in place and Adam had the advantage of surveying the room from the top of the stairway. It did not take long for him to spot Olivia. She quite literally glowed as if lit by one of the Old Master painters of the last century.

She was the center of attention in a gown of pale blue silk accented with a silver brocade panel that fell straight from the narrow silver straps to the floor. Her shoulders were bare except for the straps. Her long gloves met a ruff of pale blue lace that encircled her upper arms. She carried his silver fan and her hair was arranged to accent the sculpted features of her beautiful face. Every other woman in the room—even the notoriously glamorous and beautiful Grace Armbruster—paled in comparison. She was a vision.

Accustomed to assessing people without benefit of conversation or even direct interaction, Adam saw at once that this was not just his opinion. Every man in the room was watching her. Indeed she stood at the center of a group of admirers. She favored each of them with a smile or a nod of her head and then moved slowly across the room. The gown trailed behind her with a hint of a train and he saw that the fabric had been pressed into tiny pleats that served to enhance the illusion that the fabric clung to her form as she moved. It was perfectly proper, yet left an unmistakable aura of sensuality in her wake. Conversations stopped as she passed and more than one man followed her with his eyes, not even attempting to conceal his desire to know her better. Adam moved quickly down the staircase, speaking to one or two of his clients as he went but permitting nothing to interrupt his intention to reach her before anyone else did.

He knew that she was not yet aware of his presence and that gave him the advantage as the orchestra struck up the first waltz. He reached her at the same instant as Trevor von Dorfman did. The designer scanned her from head to toe.

"Well, Olivia, you have managed to upstage me," he said and Adam knew immediately that Trevor considered this a grave insult on Olivia's part.

To his surprise she slowly turned her gaze and smile toward the designer. "Perhaps tomorrow you will copy this design as well?" she asked sweetly.

Trevor looked as if he might enjoy striking her. His face flamed red and his fists clenched. Adam seized the moment and stepped between them. "Lady Marlowe, I believe this waltz is mine," he said and held out his arms to her. To his relief and joy she accepted his invitation and they were soon whirling around the dance floor with dozens of other couples.

"Thank you," she said.

"I thought I had warned you about Trevor."

"I am quite capable of handling this situation," she said, but she was watching the onlookers.

Adam followed her gaze. The Baron was circling the room watching her from the perimeter of the dance floor, his eyes filled with fury.

"I understand that you and the Baron have parted company, and not on the best of terms. Tell me what happened."

She returned her attention to Adam, seemed to consider whether or not to tell him, and then did.

"Are you saying that you designed every gown here and Trevor is trying to pass them off as his own?"

"It's not as if I actually *made* them," she said.

"But they are products of your imagination? Your design?"

She nodded. "I'm afraid that I was a fool. When Trevor was so kind as to assist me in getting the best possible price for my mother's jewels, I thought that the things I had heard about him . . . not just from you and your mother . . . but from others, must be exaggerated. I trusted him."

"I'll. . . ." Adam had started to say that he would handle von Dorfman, but something stopped him. "What do you plan to do?" he asked instead and knew immediately that he had said the right thing.

She smiled and focused her attention solely on him. "I plan to enjoy this waltz with you," she replied. "Thank you for asking me to dance. It has been a very long time since I have waltzed."

"Olivia, every man in this hall wishes he were standing in my place at this moment. You shall have no lack of partners this evening, I assure you."

"But, other than Mr. Rutherford, I really don't know anyone here."

"Then we'll permit my mother to remedy that. I'm quite sure that she will know exactly how to advise you on choosing the best partner."

She tilted her head to look up at him. "I came because I thought it would be good for my business," she explained, "not because I wanted to. . . ."

"I am relieved to hear that. Tell me about your business. Have you set up shop?"

Her eyes flashed with excitement. "Yes, in the apartment. Some friends helped me find a used sewing machine at a good price and I have hired my first seamstress. I am quite pleased to say that at least a few of the women here tonight are dressed in my creations."

Adam chuckled as the waltz came to an end. "You mean besides the ones Trevor stole?"

She smiled.

"Don't underestimate Trevor, Olivia. If he finds you useful—and judging by the number of ladies wearing his creations tonight, he does—he will find a way to make sure that you fail and then he will make it seem as if you have asked his forgiveness and that he has graciously allowed your return." He led her toward the refreshment table. "And then, he will work you until you drop. Ah, there's Mother."

Olivia felt a cold chill run the length of her spine at Adam's accurate description of what she had already surmised could be the result of her crossing Trevor. She did not want to tell him that she might have acted more in haste and fury than with her usual reason and caution. The truth was that she needed a dependable source of income if she was going to sustain herself, much less a business. The few customers she had managed to attract were older women like Sylvia. In that age group, there was not a great demand for a new wardrobe every season.

"Olivia, my child, how stunning you look this evening," Sylvia said when Adam had gone to get cups of punch for the three of them.

"Thank you, Mrs. Porterfield. I am very glad to see that your gown. . . ."

"Come stand next to me here so you can be seen and

so can I. Are we not the mannequins for the start of your own salon?"

Olivia looked down at Sylvia and smiled. "You have heard that I left the Baron?"

"Oh heavens, child, that is very old news. The latest buzz in this room is speculation about where you might locate your own salon."

"The apartment seems a perfectly fine location. After all, what is the point of spending additional money to rent a space when I already have one?"

Sylvia laughed and patted her arm affectionately. "Excellent. Now, maintain your composure. Grace Armbruster is making her way toward us and my guess is that you are about to receive your first order of the evening."

"Good evening, Sylvia," Grace said in her husky voice. "I wonder if I might steal this young woman away from you for a moment?"

"Of course," Sylvia agreed.

Once the other women in the room saw Grace Armbruster in conversation with Olivia, they found a way to edge closer. Within the hour, Grace was taking full credit for having discovered Olivia on the crossing from England. She ushered her from one group to the next to the obvious consternation of the Baron. By the time the last waltz was announced, Olivia had made appointments to call upon several potential clients the following week.

"I believe you have done quite enough work for one evening, Olivia," Adam said as he appeared at her side and guided her onto the dance floor. "It's time to let everyone have one more look at that remarkable gown of yours." He held out his arms to her. "Shall we?"

"I must thank your mother for her encouragement and. . . ."

"Mother was tired and left the ball an hour ago," he told her. "Dance with me, Olivia."

Olivia hesitated only an instant and then stepped once more into the circle of his arms. As he guided her expertly through the dizzying splendor of the last waltz, his dark eyes held hers. In them she saw reflected her own desire. He tightened his hold on her, drawing her closer. She did not resist.

He danced her toward the double doors that led to a balcony. As the other dancers whirled by, he drew her out into the darkness. The late summer night's breeze caught at the light fabric of her skirt as it entwined itself around the black gabardine of Adam's tuxedo trousers. Slowly he continued to turn her in a dance that was theirs alone. His cheek brushed hers. She could feel the heat of his breath mixing with the cool night air. She shivered and he drew her closer still.

"Olivia," he whispered just before taking the lobe of her ear between his lips.

She could not disguise the sharp intake of her breath, the excitement that rocketed through her at this act of intimacy.

From that moment on, words became unnecessary. She tilted her head. He kissed her temple. She placed her hand at the nape of his neck. His lips opened over hers. She released a sigh of pure surrender, and he swept her fully into his embrace and kissed her with all the pent-up passion of the last weeks.

"Let me see you home, Olivia."

She knew what he was asking, knew what agreeing would mean. She found her need for him shocking, yet thrilling. She had no doubt that in the light of day she would have regrets. However, all her life she had considered consequences. This time she would not.

"Yes," she said and met his gaze directly as she said it. "Yes," she repeated to assure him that she understood what would happen.

He led her back inside. She said her goodnights while he collected her wrap—a silver mesh shawl embroidered with gray pearls—and placed it on her shoulders like a caress. She saw several women take note of her leaving with Adam, saw them whispering behind their fans, and knew that she would be the topic of speculation over their morning tea.

In the carriage they were silent. He held her hand, their fingers interlaced, her head resting on his shoulder. When they reached her building, he paid the driver and followed her into the deserted entry and onto the unattended elevator that carried them slowly, torturously to her floor.

Inside the apartment, they might have been a couple long married. He removed his hat and gloves and stored them with his cane on the large hat rack near the entrance. She removed her long gloves and left them on the arm of an armchair near the single lamp that illuminated the large room. She moved to the sideboard.

"Brandy?" she offered.

He shook his head and shrugged out of his tailcoat as he started across the room toward her.

"Why are you doing this, Olivia?" he asked.

She found the question unsettling and her defenses were immediately aroused. "Why are you?" she countered lightly and tried to smile.

"Because I cannot stop thinking about you . . . wanting you. I have tried to abide by your rules to stay away. I can no longer do that. I don't know why you have agreed to let me be here now, but I assure you that if this is all we can ever have, then I will take this."

He took a step closer and reached up to release the single ornament that held her hair in place. "Because I can't sleep or work for thinking of you." He spread her hair over her shoulders and in the same motion pushed the silver straps off. "Because I want you . . . every moment of every hour and when I saw you tonight, I thought I had never seen anyone more beautiful, more desirable. . . ." He began a series of kisses that ran the gamut from light—even playful—to possessive, demanding. "Because I love you, Olivia."

He ran his hands over her body, down her sides, over her hips, down her legs as he knelt before her and pulled off each slipper. Then he ran his hands under the skirt of her gown, up the insides of her legs. All the while he watched her.

She closed her eyes and reveled in the sensations his touch created. Everywhere he touched her, she came alive. She clutched his shoulders to maintain her balance, the fabric of his white shirt bunching in her hands.

"Adam," she gasped.

He stood and began a fresh onslaught of kisses. She felt him open several hooks and eyes along the back of her gown, felt the fabric slide to her waist, felt his hands caressing her breasts. In another instant the dress was gone. Freed of the confines of the fabric she instinctively pressed her body to his. He cupped her hips and groaned with pleasure as he buried his face in her neck.

All of the "should nots" of her upbringing shouted for her to stop. But in the end she realized that there was no one whose standard she needed to meet . . . except her own. She was in love with Adam. She pulled back and saw that he thought she was going to stop.

She ran her fingers through his hair. "Make love to me," she whispered.

He lifted her in his arms and carried her down the hall to the bedroom. The soft yellow of the gas street lamps washed over the bed. Adam lay her on the silk coverlet and began undressing himself. When he had kicked off his shoes and removed his shirt and socks, she stretched, arching her body to relieve the tight knot of desire that had gathered as she watched him.

Adam stopped and knelt on the bed to unfasten her garters and slide her stockings down her legs in a slow smooth motion that left her breathless. He did not stop until she was completely exposed to him, the silk of the coverlet tantalizing her bare skin, and she watched him strip off the remainder of his own clothing.

Her breath caught at the sight of him standing there next to the bed, looking down at her. She held out her arms to him. Tonight, she had no doubt that he did not come to her in anger or revenge, as she now knew he had that night in the garden. Tonight there were no secrets between them. She was his lady . . . he was her love.

He moved over her and she opened herself to receive him. As he sank into her, she wrapped him in the web of her arms and legs and held him fast. She exulted in his cry of release just seconds after he had joined with her.

When she started to pull away, he held her fast, "Not yet, love," he said as he rolled with her until she was sitting astride him and he was still buried deep inside of her.

"Adam . . ." she said as he began tracing lazy circles around the perimeter of her swollen nipples.

"Two can play at this game, you know," he suggested.

She smiled and began copying his motions, tracing her fingernails over and around his nipples. Inside she felt him move.

He ran his hands lightly over her bare skin, her ribs, her stomach and around to her hips. Then he began to touch her at the very point where they were joined.

She gasped with pleasure and her breath quickened. "Adam, please . . ." she said breathlessly.

Involuntarily she began to move as she felt that once again he filled her completely. Not wanting to permit the release to come just yet, she impatiently pushed his hand away. He chuckled, a low satisfied rumble in his chest. She silenced him with a kiss—open-mouthed, her tongue plunging into the recesses of his mouth. His mirth turned to passion and he rolled with her until he was in the dominant position astride her. Slowly he slid almost free of her. She grasped his hips and urged him back. He smiled and moved into her, accelerating the motion in perfect time to her movements.

Olivia felt it coming, again tried to stop it, tried desperately to maintain some control. In the end, she cried out her release, her hips lifting to meet his thrusts, her fists grasping the silk, as wave after wave of pleasure rocked through her.

Afterwards, he pulled her against his chest, his arm wrapped around her, stroking her hair. He covered her with part of the coverlet and they slept.

Sometime later, she woke to find him propped on one elbow watching her. Without a word, they made love once again. When it was over, he did not lie down again but stood and began to dress. She understood that he wanted to leave before he could be seen by the doorman or others. She wondered where they would go from here. When he was dressed, he looked down at her and she saw that he was perhaps wondering the same.

He sat on the side of the bed and stroked her cheek. She turned her face so that she could press her lips to his palm.

"May I take you to dinner tonight?" he asked.

She nodded.

He kissed her once again and reluctantly pulled away. He tucked the coverlet around her and left the room. A few minutes later she heard the sound of a carriage pausing at the entrance and then the hollow clopping of horse hooves on cobblestone fading into the distance. Olivia sighed and stretched, luxuriating in the evidence of his lovemaking in every muscle, every pore of her body.

It took no time at all to learn that Trevor would do everything in his power to sabotage Olivia's efforts to open her own salon. Realizing that she would need the help of a second seamstress, she took the trolley downtown to the lower East side to call on a woman who did piecework for Trevor and who was an excellent seamstress.

"I cannot," Angelika Oblinski told her, shaking her head regretfully. "The Baron has made it clear that if anyone works for you, he will see that we cannot work for anyone else. Forgive me, Lady Marlowe, but you are as yet unproven as a businesswoman. I cannot take the risk."

"I understand," Olivia assured her.

The same thing happened when she tried to purchase fabric from the vendors she had called upon just a week earlier. "I'm sorry, Miss, we don't seem to have that particular fabric any longer." Or "We just sold the last of it. I have something similar. . . ." And an inferior grade of silk or velvet was presented for her inspection.

As promised, she met Molly for tea in the afternoon and found herself pouring out the entire story of Trevor's treachery to her friend.

"Come with me," Molly said, her jaw clenched as she led the way out of the tearoom and down the street.

"Uncle Bernie?" she called when they had entered a tiny shop that was so filled with bolts of fabric Olivia had to walk sideways down the narrow aisles.

"Molly, sweet Molly!" a jovial man—dressed in shirtsleeves and suspenders and puffing on a large cigar—called from the back of the shop.

Molly made the introductions and told her uncle the whole story.

Bernie frowned. "Never did like that fellow. Used to come in here when he was starting out, trying to hustle me. Well, I never sold him an inch of my goods and never will. Now, what do you need, little lady?"

Within two hours, Olivia had found wonderful goods for her work. Even better, Bernie had insisted on having them delivered to her apartment without charge.

"If you're as good as my Molly claims, I have no doubt that you'll pay the bill."

"And what if I'm not?" Olivia asked.

Bernie laughed, his cigar securely clenched in one corner of his mouth. "Then I'll let you work it off here," he told her and she understood that he wasn't joking.

By the time Olivia returned to her apartment late that afternoon to change before Adam arrived to take her to dinner, she was feeling quite pleased with herself. In the face of Trevor's attempts to sabotage her business, she had found solutions. She would be able to fill her orders in spite of him.

"I have messages for you, Lady Marlowe," the doorman greeted her.

"Thank you," she said and accepted several envelopes from him with only mild curiosity. As the elevator creaked its way to her floor, she glanced at the envelopes. She was quite certain from the return addresses that they represented orders or at the very least requests for an appointment. The return address on one envelope caught her eye. It was the Armbruster address. She tore open the envelope.

My dear Olivia,

I regret to say that I will not be keeping our appointment to discuss a gown for the ball that Mr. Armbruster and I are planning in September. I know that you will understand that as I choose a gown for an event of this import I must rely upon a proven design expert. Perhaps at some future time . . .

Yours most truly,
Grace Armbruster

The elevator halted and Olivia stepped out, but she remained standing in the hall as she opened the second envelope and the third. Inside each was a similar message from one of the women who had only the evening before insisted that they must meet with her as soon as possible.

Olivia saw the hand of Trevor von Dorfman in everything that had happened. The reluctance of the seamstress, even the refusal of the vendor to sell her goods had been plausible, but how had he managed this?

"You're very quiet this evening," Adam observed at dinner. "More so than usual."

She wanted very much to tell him everything but feared showing any weakness after her insistence on managing on her own. The truth was, she was beginning to rethink her ability to establish and manage a business of her own. "I have much to think about," she said lightly. "You of all people know how absorbing business can be."

He laughed. "And how did you spend this day?"

She sought his advice on seeking out and interviewing a new seamstress, and entertained him with tales of the fabric vendor, who just happened to be Molly's uncle.

"It would appear that you have friends in all the right places. Perhaps I should be seeking advice from you."

She knew that her smile was too weak to fool him.

"What is it, Olivia?"

She wanted to tell him, wanted to pour out all the frustrations of the day, and yet she couldn't. To do so would be to weaken her resolve to prove herself capable of living independently.

"It's nothing, truly," she assured him. "I miss Jeremy."

"Have you heard from him?"

She laughed. "A brief letter telling me little and yet everything."

"I know. I got one as well. I believe in him, Olivia. In spite of everything, he is quite resourceful and intelligent. He has a mind for business and I have every confidence that he will make a success of this."

"I want you to know that I understand why you sent Jeremy there," she said.

He looked surprised. "You approve?"

"Yes. You were exactly right in doing it. Had you forgiven him everything and permitted him to return to the firm as though nothing had happened, I don't think that would have cured him; so that he can appreciate making his own success now."

Adam covered her hand with his. "You cannot possibly know what it means to me to hear you say that, Olivia. Thank you."

"I'm not sure that Jeremy shares my approval, mind you."

Once again she had managed to trigger his marvelous laugh. "Oh, Olivia, I think that about now Jeremy would happily shoot me on sight."

She did not permit him to make love to her that night, claiming exhaustion and teasing him about not permitting her sleep the night before. He decided to walk the long distance from her apartment to the mansion. Something was troubling her. Of that he was certain. But what? Did she regret their lovemaking? Was she having second thoughts? After all, he had openly declared his love for her, but she had not responded in kind. Still, kissing her goodnight, he had felt that it would take only the least persuasion and she would have let him stay.

He covered the blocks almost without registering the distance. His thoughts were only of Olivia. He reviewed the conversation at dinner. How she had delighted him with her story of Molly's Uncle Bernie! One of the things that he loved most about her was her complete lack of prejudice when it came to other people. She seemed to make no distinction between Molly and his mother . . . to Olivia they were equals in that she cared deeply for them both.

He forced his thoughts back to her story of Bernie and his fabric shop. Why had she found it necessary to seek a supplier through Molly? She'd been with Trevor long enough to have learned all of the best fabric and notion suppliers in the city.

Trevor. He was certain that the designer was at the root of this. Hadn't he warned Olivia himself? But that night at the ball, he had seen how the Grace Armbrusters of the social set had sought her out, and he had thought that all would be well. Now he was sure that Trevor had found a way to sabotage her success and he had a feeling that it had gone well beyond threatening a few vendors and seamstresses.

"You seem a bit preoccupied this morning, dear," Sylvia said the following morning at breakfast.

"Business," he replied and focused his attention on her. "What are your plans for the day?"

"Abigail is coming by this afternoon. This morning, I'll meet with the gardener. He's done quite a good job reviving the perennials and adding the annuals as well."

"I think it looks splendid. You should have a party to celebrate its completion."

"Perhaps," Sylvia said.

Adam suppressed a smile. *Perhaps* was quite a milestone.

At the office, he closeted himself for a couple of hours. He had some important calls to make and each required his full attention.

"Good morning, Jasper. I hope you are well." He listened to Armbruster's hearty response, chatted about the market and some potential investments, then asked if he might stop by to discuss a particular offering in more detail.

"Come now," Jasper invited. "We'll discuss the matter over coffee."

Adam smiled as he hung up the phone. He took another look at several files he'd had Bertram Sanders pull for him to be sure that he had his facts straight, then left the office and hailed a carriage to take him to the Armbruster mansion on Fifth Avenue.

He did not have to wait long for the next step in his plan to unfold. Grace Armbruster appeared in the library not half an hour after he had arrived. She was dressed in a yellow summer frock that accented her flaxen hair and showed off her figure to best advantage. She pretended delighted surprise at finding him there, but Adam had long known of the woman's attraction to him. He'd just never used it to his advantage . . . until now.

"Grace, how lovely you look so early in the day," he said, standing and crossing the room to take both her hands in his and lead her back to where he and Jasper had been sharing coffee and cakes as they discussed business.

"Oh, no! If I'd known you were here I would have taken more time." She tossed her hair and lowered her lashes as she sat next to Jasper and refilled their coffee cups. "How is your mother, Adam?"

"She's flourishing. She's very involved in reviving the

gardens at the house. This morning she was talking of possibly holding a ball there once they are done."

Grace's eyes lit with excitement. "Really? How marvelous." Adam was well aware that Grace admired his mother and would do almost anything to receive an invitation to an event planned by Sylvia.

Jasper chuckled. "Grace needs only the excuse of a party to purchase yet another gown for her collection. I have no idea where she puts them all for I never see her wear the same one twice."

"Oh, Jasper," she chastised gently.

"I expect Mother will want a new gown as well. I understand that the Lady Marlowe has established quite a following. Mother and her friends talk of her as if she were an artist worthy of a museum." He paused to sip his coffee and watched Grace carefully.

"Well, she certainly made an impression at the arts ball," Jasper agreed. "In fact, Gracie, weren't you having her run up a dress or two for you?"

Adam saw Grace flinch at her husband's common phrasing.

"I . . . she . . ."

"I have heard that she's quite overwhelmed with orders," Adam said in the guise of rescuing her, but he saw that her interest was piqued.

"Among your mother's set?"

"Actually, I believe that it was the younger Rutherford daughter who was prattling on about her the other day. It seems that among the debutante set, Lady O., as Clarisa referred to her, is in high demand."

The one thing Grace Armbruster could not abide was being upstaged by some young thing. "I see," she said and Adam could indeed see that she was thinking of something that caused her deep consternation.

"On the other hand," he continued, "the Baron . . ."

"The Baron," Jasper scoffed. "It's high time someone with a legitimate title gave that impostor a run for his money. I'm pleased that you've given your business to Lady Marlowe, Gracie."

Adam saw immediately that, as he had suspected, Grace had had no intention of ordering a gown from Olivia. He wasn't sure why, but he surmised that the Baron must have threatened her with some bit of gossip she had unwisely confided in him.

Certain now that he had been right to suspect Trevor of subterfuge, he rose to take his leave. "Jasper, I shall send the final papers over this afternoon by messenger."

Jasper stood as well. "Fine, fine." He slapped Adam on the back and prepared to escort him to the front door.

"Grace," Adam said, nodding to her. "It's always a pleasure to see you."

Her smile faltered only slightly. He could see that the conversation had upset her and her mind was already on how she would handle Trevor.

His next stop was at the salon of the designer. Trevor was clearly stunned to see him, but hastily covered his surprise under a mask of solicitude.

"Adam, to what do I owe the pleasure of this unexpected patronage?"

"I apologize for not calling ahead, Trevor. Do you have a moment? I have a rather intriguing proposition to discuss with you."

Trevor's eyes lit with anticipation. For months he had been trying to get Adam's firm to invest in his salon. His tactics had been to ingratiate himself with Sylvia and her circle of friends. He led the way to his private office and instructed the young woman seated outside the door that they were not to be disturbed for any reason.

Adam nodded to her and followed the designer into his

office. Adam removed a piece of paper from his pocket and passed it across the desk to Trevor.

The designer smiled as he accepted the paper and started to read it. But his smile quickly faded, replaced by anger. "I'm afraid I don't understand," he said and stood as he tossed the paper casually aside.

"Of course, you do, Trevor. It's a letter of apology . . . an acknowledgement that you made a mistake. Think of it as a bill that you owe. The difference is that it will be paid in words, not dollars."

"I did not steal that woman's designs," Trevor said through gritted teeth. "And I defy you to find a shred of proof that I did."

Adam shrugged and removed a second piece of paper from his pocket. He laid it on the desk and sat back and steepled his fingers as he crossed his legs and waited.

Trevor ignored the second paper for a few minutes but in the end he could wait no longer. He read it and started to laugh. "You must be joking,"

"I rarely joke when it comes to business, Trevor."

Trevor's smile froze. "Exactly what are you suggesting with these documents?"

"I am offering you an opportunity . . . one I strongly urge you to take. The first is a bill you owe. You know it. I know it. Half of New York society knows it. Not a good image for your business." He picked up the second paper. "This is a letter addressed to Mrs. Armbruster and also other clients of yours. Admittedly you may wish to change the wording slightly . . . put it more in your own voice."

"Why would I write Mrs. Armbruster?"

"You and I both know why—I just don't know the particulars, but the path is clear. Mrs. Armbruster had an appointment with Lady Marlowe to discuss a gown for the ball she plans to give next month at her summer home.

Then suddenly, she cancelled it. Dry goods vendors have floor-to-ceiling bolts of fabric and yet when Lady Olivia went to purchase, they could not seem to locate a single bolt. There is a common link . . . you. I don't know what it is that you threatened to expose about Mrs. Armbruster or how you threatened the dry goods supplier . . ."

"I do resent the use of the word *threatened,* Adam."

Adam had to restrain himself from knocking the man through the window. "Resent anything you please. The only thing that matters here is that you put things right again. You have wronged people, Trevor . . . seriously violated their right to pursue a career or to do something as simple as deciding who should make their gowns."

Trevor wavered slightly and glanced at the papers on his desk.

"I have a third piece of paper here," Adam said. He laid a check on the desk. "The three papers are interwoven, Trevor, like a fine piece of silk. None stands alone. When my firm invests in a business, we expect that business to be above reproach. I have taken a long look at your business. You have had a string of good years, but in the last two years, your business has begun to falter. Your need for our support is not for expansion. It is a matter of staying afloat. Sink or swim, Trevor." Adam picked up the check and returned it to his pocket. "I'll see myself out."

At the door, Adam paused and turned back to Trevor. "One more thing," he said in a quiet, dangerous tone.

Trevor glanced up and gave Adam his full attention.

"Do not make the mistake of thinking that you are being offered this check as a kind of bribe. You have repeatedly asked for my financial backing. The price of getting it is to do everything you can to assure me that you are a respectable and reputable businessman —a man I can trust. Those," he nodded toward the two papers he'd left on Trevor's desk, "those papers are tests. Pass them and you get my backing . . . this time." He left the office, smiled at the young woman in the outer office, and went back to work.

Olivia had spent her last sleepless night. If business refused to come to her, she would go out and get it. In the first place she was tired of trying to put a positive face on things.

Every night she dined with Adam. Every night she prepared herself with small talk about the day's adventures. Blessedly he had stopped asking her about specific clients like Grace Armbruster. Her only respite was the nights she spent in Adam's arms. Words were unnecessary when they made love. He told her every night that he loved her, but it was always in the passion of the moment. She believed that he cared for her . . . love was another matter. She could not yet bring herself to say the words aloud to him, although they sang in her heart every waking moment. Sometimes when she lay in his arms listening to his even breathing as he slept after they'd made love, she whispered them in the dark.

At times it occurred to her that she would have been appalled just six months earlier to think that she would be involved in an affair, and yet she could not imagine how she would get through her day without knowing that Adam would be there at the end of it to listen to her talk, tell her of his day, make her smile, and hold her close.

In spite of this, she remained reticent about the full depth of her failure. Perhaps when she had found a way to overcome the setbacks Trevor had inflicted upon her, she would tell Adam of these events. Perhaps they would laugh about them . . . about Trevor and his treachery. But the way things were, that day would be some time in coming.

So, it was surprising to receive a message from Grace Armbruster just two weeks after the socialite had so cavalierly canceled her appointment to discuss a gown for her charity ball.

My dear Lady Marlowe,
I do hope that you will be good enough to stop by my home on Thursday afternoon at two o'clock. I should like to discuss your ideas for creating gowns for a number of events that I have on my calendar for the fall. I shall look forward to seeing you again.
Sincerely,
Grace Armbruster

Olivia read the message twice before she comprehended the immensity of it. If Grace Armbruster had changed her mind, others would follow. She hugged the vellum notepaper to her breast and closed her eyes with relief. She had never doubted her ability to create designs that would suit these women. Now that she had Molly's cousins working with her, she had no doubt of her ability to produce those designs. Her only concern was that once before Grace Armbruster had come to her and then had withdrawn. Olivia had no doubt that Trevor had orchestrated that. After working closely with him, she knew something of how he smiled and fawned when these ladies were in his salon, but how he laughed and gossiped about them once they had left. Thursday was yet two days away. There was still time for Trevor to get Grace to change her mind.

"What's all this?" Adam asked that evening when he arrived at the apartment and saw sketches strewn about the room.

"Working," she replied happily.

"I can see that." He picked up one drawing and studied it. "Who is your client?"

"Mrs. Armbruster has had a change of heart apparently. She has asked that I call on her Thursday afternoon to discuss some designs."

"Well now, that is certainly cause for celebration, don't you think?"

"Oh, Adam, I really can't. There's so much to be done. Tomorrow I must go to Bernie's and gather swatches. Then there are the trimmings, accessories, the. . . ."

He laughed. "All right, I can see that I will get none of your attention tonight, but you must eat something."

"I heated some soup. There's bread and cheese. I won't starve." She continued to sketch as ideas came faster than she could record them.

"Here, take a moment and eat something," he urged and she realized that he had gone to the kitchen, prepared a tray with bowls of soup, thick slices of bread and cheese, and glasses of wine for the two of them.

"I remember a night on the voyage over," she said.

"When we had coffee?"

"When you clanged about the café kitchen putting together a tray for coffee. I hardly heard a sound tonight. Clearly you are getting better at this."

"Do you want to know the truth of my purpose that night?"

"As I recall you were determined to keep me healthy until I could be presented to your mother."

"A ruse. The truth was that even then I wanted to be with you, listen to you talk." He reached over and ran his finger along her cheek. "The first time I saw you, I couldn't look away."

"You were quite rude, truly you were. I knew you were an American by that."

"Oh really? Rude and American in the same breath? That sounds more like my mother."

She shrugged and then laughed. "Your mother is a wise and wonderful lady."

"Do you want to know something, Olivia? When I met you, first saw you that day on the dock, I thought to myself that here was a woman who could handle anything. I thought you were quite magnificent."

She leaned across the ottoman where he had set the tray between their chairs and kissed him. The kiss lingered and lingered.

"Olivia?"

"Hm-m-m?"

"I thought you needed to work."

She sighed. "Well, yes. . . ."

He pulled away reluctantly. "I'll go and let you concentrate. I'll be out of town for a few days. I want to go and check up on the summerhouse on Long Island before Mother goes there next month. Will that give you the time you need to complete your work and make some time free for me?" he asked with a smile.

"That should do nicely," she replied.

He stood and took both her hands in his as he pulled her to her feet. "Walk me out," he said.

She saw him to the door and then returned to her work. She felt as if her life had come together in a way she could never have imagined.

Sixteen

The Armbruster mansion was an imposing edifice on Fifth Avenue directly across from Central Park. As she waited in the drawing room for Grace to join her, she could not help comparing the décor to the Porterfield house. Although the rooms were similarly furnished in the French style, there was something about the Armbruster home that showed its lack of elegance, the refinement of Sylvia's beautiful home. Like Grace herself, the room was overdone.

"Lady Marlowe, how kind of you to come. I do hope that the butler has seen to your comfort?"

"Yes, he was most kind."

"Are those the designs?" Grace asked, eyeing the portfolio at Olivia's side.

"Yes. Shall I show them to you?"

"Oh, please do. I have so many engagements coming, I hardly know how to begin getting ready for them," she said eagerly.

One by one Olivia took her through the designs, pointing out the cut, the fabric, the trimmings, and accessories. Grace made minor comments and requests, and when Olivia had shown her the last sketch, she picked up the stack and slowly went through each of them again.

"Perhaps if you could tell me your most immediate engagement, Mrs. Armbruster, I might be able to help you choose."

Grace looked up at her with widened eyes. "Why, Lady Marlowe, I must have them all. The only question is how soon you can deliver the finished gowns."

Olivia swallowed. "All twelve of them?"

"Absolutely. Of course, once we get into the actual fittings, I have no doubt that I shall want minor adjustments. Trevor always . . ." She paused and looked away briefly.

"It is quite all right to talk about the Baron's work with me, Mrs. Armbruster. He is very gifted, which makes your decision to change your mind yet again and give me this opportunity all the more surprising."

Grace smiled. "And, you're wondering why the sudden change?"

"You are certainly entitled to change your mind." Olivia smiled at her. "I try not to question good fortune."

"Well, I am not certain myself what happened. Last week I received a message from Trevor saying that he was swamped with orders at the moment and short of staff. He suggested that I see if you might be available to do something for me." She held up the drawings. "Judging by these, I suspect that Trevor will regret his generosity of spirit." She stood up, signaling that the meeting was over. "Mr. Armbruster and I plan to go to our summer home for the next six weeks. May I assume that you will be able to come there to do the fittings?" She shuffled through the sketches and pulled out three. "We'll start with these."

"Of course." At that moment Olivia would have agreed that walking on water was not above and beyond her capabilities. She placed the three selected designs on top of the rest and put them all away. "Thank you for this opportunity, Mrs. Armbruster."

"Oh, my dear, please call me Grace, and I shall call

you . . ." She studied Olivia for a long moment, then smiled. "Lady O."

Olivia went straight from the Armbruster mansion to Bernie's. Together they sorted through bolt after bolt of fabric, rolls of trims, boxes of beads and buttons. It was well after six when they finished.

"I'll have everything delivered first thing in the morning," Bernie assured her. "And, don't worry about Kathleen and her sister. I'll see that they are delivered at the same time, so you can get to work bright and early."

Olivia kissed his bald forehead. "Thank you, Bernie. I could not have done this without you."

"They all say that," he told her, wrapping a fatherly arm around her shoulders as he escorted her to the front door.

She caught a trolley at the corner and was headed uptown when she thought of stopping to tell Molly about her amazing day.

"I heard," Molly said as soon as Olivia had settled herself with a cup of tea at the kitchen table of the Rutherford house. "I think it's so terribly romantic," she sighed.

"Well, it's wonderful, no doubt. I don't know that I would describe it as romantic."

"But, how else to describe it? I mean Mr. Porterfield is like your knight in shining armor. I mean, from what Angelika told us, he came striding into the salon and took the Baron into his own office and fifteen minutes later he left and fifteen minutes after that the Baron was yelling for his secretary and dictating notes to all his best customers."

"And just what did these notes say?" Olivia asked.

"Word has it that he claimed to be all booked up and not able to take any more orders right now." She leaned closer and touched Olivia's arm. "He suggested they contact you, Livvy. Now, tell me that wasn't the result of your Mr. P. going there and having that little chat with the Baron."

Olivia's heart plummeted. So, it had been all Adam's doing after all. Somehow he had forced Trevor's hand. "Look at the time," she said brightly. "I really do have to be going."

"Going to see that handsome prince of yours, are you?" Molly sighed and clutched her hands to her heart. "It's the most wonderful thing . . . just like in the fairy tales."

Olivia smiled and gave her friend a quick hug. "Please let Kathleen and Anna know that I need them at the apartment first thing tomorrow."

Once outside the Rutherford house, she hardly knew what to do next. Across the way lights were visible in the drawing room of the Porterfield mansion. Squaring her shoulders, she marched across the park and up the front steps, where she rang the bell.

"Lady Marlowe!" Winston said, clearly surprised to see her.

"Is Mr. Porterfield at home?"

"I'm afraid not. Was he expecting you?"

Winston ushered her into the reception hall.

"No." Olivia faltered slightly. She'd had no plan in mind, but not finding him at home had thrown her into even more of a quandary.

"Mrs. Porterfield is in," Winston said kindly. "I know that she would enjoy seeing you. She's planning a party," he added with a delighted smile.

"How wonderful. Then, yes, I'll just say hello," Olivia agreed and waited while Winston went to the door to announce her.

"Olivia? Come in, my dear." Sylvia indicated the chair opposite her own and after Olivia had refused tea, she asked, "Has something happened? You seem upset."

"I really came by to see Adam."

"Ah, then it is my son who has put you in such a state. Have the two of you quarreled?"

"No . . . at least, not yet."

"Then perhaps you should. Frankly, my dear, you both seem far too content with the status quo of your relationship. People are beginning to talk and the speculation is difficult to refute."

Olivia blushed.

"Oh, for heaven's sake, Olivia, I wasn't born yesterday. I know that the two of you are madly in love and judging by the number of nights recently that Adam claims to have stayed at his club, I expect that things have gone well beyond the hand-holding stage."

Olivia had no idea how to reply to this. Fortunately, Sylvia continued. "I understand that you have some idea that you must prove yourself as an independent woman."

"I do not need your son to rescue me," Olivia said, finding her tongue at last. "It was from you that I learned the valid lesson that if I permit a man to become involved in my business, he will assume that it is because I cannot manage on my own."

"Rubbish."

"I beg your pardon."

"You heard me. As it relates to my son, that is pure rubbish and you know it. Adam is not interfering in anything. He is demonstrating his love for you as you would for him under similar circumstances. He views you as a part of his life. My son has never taken well to people who would intentionally harm someone he loves."

"But, it is my understanding that he forced Trevor. . . ."

Sylvia cut her off with an impatient wave of her hand. "Heavens, child, did you learn nothing working for that man? Trevor does what is best for Trevor. Adam presented him with a business opportunity. He decided that it would be in his best interest to accept."

"But. . . ."

"Furthermore, if you think for one moment that Grace Armbruster will sing your praises just because Trevor has said she should, you are naive beyond understanding. It is *you* who must win her patronage . . . your work that will have her friends clamoring after you. Neither Adam nor Trevor has anything to do with that. Bluntly put, Olivia, you still have the option to fail . . . all by yourself, if that is what you wish."

"Well, of course not," Olivia replied.

"I didn't think so," Sylvia replied with a quiet smile.

"Nevertheless, I could have handled things on my own."

"Really?"

"I had clients and there was always the possibility of others. It's a large city," Olivia said defensively.

"You had the patronage of two doddering old women, Olivia. It may be a large city, but the social register in it is a small, tightly knit group."

Olivia sat forward. "It's just that my . . . involvement with Adam complicates everything."

"That's the way of love, my dear, especially between two headstrong and talented people like you and Adam." Sylvia paused. "You are in love with my son, are you not?"

"Yes, but . . ."

Sylvia placed her hands on Olivia's shoulders. "In love, there can be no *buts,* my dear. The next move is yours. Adam has shown you that he loves you in the most meaningful way he can. Work has always been his life, especially since his father died. He can make no stronger statement of his belief in you than to use the resources of that business to help you achieve your ambitions."

Olivia was very quiet as she contemplated Sylvia's words. "I never thought of it in that light," she said softly.

"Olivia, I know my son. It is obvious that he loves you deeply. I believe that he has loved you almost from the time he met you. I know that he struggled with that attraction when he thought that you were part of the staff here. He is a man of deep conviction and honor. I know that his heart must have been quite heavy before he learned of your true identity."

"What shall I do?"

"Go to him."

It was a simple direction, but nothing more was necessary. "Yes," Olivia said. "Thank you, Mrs. Porterfield." She hugged the older woman to her.

"Go and pack a valise, my dear. I'll have Winston make all the arrangements."

It was nearly dusk when Olivia arrived at the Porterfield's summer home overlooking the ocean on Long Island. She had taken a train and then hired a driver to take her to the house. She climbed the path leading up to the sprawling porch that looked out to the sea.

The house was open but Adam was not there. She knew the staff had not yet arrived. Sylvia had told her that Adam always went there alone on the pretense of making sure that everything was in readiness for her arrival. In truth, she suspected that he enjoyed his solitude there.

Olivia moved from room to room taking in the unique casual grace of the home. Its cozy and inviting furnishings, its windows and doors open to sea breezes.

"Adam?"

There was no answer, although she saw evidence of his presence. His jacket was slung over a chair near the open double doors that led to the porch. The desk was cluttered with papers and his favorite pen.

She fingered the papers and then saw the beginnings of a letter . . . a letter addressed to her.

My beloved Olivia,

How can I begin to explain my love for you? How can I begin to make sense of what has happened for each of us in a matter of a few months? How can I persuade you that although it may seem far too soon, I cannot see how I will endure without you a permanent part of my life. Marry me, Olivia, for I love you beyond anything I can express in words . . .

The writing broke off there. She glanced around and saw that there were a number of crumpled sheets of his notepaper with discarded drafts of the same note. Her heart filled with love and wonder as she realized that his love for her was deep and strong . . . not based solely in physical passion, but in a connection of their very souls.

She clutched the notepaper to her breast and closed her eyes as she thought of how stubborn she had been, how foolish to have wasted even one hour of time she might have spent as his wife.

"Adam!" she cried as she ran through the house, searching for him, needing him now in a way she had denied for far too long. "Adam!" She ran out onto the porch and searched the dunes and the beach beyond for some sight of him.

And then she saw him, walking along the edge of the surf, his feet bare, the legs of his trousers rolled to his calves, his shirt sleeves turned back, his hands in his pockets, his head down. The wind whipped his thick hair across his forehead.

"Adam," she cried, running down the path toward him.

She knew she could not be heard above the wind and surf, but still she called out his name. "Adam!"

As if somehow sensing her presence, he looked up and saw her. As she ran toward him, he walked quickly toward her, his arms open to receive her. When she reached him, he lifted her and swung her around. He was laughing and kissing her and there was such pure joy in his kisses that she could not stop her tears.

"I love you," she said. "I love you more than I thought possible."

"That is all I need," he said and kissed her again. "That is all I will ever need."

They were married the following Sunday by Judge Byron Justice, an old family friend. Sylvia and the household staff were their witnesses. With his mother's blessing, Adam gave Olivia the wedding band his father had given Sylvia. After the service, Sylvia made them promise her a proper ceremony and reception in the autumn.

That night as they lay in each other's arms, they talked of the days and years to come.

"Mother will want us to live in the mansion with her," Adam said.

"Of course, we shall live there. That is your home."

"*Our* home."

They were quiet for a long time, each lost in visions of the future to come.

"Do you think Jeremy will be able to come for the ceremony at Thanksgiving?" she asked.

"I'll see to it," he promised.

"You have forgiven him?" She turned so that she could see his face.

"He's my brother now, Olivia . . . a part of our growing family."

"That sounds like a lovely plan," she said as she nestled more firmly against his chest. "Perhaps we should stop talking and see what we can do about adding a new generation."

Adam reached over to the chair near their bed and removed a small package from the pocket of his coat. "Open this," he said huskily.

She looked at him with delight and sat up to tear off the wrappings. Inside was a velvet jeweler's box. *Essinger's* was embossed in gold on the lid. "Adam?"

"Open it," he urged.

She lifted the hinged lid of the box. Inside, nestled on pale blue satin was her mother's garnet necklace. "Oh, Adam, how . . ."

"I bought them all back, Olivia. They are your heritage . . . your mother's and father's legacy to you. They belong here with you." He lifted the necklace from the box and fastened it around her neck.

She felt the weight of the necklace at her throat and thought of all the times her mother had worn it . . . how happy she had been. She thought of the ring on her finger and all that it represented of the momentous love Adam's parents had shared. Now, it was their turn.

"Why are you smiling, love?"

"Because I am so happy . . . because I thought so many times over these months since I left England that I had allowed Jeremy to lead me to make a terrible mistake."

"And now?"

"Now, I know that what I could not see or imagine all those nights I stood in the darkness on that ship is here . . in you . . . in the life we will share and it exceeds anything I could imagine." She laughed with delight at the thought of all the years to come.

Adam looked at her sitting in the middle of the bed in the moonlight wearing nothing but her wedding ring and a garnet necklace that she had sold to save her stepbrother. "Lady Olivia Marlowe, I love you," he said.

She lay down and snuggled close to him. "It's Lady Olivia Marlowe Porterfield," she reminded him.

"All I need to know is that you're *my* lady," he assured her and ended any further discussion with a kiss that was a prelude to a lifetime of devotion.